The dwarf had promised Pamela Martinez that a strike team could end the threat of the awakened King Arthur before he recovered the magical Caliburn. From the transition control room in the bowels of the Mitsutomo complex, she watched helplessly through the ComEye™ cameras as the raid into the otherworld went sour . . .

⟨⟩—⟨⟩

Martinez read the name from the monitor that had shown Sörli's disappearance while she wrenched Wilson's microphone toward her. "Jensen, what's going on?"

Nothing.

"Jensen, answer me!"

"Transmitter link is down," Wilson said.

She didn't want to hear that. Jensen's voice came through the speaker. *"Set up a left sweep."*

Pamela backhanded Wilson's shoulder. "I thought you said the link was down. How come we can still hear them?"

Wilson shrugged. "Computer says link is down."

"Damn the computer! I want to talk to them."

"Shit!" Jensen again. *"He's got the sword."* Jensen's ComEye™ showed a fuzz-edged man-shape wielding a sword. The sword slashed down and the monitor went black. Jensen's life-sign bars shortened and then dropped to nothing.

⟨⟩—⟨⟩

Also by Robert N. Charrette

A Prince Among Men

Coming from Warner Aspect in Fall 1995, the final book in the series:

A Knight Among Knaves

Published by
WARNER BOOKS

ROBERT N. CHARRETTE

A KING BENEATH THE MOUNTAIN

ASPECT

WARNER BOOKS

A Time Warner Company

WARNER BOOKS EDITION

Cover design by Don Puckey
Cover illustration by Keith Birdsong

Aspect is a trademark of Warner Books, Inc.

Warner Books, Inc.
1271 Avenue of the Americas
New York, NY 10020
Ⓦ A Time Warner Company

Printed in the United States of America

First Printing: April, 1995

10 9 8 7 6 5 4 3 2 1

For Mary, even if you are far away.

PROLOGUE

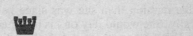

"The signal's been stable for ten minutes."

Sörli nodded at the technician's announcement, looking satisfied. Pamela Martinez had rarely seen him so positive and agreeable. She supposed she should be pleased that he was, but she was too uncertain about this whole business to be happy about anything. So much of what they were doing was a gamble. She was unsure of the reasoning behind it, unsure of its chance of success, and, most of all, unsure that she should be so involved. Not for the first time, she questioned the wisdom of being present personally.

"Put the channel on screen one," Sörli said to the technician.

She looked for approval to Wilson, the Chief Operations Officer. He nodded slightly. Reassured, the woman touched control surfaces on her console. Immediately, light bloomed on the left-hand wallscreen as a series of data windows opened. Oscillating lines writhed in multihued ripples, bar monitors charted machine capacities, and text and data scrolled through several windows. All the windows were labeled with acronyms and alphanumeric codes, but Pamela recognized almost none of them. Most of the information displayed was technical referents to machines and systems well beyond her expertise, but she knew enough about readouts to see that not everything was functioning within optimal parameters.

"Put a booster on the baseline signal, Omi," Wilson said. The technician complied, causing changes in data to cascade through most of the windows. Performed ratings had increased. Nodding, Wilson stroked his beard. "That's better."

Sörli scrutinized the data.

Lacking Sörli's comprehension, Pamela left him to it; he would be satisfied, or he would not. He was risking more on this mission than she was since he was participating physically. She would rely on his judgment.

What other course did she have?

From where she stood next to Wilson's seat in the center of the master console, Pamela could see the whole control room. She could see the great screens that were the left and right walls of the chamber. Below them, on the main floor, were a dozen workstations, all manned by their operators. Half faced the left screen, alive with data, while the other half faced the still-dark screen on the opposite wall. Beyond the consoles was the Perspex™ containing wall and beyond that transparent protection, a small section containing the raised ready platform, as yet empty.

Oblivious to anything but their own jobs, the technicians were totally absorbed with their interfaces. Even the ones dedicated to the dark screen wall were sunk in communion with their consoles though their screen was still dark and would remain so until just before insertion. Did any of them understand what they were participating in? Most likely each was only aware of his or her own small part in the system, working as unknowing cogs in Sörli's scheme. What had he told them about what was being attempted here today?

She stared through the Perspex. Inset in the wall on the far side of the platform was the silver-framed, four-by-four-meter grid of fiber-optic mesh that Sörli called the transit web. She had listened to his briefing, and had confirmed what she could of the theoretic basis of some of what he sought to do, but there was much that was unprovable and uncheckable. She still wasn't sure she believed it would do what he said it would do. The system he'd designed was just too . . . unnatural.

Unnatural or not, Sörli's transit web had better work; she'd allocated all of her discretionary budget, and then some, to this project. She wouldn't be able to keep her operations secret much longer. North American Group's quarterly review was only a week away, and there were too many people involved now, and a hundred other smaller worries. Despite Sörli's assurances that none of his hires would talk, and despite the psych profile assurances that all personnel remained steadfast, she didn't trust so many to remain silent on this endeavor. Especially if it worked. She faced a significant chance that the Charybdis Project would be exposed prematurely.

Time, time, time.

Rearden said she'd be through Sörli's data protections and into his private files in another two days. Enough time? Only if, in the wake of a success today, Sörli got careless. She had hoped to have been poised to sweep the arrogant little man out of her way as soon as the mission was completed, but Rearden hadn't gotten her what she needed. She didn't like the idea of acting before she was sure of having the secrets he'd been keeping from her, but she'd act if she had to; it was more important that Mitsutomo-sama know who was responsible for the project than to have a complete log of the technical details. With the full might of Mitsutomo Keiretsu behind her, Sörli wouldn't be keeping secrets for long. Of course, she wouldn't have exclusive control over those secrets, but she felt sure she would still be able to manipulate the situation to her advantage.

She would have to move quickly to capitalize on a success. Fortunately, she was almost ready. Passarelli in Relations said he would have the pitch for Mitsutomo-sama ready by close of business.

Sörli grumbled under his breath. Something had disturbed his composure. A glance at the screen didn't show anything obviously amiss.

"All is well?" she asked.

"Well enough."

Well enough wasn't good enough; she was risking too much here. "This *is* the signal that will lead you to Caliburn. Your strike *will* end its threat."

"It's the signal, all right," he said, still staring at the data windows. "If we're quick enough, we can keep him from drawing it. We do that and things will be better."

That was what she wanted to hear. "We will put an end to the magic."

"I never said that."

She spun on him. "You—"

"I said that there would be less of the chaos," he said brusquely. He continued speaking in a more normal tone. "And there will be. With Caliburn continuing to tie up significant magic, things will be easier to manage. Much easier." He leaned over Wilson's shoulder and reached for a bank of pressure switches. "Run the L-L scan through the clarifier program on channel C."

Batting away Sörli's hand, Wilson snapped, "It *is* on channel C."

"Then make it D," Sörli shot back. Without waiting to see if Wilson complied, he stomped down the stairs to the main floor. Halfway across the chamber, he stopped and checked the screen. He nodded at what he saw there, then co-opted a workstation's microphone to order, "Insertion teams to the platform."

A dozen men, the insertion teams, emerged from a door on the far side of the Perspex wall and marched up the stairway onto the ready platform. Each of the team members wore loose-fitting black coveralls. She looked for the circuitry fibers that were woven into the dark garments, but she couldn't see any sign of them. She had thought they should be wearing armor as well, but Sörli had said they were tasking the system too much as it was. She had countered by suggesting a smaller force, and he had said it was too small as it was.

The men chosen for the teams had been a point of contention as well. Most of them were short and stocky, a body build Sörli insisted was the most suitable to the arcane nature of the system. Only McAlister was above average height, and he was one of only three regular Mitsutomo personnel. She had wanted more regular operatives, but Sörli had insisted that the transfer system had restrictive biological parameters; there just weren't enough regular operatives available who fit the right physical profile. He'd wanted to replace McAlister, pointing out the need to transfer as many men as possible and claiming that he could take two men of the ideal phenotype in place of McAlister. She had insisted on including McAlister; the man was worth any two hired soldiers of fortune, and the fact that he was loyal to her made him worth even more than two. They'd compromised by agreeing that Sörli would select the rest of the team; she'd let him win that battle, preferring to forestall a showdown until a more decisive confrontation.

The team members were armed with Adler Arms Kar-99s. The Kar-99 was an assault rifle in 5mm caliber. Its bullpup configuration kept its length short, and a long 40-round magazine made it look oddly stock-heavy. She had been assured it was an excellent personal weapon, one common among paramilitary organizations and the militaries of many EC-dominated countries in the Fourth World; she would have been more confident in the weapon if it was built by Arisaka, one of their trading partners within Mitsutomo Keiretsu, but the insertion team members were not supposed to be carrying or wearing anything that could link them to the company. The Kar-99s, like half of the team's gear, were manufactured by the Adler corporate family, a rival to Mitsutomo; let them take the heat if things went poorly.

Aside from the assault rifles, the team members carried little in the way of armament, a standard of equipage she had not thought prudent. The "restrictive parameters" argument again. Well, Sörli must be confident of his threat assessment; he was going with them, after all.

Sörli stopped by the Perspex door that connected the control room to the insertion chamber. Hand on the handle, he looked back up at Wilson.

"Focus lock?"

Wilson tapped in a query to the computer. "Lock positive."

"Fire it up."

He stopped by Console One to check his gear. Wilson stared at Sörli, looking very annoyed. Finally asking, "Confirmation loop?"

"No," Sörli said without looking up. "I want to go right in."

"I can't sign off on this," Wilson said, stopping Sörli in his tracks. "Signal's only on the edge of the green zone."

Sörli glared up at Wilson. "You saying it won't work?"

"I'm saying that without the confirm, we'll be running outside the safety parameters."

"The probe might be noticed."

"We wouldn't be passing mass; the energy flux would be minimal."

Sörli's jaw clenched for a moment. "I said a confirm might be noticed. Fire it up."

Wilson sat back and folded his arms across his chest. His gray-shot beard jutted as he set his jaw.

"No."

Sörli's eyes blazed, but Wilson didn't fold. Slowly, Sörli said, "All right. Run it."

Wilson touched a key on his board and Pamela saw the technician on Console Five execute a flurry of keystrokes. A few seconds later Five announced, "We've got a bounce-back! Good confirm!"

"Any change in the focus lock?" Wilson asked.

"No change."

Wilson looked up at the screen, then back down to Sörli. He grinned. "Told you. We're now showing confidence well into midzone. Don't think we'll get any better. Better get your hat on."

Sörli picked up his helmet from Console One and tucked it under his arm. He took up his personal weapon, a shotgun, from where it leaned against the laminate-topped desk, and slung it. He opened the door to the insertion chamber.

"Just get us through, Wilson."

"I'll do my job. You do yours."

"We'll discuss this later," Sörli said. He walked through the door and closed it behind him.

"Capacitors charged," Technician Three announced. "One minute to insertion."

Sörli joined the men on the platform, his greetings to them being picked up by the microphones. At his order, the men put on their helmets. Unlike the coveralls, the smooth, matte-finished head coverings showed faint traceries of the gunmetal circuitry under the protective outer coating. With the dark, featureless visors down, the men lost individuality. Only the tall McAlister remained recognizable. He stood out among Sörli's handpicked squad, the only one whose loyalty was assured; the others, almost to a man, were Sörli's hires.

Sörli had opened Pamela's eyes to the danger facing the world. He'd shown her its terrifying reality, and he'd offered her a chance to do something about it. But for all his help, Sörli remained an uncommunicative bastard. And he still had too many secrets. Like where some of the equipment for this transit web came from. And just how it did what it was supposed to do. She'd once maneuvered him into explaining the principles, but she'd had to cut him off before he'd gotten very far; she hadn't been able to tell whether he was bullshitting her or not. Had this been ordinary tech, she would have called in experts for verification; but there were no experts in this field.

Only Sörli.

She hated relying on him, but she found herself concerned that he survive this adventure.

"Ten seconds to insertion."

The right screen wall came to life as the team members activated the ComEye™ systems in their helmets. Twelve windows, one for each of the men, ranged in two rows; Sörli's window stood by itself to one side. Each ComEye view monitor showed what the man who wore it saw; a smaller window displayed telemetry: the man's vital functions and insertion suit status.

The ComEye command-control telemetry system was a Tsurei product and traceable to the Mitsutomo family, but no one made a better system. Pamela hadn't been willing to compromise the success of the mission by using an inferior product, even though the system could be connected to Mitsutomo. It was a popular system; lots of companies used it.

"Three seconds."

The mesh of the transit web glowed, pulsing with varicolored light flashing through its optical fiber cords.

"Initiating," Wilson said.

A disk of flickering color appeared in the center of the mesh. It grew larger, obscuring the mesh and expanding beyond the frame until the scintillating disk was over a meter and a half in diameter. The lower edge floated a dozen centimeters from the ready platform. The colors settled into a glowing rainbow circle that encompassed a milky whiteness. A window to another world, supposedly. Pamela could see nothing through the center of the rainbow circle. Had it worked?

"Gate open," said the woman at Console One.

The technician's voice was uncannily calm. Pamela felt as if fingers of ice were massaging her spine.

"Signal strong," Five said calmly.

How could they feel nothing?

"Carrier strong," Technician Nine announced. "Go for transition."

This was the moment.

Sörli faced the color-fringed whiteness and took a step forward. He hesitated for a moment, then leaped over the lower edge of the rainbow and disappeared into milkiness.

For all he was an annoying man, he had courage.

Pamela's eyes snapped to the right, searching out Sörli's monitor on the wallscreen. Everything showed nominal. The ComEye point-of-view screen was shot through with static; nothing there made sense except the Tsurei logo in the lower left corner, which supposedly indicated that the system was operating properly. She had to believe the promise of the logo's presence; Tsurei built well.

So what was the problem?

She leaned over Wilson's shoulder and spoke into his console microphone. "Sörli?"

No answer.

"Is the commo link up?" she asked.

"All systems read nominal," Wilson replied.

"Then why isn't he answering?"

"Possibly a transmission delay. Theory suggested that there might be some temporal offset."

The speaker emitted a burst of static.

"Passage complete." Sörli's voice was distorted, barely understandable. "Looks like we caught them. First team, come through."

Five men leaped into the gate. McAlister and the second team stayed on the platform, facing the gateway.

"Map overview," Pamela ordered as the first of the five disappeared into the unnerving whiteness.

The system monitors on the left-hand screen disappeared, then reappeared in smaller versions lower down. The main screen area lit with a schematic representation of their destination, an image extrapolated from Sörli's telemetry. The confidence of the projection would increase as additional transmissions added their data. The computer sketched a map of the area around the gateway. Walls, doors, furniture, and stairways were represented in green, the intensity of the color indicating the computer's confidence in the placement and identification. The destination area seemed to be a large room, crowded with an assortment of exotically shaped furnishings and other objects.

The team members appeared on the map one by one as dots of blue, solid with the computer's certainty. Pink dots of varying color intensity showed the locations of other persons present in the target area. Some of those dots were not solid—the computer's certainty of their position less than perfect—but, as for those representing the team members, a name—where known—appeared next to each dot. The pink dots had a digital code indicating the probability of certainty that the person represented by the dot had been identified correctly. There were eight of the pink dots, but only four of them bore names: Reddy, Black, Bennett, and Arthur.

Sörli remained by the transition point while the five members of the first team spread out, fanning into a half circle that moved haltingly toward the clump of pink dots. One team member stopped by a green obstacle. His ComEye point-of-view monitor didn't have a clear picture; the pov screen showed a fuzzy image of something tall and slim surmounted by a cruciform shape.

Caliburn? The sword in the stone?

Still *in* the stone. They'd succeeded. Arthur had not drawn the sword.

Or *had* they succeeded?

No one was reporting anything and the overhead view was maddeningly frustrating; all points and dots and lines. It wasn't *real*. The ComEye screens weren't helping much; the poor transmissions made it hard to reconcile the screen images with the map. The situation discomfited Pamela. "Have we got virtuality?"

Wilson checked his personal screen. "Insufficient certainty."

"Damn."

The pink dot labeled Arthur moved toward what she believed was Caliburn. *No!* Not when they were so close.

"Go, second team! Go!" she ordered.

McAlister led them through the gateway.

"We've got a weapon discharge," one of the techs said.

Pamela checked the map. The dot labeled Arthur had gone from pink to yellow, indicating a neutralized threat. The one labeled Black was flashing back and forth between pink and yellow. Two of the unnamed pink dots disappeared.

The pictures on the ComEye pov screens remained poor, confusing images and strange shadowy shapes. Flickers of light flashed in some. The static on the speakers stuttered. The rhythm had the regularity of automatic weapon fire.

"That's not one of ours," Five said.

Sörli's voice broke through the static. "We've only got one shooter. Team one, give fire. Team two, rush him."

Pov monitor screens lit with fire as thunder rolled through the speakers.

An explosion!

Four of the ComEye monitors went black at once. Dead men. McAlister tumbled out of the milkiness and landed sprawled on the ready platform. Sörli's arm, shoulder, and part of his head thrust through into the insertion chamber. On one of the ComEye screens a silhouetted shape flailed against a disk of dazzling brightness. Sörli's arm was outstretched; his hand brushed against the edge of the gate. He screamed, the sound broadcast by his helmet mike *and* the pickups in the insertion chamber. Then the hand and arm were sucked into the rainbow and out of sight. The flailing figure on the ComEye screen vanished into the brilliant disk.

Pamela checked Sörli's monitor. Unlike those of the men who had died, Sörli's monitor wasn't black. That meant he wasn't dead, didn't it? A second look made her question her assumption; the life sign status bars remained steady, showing none of the fluctuations of pulse and respiration. The ComEye pov screen was a steady, formless gray.

"What's happened to Sörli?"

No one answered her. No one moved. The control room seemed frozen in time.

"Wilson, what's happened to Sörli?"

"I don't know." The operations officer sounded stunned.

This wasn't the way the mission was supposed to go. It wasn't supposed to be so costly.

Pamela read the name from the monitor that had shown Sörli's disappearance while she wrenched Wilson's microphone toward her. "Jensen, what's going on?"

Nothing.

She needed to know. "Jensen, answer me!"

"Transmitter link is down," Wilson said.

She didn't want to hear that.

Jensen's voice still came through the speaker. "Set up a left sweep." He was giving orders to his team. Pamela backhanded Wilson's shoulder.

"I thought you said the link was down. How come we can still hear them?"

Wilson shrugged. "Computer says link is down."

"Damn the computer! I want to talk to them."

"Shit!" Jensen again. "He's got the sword!"

It couldn't be! Pamela eyes snapped to Jensen's monitor. The pov screen showed a fuzz-edged man-shape wielding a sword. The sword slashed down and the screen went dark. Jensen's life sign bars shortened and dropped to nothing.

The audio transmissions from the insertion team were suddenly clear. Shouts, screams, and gunfire filled the control room.

Two more monitors went dark.

Pamela was terrified. What was happening? Sörli kept too many secrets. Now he was gone and things had gone sour. What would happen now? Everything was in chaos. Everything was falling apart.

No!

Panic wouldn't help. Panic never helped. She had to get a grip. Someone had to take charge or everything *would* fall apart. She locked up her fear.

"Bring them back," she ordered. "Use the rebound code."

"Don't have to." Wilson pointed at the ready platform. "Look!"

Two stocky figures emerged from the milkiness and collapsed on the platform. One sprawled atop McAlister's prone and bloody form.

Three. Only three had come back.

And Arthur had the sword.

Very bad.

An alarm began to hoot.

"Shut the grid down!" Wilson shouted. "Shut it down before it overloads."

The technicians responded with frantic activity. The rainbow ring contracted. She watched the slowly shrinking circle with dread. As the rainbow closed off the whiteness, someone standing behind her cleared his throat.

There wasn't supposed to be anyone there. She turned.

A tight knot of business-suited men stood facing her. The Mitsutomo pin gleamed from each lapel. None of the faces were friendly, and she recognized the foremost one.

Ryota Nakaguchi.

She swallowed hard. Nakaguchi was a *kansayaku,* officially a free-roaming auditor for the corporation, but in reality a hatchet man. Nakaguchi was rumored to have direct access to Mitsutomo-sama himself. He was the old man's facilitator; he also cleaned up messes. Efficiently. More than one departmental chief's head had rolled under his hatchet. Until now, she had thought her position as head of North American Group made her immune to Nakaguchi.

Something exploded beyond the Perspex wall; she could hear fragments pelting the barrier. She was afraid to look.

Nakaguchi's cold eyes told her she was not immune.

"Konichiwa, Ms. Martinez. I believe you have some explaining to do."

Part 1

CONNECTION WITH THE SUPERNATURAL

CHAPTER
1

It was Friday night and the Rezcom 3 mall was busy, which was just the way he hoped it would be. He was a little worried about being recognized, but not much. It had been almost a year since he'd been here. He dressed differently now and wore his hair differently, too. It would take more than a casual glance to recognize the John Reddy who used to live here. But then, he wasn't that John Reddy anymore. That John Reddy had been buried after being killed in a break-in at the Woodman Armory Museum, where he had worked as a security guard. It had been in all the local media and it was in the police files. Condolences due to the bereaved mother for her son gone to join his long-dead father.

Condolences were a bit premature.

There were lots of people thronging the mall, too many for the security guards to watch individually. He was just one among many. He walked casually, trying not to make it obvious that he was headed for the doors to the south residential tower. No one accosted him. No one called out his name in shock or surprise.

He felt a little disappointed.

He felt a lot more disappointed when he reached the entry to the tower. He'd been hoping someone would have propped the door open, a common occurrence on a hopping Friday night. It wasn't. It was shut, sealed. On the wall beside it, the brushed metal and plastic screen of the security panel gleamed softly. The computer behind the security system glared at him with the brazen red eye of the active light. It would know who he was if he put his hand on the recognition panel, a necessary step in activating the system. The computer didn't care about his new clothes and haircut.

The problem was that he didn't want to tell the computer he was here. The computer was Mitsutomo. He had no interest in letting the paternal corporation know its prodigal son had returned.

Standing around dithering was only going to attract attention. Just in case someone had noticed him stop, he looked around, switching the line of his gaze randomly and trying to look like a fuzzed-out kid who'd just happened to stop in front of the access corridor. He shuffled away, walking a little unsteadily to keep up the illusion.

Just in case.

It might be, probably was, pointless, but he did it anyway. He had taken too long to screw up enough courage to come back here to have it blown just because he was an amateur at this sneaking and poking stuff.

On his third pass near the corridor, he spotted a couple of mainline straightline wage slave types just as they took the turn. He angled his path and started down the corridor just about the time they reached the door. Still looking at his pal, one of them pressed his hand against the recognition panel. The other caught sight of John approaching.

John saw the calculation in the man's eyes. What was he facing here? A scuzzy kid coming home, or a mugger? Or worse, a street kid about to lay guilt on them for their well-earned, easy lifestyles and ask for a handout?

John didn't look Mr. Corporate in the eyes. No threat, Mister. Just a kid. Don't want nothing from you.

Except that you hold the door.

John was close enough, and the man's corporate politeness made him hesitate just long enough that John grabbed the door before it clicked shut.

"Sorry," Mr. Corporate said. His smile was full synthetic and vanished faster than Foamnut™ packing in a heavy rain.

"Null," John replied.

The street slang got a twitch from Mr. Corporate and his pal. Mr. C was thinking he'd miscalculated and should have shut the door. His pal was clearly feeling the same way. They were two to John's one but they were still edgy. Too safe, they were. Entirely too safe.

He gave them a grin, showing a little teeth. Not mainline straightline safe, the smile said. They twitched.

The elevator car arrived and Mr. Corporate's pal slipped in and punched the door closed. The closing panels nipped Mr. C's heels as he boarded. John let them go; they'd had their thrill for the day. He took the stairs.

The stairway didn't have buttons to push that might get logged in the computer. The well was all concrete, with steel handrails and steel steps. It was all echoes and chill. He paced himself going up, knowing it was a long climb. No need to rush. Not now.

On the twenty-third floor landing he stopped, staring at the big "23" painted on the concrete. He could see the faint outline of black that had once closed up the three and turned it into an eight. That had been Yael's idea. How long ago? A lifetime. He wasn't a kid anymore.

At least not that kind of kid.

Too bad.

He tugged on the fire door and froze before he'd gotten it more than a couple inches open. An elevator was arriving in the lobby, the doors already opening. It couldn't be his bad luck that those two wage slaves lived on twenty-three. No, they'd have reached it a long time ago if they had. He caught sight of a bent figure with a familiar shuffle. It was worse: Mr. Johnson, a neighbor who knew him. He let the door slip closed, holding on to make sure it would be quiet.

John gave the man time to make his way to his door, more time to open it and go inside, and a little more time just to be sure. He was certain Mr. Johnson would recognize him, and he didn't want to be recognized. When he thought he'd waited long enough, he headed down the corridor Mr. J had taken. He didn't count doors or look at apartment numbers; he knew exactly how many steps it took. He stood, at last, in front of the door.

There was no name card in the slot above the lock.

Did his mother still live here?

The missing card wasn't an answer. That sort of thing had happened before, petty vandalism by the Rezcom kids. Hell, he'd done it himself.

So here he was. Now what?

Getting past this lock wouldn't be as easy as the one downstairs. This was a private residence door; the lock would only recognize the registered inhabitants. He didn't know too many dead people living in Rezcom 3 and registered with the security computer. It would have been part of the normal practice for the filing of his death report to result in his access authority being wiped from the computer's memory.

He could press the visitor's button and call the resident to let him in. If his mother wasn't here anymore, he could say that he'd gotten the wrong floor or something equally harmless. But if his mother *was* here, it didn't seem like the right way to announce his return.

Should he try the lock? Systems glitched sometimes; his recognition code might still be in there. What would be his mother's reaction if he just walked in alive and whole and missing for nearly a year without a word? And what if someone else had moved in? He'd been told that his mother had moved, but his source was a proven liar. Standing stupidly in front of the door like a fuzzed dode wasn't getting him anywhere.

He pushed the visitor's button.

Ten seconds.

Twenty.

Thirty.

A minute went by. No one answered.

He knew his mother's habits well enough; she'd have the call set to repeat in the bathroom, in the bedroom, and even as an interrupt flasher on the wallscreen. She hated missing visitors. Of course a stranger might do things differently. He pressed the button again.

Nothing.

He looked at the card slot and palm plate of the lock. He didn't have a card anymore, but the lock was supposed to open when the system recognized the handprint of a resident and the person punched in a code; a safety feature for lost cards. He remembered the code well enough and his handprint hadn't changed. Did the safety feature mean that the apartment's system had a link with the building's mainframe, or did it keep the codes in its own tiny silicon brain? He'd never worried about such things when he lived here, but hidden computer links were the sorts of thing he had to worry about now. Would an attempt to open the door be logged somewhere in the Mitsutomo computers, where people interested in finding him would see it? He wished he knew. He wished he knew a lot of things. Like how to force the lock or hack the codes.

Hell, he hadn't come here to stand in the hall.

He palmed the plate and punched the old code. Almost immediately, he heard the sound of the bolt snicking back. Still not quite believing his luck, John tried the handle and found that it moved. Some security tech somewhere had saved himself some work by not bothering to cancel a dead person's codes. Not surprising; most people coming back from the dead wouldn't need to open a door. At least none of the ghosts he'd read about ever worried about such things; they just walked right through doors. Maybe the tech had read the same stories, maybe not. But however it had come to pass, he had his entry. He opened the door and went inside.

The apartment looked exactly as he remembered it, save that it was dark, empty, and the vid wall was on standby mode. His mother never left the vid that way; it was always on when she was home and recording when she wasn't. But it was the sameness of the furnishings that told him he was not likely to find his mother here; she'd never go even six months without some sort of redecorating. The apartment was still dressed in last year's autumn colors. How long had she been gone? There wouldn't be any layers of dust for clues; the cleaning 'bots would take care of that. The computer would know the date of the last use of the apartment's systems, but he wasn't about to ask it; he had chanced enough in getting in.

But if his mother was gone, why wasn't the apartment empty or rearranged for a new tenant? And if she wasn't gone, why hadn't anything changed? Some people kept things the same after the death of a loved one, but Marianne Reddy hadn't done that for her husband, as much as she had loved him. She had loved John, too, but he didn't think she'd show such obsessive behavior for him, either.

He thought about the computer again. She might have left a message. A stupid thought, really. Not for him anyway. He left the computer alone.

He looked into her room. It was neat and tidy, with the same frozen-in-time look about it that the main room had. He checked the closet. There were clothes, but the selection looked incomplete somehow. He wasn't sure, though, because he had never really paid all that much attention to his mother's wardrobe. He tried a couple of the drawers and found only a small selection of underwear and such things. Her toiletries and her favorite jewelry were gone. It was as though she had packed for a trip and never come back.

Where had she gone? Was she coming back? For that matter, was she still alive? Recalling the ruthlessness of those who had come looking for John and his friends, John knew that he couldn't be sure. His hope of finding her here and safe had fled. Maybe if he'd come sooner. But he hadn't. He'd put off trying for so long, and now that he'd worked up his nerve and come back, he'd found nothing. Bennett had told him she was no longer here, but John hadn't wanted to believe that. Bennett was a manipulative liar. Bennett had also said she was safe, which was something that John *did* want to believe, but Bennett had lied about so many things that John just couldn't know what was truth and what was lies. Now he knew the truth of one of Bennett's statements and could only wonder about the other.

He felt depressed.

When this had been his home and he'd felt this, he had always retreated to his room and lost himself in a good book or vid. Maybe seeing his room would make him feel better now. If it was as unchanged as the rest of the apartment, he could pick up a thing or two he would like to have; he hadn't had the opportunity to take anything with him when he fled last fall.

His room wasn't quite the way he remembered it. His usual mess on the floor and desk had been cleaned up and things had been moved around. His mother did that sometimes. Even without the familiar chaos, the place felt welcoming. He wandered about, picking up things and putting them back or into his pockets. There were a lot of memories here, but, strangely enough, that didn't seem to be why the room did not feel empty.

As the sense of his mother had permeated the rest of the apartment, another feminine presence dominated here. A familiar presence. Faye's presence. John's room was the only place in the apartment where Faye would spend any time. He hadn't seen her since his return from the otherworld. Having a sense of her proximity seemed a taunting echo of his safe, homey past.

Faye had been his companion for as long as he could remember. Throughout his childhood and adolescence no one else believed she existed, for she was invisible and no one but John could hear her speak. An imaginary friend, they had said, but John had always known she was real. They'd sent him to psychiatrists to rid him of an unhealthy attachment to a childish fantasy, but John had remained steadfast. He had known Faye was real, despite all they said. Faye had been that touch of magic he knew the world needed to be complete. John had learned to tell the psychiatrists what they wanted to hear. He and Faye had laughed many times over the gullibility of such supposedly learned shrinks.

In the otherworld she had been real enough to see, and hear, and touch. Real enough for him to know she was a woman and he was . . . Well, there was no point in thinking about that. When he'd found himself again in the real world, she wasn't there beside him. He'd wondered why for weeks. He'd been trying to convince himself that he shouldn't expect to see her again.

Memories stirred his feelings. Even if he never saw her again, he could never forget her. She was a part of his life he'd never forget. He wished she was here. Now.

He almost felt she was. Though there was no reason she should be here, John couldn't keep himself from speaking.

"Faye?"

He felt a stirring. It wasn't a sound or flash of movement, but it was there nonetheless. His eyes darted about the room.

"John?"

Her voice was faint, as though she spoke from a great distance. He was startled to realize that he heard her voice with his ears.

"Am I dreaming, John?"

It was her voice! She *was* here! But where? There really wasn't anyplace she could hide.

"Where are you?"

"Here, John."

He turned toward her voice, but didn't see her. But he felt her. She was beside him, enfolding him in an ethereal embrace. Her caress might have been a cool, spring breeze. He tried to hug her back, but here was nothing for him to grasp.

She laughed. "You know better than that."

Did he? "What's happened?" When last he'd seen her she had been as real as he was. Real enough to touch, to hold, and to make him react as he was reacting now, straining against the tightness of his jeans.

"This is the sunlit world, John. I'm not very strong here."

Strong enough to affect him, despite what he feared about their possible blood relationship. Her words weren't meant to refer to the attraction he felt; they had something to do with her magical nature. "I don't understand. I thought things were supposed to be different now."

"They are."

"Then why can't I see you anymore?" Or touch you?

"We're no longer in the otherworld."

"You mean that's the only place I can see you?"

"I think so."

"You don't know?"

She laughed again, melody in his ears. "I'm not one of the great ones to understand the heart of the world. Be happy that we're together again. I am."

"So am I." Though he still wanted to touch her.

"I'm glad you came back. I've been here since the Lady returned me to this realm. I didn't know where else to go. It's been very lonely."

"No one's been here?"

"Not since the Rezcom men locked the doors."

"You haven't seen my mother, have you?"

"Your mother? Oh, you mean Marianne Reddy?"

He almost asked who else, but thought better of it and just said, "Yes."

"I don't know what happened to her. There was no one here when I got back. Just the Rezcom men since. I kept hoping you'd— John, there's someone coming."

He'd guessed as much; his scalp was prickling. During the last few weeks on the street, he'd often gotten such a sensation when someone was looking for him.

He heard the door unlock.

"There are two of them," she whispered.

John caught a reflection of light and image in the main room's window before he eased the bedroom door shut, cutting off the line of sight. He'd seen two men in Rezcom security uniforms, the Mitsutomo logo bright on the left shoulders of their shirts.

Damn, the lock did have a link to Mitsutomo security.

"I'll hide you like at MaxMix Manor," Faye whispered.

Having experienced it before, John was more confident this time. He stood still when one of the guards approached the door to his room.

"Wasn't this shut?" the man asked in a whisper.

"Don't remember," his partner replied.

"I think it was."

"Okay, okay. I'm right behind you."

The door flew open, revealing a tall security guard. He had his gun drawn. The other man had a weapon in his hand as well. The tall guard took a step into the room and looked around nervously. His gaze passed across John without stopping.

"You're getting jumpy, Floyd," the backup man said.

"This place gives me the creeps," Floyd said. "You weren't here the last time, Charley, or you'd be as jumpy as me."

Charley shrugged and holstered his pistol. "Let's check the rest of the place."

Floyd backed out of John's room, holstering his gun and joining his partner to search the rest of the apartment. When they were done, Floyd raised his hand unit. "This is Kendall. We're in South 23G. There's no one in the apartment."

"You're sure?" responded a voice from the speaker.

"I told you we didn't find anybody."

"Stay there," ordered the voice. "Don't touch anything until Gower and his crew get there."

"Wilco." Floyd switched off the hand unit. "God, I hate this spook stuff."

"Relax," said Charley. "There's nothing to this spook stuff. It'll take at least an hour for them to get here. At least we don't got to do patrol now." Charley flopped himself onto the couch and ordered the vid wall awake. He jumped channels until he found a rehash of the last Middle Eastern war. Floyd joined him on the couch and helped him watch the show.

Faye's presence nudged at John.

"John, they're going to stay and I can't keep this up forever. We ought to leave."

"Let's go then."

The door swung into his path.

"We can't just walk past them," Faye said.

"Why not. They can't see you, and you're not letting them see me."

"If you start moving around, the spell won't work."

"Oh."

"I can distract them, though. Then you can run for the door. I'll meet you outside."

"What have you got in mind?"

She didn't answer; she was gone.

Something clattered in the kitchen.

The two guards looked at each other. "Cleaning 'bots?"

"I shut 'em down," Charley said.

"I was afraid you had."

"We'd better check it out."

"Damn, I hate this apartment."

They drew their weapons and advanced on the kitchen.

"Shit!" Floyd exclaimed. "Look at that."

John didn't; he ran for the door. The guards were too focused on the kitchen to notice him. There was another loud clatter as he opened the door. Charley shouted, "Look out!" John stepped into the corridor. The door slammed shut behind him, cutting off Floyd's cursing.

"Where are we going, John?" Faye asked. She was beside him again.

"Out of here," he said. He didn't know where, but anywhere was better than here. There was nothing for him here now, nothing but trouble, and he was not very fond of trouble. But somehow he was getting the feeling that trouble had become fond of him.

He and Faye took the elevator down. No point in worrying now; Mitsutomo knew he'd been here. They didn't see any more security guards nor any sign of Gower's crew on their way out of Rezcom 3.

The elf walked between the worlds. It was easier now than it had been a few months ago. It would get easier still. For the moment, however, only certain folk could find the way. He reminded his companion to stay close to him, where the magic of passage would enfold him.

They emerged in a small park overlooking the old heart of the city. Providence, they had named it. What a mockery that was! Like so many of their cities, once it had been an island of blight on the land. Now, the blight had spread until it merged into a pustulant stretch of the lifeless and the life-taking. The green and the life-giving were now the islands. They called it urban sprawl. His word for it had no translation into any of their languages; they did not have sufficiently obscene words.

"Uh-gly," his companion said, looking out over the skyscrapers and roads and lights.

"But your kind can find roosts among their towers. That is why you are useful to me."

"Air naaht riight."

"Yes. You must be careful. The magic is not yet strong enough to support your flight everywhere."

His companion unfolded his wings and gave them a tentative flap as if to test the statement. He grunted agreement.

"Take this." The elf held out a scrap of garment. The rest had gone to other hunters. "Find him if you can."

"Wiill. Wiill naaht fail you, loord."

"See that you do, Gorshin." The elf had heard that promise before. He hoped that it would be so. "Go."

Gorshin left him in a fluttering, awkward glide, heading for the city. The elf turned and walked back the way he'd come. There were matters that needed his attention.

CHAPTER
2

"Your personal interest in this operation is commendable, Ms. Martinez."

If Nakaguchi hadn't shouted, Pamela wouldn't have heard him over the roar of the engines. There was nothing to be gained by shouting back. She gave Nakaguchi a polite smile he didn't deserve. He seemed satisfied and continued on his way to the cockpit. Pamela went back to staring out the window at the mountains through which they traveled.

Just how much did *kansayaku* Nakaguchi know? Certainly he knew enough to name some names that Pamela had thought sufficiently concealed from her superiors. How much more? If he knew *all*, as he claimed, why had he not exposed her operation? Instead Nakaguchi had involved himself in the Charybdis Project without cutting her out of the operations. An unusual course. What did he have in mind?

She intended to find out, and this trip had offered her the first chance to uncover his agenda. Investigations in this part of the world hadn't been part of *her* program, yet Nakaguchi had arranged the trip here using Charybdis resources. She had been surprised when he had agreed to let her come along.

Foolish of him. She planned on taking advantage of the opportunity.

The noise level in the Aureohuída Caballo™ helicopter was abominable. Company equipment would have been quieter, but while Mitsutomo Keiretsu was one of the dominant megacorporations of the world economic community, the Keiretsu didn't have a very strong presence in South America and some of the usual travel amenities were lacking. She half suspected that Nakaguchi had deliberately chosen such substandard transport.

The Caballo began to buck in the treacherous mountain winds as the rotary-winged craft dipped in closer to the granite claws reaching up from below. Pamela gripped her armrests tightly. She already had her harness in place and watched as the unwise among her fellow passengers hastily sought to fasten theirs and maintain some decorum. Nakaguchi seemed to be enjoying the lurching flight, but most of the others looked sick. Pamela didn't find the gut-wrenching ride to her liking either. She heard the nauseating sound of someone vomiting behind her and hoped the unfortunate had managed to reach his airsickness bag in time.

The jolt of the first wheel striking ground was little different from the more energetic bounces the helicopter had taken during its descent. Pamela didn't even think about releasing her harness until she was satisfied that all four wheels had touched down and the craft was firmly on the ground.

Duncan Middleton, her personal assistant, joined her as she unlatched the last buckle. He was the only member of her staff that Nakaguchi had cleared for the trip.

"Mr. Hagen's not much of a flier," Duncan said, smiling smugly.

Pamela glanced back as she stood and stepped into the aisle. Hendrik Hagen looked sick, pale and strained. Pale flecks in his dark beard marked him as the passenger with the weak stomach. If he'd been one of hers, she would have felt some sympathy, or at least said something sympathetic. As it was, she felt vaguely pleased with the man's discomfort.

Hagen had shown up with the second wave of Nakaguchi's invasion. The roster listed him as a public relations specialist, obviously a cover for his actual function in Nakaguchi's organization. Her people still hadn't sorted out exactly what he did for Nakaguchi.

When he was more composed, Hagen looked a lot like Sörli. In fact, the first time she'd seen him, Pamela had thought he might *be* Sörli. Only he hadn't shown any sign of recognizing her, and the Sörli she'd known wouldn't have let the meeting go past unremarked. Nevertheless, the resemblance was so strong that she'd done some checking, just to be sure, and found that Hagen had been with Nakaguchi's staff almost as long as Sörli had been on her payroll. As far as her sources had been able to tell, the two men were related by no more than the fact that both were afflicted with dwarfism.

A smiling Nakaguchi emerged from the cockpit. "The pilot wishes you all to know that our landing was not something of which he is proud. He did the best he could under the circumstances. Something about excess baggage."

That Nakaguchi ended his survey of the assembled passengers by looking at Pamela was surely no coincidence. What was he playing at? He could have denied her permission to come along.

"If this find is as important as you seem to think, it is only appropriate that I be there."

"Did I say otherwise?"

His look of innocence was probably very effective with office ladies, but Pamela wasn't buying. "Not directly."

He gave up on the pretense and shifted to a more confidential tone. "Ms. Martinez, you are still in charge of the North American Group. Nominally. I am sure you know your geography well enough to realize where we are."

She did. What she didn't know was why he was being so lenient. Did she hold some advantage of which she was unaware? Only time would tell. Meanwhile, she would hold on to—and use—every advantage that she *did* have. "The location is unimportant. This is a Charybdis Project operation."

"Of course it is. And the Project is still listed under your table of organization. However, I don't think I need to remind you of who is actually in charge."

"My name is on the appropriations. I have a right to be here."

"And so you are here. I have to ask myself why. You were content before to let others do the work and take the risks. What prompts such intense, and personal, interest now?"

"Times change."

"Indeed they do. Now more than ever before. But your Charybdis Project has taught you something of that, hasn't it?" he asked, smiling knowingly.

He didn't seem to really expect an answer, so Pamela didn't give him one. She just smiled back at him. Let him wonder what was behind that!

With a bang and a clatter, the hull door opened and the access stairway rattled out. Someone clumped up and called for "Señor Nakaguchi."

"Here," he said.

Nakaguchi proved himself as boorish as the local by casting corporate etiquette to the wind. The two of them spoke briefly, softly enough that the noise of the dying engine masked their words. Nakaguchi left the helicopter without speaking to anyone else on board. Annoyed, Pamela sat down and watched Nakaguchi's aides depart. Hagen was the last to leave. He stopped by her seat.

"He'll be in a hurry," he said.

"So?"

"You might want to change into something more suitable for climbing."

"Climbing?" she asked, pretending she didn't know what he was talking about. Duncan had intercepted Nakaguchi's predeparture memo instructing his aides to bring mountaineering equipment, and they had come prepared.

"We will be going up the mountain."

"I see. Why are you telling me this now?"

"Trying to save trouble. I can arrange some gear if you'd like."

"No, thank you. That will be unnecessary."

Hagen shrugged. "Suit yourself."

"I will," she said to his back as he left the helicopter.

When Nakaguchi returned, Pamela and Duncan were already attired in their tight-fitting Mountaineer HiClimber™ suits, their packs and harnesses loaded and ready to don. His aides were still fumbling with their less hi-tech gear. Nakaguchi seemed surprised—from the way he looked her over twice as much by the form her HiClimber revealed as from the fact that she was wearing it and ready to go. Characteristically, he hid his surprise with an attack.

"Do you even have the slightest comprehension of what we are headed for?" he asked.

She matched his condescending tone with her own. "A little hypocritical to berate me for not knowing what's going on when you won't release reports to me."

"You haven't received reports? I'm shocked. Isn't Charybdis Project under your direct supervision? Of course it is, isn't it? You told me so yourself only today. Clearly there has been a slipup somewhere along the line. Perhaps you should reevaluate your staff. I'd assumed you were aware of why we are here."

"I am in no mood for your games."

"Games. You think I'm playing games?"

"You seem to have a great fondness for them."

"I do. It's true. And you know, I always play to win. It's an attitude with which I'm sure you empathize. But games are not the issue here today. History is the issue. Or, more properly, time is the issue: the past meeting the future."

"Save the advertising slogans for the proles."

"They are not the only ones needing inspiration, Ms. Martinez. Mitsutomo is embarked on a great enterprise here. We stand on the verge of a new day, a new way of life." Nakaguchi began to take on an uncomfortable resemblance to one of the Bible-thumping preachers from the religion channels. "The world was not always as it is today. There were giants in the earth once. All in a time when being a giant meant something other than being a megacorporation. Men were heroes then, able to stride across the world and make it their own in ways that modern people scoff at and call magical.

The uninitiated consign such stuff to legends, to fantasy. But you have already had a taste of the reality that underlies the stories. You know that some legends are more than fairy stories. That knowledge puts you among the pioneers charting the course into the future. You have had a taste of the power that awaits those who are bold enough to reach out and seize it."

What she'd had was a taste of disaster. "Legends are unsubstantiated fantasy. Very dangerous in the modern world."

"Unsubstantiated? Not at all." Nakaguchi continued his patronizing speech. "Have you never wondered why there are certain myths that have analogues all over the world? The very persistence and pervasiveness of such myths give weight to their truth. At the heart of such persevering stories there must be a foundation of reality, something true and concrete upon which the stories are built. Consider the legends from all over the world about heroes who lie asleep, awaiting the time that they will walk the earth again."

"The age of heroes is over," Pamela told him. If there had ever been one.

"Is it over? The myths say that the time for heroes will come again. Look at the state of the world today. Could we not use a hero or two? Say, an Arthur with his dream of Camelot, or a Charlemagne to stand against the hordes seeking to tear down civilization. Or a Siegfried, slayer of giants and dragons. Consider what such a man could do today."

"There is not much call for dragon-slayers today. A knight in shining armor can't do much against an automatic weapon."

"Your view is excessively narrow. Such a man was not a hero because of mere physical capabilities. A man nearly deified in the memory of his fellows had to be more than a simple warrior. He would have had attributes and skills necessary to make him a great man, a leader. At their core such skills are as applicable today as they were then; people are still people. Such a man would be capable of changing any world he was a part of." Nakaguchi's tone became conspiratorial. "But such a man will need guidance to understand the changes since he last walked the earth, guidance that we must stand ready to provide."

Stand ready to provide? Despite the sun's heat, Pamela felt a chill. "You have found a sleeper."

"Very good, Ms. Martinez. Yes, we have found a sleeper, a man who has been in suspended animation through the power of magic. I believe that he is a man who can change the balance of power in the strange new world we face."

"For the good of Mitsutomo?"

With only the slightest hesitation, he responded, "Of course."

"And who is this sleeper?"

Instead of answering, Nakaguchi directed his gaze over her shoulder. She turned to see a heavyset man approaching. The man wore soiled fatigues and a battered hat and looked more than a little disreputable. He spoke, loudly, before he reached a normal conversation distance.

"It's good you're here." The man spoke Mexican, but his accent wasn't that of the city. His dark skin and hooked nose said he had some of the old blood, so she guessed he was from the southeast part of the country. He gave her a quick, leering glance and spoke to Nakaguchi. "Traveling with amenities, Patrón Nakaguchi?"

Did he know she understood him? Did he care?

"Ms. Martinez is an officer of Mitsutomo," Nakaguchi said.

"Sorry, señora. We see few company officers out here." He didn't sound sorry at all.

"Ms. Martinez, this is Joaquín Azaña. Joaquín is the head of the discovery team. He is very well known in certain antiquities circles."

A polite way of saying he was a tomb robber. He certainly had the manners of one. He gave Pamela only the slightest of nods and focused his attention entirely on Nakaguchi.

"You want to see the site today, we must climb now, patrón. There is little time to reach it before dark."

"Surely you have lights up there."

"Ai, yeah. Battery lamps only. Not enough for all night."

"Then we will bring more with us."

Azaña shifted his footing. "There's not a lot of room up there. Best we come back down to the camp before dark."

"Afraid of the dark, Mr. Azaña?" Pamela asked.

"No," Azaña said rather quickly. "It is just the desk people. They will not fare well on the mountain in the dark."

Pamela tucked her hair up under her climbing helmet and tightened the strap. "Then we'd best be going, hadn't we?"

Azaña looked from her to Nakaguchi.

"Ms. Martinez is right."

"Yes, patrón."

They left the camp, walking in a disorganized clump until the path forced a more linear arrangement. Azaña took the lead, with Nakaguchi second. There was a moment of tension when Hagen moved to follow on the heels of his boss, and Duncan stepped in his way. The little man glared, but subsided after a glance at Pamela. She took the third position and Duncan stepped in immediately behind her, leaving Hagen standing there. When Pamela looked back the little man was still standing there, glowering; the rest of Nakaguchi's people had filed past him.

Azaña swarmed up the mountain like a llama and his previous concern for the "desk people" didn't seem to extend to making allowances for their slower speed. Nakaguchi followed close behind the Mexican and, not to be outdone, Pamela pushed herself to keep up. The Breathe-EZ™ acclimatization tablet she'd taken was improving her oxygen uptake, making the climb less dangerous than it would have been, but the headache starting to pound behind her eyes almost made her long for the altitude sickness she could have otherwise expected. At least then she could have passed out and taken a rest without losing face. As it was, she pushed herself, feeding the headache with her exertion. She wasn't overheating, though; the HiClimber suit was doing its job and keeping her body temperature comfortable.

The path, where there was a path, grew narrower and more treacherous. The climb became steeper and their pace slowed. Each time she looked back, Duncan's red-and-white HiClimber was farther and farther behind. One by one, Nakaguchi's drones in their matching blue Rocker™ climbing suits passed him. An hour into the climb, he was trailing the entire group. Hagen, on the other hand, proved to be a superb climber, passing the other aides easily. He slowed his pace as he came up behind her.

"Nice suit," he said. He wore one of the blue Rocker suits, but she noted that his harness held some nonstandard accessories. "How'd you find out?"

"I've played these sorts of games before."

"I'll remember." He dropped back to leave her climbing room.

The Mexican angled around to the shadowed side of the mountain, leading the troop away from the warming sun. Almost immediately after she stepped out of the sun's direct rays, Pamela felt a warmth spreading from her fanny pack as the HiClimber's heater kicked in. It was cold up here, and only the HiClimber was keeping her from noticing just how cold.

The slope here was gentler, easier to take, but they still climbed for another half hour. If the trip down took as long as going up, she doubted they'd be back to the camp until well after dark.

Ahead she could see Azaña sauntering across a high meadow. By the time she reached it, the Mexican was essaying an almost vertical climb past an old rockfall. Nakaguchi was close on his tail. Azaña reached the top of the sheer stretch, clambered over a mound of small, loose rocks, and seemed to disappear into the mountainside. Nakaguchi dodged a couple of fragments that the Mexican had dislodged and followed, disappearing as well. Pamela trotted across the meadow and scanned the rock above her. No sign of them. She started up. As she neared the top of the old fall, she saw how the pile of small stones had kept her from seeing a small dark opening in the rock face. There was a cave.

She managed to get over the piled rocks without kicking any down on Hagen, who had just reached the base of the fall. Nakaguchi hadn't shown such consideration for her.

The cave entrance was barely a meter high. Piled stones stood in the corners of the opening, suggesting a breached wall. She guessed that the cairn over which she clambered had been made from stones that had once walled over the opening. She crawled into the darkness to join Azaña and Nakaguchi. There was more room inside, enough to stand up. She did, brushing dust from the knees of her HiClimber. Azaña was just turning on a battery lantern.

The light reflected from the walls in thousands of tiny sparkles from the minerals embedded in the stone, revealing a cramped space, barely bigger than a public washroom. It smelled of dust. Scattered about the floor were more stones, many encrusted with what looked like hardened mud. Adobe? More stones still embedded in an earthen matrix were part of a second wall still partially closing a narrow cleft in the far wall; there was enough debris to have completely filled the gap. The lantern's light didn't reveal anything beyond the partial wall; she could only see deep darkness through the narrow slit.

"This is where the offerings were?" Nakaguchi asked.

Azaña nodded.

Nakaguchi examined a mud-encrusted rock. "The second wall was intact?"

"As I told you, patrón. Solid and undisturbed. Only the ritual holes."

Stone grated outside the chamber and Azaña jumped. Hagen's short, broad shape appeared in the entrance. He stepped inside, further crowding them, and swept the chamber with his gaze, a disapproving frown on his face. He picked up one of the encrusted stones and poked at the hardened mud. His frown grew deeper.

"Well, Mr. Hagen?" Nakaguchi asked.

"Looks plausible," he declared. "Been inside?"

"Not yet."

"It'll be awhile before the others get up here."

Nakaguchi nodded. "Show me the inner chamber," he ordered Azaña.

Azaña edged past him, the lantern throwing strange shadows on the rough walls of the chamber. They had to squeeze sideways to move through the opening into the mountain. Azaña led them through the darkness, his lantern the sole, feeble source of light. Pamela didn't like the idea of following Nakaguchi into the darkness, but it was preferable to staying behind and waiting for him to come back and tell her secondhand what he found; he was not exactly a reliable source. Pamela slid down the goggles of her helmet and dialed up the light amplification circuits. It helped some. The lantern now provided enough illumination for her to see where she was going. She was careful not to look directly at the lantern.

When the sounds of Azaña's passage began to echo, she knew they'd come to a less closed-in area. She was relieved. New light blossomed as the Mexican turned on a second lantern. Pamela quickly slipped off the goggles; there was no need to be blinded.

Azaña had led them to a nearly circular chamber almost ten meters across. The walls had been smoothed by human hands and plastered over. They were covered in paintings and glyphs that looked a lot like some of the decorations she'd seen in Mexico City. The paintings were old; a glasslike sheen of calcite lay over some of them where mineral-bearing water had seeped from the rock. It was clear from the tools lying about that some work had recently been done to uncover one of the more obscured paintings.

"They look Aztec," she said.

"They are," Nakaguchi answered absently. He seemed absorbed in examining a particularly convoluted glyph. Hagen took up a lantern and stood by his shoulder, grumbling.

Pamela didn't understand. What were Aztec paintings doing here? "Wasn't this Inca territory?"

"As much as it was any tribe's," Hagen said.

"What do you mean by that?" she asked him, but the little man ignored her.

Nakaguchi abandoned the glyph and moved to a door-sized patch of almost undecorated wall. A dark circle was centered in it about ninety centimeters from the floor and there were three smaller dark circles at the bottom, touching the floor.

Nakaguchi ran his fingers along the wall's surface and then across—no, into—the central dark circle, revealing it to be a hollow.

"It is intact," he said dreamily. "The oracle hole. The paths of the lesser life. Everything."

"As I told you, patrón. The workers will not break the wall. Oliváres has told them this is a bad place, great magic."

"What would this Oliváres know about it?"

"The workers, they say he is a sorcerer."

"A what?" Pamela asked. She didn't believe she had heard correctly.

"A sorcerer," Azaña repeated.

Two years ago she would have laughed in the man's face. Now, she held her tongue.

"And is he a sorcerer?" Nakaguchi asked.

"I would not know, patrón."

Hagen looked up from the glyph he'd been studying. "Dynamite the cave," he said abruptly.

Nakaguchi snorted. "Don't be ridiculous."

Pointing at the glyphs, Hagen asked, "Can't you read it?"

"Well enough."

Pamela was surprised. "What does it say?"

"It says that this is the place where the feathered serpent awaits death," Nakaguchi replied.

"Dynamite the cave," Hagen repeated, this time more insistently.

"No," Nakaguchi snapped.

Pamela found the split between the two interesting.

In a more reasonable tone, Nakaguchi continued. "If it hadn't been for your help, we would have never have found this cave. Now you want to destroy it?"

Hagen glared for a moment, jaw working beneath his beard. "I thought you understood the danger that the sleepers pose."

"I understand the power they offer."

"You're a fool."

"And you're in danger of losing your job."

Perhaps with you, Nakaguchi. Pamela was beginning to see Hagen as a potential ally. But she needed a lot more information. "I asked once before, Nakaguchi. Are you ready yet to tell me who you think this sleeper is?"

"I thought I knew before. Now I am sure."

"And he is?"

"The Mayans called him Kukulcan. The Guatemalans called him Gugumatz. I suppose he is best known by his Aztec name, Quetzoucoatl. Their languages were different, but to all of them, he was the feathered serpent."

"Quetzoucoatl?" Pamela couldn't quite believe it. These sleepers were supposed to be men. Wasn't Quetzoucoatl a god?

"Surely you've had some contact with the legend?"

She had heard stories, but it had been a long time ago. Legends about gods were things of her childhood, long abandoned.

Nakaguchi didn't wait for her response.

"Quetzoucoatl was quite influential in the Central American region, though he wasn't a native. He and his companions arrived by ship from a place far to the east. Since he was black-skinned, you should have a good idea of where he actually came from, in a continental way, at least. He was a being with godlike powers who brought an age of peace and plenty. The primitives were saddened when he announced that he could not remain among them, but they were cheered when he said that he would return. They waited for him, making his doings into myth and always remembering his promise to return. When the Spaniards came, the Aztec coast watchers mistook the shining armor of the soon-to-be conquistadors as his sign, their coming a fulfillment of the prophecy of his return. They were wrong, of course."

Pamela knew how wrong the Aztecs had been. Mexico still groaned under the legacy of that fatal error.

Nakaguchi shrugged. "And, of course, he is not a god. Godhood, for him, was merely the inspired awe of a primitive people who had no true understanding of his nature."

Had Pamela heard correctly? "You said *is. Is* not a god."

"Of course I used the present tense, Ms. Martinez." Nakaguchi turned back to the undecorated wall and ran his fingers along the edge of the hollow. "Quetzoucoatl is not dead. He merely sleeps, awaiting the time of his return."

Nakaguchi detached a climbing hammer from his belt. Hagen stepped up to him and, disregarding all corporate etiquette, laid a hand on Nakaguchi's arm.

"If you won't destroy it, at least leave it be."

"Take your hand away," Nakaguchi said coldly.

Nakaguchi's voice was hard as steel and sharp as broken glass. Hagen removed his hand and took a step back. Hefting the hammer in his hand, Nakaguchi stared at Hagen until the small man took another step backward.

Nakaguchi turned back to the wall. Thrusting tool and hand into the darkness of the central aperture, he twisted his wrist to set the alloy spike against some unseen resistance. He tugged. A spidery crack ran from the edge of the hole. Nakaguchi tugged again. Powdery adobe exploded out as a stone shifted in the wall. Nakaguchi wrenched until he ripped the stone free from the wall to fall behind him. Attacking the wall again, he jerked and yanked until he tore another stone free, and another, until he had opened a half-meter hole. He peered through.

"Azaña, the lantern!"

The Mexican stepped up. Pamela crowded closer as well. She had come this far to be in on the uncovering; she wanted to see. Azaña shoved the lantern partially into the opening. Light speared into the space beyond, to be reflected in a dazzle of ruddy glints from something within the darkness. Pamela gasped when she realized she was seeing a golden face, serene and perfectly composed. Turquoise and emerald studded a headband from which a riot of plumage emerged. The regal face did not so much as twitch or lift an eyelid.

"Quetzoucoatl!" Azaña gasped.

The Mexican jerked back and dropped the lantern, but Hagen caught it before it struck the floor.

Nakaguchi attacked the wall with a will, ripping and tearing until he had removed enough of the stones to squeeze through. Pamela and Hagen exchanged worried glances. Nakaguchi's hand thrust back from the other side.

"The lantern!" he shouted. "The lantern!"

Hagen handed it to him, then squeezed through the gap himself. Pamela had no desire to meet a god, but neither did she want to remain behind with the cowering Azaña. Wondering what sort of fool she was being, she slipped through the opening.

Like the chamber on the other side of the wall, this one was plastered and painted. Nakaguchi stood in the center, bowing to the seated figure and throne that dominated the small chamber.

The sleeper gave no sign of awareness.

Pamela realized why: the gold visage was not a face but a mask. A death mask? She looked closer. The figure on the throne appeared to be enfolded in a cloak of feathers. Appropriate for Quetzoucoatl. Where the figure's limbs emerged from the covering they were sticklike and shrunken, like a mummy's. Was Nakaguchi wrong? Was his sleeper just another royal mummy? Such a find would have archaeological significance, but it was hardly the sort of thing the Charybdis Project sought.

But it was the sort of answer Pamela preferred when told an ancient god had just been rediscovered.

"The museums will be pleased with your find," she told him.

"He is not for the museums."

"Open your eyes, Nakaguchi. It's just a goddamn mummy!"

Nakaguchi continued to stare at the mummy. "Open your own eyes, Martinez."

Pamela looked more closely at the withered shell of the ancient Indian ruler. The mask was magnificent, a work of art. The cloak would have once been magnificent and might be again after the restorer removed the dust of the centuries. This ancient king must have been a powerful ruler to rate such an elaborate robe; it fell in heaping folds around his legs. Too bad the feathers there had become so dirty.

The feathers there?

She looked closer. What she had assumed were feathers were not feathers at all, but a pile of insect husks tumbled in a talus slope from the throne. Tiny dry corpses. Pale bones of small animals lay among the empty shells, tumbled in piles on the floor around the throne, and lay in windrows against the arms of the mummy, white against the body's dark skin.

A breeze puffed into the chamber, stirring the dust. The feathers of the crown rustled. Did that masked head nod? Or was it a trick of the light and the wind?

Nakaguchi turned to them.

"Gentleman and madam, may I present you to the Lord of Wind. His will be a wind of change, and it will fill our sails as we set our prows to the future."

The stirring air felt very, very cold to Pamela.

He became aware of others, nearby.

Time had passed.

Much time.

How much he did not know.

He was weak.

Very weak.

Their auras burned like distant fires in the night. Beckoning him. He reached out, all too aware of his weakness. He was eager, hungry. He—

Stopped.

The aura of the nearest one was different. He was not sure at first why, then he understood.

This one bore the sign.

The need would remain unfulfilled. For the moment. The hunger was strong, but his will was stronger. He had waited so long.

He could wait awhile longer.

Officer Shirley Hamett swung open the door of her GM Urban Patroller™ and looked around before she got out. Things didn't look any better outside the tinted Perspex windows. Something had gone down since she passed by earlier on her patrol. Whatever had happened had left the area looking more trashed than normal for this stretch of urban blight. A fire burned in a pile of trash spilling out of the alley behind the old Mallon Brothers warehouse. The fire made a mystery of the alley; the glitched thermal circuits on her Tsurei ComEye helmet couldn't handle it. The starlight circuit wasn't much better; at least not from this angle.

She got out of the car and listened.

Quiet. The streets were quiet and empty. The lack of streetlife was the strongest sign that there had been something going on down here. The only activity she could see was the crackling trash fire. So where was the fight that had been reported?

"This is one-Zulu-twelve," she said into her helmet mike. "I'm on scene at Harris and Lovatt. It's quiet here. Over."

"*Zzzchk* Zulu *crkkkk. Kckckzz* Dispatch. We've got no picture. *Bzzzz.*"

What a surprise. Seemed like the damned Tsurei ComEye helmets didn't transmit more often than they did. So much for milspec quality. She knew that it didn't help that she was down by the old rail yards, which put a lot of buildings between her and the tower, but that didn't ease her anger. The damned corps thought that they could slough off any old junk on the cops just because they worked for the government, and the government didn't care what it bought so long as the corps paid their nice fat kickbacks. And the media said that *cops* were corrupt.

Of course, it also didn't help that Fumble Freer was on the dispatch console. Freer was a techno disaster; he'd probably spilled coffee on the keyboard again or cross-linked his entertainment program to the report channels and fritzed out the system.

"This is one-Zulu-twelve. Trying alternate channels. Let me know if you get something."

"*Zzzchkzz*-twelve. Still noth-*ikkkk crkkkk.*"

Great. Why couldn't they have a satellite-laser link like she'd heard they had down in the Balt-Wash sprawl? Probably 'cause it wasn't the kind of half-assed solution that the New England Cooperative's oh-so-wise politicians favored.

Bitching didn't get the job done. "Dispatch, I'm gonna take a look around and check it out."

"*Nkatck,* one-Zulu-twelve. *Bzz-chratckkk. KKanzz* [pop] *xck* backup on the way."

"Say again, Dispatch. What was that about backup?"

Fuzz and static.

That was the way of it. Backup was people and things you could rely on. You had to work with what you could count on; Freer's promises of more cars weren't something a smart officer relied on. If she waited and the promised backup didn't show, she would be the one explaining why she'd spent time unproductively. The brass upstairs didn't like timid officers, especially timid female officers.

Shirley switched her commo to her car's channel. "Hey, partner, give me some light down here. High beams."

Her link with the Patroller's dogbrain was good; she'd made sure of that. The rent-a-nerd's fee had come out of her pocket, but it was money well spent.

Gravel snapped out from under the tires as the Patroller shifted to bring its headlights to bear on her position. The patrol vehicle was small enough but its computer wouldn't allow it entry into the alley; its motion controllers weren't sophisticated enough, another economy. Still, the car could sit at the entrance and block it while giving her some support. The Patroller's lights blinked onto high and flooded the alley with daylight, throwing stark shadows against the building and casting deep pools of dark deeper into the alley. Halfway down the alley something scurried out of the sudden illumination. The filters on her visor were still adjusting and she didn't get a good look.

Too big to be rats.

Somebody was still around. A witness, maybe. She ought to find out. Skirting the fire, she entered the alley.

She found the first body twenty feet into the alley. He wore a shredded synthleather Beasts jacket. The Beasts were a powerful gang in the district. Whoever had messed with them was asking for trouble. She hoped this wasn't the start of a gang war.

The second body was a Beast too. So was the third. She counted half a dozen and no sign of any other casualties. Shirley recognized one of the corpses as Mag Quidellia, one of the Beasts' toughest warriors. There'd be a war for sure.

But who could have taken on this squad of Beasts and come away clean?

"Hey, hey, the lights are itchy making," said a voice from the darkness.

She turned, searching for the speaker. Even with her enhanced vision, spotting him wasn't easy. He was a shadow within the shadow of a dumpster.

"Come out where I can see you," she ordered. She didn't reach for her weapon; that would be premature.

The guy who emerged was a dark-skinned, lanky sort, who moved with surprising, catlike grace. Shirley slipped the restraining strap off her weapon. The guy wore a sleeveless Beasts jacket; by the fit, it wasn't his.

As he stepped forward he raised a long-fingered hand with pointed nails that glistened in the light. Implants? He turned that raised hand back and forth in the beams from the Patroller. "It kinda burns, you know. Makes me feel nasty. Like somebody ought to be hurt for making night into day. Ain't right, you know. The world's got a proper order. Ain't right to mess with the order. We don't like it when people mess with the proper order. Do we?"

Gravelly voices mumbled agreement as more lanky forms emerged from the shadows around Shirley. There were eight or nine of them. She wasn't sure what they were wearing; somehow they were hard to see. This was trouble. She hoped Freer hadn't been blowing air when he'd said backup was on the way. She needed help. She needed time for the help to get to her.

"Proper Order? That what you guys call yourselves?"

Their laughs were metal-on-metal screeches. They grinned at her and light reflected from their teeth, teeth filed to sharp points. They all wore red wool caps as their colors and they all had mutilated themselves; these were hard-core types, but they weren't a gang she'd heard about.

"We're new in town," one of the gangers said. "Just out for a good time. You gonna show us a good time?"

She unholstered her weapon. "I think maybe you better go looking elsewhere."

They laughed at her.

Without warning one of them launched himself at her, hurtling toward her with his clawed hands outstretched. She reacted. The Arisaka Enforcer™ bucked in her hand. Her helmet filters cut the sound of the gun's report. She knew she hit him. She also knew the 10mm slug wouldn't stop his flight. She threw herself back, barely avoiding him. She felt his claws rake against her Arm-R-Plast™ vest.

The others stood and watched as he landed in an awkward heap.

"You don't want the same," she told them. They laughed at her again. Lord Above, she was dealing with wonkheads.

The one that had jumped her was getting to his feet. Definitely wonkheads. Snarling, he stalked toward her. She shot him again. He spun around and landed facedown on the pavement, but only for a moment. He got to his feet, laughing.

She was in deep shit.

Twirling around, he capered in front of her. "Too much strength for you just now. Too much! Too, *too* much," he crowed.

Then they were on her and she was fighting for her life.

"You are assaulting an officer of the law," boomed the loudspeaker aboard her Patroller. "Cease and desist at once. Your actions are being recorded and will be used against you at your trial. Cease and desist. You are assaulting . . ." The car droned on. It was all the Patroller could do; NEC hadn't authorized the more expensive, armed versions.

Claws shredded her uniform and dug into her flesh. They tore off her helmet and took part of her ear with it. That was when she got her first good look at their faces. Lord Above, they weren't human! Teeth sank into her throat.

"Officer down," reported the Patroller. It was the last thing Shirley heard.

CHAPTER 3

Chardonneville was a tiny hamlet just north of Metz. No one had lived on the site for over seven hundred years until an eccentric billionaire by the name of Gourgaud decided to make it his own. He had wanted to build himself a bucolic village as a rustic getaway, a haven from the twenty-first century, but the ground breaking had uncovered a medieval village and an even more ancient settlement beneath that. The excavations had been a sensation in archaeological circles twelve years ago; there had been conferences and exhibitions. There had even been some talk of an *in situ* museum, but Gourgaud had wanted nothing of that. He made sure that the whole area was excavated down to the Neolithic layers until nothing was left in the ground; everything was mapped and cataloged and preserved. Some of the stuff went to Aachen, but most of it was shipped off to Cluny. Gourgaud had financed the digging and the cataloging and the publishing, setting up an endowment which specified that all work on the Chardonneville material was to take place anywhere but Chardonneville, and that no further excavations were to be allowed. He wanted no museum, no tourists; so he made sure there was nothing left to interest them. He wanted his tiny fiefdom to be left alone.

But Gourgaud died before getting a chance to move into his little village. The people he'd hired to populate his fiefdom had already moved in, and when the word came that the dreamer had died, a lot of them packed up and left, but some stayed, taking to the bucolic rural life. Chardonneville had become just an ordinary, sleepy little village, too small to be of interest to anyone but the inhabitants. The media coverage of the excavations was forgotten now. Chardonneville remained a revered name among a tiny circle of archaeological cognoscenti, but they cared little for the kitschy little faux-medieval hamlet the billionaire had built. They had the finds, the site plans, the dating data, and the maps—what interest did they have for a billionaire's fantasy village?

Chardonneville's history was an entertaining story, a fine tale of the eccentricities of the rich.

It was also a lie.

Chardonneville might look like an ordinary village, but, as had been planned from the beginning, every person who lived there was part of the European Community Secret Service or of an ECSS agent's family. The sleepy-looking village was a cover for the underground complex that was the European headquarters of Department M, a clandestine operation dedicated to unraveling and controlling the mysteries of magic and the ancient heroes whose awakening seemed to herald a new age.

Elizabeth Spae worked for Department M; a situation that she was considering changing, and not for the first time.

The lights were harsh and hurt her eyes. She knew that her discomfort was intended because she had complained after each of the previous sessions. The lights, the sort used in prisoner interrogations, remained, glaring and unpleasant. Though she was no prisoner, this certainly was an interrogation, the third in as many weeks since she and Holger Kun had returned to Chardonneville.

Spae didn't like being interrogated. She didn't like the glare of the lights, or their baking heat. She didn't like the harsh echoes from the room's hard walls, or the cold floor underfoot. She didn't like not being able to see her questioners, hiding behind the wall of dazzle.

She knew that all of Magnus's team was assembled in the shadows behind those lights; she'd seen them before they switched on the blinding lamps. Reinholt Gere, Doctor Essenbach, L'Hereaux, the insufferable Dagastino, and Magnus himself. Because *he* was present, she stayed. Of all of them, only he commanded her respect. But there were limits, and she wasn't sure her sufferance would last much longer. Still, she listened when Magnus interrupted his colleagues' questions and spoke to her for the first time.

"Dr. Spae, your continued insistence that the American sleeper is King Arthur puts the Department in a very difficult position."

Sitting in the glare and heat, Elizabeth Spae wasn't impressed by the Department's difficult position. How difficult was it to accept reality and admit that they had been wrong about Arthur? The Department was supposed to find sleepers and help them adjust to the twenty-first century, not pretend they weren't who they were because it was embarrassing to admit to a mistake. "I said all I had to say in my report. And his name is Artos, by the way."

"What he calls himself is not really important. Is he or is he not the man known to legend as King Arthur?"

"I believe he is."

"We do not deal in beliefs," Dagastino said. "We deal in facts. Your *beliefs* are not admissible. We need proof."

"If only you could offer us some solid evidence." Spae could almost see the concerned look on Essenbach's face. Essenbach was a mage, and a decent one; of all them, she should understand the best. The others only *observed* the magic rising in the world; she, like Spae, could feel it. Spae had difficulty understanding how Essenbach could go along with this outrageous and pointless questioning when there was important work to be done harnessing the magic. Wasn't that as much a part of the Department's mandate as the searching out of sleepers?

"You know our resources are stretched, Doctor." Gere spoke with a deliberate slowness that put Spae in mind of one of her college professors. That professor had been overly fond of lecturing, too. "We can't afford to chase phantoms. If this sleeper is Arthur, we need him."

"We need all the sleepers," L'Hereaux said. His brusque voice came from her left; he'd moved since he'd last spoken. "If this man is Arthur, the Department must have him in its corner."

Spae didn't like the security man much. She didn't trust his reasons for wanting access to the sleepers. "For the propaganda value, or do you have something else in mind?"

"We do this for the world's sake. The threat we're facing—"

"Is largely undefined," Spae pointed out. Everyone felt certain that the sleepers were being woken to face a great peril, and so the Department collected every sleeper they could locate. The problem was that no one—including the sleepers—knew *what* peril they were supposed to face.

"All the more reason to find this sleeper. If he is Arthur—"

"Which remains to be proved," Dagastino insisted.

"Holger Kun will corroborate that he is the real Artos," Spae said.

"Even were he a reliable judge, Agent Kun is in no condition to corroborate anything."

Spae turned to face Dagastino's disembodied voice. Where was Kun, anyway? Why wasn't he here? For that matter, why hadn't he been at any of these sessions? "What do you mean, in no condition?"

"He's had a breakdown," Gere answered.

Spae was aghast. "A what? He's a damned bullyboy. Bullyboys don't have nervous breakdowns."

"The trip to the otherworld—"

"Or whatever actually happened," Dagastino cut in.

"—unsettled him," Gere finished.

That wasn't surprising; she'd been unsettled herself. Kun hated magic and magical things, but he dealt with them, and dealt with them well—because he was a complete professional. She admired him for that. A breakdown? "He was fine the last time I saw him." Before her first interrogation. Before his as well?

"Mr. Kun is in good hands, Doctor," Magnus assured her. That was something she'd like to know for herself, but rather than making an issue of it now, she let Magnus continue. "Mr. Kun is not why we are here. You are, Doctor. Or rather, the sleeper with whom you have had contact. By all indications, his was an important awakening."

"He's not Arthur," Dagastino interrupted.

"I do not wish to debate his identity at this time," Magnus said, although he didn't sound as if the issue was unimportant to him. "Whoever he is, one thing is clear. Since his awakening, the incidence of supernatural occurrences has risen. There is more magic loose upon the world now, and we must concern ourselves with that. We must concern ourselves with recovering this sleeper."

"If that's your real concern, why do you keep interrupting my work? Let me finish my rituals. I think I can locate him."

"Your rituals are untried," Dagastino pronounced. "And on shaky theoretical ground."

"What would you know about it, Dagastino? You can't even keep your conjurations separate from your abjurations."

"This is intolerable," Dagastino sputtered. Dagastino had been a thorn in her side since she'd been recruited by the Department; they had taken an instant dislike to each other. But it was only after she'd had time to observe Dagastino in action that she had come to truly despise the man. Spae could imagine him red faced and wide eyed behind the glare, sputtering from her insult and on the verge of a fit of indignation; it was a small consolation. "I don't have to sit here and be insulted by this woman. Even before this American affair, she was a proven troublemaker. She is unreliable, inept,—"

"That's enough, Dr. Dagastino," Magnus said. "Dr. Spae, I am informed that there are certain techniques that might enhance your memories. Perhaps you will be able to recall additional details under such a controlled questioning."

Dagastino's voice emerged from behind the shield of the lights like a striking weapon. "Pentatell™ will give us the truth."

Pentatell! "Is that what you did to Kun?" She'd read about what the truth drug could do and about its side effects. It wasn't supposed to be dangerous to a stable personality, but none of the articles had defined "stable."

"We did nothing to Mr. Kun," Magnus said.

Could she believe that? "He was fine before we got back here."

"That did seem to be the case," Gere said. "However, Agent Kun does seem to be suffering from delayed trauma derived, at least in part, from his sojourn in the otherworld. Given his history, I am told that such a reaction is understandable."

She knew Kun's history, too, and she'd seen how he'd taken facing it in the otherworld. These bastards had done something to him. They must have. Given him Pentatell, at least. He'd have taken it if they'd asked him to; he was a good soldier. Her respect for Magnus's leadership was faltering.

Well, Kun might be a good little soldier, but Spae wasn't any kind of soldier, good or otherwise.

"I'm not taking any drugs."

"Consider our position, Doctor." Magnus sounded reasonable. Spae wasn't interested in being reasonable if it meant having chemicals pumped into her system. "We can't force you—"

"Damned right!"

"—but I wish you would consider the bigger picture. We need corroboration and have limited sources to rely upon. Mr. Kun offered his full cooperation, but his condition was a problem. You yourself admit to experiencing unusual and surreal phenomena. Consider the possibility that you may be a victim of delayed trauma yourself. The effects of transport to the otherworld are unknown. Even setting aside the possible effects of the concussion you received during the firefight with the Mitsutomo operatives, your memories are suspect. We need verification."

"We need *facts*," Dagastino cut in.

"Consider our situation, Dr. Spae. Only you and Mr. Kun seem to have survived your trip—"

"Alleged trip," Dagastino interrupted.

Magnus resumed his speech after the barest of hesitations. "You are one of two visitors to the otherworld to whom we have access. Mr. Kun's unfortunate condition has rendered him nearly useless as a source of information. As to the rest of your traveling party, they are all dead or missing. This Bennett, the elf—"

"*Alleged* elf." Dagastino again.

Magnus cleared his throat. "Bennett remained in the otherworld. Harold Black is dead. We have no information on the whereabouts of the sleeper. John Reddy, who you say accompanied you to the otherworld and survived, is listed as dead, killed in the awakening of the sleeper."

All old news. "I explained that. It was even in the prelim report. The body wasn't his."

"Then whose body was it, Dr. Spae?" L'Hereaux asked. "Computer records map the physical characteristics of the corpse exactly to those listed in John Reddy's profile."

"The body was a mundane," Dr. Essenbach said. "There was no indication of any connection with the supernatural other than the cause of death. Didn't you say that Reddy claimed to be the son of an elf lord?"

"Bennett claimed that," she corrected.

"Bennett? The elf?" L'Hereaux's suspicious tone all but accused her of lying.

"Yes, the damn elf!"

"Reddy did not claim such a heritage, then?"

"He believed what Bennett said."

"But you do not?"

Did she believe it? Reddy hadn't looked like an elf, but there had been an aura of magic around him. "I don't know. It's a possibility."

"Couldn't you read his aura?" Dagastino asked maliciously.

L'Hereaux didn't let her get a word in. "Do you consider yourself on good terms with this Mr. Bennett?"

"After what happened? I don't think so."

"Then you have lost the Department a contact with a lord of the otherworld."

"*I* didn't lose anything."

"Oh, no? Who else was there? You were our specialist on the spot, Doctor. Who else had responsibility? Where is the sleeper? Where is Reddy?"

Why was L'Hereaux being such a badger? She had answered all these questions before. "I don't know."

"Don't know or are not willing to tell?"

Lord, the man wouldn't let go. "I *said* I don't know."

"Do you know who else is involved in this affair? Do you have connections with outside interests, Doctor?"

So they were back to that. "Are you referring to Mitsutomo?"

"I asked you the question, Doctor," L'Hereaux said harshly. "What role is Mitsutomo taking in this affair?"

"How should I know? I'm not on their payroll. If anything, I'd say that they seem to be antagonistic toward Artos."

"And why would that be?"

"Ask them!"

"We are asking you, Doctor." L'Hereaux's voice was annoyingly calm.

"I don't like what you're implying."

"Neither do I, Doctor. Neither do I. Mitsutomo seems to know more than they should. How might that be? Agent Kun seemed to think they had a secret source of knowledge."

The Department couldn't control every bit of data about the resurgence of magic in the world. Mitsutomo was a powerful megacorp; a corporation didn't get that big without smart people, and smart people made connections when presented with evidence. Who could guess what they knew? "Look, I don't know anything about Mitsutomo other than they kidnapped Reddy and Black and that they planted a transmitter on Black. That's how they were able to follow us to the otherworld."

"But you haven't explained how they managed to bridge the gap between the worlds," L'Hereaux said.

"Bridging the dimensions would take a mage," Dagastino added.

"What do you know about it? You ever done it?" Spae asked contemptuously.

"I'm afraid I have to agree with Dr. Dagastino," Essenbach said. "A mage is necessary. We do not have the ability to breach the dimensions with mere technology."

"Look, I don't know how they did it, but they *did* it. Mitsutomo raided the otherworld and tried to kill Artos. There was a raid on the awakening site as well. Maybe *that* was Mitsutomo, too. I've told you before that I don't know how they knew about Artos, or why they wanted to kill him. I am not involved with them."

"So you say," Dagastino said.

L'Hereaux stepped to the edge of the lights, becoming a silhouette against the dazzle. "Agent Kun's report does corroborate the raid and the transmitter. We know that Mitsutomo is at least partially aware of the magical upsurgence."

"How could they unless *someone* informed them?" Dagastino's tone made it clear who *he* thought the someone was.

"Accusations are not called for at this time," L'Hereaux said. "Mitsutomo is involved. Consider the implications: a megacorporation aware of the sleepers and what they represent. This could have profound consequences. Mitsutomo's interests are not the world's interests."

"There is the matter of the man Sörli," Gere said. This was new; they hadn't brought Sörli up in the previous sessions. "His involvement is something that concerns me, Dr. Spae. One of Agent Kun's field reports stated that you identified Sörli in Worcester shortly before the awakening of the sleeper. Is that correct?"

"Correct." Just as in my report.

"Your final report does not mention him. Why is that, Doctor?"

"We didn't see him again."

"I find it most interesting that you encountered Sörli at the beginning of this affair and never again," Dagastino said.

Gere cleared his throat. "How shall I say this? Such an encounter is uncharacteristic, judging from our previous dealings with the man."

L'Hereaux spoke from behind her; he had shifted position again. "Sörli has more than once disrupted our operations. We must consider the possibility that he has acquired the sleeper.

Do you think that is possible, Dr. Spae?" He paused, then spoke from yet another spot. "Perhaps Sörli has persuaded you that your best interests lie elsewhere."

Spae felt herself tense. So if Mitsutomo hadn't co-opted her, Sörli had, eh? They seemed to have convicted her already. "What are you saying, L'Hereaux?"

"I think it's obvious."

"And uncalled for," Magnus said.

"Dr. Spae is loyal," said Essenbach.

"There remains the question of Sörli's employers," Gere said.

"I should think that answer is obvious," said Dagastino. "Mitsutomo."

Magnus sighed. "If Mitsutomo is Sörli's master, Dr. Dagastino, they've been aware of the magic longer than I'd care to think about."

"I would think Sörli's association with Mitsutomo, if it exists, is a rather recent thing," L'Hereaux said. "As recent as some other associations. Wouldn't you agree, Dr. Spae?"

"Sörli is not the issue here." Essenbach's voice cracked a little. "Can we get back to the important issue?"

"Sörli *is* the issue," Dagastino snapped. "Especially if Spae has fallen under his influence."

"Stuff you," Spae told him.

For once Dagastino didn't rise to the bait. "But I think we have a more likely villain. Consider how she consorted with the elf Bennett, against Agent Kun's advice, and lost the sleeper to the otherworld."

What a little slime. He didn't care which side he took as long as he could get in a shot at her. "So you're willing to admit I really went to the otherworld, if it lets you drag me down." Spae kept speaking, overriding his next comment. "We don't know Artos remained in the otherworld. I believe that he was returned as Kun and I were, so he's not lost."

"We have no evidence the sleeper ever left the Faery realm," L'Hereaux said.

"The Lady of the Lakes gave her word."

"And what value may we place on that?"

"I believed her," Spae said with firm conviction.

"And so *we* should believe *you*?" She could imagine Dagastino's lip curling as he spoke. "You are stretching our credulity, Spae."

"And you're stretching my patience," she shot back.

"No more than you are stretching ours." Magnus scraped his chair back and stood, a shift in the shadows beyond the lights. "Dr. Spae, your reports make some strong claims for this Bennett, but they are claims without substantiation. Where is the proof? Is this elf truly a prince of Faery?"

"Alleged elf."

"Enough, Dagastino!" More calmly, Magnus continued to speak to her. "Mr. Kun reported that he urged you not to consent to the expedition to the otherworld. Is that true?"

"As true as it was the last time you asked."

She was tired of this, tired of their games.

"And yet you proceeded anyway."

"I did."

"And continued on, even when Mr. Kun advised a withdrawal to our own reality."

"Yes."

"For what purpose, Doctor?"

"You know why."

"Tell me again then. Convince *me*, Doctor."

She sighed. The great man was proving no better than the rest. He'd become as untrusting and paranoid as the others. You couldn't trust someone who didn't trust you. She'd been trusting the promises of liars and doubters.

She felt hot, from more than the lights. She was angry, very angry. Letting the emotion flood her, she pulled the energy together. The heat of the lights was searing; she imagined it hotter still, hot enough to melt and crumple the reflectors, twisting them around to hold in the heat. With a popping like a burst of automatic weapons fire, all the lights exploded. For a few seconds it seemed as if the room was plunged into darkness, but at last her eyes registered the room's ordinary lighting. Blackened reflectors stood at intervals smoking. Magnus's team stood or sat still, staring at her. Magnus didn't look amused.

"I want to know why you listened to Bennett and not to your associate."

What could she tell him that he'd understand? "How could anyone pass up a chance actually to visit the otherworld? Don't you want to know what it was like, Magnus?"

"No," he answered, cold as ice.

"Well, some people have more intellectual curiosity. Would you pass it up, Dr. Essenbach? *Would* you? Of course you wouldn't. Don't bother answering, Dagastino. *You* probably would throw away your chance, unless you had the blessing and encouragement of everyone around you, especially your boss." Dagastino gave a nervous glance at Magnus, who didn't seem to notice. "Hell, until recently we weren't even sure the otherworld existed. Well, now we know. I've been there. I've seen it."

"And perhaps fallen under its spell?" L'Hereaux suggested.

She rounded on him. "What would you know about it? You've never shown any more sensitivity to the arcane than your average lump of mud. You and your goddamned bully-boys have trampled on and destroyed more occult evidence than you've ever brought in."

"Now, Doctor . . ."

Magnus's tone was cautioning, but Spae no longer cared. She'd seen enough to know that the spy games weren't going to stop; they were only going to get worse. She was tired of the suspicion, tired of the distrust. She didn't need it. Or them. Or their bloody Department!

"I've had enough of your 'now, Doctor'. I volunteered to work with the Department when you came knocking on my door, crying about needing people who could deal with the arcane. And I have worked with you. Honestly. To the best of my ability. But, you know, when I said I'd work with you, the emphasis was on the *with*! I'm not a servant, and I'm not a pawn to be pushed around in your stupid games. Most especially I'm not some faceless work-prole who will take all the bullshit you dish out and ask for more!"

"Doctor, sit down," Magnus ordered.

"I will not! I've had enough of this! You can take your damned Department and shove it!"

She glared wildly around the room. Dagastino and Gere were still stunned. Essenbach looked utterly appalled. L'Hereaux was the only one doing anything; he was leaning over a console, whispering—calling for his bullyboys, no doubt.

Oh, no! They weren't going to lock her away in their see-nothing, know-nothing places. She wasn't about to stand still for that! They were afraid of what had happened in the other-world. Well, she'd show them that they had something to be afraid of.

She raised the power in a flaring burst of energy, all dazzle and incandescence. They cowered from the light, shrinking back as the brilliance cast their inky shadows in elongated caricatures on the white walls.

Let the light blind them to her doings! Let their thoughts be as twisted as their shadows on the walls! They would not see her as she walked, nor move to oppose her.

The effect wouldn't last long, but it would hold for long enough for her to leave. She turned for the door and out of the corner of her eye noticed one shadow that did not match. L'Hereaux's shade did not match the security chief's crouch. She looked at him and saw that he was not really crouching; he was looking back at her.

She threw him the finger.

He smiled and she almost stumbled, for in that moment he looked like Bennett. She caught herself and looked again. L'Hereaux was L'Hereaux.

There wasn't time to think about it.

She ran for the door. No one moved to stop her. She kept going.

Had she actually seen what she thought she'd seen? Was it her imagination? It must have been a trick of the light, an illusion based on fears and congruities. It couldn't have been real.

But what if it was?

If L'Hereaux was Bennett in disguise, had he always been, or had the elf only recently displaced the true L'Hereaux? In either case, why? What did the elf prince want? Had he wanted her to recognize him? And if so, why?

Thinking about Bennett's involvement made her head hurt. She didn't have time to deal with it now; she had to worry about herself. She had to get out, or waste the effect of her spell. She headed topside, longing for the clear air and open sky. No one moved to stop the angry doctor. They knew better; she had top clearances. For a few minutes more, anyway.

No one barred her way at the entrance, but the wary-eyed guards watched her as if she were some kind of wild animal. She didn't care what they thought as long as they let her go.

She left the complex.

They weren't going to be happy with her after this. They'd wanted to know what she had learned in the otherworld, and she'd given them a demonstration of what she could do now. Maybe she'd best consider it her resignation.

Would they let her resign?

They could try to stop her. She was still hot with anger and indignation as she stamped down the lane toward her cottage. Let them try!

CHAPTER
4

Time had passed.

How much?

It was hard to tell without sight or sound or scent.

Dust was a taste familiar. Motion a feeling grown strange over . . . time. How strange time had grown.

Time passed.

He knew he was drifting. He knew he was hungry. He knew he needed nourishment.

There were auras around him, nearing him and drawing away, darting about like hummingbirds seeking nectar.

Too fast, too fast.

He waited. Time was his. Patience was his. The reward, when it came, would be his.

The bright hummingbirds brought him to a place of cold and dark. Abandoned him, taking away their light and heat. A ploy to entrap him? No. They returned with a cold artificial light that he felt though he could not see it.

His hunger returned as well. He felt its heat.

He felt their heat. The light beckoned him.

He wanted.

He needed.

One flickered close, lingering.

Unaware.

There was no sign to avoid on this one.

He rejoiced.

He took the light, sucking it down, feeding his hunger, warming his self.

Light beat against lids long closed. He had sight again. He declined to use it. He had strength again, but so very little. He was still so very weak.

The hummingbirds flitted about, still too quick.

He could wait.

Pamela Martinez was surprised that Nakaguchi invited her to attend the installation of his prize. Presumably he wanted to demonstrate his command of the Project. Pamela had considered finding something else to do, but Nakaguchi was going to be using the Nieumann Lab at the Brookfield Chemogenics Facility, a lab which, prior to Nakaguchi's usurpation, she had shepherded. She had personally approved the purchase orders for every item of equipment that had gone into the lab. She had seen to it that the Nieumann Lab was one of the best in the world, a cutting edge facility for biochemical and biomedical research. She wanted to know what Nakaguchi had done to it.

And now, standing in the observation bay of Lab 1, she did. The dark and shriveled thing Nakaguchi had hauled back from the Andes looked totally out of place on the shining lab table. Its ugliness dominated the chamber. It looked as dead as any mummy she'd seen in a museum. Deader, possibly. Or maybe it was just the contrast with so much shining machinery dedicated to life.

A bevy of technicians in green medical scrubs complete with masks were scattered around the periphery of the lab, setting up monitors, manning workstations, and adjusting machines. Some stood in clumps, discussing things in voices that carried over the interphone as no more than a buzz. One figure separated itself from a clump and walked toward the observation window. The man bowed toward the observation bay. Pamela noted the caduceus symbol on his greens and read the name tag: Hasukawa.

"I am ready to begin the preliminary examination, Nakaguchi-sama," Hasukawa said.

"Proceed, Hasukawa-san."

"Is that Matsuo Hasukawa?" Pamela asked.

Without taking his eyes away from the scene in the lab, Nakaguchi replied, "None other."

Hasukawa was a world-renowned geriatrics specialist. What expertise did he bring to the examination of a centuries-old corpse? Why was he here at all? "Just what are you trying to prove here, Nakaguchi? Your 'sleeper' hasn't shown any sign of being more than a well-preserved mummy."

"You're mistaken, Ms. Martinez."

"Unfortunately," Hagen said.

Hasukawa moved to the table and began his examination. Whatever the doctor was doing, it wasn't particularly visible from the observation bay. She turned her attention to the others in the lab, trying to make sense out of the collection of machines and the contents of the displays. One of the untended monitors blipped to life, a green squiggle tracing a sluggish path across the screen.

Someone in the lab shouted.

Hasukawa was staggering away from the examination table, clutching at his chest. He fell to the floor. Technicians abandoned their stations and rushed to the fallen doctor.

"It looks like a heart attack," said someone. "He's fading fast."

Nakaguchi leaned over the mike for the interphone. "Get him to the hospital."

One of the green-coated men around the fallen Hasukawa looked up at the window. He had a caduceus on his greens. "I don't think there's time. Best we work on him here. We have everything we need."

"Respiratory arrest," one of the others said.

The doctor started to turn back, but Nakaguchi's shout froze him.

"I said get him to the hospital. That is standard procedure. That is what you will do. You may accompany him if you wish."

The doctor gave the window a last glance and went to work on Hasukawa. Nakaguchi turned to one of his aides, Kurita, the security specialist. "See that my orders are carried out."

"*Ho!*" Kurita said with a sharp bow. It was the sort of precision you saw in old samurai vids and it chilled Pamela. The aide left the observation bay at a run. In seconds he was in the lab with a squad of security men and a gurney. They pulled the doctor away from his resuscitation attempt and loaded Hasukawa onto the gurney. The doctor glared at the window for a second, then ran after the departing security men.

Pamela stared at Nakaguchi. The doctor in the lab was right; by the time they reached the hospital, it would likely be too late to revive Hasukawa. Nakaguchi was condemning him to death.

"You'll be to blame if he dies."

Nakaguchi turned to look at her. "Doctor Hasukawa was an old man. It is unfortunate, but old men die."

Pamela had a sudden realization. "You knew this was going to happen."

Nakaguchi maintained an infuriatingly bland expression.

"Was it something about the corpse? Is that it? Is it some sort of bacteria?"

"First of all, Quetzoucoatl is no corpse. Second of all, there are no bacteria involved. That should be obvious even to someone of your limited vision. We were all exposed to him in his resting place and none of us fell ill. How could you even imagine that bacteria might be the explanation?"

"If it's not a disease, then what's going on?"

Hagen mumbled something so softly that Pamela wasn't sure that the man had actually spoken, although it sounded as if he said, "Evil."

Nakaguchi snorted. "The sleeper awakes."

He had been slow, locked in the sluggishness of sleep. He was still slow, torpid from the time of deep dreams. He could feel the hummingbird lights flitting about him. He wanted their heat, needed it, but he was slow and they so quick, so vital.

What he needed fluttered just out of his sluggish reach, as yet unattainable. The hummingbirds danced near, tantalizing him, then flitted away out of reach. He ached with frustration, thwarted by their confounding speed.

He needed.

He waited.

He hungered.

He waited, preparing himself.

One of the hummingbirds approached him. Slowing its rushing flight, it lingered. He felt its feathery touch upon his paper-dry skin. The touch was enough.

He struck as the viper strikes, uncoiling with unexpected speed.

The little bird crumpled at his touch. His first taste of the warmth tingled, exciting him. Ravenously, he pulled harder until the heat flooded him. He almost heard the humming-bird's cries. He drained it dry. His hunger was barely slaked, but he was stronger than he had been in—

Centuries!

How could it have been so long?

Frightened by what he had done, the hummingbirds dragged the husk of their companion away. They were still too quick for him. The strength he'd gained was greater than any he'd had from the little fires that had sustained him for so long, but he was still weak and slow. Still half-adream.

He knew how to wait.

In time—not so much as before but strangely seemingly longer—they returned. They had armored themselves against him. Foolishly so. They used dead, flimsy stuff that barely covered the beckoning light of themselves.

He took the first to present itself.

The hummingbird sang, a warbling song that had little of intelligence about it, but did occasionally strike a familiar chord. A mistake, it seemed to be saying. He wasn't sure what it was saying; its language was strange.

Had so much time passed that language itself had changed?

What did it matter? The little bird's struggles grew feeble. He felt stronger as the fire infused his veins. His sense of the surroundings grew clearer.

The hummingbird was pleading, promising. What? More than it could deliver certainly.

Was he making a mistake? Perhaps. It wouldn't be the first time.

Strength first, subtlety at leisure. It was an excellent paradigm to impress; it had served him well in the past. It had served best when applied in accordance with current circumstances. But what were current circumstances? In so much time, much was sure to have changed.

Reluctantly, he ceased draining the little bird. Its light flickered, but did not gutter and go out. Satisfactory. Before he released it, he put his mark on it, to keep it true. He didn't have enough strength to make the mark truly effective, but this one was weak. What he had done would serve for now.

He opened his eyes to gaze upon the first of his new servants.

Pamela gasped when the mummy opened its eyes. She stared in frozen horror as it reached out a withered hand to lay upon the brow of the technician slumped against the table. Gaunt-faced, the technician rose unsteadily to his feet.

"Joel, you okay?" one of the others asked.

Joel didn't answer her. Instead he said, "Bring in the first subject."

The technicians looked to one another in consternation and confusion. A few looked to the observation window.

"Do as he says," Nakaguchi ordered.

A few minutes later, the "first subject" arrived. By the look of him he'd be one of the homeless derelicts Chemogenics sometimes used in medical testing. He would have been required to sign a consent form, releasing Chemogenics, and the whole Mitsutomo Keiretsu from all responsibility should there be some unfortunate occurrence during the unspecified medical experiments in which he agreed to take part. From the way the derelict turned his head around and grinned idiotically, she doubted he had the competence to understand what he'd been told, let alone make a voluntary decision. His two attendants wheeled the chair up beside the examining table. The derelict grinned at the mummy and said, "Howd'ya do, pal. Ya sign up too?"

The attendants backed away with unseemly haste when the mummy's dark hand rose quivering.

Joel stepped forward and released the restraining strap on the derelict's right arm. He brought the man's hand up into the path of the mummy's groping fingers. The derelict started to squirm as soon as the gnarled fingers closed over his wrist. He began to struggle, bucking in his chair and tugging against the iron grip. Within seconds he was panting. He slumped, exhausted. Pamela could see the sweat coating the derelict's face as he rocked his head back, mouth open to scream. Only a tortured moan emerged. The old man's head slid to the side, turning his face from her view. For several minutes nothing visible occurred, then it was over.

Pamela wasn't sure how she knew, but she knew.

The mummy opened its hand and let the derelict's limp arm fall. Hitting the arm of the wheelchair, it made a sound like a dry stick hitting metal. Pamela half expected the limb to shatter; it merely fell, lifeless, into the dead man's lap.

"Another," Joel ordered.

By her side Nakaguchi chuckled.

"You see, Ms. Martinez. It is possible to deal effectively with sleepers. All you have to do is keep them happy."

Pamela forced herself to maintain a neutral expression. Nakaguchi had gone beyond the boundary by bringing this monster to life, but now was not the time to challenge them. She would have to marshal her resources and wait for the best chance. She didn't think she'd get more than one try.

Charley Gordon pulled up the collar of his coat and managed to shut out the drizzle of icy rainwater that was worming its way down his back. A Chrysler Compel™ entering the parking structure hit a puddle and splashed him as it took the turn. He gave it the finger. There was no telling who was behind the opaqued windows of the car, but he didn't care. The bum probably hadn't even seen Charley.

He walked down the lane between the Sobanski Rezcom and its parking garage. The Sobanski was one of the first of its kind in the Attleboro District. Like a lot of the district, it was pretty run-down. Pulverized curb crunched under his shoes as he turned into the service alley. It was the third one he tried. Jimmy Kravatz hadn't said which alley in the message he'd left.

Kravatz was one of Charley's best ears in the Foxboro District. If the word was on the streets, Kravatz heard it. The ear was spooked about something, meaning that whatever he wanted to talk to Charley about might actually be important.

The recording Kravatz had left on Charley's box said he needed to see Charley right away. He'd left an address, too: the service alley behind the Sobanski Rezcom. He hadn't said there was more than one. Still, it was a Kravatz kind of address, but it was a little out of his usual territory.

He found the ear huddled in the lee of a dumpster and stinking of booze. He roused Kravatz with a boot in the leg.

"What is it, Jimmy? What's so important I gotta come down here in this shit?"

Kravatz scrambled to his feet, polluting Charley's space with his breath. "It's Marabeth, Officer Charley. She's been taken away."

Charley hadn't been just an officer since he'd transferred to the special crimes unit, but there were some things you put up with rather than queer an arrangement with a good ear.

"This Marabeth, she got a last name?"

Kravatz had to think about that for a while. "Lankster, I think. We don't use them kind of names much."

"I'll check on her." Charley reached under his coat and punched in a request for status on Marabeth Lankster, spelling optional.

"Ya won't find nuthin'," Kravatz told him. "They got her."

A truck turned into the alley, sweeping them with its lights. They had to huddle behind the dumpster as it ground its way down the pavement. The trash container screeched as the vehicle scraped it. Kravatz cowered behind Charley, howling in accompaniment to the sound. Charley shouted at him to shut up. For a change, he did. Too well. For several minutes after the truck had passed, Kravatz just shivered, unwilling to talk.

Charley's belt unit beeped that it had a response to his request. He pulled it out, shielding the screen from the rain so he could read it. The list was short. The closest name was a Marabeth Lancaster with a status on file of Unregistered, Criminal. That was likely the one. Just like Kravatz, an outcast from the system on every count except criminal. Lancaster's rap sheet was an assortment of drug charges, a welter of Vagrancies, a couple of Solicitings, and a single count of felony Harassment. She wasn't unusual for a streeter.

"This Marabeth, she a close friend of yours?"

"We—she and me—I mean, we kinda know each other from way long time ago. Two years maybe."

"You say she was taken away?"

Nodding furiously, Kravatz said, "Snatched! Right outa her box!"

The last time Kravatz had reported a missing person the guy in question had gotten himself wasted and fallen down in the wrong alley. "Bottle fairies again?"

"Ain't no fairies, Officer. I seen 'em. Ain't fairies at all."

"Who'd you see, Jimmy?"

"Trolls. Trolls, they was. Big hulking things."

Swell. "What did these trolls look like, Jimmy?"

"I—I didn't get too good a look. They was wearing uniforms. Nice white ones. They looked warm."

Uniformed trolls? Better and better. "Listen, Jimmy, I don't got time for this."

"I'm telling ya, Officer Charley. Them trolls took Marabeth. Ya gotta get her back. I think they're gonna eat her."

"You know where these trolls took Marabeth?"

"They put her in their truck. Honda Losquit™, last year's model. You know, the one right after they dropped the bumper strips."

Kravatz was a loony but he had a way with vehicles. "You catch the plate?"

"Naw. Corporate though."

Uniformed *corporate* trolls. How nice. "Look, Jimmy. You haven't given me much to go on, but I'll put it in. We'll do what we can, okay?"

"Ya gotta get her back, Officer Charley. Ya gotta do something."

"I'll do what I can, Jimmy."

Charley did what he could. He turned off the recorder on his belt unit and assigned the file number. Opening a line to the station house, he transmitted the MP report and tagged it with a "notify officer." He'd file a full when he got back. Not that there'd be anything else to do with it. Streeters got themselves lost every day; it didn't take trolls, corporate or otherwise. If Marabeth Lancaster was ever heard from again, it'd be a miracle. Charley had given up believing in miracles a long time ago.

"You take care of yourself, Jimmy. Stay away from those trolls. And if you see them again, you give me a call, okay?"

"You bet, Officer Charley."

Not one worth taking, Charley thought as he slouched back to his car. *The things you got to put up with to humor your ears.*

Kemal was a mage.

Or at least he was going to be. Tonight he was going to prove it. He'd been purifying himself for weeks, getting ready for tonight, and now the time had come. The stars were right, the moon was in the right phase, and he'd gathered everything he needed for the summoning.

The dagger had been the hardest. He didn't know much about forging but then he didn't have to know all that much; the important part was that he make it himself. He was convinced that was the reason that all his other rituals had failed. Every tool—*every* one—had to be made by the magician. Just purifying the tools wasn't enough. So he'd done it; he had the scars from handling the hot iron to prove it. The dagger might not be meteoric iron, but the next best thing. The metal was preatomic, reforged from a piece of a Victorian wrought-iron fence he'd cut free from the barrier around an East Side mansion in the dark of the moon.

The time had come. All his reading, all his studying, all his preparations were going to come to fruition tonight. He started to undress. Naked as the day he had come into the world, he took his place in the circles of power. Slowly, carefully, he closed them and said the proper incantations to activate his protections.

Was that the power he felt making his skin tingle?

As he started the summoning, he was sure of it. The power was rising; he could feel it.

He had teased the name of a still-summonable demon from the ancient texts. He had practiced speaking each syllable of the name, but never the whole name; he wanted to take no chances. Now, he spoke the name of the spirit. There was no response, but he didn't expect one. Yet. He called the name again. For the third time he called the name.

He waited, growing surer that something was nearby.

He heard the window to his bedroom slide open. Did demons have to come through the window? Something thumped in his bedroom as he turned his eyes toward the door.

A figure emerged. It wasn't human; nothing human ever had such a sharp-featured face. The demon was a lot smaller than he expected. Kemal hadn't expected it to be clothed either; none of his grimoires talked about that. This spirit was dressed in studded biker leathers and wearing a stupid Shriner's hat, not what he thought proper demon wear at all.

"Stand, spirit. I command you in the name of the Lord of Hosts. Stand lest I hurl you into the pit forevermore by the use of His name."

"Spirit?" His visitor gave Kemal a toothy grin. "Got the wrong number, Chuckles."

It stepped across the first of his protective barriers.

That wasn't right. A demon wasn't supposed to do that. It could only do that if Kemal hadn't gotten the protective sigils correct. He had been meticulous. He couldn't have made any mistakes. Could he?

The demon stepped across the second barrier. It had talons on its hands.

Kemal turned and ran for the door to the hall. He hadn't gone three steps before he felt its claws in his back.

CHAPTER
5

John woke from the dream with a start. His sudden movement startled a rat prowling the perimeter of the room and sent it scurrying into the wall. John lay still and watched it scamper. Had it really been less than a year since just the thought of a rat in a building had creeped him out? They were just part of the ecosystem here. Admirable in their own way. They'd found themselves a secure niche in the world, a place where they could be what they were and live their lives in their own way. He sort of envied them.

"Are you all right, John?"

He felt the feather touch of Faye's invisible presence, a rustling of his skin hairs, little more than a breeze might do. He kicked away the sheet that had wrapped itself around his legs and heaved himself up from the mattress.

"John?"

"Yeah, yeah. I'm fine."

She'd know he was lying. She always knew. But that didn't stop him. It was better to pretend that the dream hadn't upset him, better to pretend that he wasn't frustrated by her untouchable nearness. Maybe she'd pretend, too; they'd played lots of pretend games when he'd been growing up.

Life just hadn't been what he'd expected after his return from the otherworld. The magical sensitivity he'd felt in the other realm seemed to have deserted him. He felt it in the dream, but it came associated with unpleasant things there. He wished that he could feel it when he was awake and without all that other baggage.

The dream had terrified him, as usual. His body was slick with sweat that the faint breeze from outside made chill and clammy on him. He shivered, knowing it was from more than the chill. It seemed that he could still hear the guns firing and the screams of the wounded, but what he'd first thought was screaming turned into the howling sirens of cop cars racing along the highway outside. He found himself staring out the window. The guns were real too, but far away. Something nasty was going down out there in old Providence's little corner of the sprawl tonight.

Up in his tower in the middle of this little patch of decayed and mostly derelict buildings, he was isolated from the violence out there.

There were advantages to being isolated from the world.

And a lot more disadvantages.

For good or ill, he'd been on his own since his return from the otherworld. He'd spent days waiting for Bear and the ECSS agents to show up where he had. They hadn't, so far as he could tell. He'd spent some time thinking he'd been tricked, but couldn't see any point in it. The Lady of the Lakes had said she'd send them home, and since she transferred John into the Northeast sprawl—probably as close as she could get to John's home—he guessed that she must have sent the others somewhere else closer to their homes.

Being on his own had frightened John. He'd been too afraid of Mitsutomo to go back to Worcester right away. He'd found himself a slump in an abandoned building and spent weeks living on tricks learned from Trashcan Harry, trying to figure the angles and work up the courage. He'd gone back to the rezcom now, for all the good it had done. He still didn't know what had happened to his mother—foster mother, according to Bennett. But blood relative or not, she was all the mother he'd ever known, and he loved her. Nothing Bennett could say would change that.

And it wasn't like Bennett had never lied to him.

At least he'd found Faye again. Sort of. Like him, she wasn't the same as she'd been in the otherworld. They might never have been there for all the trip had changed their lives. They were no better off than when they'd fled Worcester the first time.

Except that neither Bear nor Trashcan Harry was here. Harry never would be, and Bear was God knew where. It was just he and Faye. Alone and isolated.

And different.

Faye had been corporeal in the otherworld, a woman of unsettling beauty. All their friendly intimacies of his childhood had seemed on the verge of becoming something more. He'd wanted it, but he'd backed away. Believing that he was an elf, and knowing that she was, he had been terrified that they were related somehow. Sister and brother even. They'd grown up together, hadn't they? Wouldn't anything they did together be wrong? He'd feared so, but Faye hadn't seemed bothered by the issue at all. There hadn't been time to wonder why then, and he'd lost her on his return to the real world. Now they were together again, and what did it matter? She was his invisible playmate again.

Was this her choice, or could she only be corporeal in the otherworld? She'd said things were different here, and he hadn't asked her what she meant by that. He was too afraid to ask. Without a way back to the elf realms, the answer might be too painful. What if she was intangible because she wanted to be? What if she would only be real for a real elf, and not a counterfeit like John was coming to believe he was?

Was his elven heritage just another of Bennett's lies?

What could he be but a counterfeit? He still looked like he always had. There was none of the gauntness and fey beauty of an elf about him. His ears had no points, his eyes no nacreous luster. He looked to be the same tall, gangly John Reddy he'd always been. What did it matter that he'd seen himself with a different face in the otherworld? Bennett had been the one who'd sent him to that otherworldly reflecting pool. He felt that what he'd seen was true, but what if it wasn't? What was he supposed to believe? He didn't look any different now. No one he knew on this side of reality thought he was an elf. To them he'd looked as he always had, was what he'd always been.

Of course, there was Bear, the great King Arthur. Bear, being Bear, saw things differently. *He* had believed John was an elf, and he'd cursed John for it, calling him a "serpent in my camp." Damn Bear anyway! What right did he have to judge John? To curse him just because of what he was? Especially when even John couldn't be sure it was true. Bear should have trusted him more. Bear should have known John was the same John he'd always been. Bear should have believed that he was the same person who had saved Bear from blundering his life away in the weeks after his awakening, believed in the person who had stood by him right up until the end. Even when Bear had accused him of being a traitor, John had stood by him. Saved him, even!

And gotten not so much as a thank-you.

But Bear had seen John as an elf. Hadn't he? He'd certainly acted and spoken as if he had. Or was even that another of Bennett's tricks? They *had* been in the otherworld at the time.

The otherworld was the past now. The present was a dirty, smelly slump on the West Side of Providence; John's life was that of a maybe-orphaned, urban castaway with nowhere to go and no one to turn to. One thing his adventures with Bear had done was to kill his old life. Too bad they hadn't quite prepared him for his new one.

Another cop car wailed along the highway, sounding like a damned soul rushing to oblivion. He almost howled along with it.

"What's the matter, John?"

Everything. "Nothing. Just thinking."

He felt her feather touch about him, a tantalizing mockery of her real embrace. Her voice was real enough, though. Real enough to remind him of other times, other chances.

"I know." Her tone was honestly sympathetic. Did it have a hint of pain as well? "You've been thinking about things that make you unhappy. I don't like to see you so fretful."

Fretful? Yeah, he supposed so. "Life's not so great around here."

"We're together again. That's what's important."

Together? When they couldn't touch? "How can we—" He stopped, realizing how stupid what he'd been intending to say was. They'd been together for years without physically touching each other and it had never bothered him. They'd been the best of friends, happy and content with each other. Had so much changed?

"How can we what, John?"

He was too embarrassed to answer honestly. "How can we—ah—how can we make it better? Life around here, I mean?"

"This is a good place, John. It feels a little like home."

Rezcom 3 of the Benjamin Harrison Town Project was never like this sprawl-blighted abandoned factory. The place was half a dozen floors of ravaged masonry, smashed windows, vermin nests, graffiti, and refuse. There was no power and no climate control. No mall with a gazillion things available on your corp card. There were also no crowds, cleaning 'bots, security doors, sec-cams, or Mitsutomo-owned watchmen—so maybe it wasn't so bad after all. But *home?* "How can you say that?"

"Can't you feel it in the air?"

There *was* something about the place; John felt it when he'd first stumbled in out of the rain. He'd put the feelings down to just being glad to have shelter. He'd stayed, thinking it just a matter of convenience, but now that Faye had drawn his attention to it, he realized that there was something—not exactly friendlier, but—easier about being here. Maybe it was Faye's presence.

"I don't know what I feel," he said, realizing that he'd felt *something* about the place even before Faye had come back with him. Maybe he'd have to look a little harder at the place and see what lurked behind the debris of abandonment and decay. Why had he decided to slump here? Beyond the fact that it was available and free. Why here out of all the derelict sites of the sprawl?

Thinking about the place made him aware of an itchy, uncomfortable feeling that hovered on the edge of his consciousness, the sort of thing he'd felt as a kid when he was sure that his mother was about to find out something he'd done. "It sure doesn't feel like home to me."

"It could be. You could make it your domain."

"My domain, eh? Not exactly a palace suited for an elven prince. But then I'm not exactly an elven prince, am I?"

"You are my prince, John."

Her voice made his knees quiver and her words made his head spin. All the frustration of her intangibility rose up and strangled his eyesight, narrowing it until he could only see straight ahead, out the window in front of him. In the night sky only a pitiful few stars were visible against the sprawl glow, a tantalizing hint of what was hidden. It wasn't right!

One of those lonesome stars blinked as something occluded it, breaking his frozen stare. His vision returned to normal, but he didn't want to turn around. What was there to see anyway? He gazed out at the street, quiet now in the early morning. Dawn was only a few hours away; even the night creatures were abed. A flicker of motion told him that he was even wrong about that.

"Someone's coming," Faye said.

It was true. The face of the building was in shadow, but John's night vision was very good; he could make out darker shapes moving in the darkness below. He couldn't tell who they were, but he counted four. He hoped they would go on by, taking their dark business away with them, but they stopped near the main entrance, huddling in a clump of congealed night. One moved away from the bunch and continued on, slipping around the corner of the building. One by one, the others slipped inside.

The little bits of magic he'd learned in the otherworld hadn't worked for him in the real world. He couldn't turn himself invisible and scout out the intruders. But Faye was already invisible. . . .

"Check them out," he ordered as he snatched up his pants. Faye went. He dressed as quickly as he could, pulling on his jacket and strapping on his belts. Stuffing his bronze-headed defense stick in his waist belt, he headed for the stairwell. The top floor was the most comfortable sleeping area, but there were too few ways down, and he didn't want to be trapped.

Whatever the old corp had done in the factory involved huge machines; most of the building's first three stories were devoted to an open work space. A maze of catwalks hemmed in the rusting hulks of the old machines and offered aerial access to almost the whole of the main area. Faye rejoined John as he crouched on one of the higher catwalks, watching two of the intruders pick their way across the ground level debris. It was forty feet to the floor, but the height didn't bother him; people in his building bothered him.

"There are only the four," Faye reported. "The one who didn't come inside is a female; she's waiting on the loading dock by the door. The ones inside are all males. One stayed in the lobby. The other two are searching the lower floor."

He could see that. "What do you think they're looking for?"

"You."

Somehow, the answer wasn't a surprise. "Anyone they can find, or me specifically?"

"You specifically."

"How do you know that?"

"One of the searchers said, 'This Tall Jack's gonna be easy money.' "

Some of the locals called him Tall Jack. Easy money? Bounty hunters or ordinary hunters? "Did they let slip why they're hunting me?"

"No."

Of course not. "Are they streeters or corporate?"

"Streeters, by their look and talk."

"Even the woman?"

"I haven't heard her say anything, but she looks it."

John was indignant about the intrusion. This was his place, his domain, as Faye would have it. These intruders had no place being here. He was even more incensed because they had come seeking him for money. He shifted catwalks, keeping the two intruders in sight. The searchers were still working the north corner; they showed no signs of noticing his move. He had half a dozen escape routes planned; he could be gone before they got off the first floor. He could be, but he didn't want to be; he was tired of running.

"Guns?"

"I didn't see any," she said.

Fine. If they didn't have guns, any fighting would be more even. From the searchers' awkward pattern, John could tell that he knew the place better than they did. Another advantage. Maybe he wouldn't have to run. If he could catch them one at a time . . . They were already cooperating by keeping half their numbers at the doors.

"Comlinks?"

"No."

Better still. If they couldn't talk to each other easily, it'd be harder for them to call for reinforcements.

John moved along the catwalks, passing over the two below. He stopped near one of the taller machines. Carefully, he climbed over the rail, and lowered himself until he was hanging, gripping the walk with his hands. His feet dangled in open air. He waited until his body stopped swaying before dropping. He landed silently, but awkwardly, on the uneven surface of the machinery, and almost lost his balance. He had to grab a stanchion to steady himself and avoid an uncontrolled plunge to the floor, still a good twenty feet below. The maneuver wrenched his defense stick out of its snugged position. The stick started to shift, to fall. John twisted, knowing he'd be too late to keep the heavy bronze head from gonging on the machine but trying anyway. The stick never struck. It hung in the air, head hovering less than an inch from the metal surface.

"Thank you, Faye," he whispered as he closed his hand on the wooden shaft.

"You're welcome," she whispered back.

Climbing down the machine was harder with the stick in his hand than it would have been otherwise, but he didn't want to risk having it slip again; he couldn't count on Faye's being close enough to catch it. He reached the floor without attracting the attention of the searchers. John crept closer.

"Hey, Roscoe, how come we're doin' all the work?" one of them complained in a whining voice.

"Cause we're gettin' paid, stupid," Roscoe answered absently.

"Yeah, I know that."

The two of them continued their probe of the darkness around the machines. They were not very thorough; they missed more than a dozen places where someone even of John's height could have hidden. Flashlights would have made their search more effective, but would have made their movements more obvious as well. Despite their talking, stealth seemed to be part of their plan.

John crept closer, hoping they would soon find it necessary to separate.

"Hey, Roscoe."

"What now, Flake?"

"How come she's waitin' out back doing nothin' while we're doin' this?"

"The geek might go out that way."

"Yeah, I knew that."

Flake tripped over something and stumbled into one of the machines. John used the opportunity to cross the aisle. By what he was observing John guessed that Roscoe would be the more dangerous one; he'd have to be taken out first. But not just yet—the two were sticking too close together.

"Hey, Roscoe, you know what I think? I think she's gettin' ideas. I think she thinks she's gettin' too good to do the rough stuff."

"I think you're thinkin' too much. She gets to do what she wants 'cause she's got the connections."

"We could get our own connections."

"Now I *know* you're thinkin' too much. We're gettin' paid; that's enough. Now shut up, Flake, or the geek'll hear us comin'."

"Aw, Roscoe, we been all over most of this place. Tall Jack ain't down here. He ain't gonna hear us."

"Talk any louder and he'll hear even if he's on the roof. Now shut up!"

Flake shut up, mostly. He grumbled as he continued poking about. The two intruders worked their way to the old warehousing area. It was more open in the upper levels—no catwalks—than the main area, but just as clogged on the ground level because of all the old crates and debris on the floor. John still had cover. He moved closer still, angling toward Roscoe. He lost some ground waiting for Flake to turn away from an area illuminated by a streetlight's amber glow shining through one of the windows. The delay made John nervous. They were finishing their search of the main floor and would be heading up the stairs soon. It would be easier to separate them upstairs, but harder to sneak up on them; there were fewer places to hide.

A shadow flickered across the floor.

Flake jumped back. "What's that!"

"Shit, Flake!" Roscoe spun and crouched. Seeing nothing untoward, he straightened up. "Will you cut it out?"

"I saw somethin'."

"What?"

"I don't know."

Flake's head jerked about as he tried to see everywhere at once. Roscoe scanned the dark more slowly and carefully.

"I don't see nothin'."

"I'm tellin' you I saw somethin'." The shadow flickered again. "There!"

Flake pointed at the floor, where the shadow had been. John shook his head. Though he hadn't seen whatever had cast the shadow, whatever it was wasn't on the floor; it had been somewhere behind the two. He knew it wasn't Faye; she didn't cast shadows.

"It's outside," Roscoe said. That was John's conclusion as well. "Somethin' flew past the streetlight."

"I ain't so sure." Flake sounded scared.

"It's just a bird or somethin'."

"Birds don't fly at night," Flake snapped.

"Ain't you never heard of owls?"

Flake thought about that for a moment. "Ain't never seen no owls 'round here."

"So it was a bat. You seen bats, ain't you?"

"A bat? I dunno. Ain't so sure it was a bat."

"Just shut up and come on." Roscoe sounded impatient.

"I'm tellin' you there's somethin' in here with us!"

Roscoe grabbed Flake's jaw and turned his face to the light. He started intently into his partner's eyes. "You drop somethin' before we came in here, Flake? Shit, man, you know better than that."

Flake yanked his head away. "I didn't take nothin'!"

"Better not have."

"I didn't!"

"Then you ain't got no cause to see things that ain't there. Now come on, we got things to do here."

Roscoe turned away and went on to the next tumble of abandoned crates. Flake gave the window a glance before following. The intruders' search took them through the storage area without offering John the chance he was waiting for. Roscoe started across the open area by the loading dock. Flake was slower, more wary. The gap between the two increased, but Flake stood between John and Roscoe, spoiling John's plan to take Roscoe first. John might have to settle for what he could get. Roscoe was across the loading area and nearly to the stairway. If he didn't stop to wait for Flake . . .

Roscoe entered the stairwell.

John didn't think he'd get a better chance.

He stepped out from behind the stack of crates that had shielded him and crept forward. He held his defense stick before him, the bronze head heavy in his hand. The stick wasn't as fast as the swords he had used when fencing nor did it have a point or edge, but it did have an authoritative weight that had proved itself more than once on the street. There had been times he'd regretted that the stick was blunt, but not often. He hoped this wasn't going to be one of those times.

Flake turned when John was four meters away, warned by some premonition, certainly not by any sound John had made. The intruder's eyes went round as he saw John; he made a strangled sound, but he didn't yell. That suited John. Flake jumped away and John's first strike missed.

Seeing John extended in his lunge, Flake found some nerve and came after him. John recovered to stance with a speed that seemed to baffle Flake rather than serve as the warning it was. Flake charged forward, swinging a wide, slow round-house punch. John grasped his stick at both ends and side-stepped outside the blow. Using the stick as a baton, he directed Flake's punch away before shifting his grip and swinging the bronze weight down along Flake's temple. The man went down like a sack of laundry.

John could have put the blow on the top of the man's head and probably killed him, but he hadn't. There were still some questions John wanted answered. A concussed villain was a villain who might answer some of them, but a dead one wouldn't have anything at all to say; Flake didn't seem to be the sort who would be able to avoid answering questions.

A loud noise, halfway between a squeak and a shout, echoed through the building. Briefly. The sound cut off almost as soon as it began. Startled by its strangeness, John turned to look for its source. It had seemed to come from somewhere near the front entrance.

Had he been the only one to hear it?

"Behind you, John!"

Faye's warning was timely. John turned to see Roscoe rushing him, something dark and heavy-looking in the man's hand. Acting on reflex, John met him with a stop thrust, the narrow tip of the stick taking Roscoe in the solar plexus. Breath whooshed out of the intruder and he doubled over, gasping. If John had been armed with a sword, Roscoe would have been spitted.

John brought the stick down on him. There was a cracking sound and the man collapsed. John found himself holding only the weighted end of his broken stick. He hadn't thought he'd hit Roscoe very hard. John bent down to see if the man was still breathing.

He was, raggedly. That didn't seem good.

"You did what you had to do, John."

Had he? He looked around for the object that Roscoe had carried into the fight. He found himself hoping that it was something lethal. He saw the thing; it was a sap. The two men had wanted him alive. Was it right to kill one of them for that?

"You think he'll be all right?"

"He's a human, John. They're not very resilient. The one at the front door wasn't."

The one at the front door wasn't what? John decided he didn't want to know. "I don't want him to die."

"He had no business being here," Faye said matter-of-factly.

"Isn't that a little extreme?"

His answer was a creaking noise that he recognized as the door to the loading dock. The woman. He'd forgotten about her. She must have heard some of the noise and come to investigate. He didn't want any more trouble. Maybe she'd see how things stood and he could bluff her off. He rose, hoping to take advantage of his height and look impressive.

"You're the only one left," he said, as she barreled out of the deep shadows near the door. "Best you just leave."

She didn't stop, but she slowed down, her rush transforming into a strangely casual stroll. She took in the sprawled bodies of her fellows without any sign of alarm. She spoke as casually as she walked.

"Looks like ya caught Roscoe and the Flake by surprise. I'm not so easy."

"Don't be so sure."

Without a pause she said, "Yer a little short."

"Huh?"

She nodded at the splintered stump of the defense stick that he still held clenched in his hand. "Ya ain't got what ya used ta have, tall, pale, and comely. It'll take a bigger tool than you've got ta impress me."

Tall, pale, and comely? He'd heard that phrase before. Could it be? He took a closer look at the figure confronting him. She was tall for a woman and broad enough in the shoulders that she filled the shoulders of the baggy milspec jacket she wore. The pants were milspec, too, but the shoes, a mismatched pair of Aeroboks™, weren't. Her face was shaded by a broad-brimmed, floppy hat that had clearly seen better days even before she'd recovered it from the trash. A stray beam from the streetlight reflected triple flashes from three tiny chrome studs on her cheek. He knew this woman; she was a zip artist from down near the Barrier. He'd heard she was a kicker.

"You're Spillway Sue."

She squinted at him, frowning. "Man's got good eyes. Zeiss?" She reached into a pocket and pulled something out. A flick of her wrist unsheathed a twenty-centimeter blade. She held the weapon with a casual confidence. "Good price for top-grade eyes."

She took a step forward, moving cautiously enough that John knew she was not as unconcerned about facing him as she pretended. He found reason to be concerned himself; her stance was very good; she was no novice knife fighter. He flipped his stick in the air and caught the splintered end. It would be more useful as a club now. It would pack a significant wallop, but would still be slower than the knife. They began to circle each other.

With a squeal of rusted metal torn free from its encrusted moorings and a rumbling thunder, one of the loading doors began to rise. Harsh light flared into the building, washing both combatants in actinic glare. John put up his free hand, trying to shield his eyes. Spillway Sue stood frozen, staring into the light like a rat caught in a flashlight beam. A rat never would have looked so put out.

A squat figure stepped into the light. Whoever it was wore a long coat that made his figure look like an animate box with a ball on top. The intruder must have been confident that they didn't have any guns; silhouetted as he was, he made an easy target. An armed target, however, as John saw when the man advanced; he held a heavy caliber pistol in his right hand. As the man stepped into the loading area, John realized that he was quite short. His voice was deep and gravelly, so much so that John suspected the man might be deliberately trying to hide his normal tones.

"I suggest that you drop your weapons and stay put."

Unfrozen, Sue spoke. "This is a private party."

"Not anymore," the man said. "Don't try to run. I have men covering the exits."

Spillway Sue made an elaborate show of looking around. "I only see one of ya. Maybe ya got everything covered and maybe ya don't. Suppose I just go check it out."

She took a step away from the man and toward the shadowy safety of the warehouse area. The gun muzzle shifted slightly in her direction.

"Suppose you don't," the gunman said.

Sue stood still. Her tongue flicked along her upper lip. John figured she was calculating the odds. Did she think she had any chance of outrunning a bullet? For his part, he stayed very still. When the man demanded they drop their weapons, he let go of what was left of his stick. The clank made by the bronze head covered whatever Sue said in response to the man's command. She gave John a hard glance and slowly opened her hand, letting her knife fall to the floor.

"My name's Wilson," the man said. "You don't know me, but we have a friend in common. Big fellow. On the street, he goes by the name of Bear."

"I don't know ya from Adam. Ain't never heard of Bear," Sue said.

"I wasn't talking to you," Wilson said.

Wilson bent down and placed something on the floor. He shoved the object with his foot, sending it sliding toward John. It was a vid reader. "There's a disk in this. Run it."

John picked it up and pressed the button. In a moment the screen lit, showing a head and shoulders shot of a bearded, blond man. John recognized the face at once. It was Bear, all right.

"Jack, it is important that we talk," the recording said. "Go with this man."

The screen went blank.

John stared at the screen. *That's all? Two sentences!* John slammed the reader onto the floor. It shattered into a thousand shards of plastic and silicon chips.

"What's this all about?" he demanded.

"Good question, dode," Sue said.

"You shut up and stay out of this," John snapped.

"Hey, hey, it's null. So, ah, I'll be going."

"I think not," said Wilson. He shifted slightly and let the piercing light illuminate his gun. "For the moment it will be safer for everyone if you accompany us."

Sue shook her head. "I ain't going nowhere."

"What *us* you talking about, Wilson? I didn't say I was going with you," John said.

Wilson cleared his throat and shifted his weapon slightly. Light glinted from the metal. "I suggest you reconsider."

"Whatcha gonna do?" Sue asked mockingly. "Shoot us?"

Wilson gave them a tight smile. "That was suggested as the path of least resistance."

"We won't be much for conversation if we're dead." Sue didn't sound quite so confident as she had a moment before.

Wilson's smile opened up. "Who said anything about shooting you dead?"

A red dot appeared above the barrel of Wilson's gun. Another appeared on Spillway Sue's knee. Seeing that John was looking at her legs, she looked down and saw the spot. She didn't flinch away, which John thought showed real nerve, but her voice did start out a little weak when she asked her next question.

"What about Roscoe and the Flake?"

Wilson shrugged. "Since they have been so kind as to sleep through our meeting so far, I see no reason to take them along."

"Ya gonna kill 'em?"

Wilson didn't answer.

"Ya are, ain't ya? Ya already done Cholly, ain't ya?"

"Who's Cholly?"

"Ya know. Ya took him out up front before ya came back here, didn't ya? Ya killed Cholly, now yer gonna do these guys. How long we got?"

Faye's earlier words about the man who had been on the front door were now explained; Wilson was the reason. John was glad that Faye hadn't been involved. Unfortunately, now *he* was facing this Wilson.

"You do seem obsessed with death, young woman," Wilson said.

"Occupational hazard," she mumbled, essentially to herself. Louder she said, "Hey, dode. What's Shorty want with ya anyway? Ya know, as far as I got interest, the two of ya can just buzz on off, eh?"

"I think not," Wilson said.

"Why not let her go, Wilson? She's not part of whatever Bear sent you here for."

"Tall Jack's right," Sue chimed in. "I got no interest here."

"Young woman, I am here as an escort for Jack. By being here, you are involved. Your presence has complicated the matter by jeopardizing security."

"I'm sooo sorry."

"As am I, young woman. I intend to complete this mission with minimal trouble. There is no threat to those who are no threat."

"What's that supposed to mean?"

"It means that you should now move on out to the dock."

He gestured with his gun. Spillway Sue looked unhappy as she moved to comply, but she did move. John was relieved. She might have been here on some unspecified mission to do him ill, but he didn't want to see her gratuitously maimed. He followed her toward the glaring light. He could hear the soft scuff of Wilson's shoes behind him.

As she stepped onto the deck, Sue asked, "Gonna leave the wet stuff ta yer partners, Shorty?"

"Just proceed on down the stairs," Wilson said.

There were two vehicles in the yard. One was a high-bellied off-road truck, the other a long, low-slung limousine. The limousine's back door opened, revealing a softly lit interior.

Bear wasn't waiting there. In fact, no one was there. John looked at the vehicles. No one stood next to either, and both vehicles had opaqued windows; their interiors and any riders were screened. For all John could see, Wilson was alone.

The light that had heralded Wilson's arrival was on the roof of the truck's cab. As they started down the stairs, the lamp went dark. The sudden change in illumination almost made John stumble. Spillway Sue missed a step and fell to the ground. Her head swiveled around as she got back to her feet.

"I don't see anyone backing ya, Shorty."

John didn't either.

"The tower," Faye whispered.

That had to be the Lantham Building; it was the tallest structure nearby. The loading dock would be visible from there. John ran his eyes up the spire. Most of the windows were dark pocks in the surface of the building. From one of those dark pits near the top, something looking very much like a long-barreled sniper rifle protruded. He felt confident that someone sat hunched behind the weapon: a sniper. Spillway Sue followed his gaze. John didn't know if she saw the sniper, but she stopped objecting and stepped toward the car. John followed.

As he neared the vehicle, John whispered, "Stay out of this, Faye."

"John—"

"No arguments," he said as he bent over to get into the car.

"That would be a good choice, fairy," Wilson said.

John froze halfway into the car. He stared at Wilson. "You know about her?"

"I know about a lot of things. Arthur's waiting and we're wasting time. If you want your questions answered, you'd better get in the car."

John did want his questions answered. He slipped into the soft seat. Spillway Sue had slid all the way across and was fiddling with the controls in the armrest, with no visible results. Wilson closed the door on them. A moment later John felt the limousine shift as a new weight was added on the passenger side. A second later they were rolling.

It was only then that John remembered: Bear's real friends didn't call him Arthur.

CHAPTER
6

The bed they'd had prepared for him was supple, covered in a smooth fabric that felt cool and soft on his dry skin. The coverings were of the same lightweight fabric. Something hummed beneath the mattress, something that provided heat to warm him. That was good; it allowed him to use his resources for more important purposes than maintaining the heat of his blood.

The pillow was good too, fluffy and soft, although it smelled like nothing he knew. It was not stuffed with down or cotton wool; he knew those smells. Whatever cushioned his head so comfortably had never been alive, so far as he could tell. It was too soft to be mineral, its character too yielding. A wonder of this new age, no doubt. Like the lamps that smelled of lightning. An age of wonders, for truth.

Joel Lee relayed his orders, and he listened carefully to the words that his new slave used, learning. He noticed that those to whom Joel Lee spoke looked to another before fulfilling the slave's orders. Normally he would have been incensed by such presumption, but he was not yet normal; he was a spirit locked in a body stiffened by the passage of time, not yet limbered by the rush of fresh energy. When his strength permitted, he turned his head to observe this other, this source of authority.

Two stood where the servants had looked. A man, an Asian, dark of hair and solemn of mien, and a woman of Latin blood, dark also but in a different way and grim of demeanor. She had something of the beauty of the finest of the New World primitives who had hailed him as king and god. He could feel that one of them was the one with the sign, the one who had come to end the long sleep, but his perceptions were still weak and so clouded that he could not tell which.

So, he had not dreamed that a follower of the Path had come to him. This place was so foreign and barren that he had feared—no, fear was too strong—*conjectured* that the disturbance of his sleep had been some sort of mistake. He was pleased to see that his memory of the sign had not been a fragment of dream, a hopeful imagining. Here was vindication. The followers had been true, biding in the passing world until the time of the awakening had come, and arriving at last to wake the sleeper.

Had his mind not been so muddied by the ages of sleep, he would have known at once which of the two was the follower. He studied them, observing the subtle play of expression and stance and gesture. He could see which was the superior: the man. As was appropriate.

The power need not be squandered when the mind would serve.

But some squandering could be excused. Strength at the first. It would be best that they not think he was as weak as he was. Though his strength was still wanting, that was no longer of such concern as it had been; Joel Lee assured him that there were more to feed his hunger. The followers would provide. A show of strength then. He reached out, kindling the fire in the sign.

The Asian jumped.

Had not his body been so locked in the deep sleep, he would have laughed. Had not the Asian known he could do that? How could a follower not know? How much had they lost? He had Joel Lee call the Asian forward and ask his name and degree.

"Ryota Nakaguchi, Venerated One." The Asian spoke the honorific in the secret tongue. Perhaps they had not lost so much. "Fifth degree."

Fifth? And yet he knew so little of the link between the sign and the sleeper. The followers may have persevered, but they were not all they should be. He would see that changed!

But not in his current condition.

Nakaguchi interrupted his thoughts. "Venerated One, how may I address you that I not dishonor you?"

It was a question that ritual demanded he answer personally. He focused his sparse strength, forcing his first word in centuries. It was appropriate that the word be his name.

"Quetzal," he said.

"Not Quetzoucoatl?" Nakaguchi sounded upset.

Fool.

"The Awaited One, the Lord of Change," he had Joel Lee say, feeding him the ancient words.

Nakaguchi's eyes widened, his aura flaring with respect. The man bowed deeply, a pointless gesture. Joel Lee issued Quetzal's demand for sustenance. Nakaguchi bowed again and saw to it. Nakaguchi's servants brought an old man before Quetzal. Not the woman? He was disappointed; she would have been tasty.

The room was lit only by the backflash of the data windows open on the wallscreen and the glow of the half-dozen screens and submonitors on the C-shaped console. Pamela stood for a moment after closing the door behind her, waiting for her eyes to adjust. The room's occupant gave no sign that she knew Pamela had arrived, but Pamela knew her entrance could not have gone unnoticed. As Pamela became used to the dim light, she made out the form of the woman seated in a Console Queen™ office lounger in the center of the console board that filled the room. Sheila Rearden, her flabby flesh supported and confined by the CQ chair, was still save for her fluttering hands. Her flexing fingers hit the keys of a virtual keyboard and her rotating hands tapped and twisted controls that only existed within the computer's world. Rearden was a technomancer, a wizard within the context of the machine; that was why Pamela employed her.

Pamela couldn't remember the last occasion she had seen Rearden standing upright on her own two feet; the decker rarely stirred from her office, and Pamela had yet to see Rearden in the corridors of the building. But it wasn't Rearden's athletic prowess or command of etiquette that Pamela found interesting. Rearden got results.

"Have you anything for me?" she asked the supine form.

"Maybe." Rearden remained focused on the wallscreen, refusing to look in Pamela's direction. The console cowgirl wore virtuality goggles, but Pamela didn't have to see her face to read Rearden's anxiety; she could recognize the tension in the decker's body and hear it as she said, "I think I can get in, but he's got his stuff under a personal access code with a front office protection chop. Ruffle big bird's feathers if we go after this stuff and get caught with our hands in the cookie jar. You sure this is important enough?"

"It may be vital."

The writhing fingers stilled. "It's my ass gonna be fried if his deckers trace my footprints."

"Just don't leave any footprints."

"Not like I want to, Ms. M. I got a real attachment to my ass."

"It's not just yours on the line."

"Yeah?" She turned slowly in her chair until the mirrored surfaces of the virtuality goggles pointed at Pamela. "This really big enough to chance pissing off the sama-san?"

"I believe so," Pamela said firmly.

"And you ain't gonna cut me loose if they come hunting heads? I know how easy it is for a suit—no offense to you personally, Ms. M, you're okay—to blame it on us anarchist decker types."

Pamela leaned over the nearest console and touched her portacomp to the input panel. A new window opened, bearing her personal seal and showing a standard-format approval file in the transfer box. She touched the screen and initiated the release to Rearden's databank. "My own codes to authorize your actions."

"Sub zero." Rearden smiled. "You're radiating all kinds of positive waves. Like with that kind of attitude, maybe we can't lose."

"I don't intend to lose." *Or take the blame.* Anarchist decker types were notorious for stealing authorization codes to lend legitimacy to their actions. Pamela had already logged a report of suspicious activity in her database; that would support her denial of Rearden's decking should it become necessary.

Rearden swiveled her chair back to face the wallscreen. Flickering fingers danced in the air as Rearden did her magic, but Rearden's mystic passes were purely technological magic. Pamela waited.

"In." The console cowgirl's body shuddered with released tension. "All quiet."

Pamela breathed a sigh of relief. They'd opened the door without setting off an alarm. Rearden was earning her pay.

"Bringing up his inventory on screens three and four."

"Which?"

"Sorry." Two of the windows on the wall changed color. "Yellow screens."

Pamela scanned the titles and codes of the files displayed. Most were standard company files, a familiar format; some few suggested interesting possibilities; but nothing appeared to be what she sought. It would be foolish of him to label his vulnerabilities. Which among all of these things concealed what she needed to bring Nakaguchi down?

Pamela leaned over the console and tapped in commands. A facsimile of her own databanks appeared on the center window. "Run a gross comparison using this stuff as a baseline. Bring up anything with anomalous storage parameters. I'm especially interested in anything with private access windows."

"Righteo!"

The wallscreen dissolved into a chaotic jumble of shifting windows mutating through an avalanche of sizes, colors, and scroll speeds. Pamela assumed Rearden was keeping track of it all somehow, but she was lost. Computer expertise was why she employed Rearden; Pamela let the expert work. Finally, the turmoil slowed, as did Rearden's flashing fingers. The decker grinned and folded her hands, smiling in a self-satisfied way. Screens three and four returned to their saffron steadiness, with an inventory sparser by far. Pamela scanned the file and database names. She was not surprised to see the Charybdis Project databank as one of the suspect units. She used a laser pointer to highlight it.

"We'll start here."

Rearden made no move to unfold her hands. "He's got locks."

"Open them."

"They're complex."

"You like to say you're the best at what you do. Can you get into his system or not?"

"The run's been pretty clean so far, but I'm deep into it now. It's getting a lot more complex. He's got himself a pretty good cowboy, too. Nice work, real slick."

"Are you saying you can't do it?"

"Didn't say that. I'm just saying that Naki's decker's got crossfiles and tagalongs all over the place. Can't guarantee I won't leave traces."

And traces could and would be tracked back to their source, to Rearden, and ultimately to her. Nakaguchi would explode when he found that someone had rifled his private files. He had earned his reputation as a hatchet man; heads would roll. Hers, if he found her denials implausible. Were the contents of Nakaguchi's files worth running the risks inherent in this attempt? Could whatever was hidden in them offer enough compensation?

She didn't know. She had her suspicions, though. She couldn't afford *not* to know what was in those files; she needed *any* ammunition she could get.

"Do it," she ordered.

It had taken three of Nakaguchi's pitiful offerings before Quetzal had felt energized enough to stand. And stand he had. It felt glorious! To move again! To stand! To walk!

Exhaustion had come quickly, and he had dismissed all save for Joel Lee and slept. Normal sleep, though, not the deeper sleep. When he awoke, he consulted the time device. Hours had passed. Only *hours*.

He felt liberated.

He *was* liberated. Free again to walk the earth, free to reclaim what had been his, free to exercise his rights as a master of the mysteries, but most of all free to enjoy life again.

He was still hungry, though, but it was not the ravenous craving that had consumed him earlier. He could wait.

From his deliciously soft bed, he surveyed the room, marveling at the strange furnishings. Everything was so plain and undecorated. Some little of what he saw was familiar, and he had Joel Lee name the exotic items. Later he would pursue the meanings of the strange objects; for now he was content to know their names. Knowing names was important.

Nakaguchi appeared within minutes, unsummoned.

"How are you feeling, Venerated One?"

"Eager to be about."

"The doctors advise that you regain more strength first. Your body is weak."

That was a matter easily rectified. He could improve his strength immediately, but he needed Nakaguchi still; the Asian remained the only follower he had seen. He counseled himself to patience, to a gradual increase of his bodily strength.

However weak his body, his will remained strong and his mind need not remain idle. There was much to learn about the era into which he had awakened. How much? Well, that was to be learned as well. Even abed, he could learn. His link with Joel Lee suppressed the slave's mind, rendering it useful for only limited information; but Nakaguchi, still independent, could answer far more complicated questions. But passive learning was best undertaken in a safe place and he had yet to determine if this place was safe enough. Nakaguchi seemed to think so, but with the Asian only barely initiated into the mysteries, his confidence might be misplaced. For the moment, safety was of paramount concern; there was much Quetzal could not anticipate about this new age.

"Where is this place?" he asked.

With only the slightest prodding, the Asian began to babble. He was clearly eager to please.

"We are in Massachusetts, a member of the New England Cooperative and one of the founding states of the United States of America. The United States is the dominant political entity in the North American free trade zone. This particular facility is situated in the Brookfield District of what is commonly referred to as the Northeast sprawl. It is the property of a company called Chemogenics, one of many companies belonging to the Mitsutomo Keiretsu, the greatest of the world's megacorporations."

Nakaguchi made his statement with pride. It was full of the details Quetzal wanted, as Nakaguchi must have known, but there were important details lacking, including the most important one. "You control this Mitsutomo Keiretsu?"

The Asian's pale skin tone grew darker as he flushed. "Regrettably not, Venerated One. But I am high in the councils of the one who does. He listens to me."

A councilor only? The situation was not what it should be. "Who rules?"

"The old man, of course. Hiroto Mitsutomo."

So, it was a personal empire. Quetzal understood those. A trusted councilor had influence, if not power, and stood high in such an empire. Still, all was not as it should have been. He had expected that the followers would have established themselves as significant powers in the world as part of the preparation, but they should not have made themselves so self-important that they sent their flunkies to do what was rightly their job. "What is Hiroto Mitsutomo's rank?"

"Regrettably, Mitsutomo-sama does not follow the Path."

Quetzal didn't care for the answer. This was not as it should have been. He was still weak from his awakening, vulnerable. To find that he was here at the mercy of the uninitiated Hiroto Mitsutomo, dependent on the sufferance of an unbeliever, was disturbing. Definitely not as it should be. The situation would have to be changed, soon, but how? To act in ignorance was to fail.

He noted that those accompanying Nakaguchi wore the long white robes of this age's wise men.

"I see that you have brought wise men with you. Are they to tell me of this era?"

Nakaguchi was momentarily confused by the change of subject, but recovered quickly. "They are doctors, not teachers. They are here to observe and to minister to you as necessary. They will monitor your physical condition during the educational program that I have prepared for you. The technique is strenuous and we are concerned for your health."

Quetzal was confused by the Asian's speech. Learning had never been strenuous; exciting, perhaps, when he had disagreed with a teacher. Especially when the teacher had been an inferior. "You propose to teach me yourself."

"I would not so presume, Venerated One."

"Then you have brought books?"

"Books would be quite useless until you learned the language. There are very few books in the old tongues and none of them concern current events. We will be using the computer."

Computer? The word was strange. Was it a ritual spell for learning? "Explain computer."

"That would take words you lack, Venerated One. Once we have you comfortable with speaking a modern language, we can discuss computers. I think you will find them fascinating."

They led him to a throne of strange design, padded better than any he had seen; even the arms were padded. At the urgings of the doctors, he sat, sinking into the soft cushion. The doctors left to fuss over their machines. Quetzal watched, trying to make sense of their actions. After a moment he felt a prickling sensation wherever he was in contact with the chair. He lifted an arm to see what afflicted him and saw nothing, but the sensation on his arm stopped.

"Part of the monitoring mechanism," Nakaguchi explained. "A biofeedback system."

So many strange words. The Asian had been expecting Quetzal's reaction and did not seem to be concerned. Very well. For the moment, Quetzal would also be unconcerned.

The prickling began again when he lowered his arm, but within a few heartbeats the sensation stopped.

One of the doctors stepped from behind the throne. He held a helmet in his hands, a shiny thing with a visor and a crest of cords that stretched back behind the throne and out of sight. Another doctor approached him from the other side. This one held a small cylinder in his hand. The doctor lifted the cylinder and sprayed a light mist of wet vapor onto the side of Quetzal's head.

"Camel spawn!" Quetzal snarled. He raised his hand, ready to summon a wasting spell. The doctor recoiled. Nakaguchi stepped between them.

"Do not be alarmed, Venerated One. It is merely an electrolyte spray to improve the conductivity for the helmet."

More strange words. It did not matter whether the watery insult offered improvement or not, he resented the liberty they took. "It is offensive."

"I apologize, Venerated One, but it is necessary for the computer."

Quetzal lowered his hand. With a moment to think, he was not sure he could have gathered the energy for the spell anyway. Let them think he was being magnanimous. "I dislike the feel of the water."

Nakaguchi smirked at Quetzal's failure to remember the strange word for what had been sprayed on him. "The discomfort of the spray is only momentary. There will be interference in the interface without the electrolyte."

"This is a difficulty?"

"A significant one, Venerated One."

"I shall allow myself to be sprayed."

He submitted himself to the indignity of the doctor's cylinder of mist. The scent was fruity but not altogether pleasant. There was an underscent of decay which, combined with the coolness the spray brought to his scalp, reminded him of climbing into the mountains from the steamy jungles below.

"Will you don the helmet now, Venerated One?"

"Is it important for your computer?"

"It is."

"Very well." Quetzal took the helmet from the doctor, though, and set it upon his head unaided. The visor was solid, with no vision slot. "It blocks my vision."

"The body's eyesight only, Venerated One. The computer will give you sight much like a vision."

"This computer knows the mysteries?"

Nakaguchi chuckled. "The computer knows a different sort of mystery. Are you ready?"

A different sort of mystery? Quetzal's curiosity was aroused. *Like* a vision? He nodded permission. "Proceed."

Nakaguchi said something to the doctors. Without warning, Quetzal's mind expanded, exploding outward. By the worm at the heart of the world! His head was afire! A thousand images assailed his eyes. Sounds filled his ears in near-senseless cacophony while, unbidden, foreign words and concepts occurred to him. What was happening? For a moment he knew fear. Had Nakaguchi betrayed him? Was this what it was like to be possessed? Was there a mind behind this invasion, a will that would overpower his own? He felt assaulted. The speed of the strangeness fired his brain, burning it. He felt the flames eating at his will, threatening to reduce him to cinders. He resisted, forcing control and serenity upon himself.

The attack abruptly ceased.

His mind was his own again; the alien presences gone.

"Are you all right, Venerated One? You cried out."

"Surprise," he lied. To admit weakness to an inferior was a great folly. "I was merely surprised."

"You sounded in pain."

"A misunderstanding on your part." Admission that he had felt pain would be folly, too.

"I am pleased to hear that, Venerated One. There was some concern as to whether you could handle the input."

Input. A word for what he had experienced. "It was . . . confusing."

"Then the concern was well founded. Fortunately I ordered a reduced feed. I could have the technicians adjust the input level to a still-slower speed if you would find it more comfortable."

There was a hidden satisfaction in the Asian's voice, a hint of pleasure at superiority. Quetzal could not afford to demonstrate weakness to this one. "There is so much to learn."

"Very much," Nakaguchi agreed. "We only wish to help you adjust. You must take our advice and proceed slowly."

Must? Must! He restrained his outrage with the knowledge that he was still weak. For the moment he needed this worm.

"Your computer babbles like a fever victim, the important jumbled together with the inconsequential. How could I not find that confusing? Tell me how I may sort through the voices to select the wheat from the chaff."

"We could confine the feed to specific areas. Build up a selected vocabulary."

"Do so."

"It shall be done. What aspect of our age do you wish to study first, Venerated One?"

A stupid question. "The state of the mysteries."

Nakaguchi gave orders to the doctors, whom he heard busy themselves with their machines. Once again he allowed them to open the way to the computer. He was more confident now. He had experienced what the computer could do; he would deal with it. He would wrestle with it until he mastered it.

The images and concepts burned once again in his mind, but they came more slowly and in fewer numbers. He had time to meet each one and master it. From the computer he learned the forlorn state of the magical arts in this new age. As foretold, men had forgotten and abandoned the Great Art as the stars had aligned themselves unfavorably and drained the world of its vitality. Being men, they had forgotten most of what had been known, forgotten it so completely that many no longer believed in the power of the Great Art. Of late there had been a change, some shift in the stars, no doubt. [How he longed to see them again in all their cold, knowing glory!] This age was reawakening to the mysteries.

They knew so little. That too was as it had been foretold. His awakening had come at a fortunate time, perhaps even the most fortunate. [The stars would know; they would tell him when he gazed upon them again.] In these days, when the uninitiated struggled to comprehend what was happening around them, an adept would have a powerful advantage.

Soon he would walk among men in the robes of power. King he had been, king he would be again. King, and more. How much more depended only upon his will—and had it not sustained him through the long sleep? He would be much more than a mere king!

The flow of images and sounds stopped. Why? His sight dimmed, returning him to the dark, ordinary world inside the computer's helmet. He tore it from his head to find Nakaguchi leaning over him.

"You stopped it," he accused the Asian.

"Your vital signs were beginning to fluctuate, Venerated One. The doctors thought it best to abort the session. We can begin again once you have had a chance to rest and regain a little strength."

"Yes, strength. I am hungry."

"I will have some food prepared for you."

"Another."

Nakaguchi nodded in understanding and departed. The fare that the Asian eventually provided was poor, another pitiful castoff, but the rush of strength invigorated Quetzal. He was ready to learn more, but Nakaguchi and the doctors said that tomorrow would be better.

He let them go without complaint, but he did not abandon his desire. Who were they to dictate when he should follow his will?

"Joel Lee, show me how to access—that is the right word?—whatever information I desire."

The slave demonstrated how to control the machines. Quetzal discovered that his control of the machine was partial, but it was enough for now. He gained access to the historical files for Mitsutomo's involvement in the mysteries. As he drank in what the machines laid before him, he began to formulate his strategy.

He would place himself at the heart of this Charybdis Project, Hiroto Mitsutomo's program to study magic. His skills and knowledge would make him invaluable, indispensable, until he controlled Charybdis. From there, it would be but a small step to controlling Mitsutomo.

There was one section of his e-mail that Charley Gordon always saved for last: the anonymous transmitters. As usual, most of them were junk. One wasn't.

>>21.10.09 * 15.01.58.22 * xxxxx.xxx
LOG #1009.121
TO: GORDONC@NECPOLNET*0004.03.874334
FROM: <UNKNOWN>
RE: MODUS 112.
MESSAGE:
    ENTRY. JANE DOE 12 * 45.23 * 211008.4.

The "Modus" notation told him that the message wasn't exactly anonymous. This message was from a network contact who had adopted Charley. Whoever the guy was, he had a good sense of what was and what wasn't weird—in other words, what was business for the Special Investigations Unit. Twice already this year he'd supplied Charley with data that had helped Charley close an investigation that had been going nowhere. The guy was a regular console detective. Sure he made a lot of intuitive leaps, but more often than not they paid off once Charley had done the legwork to tie the pieces together.

Every communiqué from him was transmitted anonymously, lacking even the usual hacker handle. The guy dropped his messages into Charley's box and picked up any replies from random cyberspace locations, each week posting his new "address" to Charley. That kind of sourcing had made Charley suspicious at first. The guy was a regular ghost in the machine. Because he was a friendly ghost, Charley had dubbed him "Caspar," a combination of spook and wise man.

Caspar was a reticent fellow, apparently satisfied by his good deeds; he'd refused to step forward for the reward he'd earned for providing data in the Billingsford case. In fact, Caspar had demanded that his participation be kept quiet, under threat of deserting Charley. Charley had gone along. Good contacts were priceless, even when they were cyber-cowboys; a smart cop kept his good contacts happy. And Caspar was a good contact.

The "112" was Caspar's case number; Caspar had assigned modus numbers to each collection of data he thought was related. Offhand, Charley couldn't remember what 112 was about, so he called it up.

Dead streeters.

Not an unusual piece of business for Charley, but not necessarily business for the Special Investigations. Looking at the official case file tags for all the previous entries, Charley saw that only one had been referred to SIU, and that one wasn't on his caseload.

Right.

What was Caspar seeing here?

Dutifully he logged in the new stiff and set up a data transfer from the morgue records. He read them as they dumped to his file. No witnesses. No suspicious circumstances. Routine autopsy scan listed myocardial infarction as cause of death, heart attack; not unusual with an age of sixty, approximate. Routine genetic typing in progress, to be matched with missing persons. On the whole, nothing to warrant SIU attention.

Even Caspar chased a few wild hares.

Streeters were found dead all the time, and the taxpayers of the New England Cooperative didn't like seeing their money squandered on justice for nonproductives and unregistereds. His console started buzzing, reminding him that there was plenty for him to do which *would* be satisfactory to those fine upstanding citizens who paid his salary. He closed the file and answered the call. It was the manager of the Norwood Hilton, reporting another incident of poltergeist damage.

Jerry Constantine liked debunking. Too bad it was only his hobby and not his job. There was nothing quite like the thrill of showing up a charlatan for what he was. It gave Jerry a real sense of victory, a sense that he had done something that the world needed. There were too many nut cases peddling their nonsense and booga-booga foolishness to too many gullible people. Tonight he was sure he had a live one.

The carnival's advertising didn't use any pictures of "The Wild and Wonderful Fairy Goblin." Of course. That was a normal teaser. Gotta pay to see it. Gotta pay, gotta pay. Of course, you gotta pay; money was all that was behind these scams. Jerry insisted the admission booth take his card; he wanted a record that money had been taken for this fakery.

Jules from the office had been out here last night and had seen the fairy goblin. Jules had done nothing but rave about how strange it was all day. Everybody listened to Jules. All the talk had just made Jerry mad. Jules was supposed to be bright. Hadn't he just gotten the promotion Jerry had been promised? God, that Jules was an idiot! Busting this scam would have been fun all by itself, but being able to show everyone at the office just how stupid Jules was would make it even sweeter.

"All right, folks. The doors are about to open," the barker said.

Jerry was ready!

"Stay quiet, folks, and please don't tap on the glass," the barker's assistant said as the line filed past her. "Please keep moving. Lots of people want to see the wonder of the fairy goblin."

I wonder how many people will want to see it after I'm through. But Jerry didn't say that aloud. He'd have plenty to say in a bit though; *after* he'd seen the fairy goblin.

The passageway was dark and filled with music—some crystal-loving, cosmic shit—all carefully calculated to add to the mystery. A recorded voice was dumping bilge about the supposed lifestyle of the fairy goblin and how difficult it had been for the carnival to obtain and how selfless they were being in offering the public a chance to view the wonder. Jerry wanted to barf.

This scam used the one-way window shtick. The rubes were supposed to be hidden from the strange wonder, watching it while it couldn't see them. A little added voyeuristic titillation. Good for business. Jerry had seen it before.

Jerry was a little taken aback when he reached the window. He had been expecting a dwarf or a kid in a heavy makeup job, but the fairy goblin wasn't that. It was too lean; even a starving kid wouldn't be so skinny. And the proportions were a bit off for a human. The damned thing was naked, not that it mattered much—it was pretty hairy down there—but that would make the scam harder to play in the Bible Belt. Did they have a different version for more straitlaced rubes?

The carnival scammers had taken an unusual tack with their fairy goblin. He had to concede that it was clever not making it look like a post-Froudite keebler. Having it not be what people expected gave them an edge; maybe it was a little less commercial, but it caught the debunker off guard. Good move, but not good enough to stop Jerry. He gave the fairy goblin a good look over. He didn't care about disgruntled rubes pushing past him and complaining about him hogging the tiny window.

The fairy goblin was about the size of a twelve-year-old boy, but far leaner and more muscular. No, cute wasn't their goal in this exhibit. Again he silently congratulated the planners of this fraud on their cleverness.

The fairy goblin had a gaunt, narrow face, that Jerry found oddly attractive despite the slightly jutting jawline. The big, dark, slanting eyes and the long, pointed ears gave it a lupine look. It looked very real, very alive.

He was having a hard time figuring out how they'd done it, until he recognized that the window was the answer. It wasn't a window at all. It had to be a holoprojection screen. He was impressed again. The guy who programmed the holovid was good, real good. The texture mapping and the interplay of lighting was superb, with a subtlety Jerry had never seen before.

"Keep moving, folks." The attendant had come and singled Jerry out; he'd outstayed his admission fee. "Lots of folks want to see the wonderful fairy goblin."

Jerry nodded and moved on. He wanted to see the wonderful fairy goblin all right. He wanted to see the real thing. He hadn't been able to spot any projector lenses; so they had to be working it from the other side of the wall. That meant getting backstage.

Once out of the tunnel, he left the line of rubes and their dim-minded babbling about the amazing fairy goblin. No one saw him slip through the door into the back. Maybe the scammers weren't so clever; they'd left the door unlocked and they didn't have anybody watching the place. Good luck for Jerry.

It didn't take him long to find the projection booth. It was big, big enough to actually be the fairy goblin's living quarters that he'd seen through the window. Did the size have something to do with the success of the tech that they were using? They were trusting a magnetic-key lock to hold their secrets. Clearly they hadn't counted on Jerry. He dug his unscrambler from his pocket and slipped the contact card into the slot. It didn't take him long to spoof the lock. The bolt clicked open, offering him access to the scammers' secret.

He opened the door and his smile melted from his face. There were no lenses, no projectors, no computers. Just the fairy goblin, looking at him with its deep, dark, hungry eyes.

Grinning at him, it showed its pointed teeth.

CHAPTER
7

Resigning from the Department wasn't as simple as walking out, Spae discovered. She should have guessed that her display of pique—let alone her improved magical ability—would have repercussions. She shouldn't have done it; she knew better, but her temper had gotten the better of her, and now she had to live with the consequences.

She'd been barred from access to the underground facilities, including her workshop. That was criminal; almost everything in that lab was her personal property. When she'd logged a demand that her property be returned, the synth secretary who'd responded had said that there were a few forms. So far they'd transmitted thirty different forms for her to fill out. The forms were now "in process," which she knew from past experience was bureaucratese for lost. Fortunately she'd brought some of her most important items home from the workshop the night before for a private ritual. She suspected she'd never see the rest of her equipment and books unless she reentered the fold.

Which she was not about to do.

She'd had enough of those pompous asses, and she knew they were not fond of her. Still, they weren't about to let her go. She'd learned that when she'd tried to arrange transportation out of Chardonneville. Every airline she'd tried rejected her requests for tickets on international flights, citing an invalid passport. They all offered to process a passport application and append her ticket purchase, of course. She hadn't bothered. What good would it do to file a new one? The Department would get it canceled as soon as it was issued—if it was even issued at all.

When she'd set her sights on a less-distant escape she'd found they had anticipated her. By what couldn't have been coincidence, the cross-country buses had changed their schedule the day of her resignation and no longer stopped at Chardonneville. There were no rental car offices in the tiny village, and she was not yet ready to stoop to auto theft. She had been furious. Once she had calmed down enough to think, she had actually considered walking out of the village. When she calmed down further, she realized that such a method wouldn't be practical either—or any method for that matter— if they wanted her to stay as badly as it appeared, she would only force them to get physical, and she doubted she'd win that sort of confrontation.

At least they weren't being total barbarians. She was still able to move freely around the village, and so far her cottage remained inviolate. At least as far as she could tell. The electronic systems continued to say that no one had entered, but those systems had been installed by the Department and were suspect. Her wards agreed, but even with her increased understanding of magic, she wasn't sure that they were completely reliable.

Chardonneville made a small world. By her third day of village arrest, she was contemplating mayhem.

The perscomp buzzed as she was pouring her second cup of morning coffee. She was going to ignore it, but she noticed the incoming ID: Essenbach. Curious, Spae tapped the code to accept, but left the transmission on audio only. Essenbach's face appeared on the monitor. She stared expectantly at the screen for a moment until she realized that Spae wasn't transmitting video.

"Dr. Spae?"

"I'm here."

Essenbach looked a little confused. "Is there something wrong?"

"That's a stupid question."

"Yes, I suppose it is, considering the circumstances. I meant something more immediate."

"What is it you want, Doctor?"

"It's been several days since we heard from you. I was concerned about you."

"How kind."

"I know we haven't been close, but I like to think we have a good professional relationship. We have a lot in common."

"Such as a certain interrogation room?"

Essenbach pursed her lips, clearly upset, but Spae didn't know whether the woman was concerned about what had happened or merely because Spae had upset her conciliation speech.

"I'm not happy about that, Dr. Spae. It was not an approach that I thought warranted."

"So you didn't participate."

Essenbach had the decency to look guilty. "I am sorry about what happened. I know you've been under a lot of stress lately. I just wanted to let you know that I understand. I also wanted to let you know that I think the Department's being a little off base in their treatment of you."

"Just a little."

"More than a little, really. You are one of the best hermetic scholars I know. Your expertise is invaluable, and we need you in the program, now more than ever. I was hoping to convince you to reconsider your resignation."

Not likely. "Magnus put you up to this?"

The question seemed to catch Essenbach off-balance. "He doesn't know I'm contacting you."

"Don't bet on it."

"What do you mean?"

"How long have you been with the Department, Dr. Essenbach? A little less than five years, I think. Have you ever done any field work for the Department?"

"What has that—"

"Have you?" Spae sounded strident, even to herself.

"I worked with Dr. Dagastino on the Cornwall Project."

"That fiasco doesn't count. Have you ever been on a real sleeper hunt? I mean out in the streets or the boonies or the nuthouses. Have you ever even seen a sleeper before he's gone through orientation?"

"No, of course not. I'm a psychometric realization specialist. The sleepers, per se, are not my field. Why, other than Magnus, I don't think I've ever met one."

"The sleepers aren't the issue. It's what's going on around them. It's the people around them, the ones that want to use them."

"I don't understand."

"Exactly my point. You've spent your time buried in your workshop and in the library. As you said, we have a lot in common. I did a lot of head-hiding myself, but I have had the real world brought rather forcibly to my attention. In the last couple of years, I have seen a lot of the people you're dealing with and how they operate. In the last few weeks, I've gotten a pretty clear view of their care and concern. If they don't have a tap on this line, the weather forecast is for snow in hell."

"Magnus wouldn't permit it."

"Think he's too noble for it? If he hasn't fallen under their sway it's only because he was playing these sorts of games before any of them were born. The settings, costumes, and props change, but the play remains the same."

"Well, I can see that you are still overwrought. Perhaps we can have a more rational discussion when you've had more time to think things through. I'm sure you will—"

Spae cut the connection.

"I'm sure I will, too."

She called up the perscomp's atlas program and requested a detailed local map. She studied it until her stomach reminded her that there were more immediate things.

Wanting some fresh air, she decided to take her lunch at the café. She sat alone, as befitted a Departmental pariah, an island in a tiny sea of a half-dozen occupied tables. With a full stomach, a cup of cappuccino on the table before her, and a reader in her lap, she was as content as she had been for days.

She should have looked as though she was reading, idling, wasting time, but she was in fact contemplating the layout of the road net and memorizing the salient points. Someday, she'd be leaving.

Although she was not yet ready to depart, her walking stick, the one she'd taken to the otherworld, leaned against her knee. She felt better for its touch against her skin. Her ankle maintained contact with her heavy canvas shoulder bag. The satchel was stuffed with irreplaceable equipment and materials, things she hadn't felt safe enough to leave at the cottage. She didn't completely trust this truce between herself and the Department.

A man stepped up to the table. Expecting to have to shoo away the waiter again, Spae was surprised to see a stranger. The dark-haired man wore a flannel shirt, light-colored twill slacks tucked into crumpled socks, and scuffed ankle boots. He had a rucksack slung over one shoulder and carried a walking staff. Everything was covered with a light layer of dust, as though he'd been tramping through the countryside. It was a look she'd seen before, typical of the sort of vagabond students that wandered the countryside on their *wanderjar* hikes, but this one seemed a little older than the ordinary student.

"Excuséz-moi, mademoiselle," he said. *"Quesque c'est s'asseoir place?"*

Spae shook her head at his abominable French. He took it for an answer to his question, smiling a thank-you and swinging his rucksack down as he pulled out a chair to seat himself.

"Je ne sais tout pas l'habitude, ah, *accepter sa part de la table,"* he said.

"Not much used to French, either."

"You speak English!" His face lit up. He really did have a nice smile. "How delightful!"

"I'm sure."

Her abrupt comment shut him up and she went back to her pretended reading. When she reached for her cup, she noticed he was staring at her. He had deep brown eyes. She took a sip of her cappuccino. Before she put the cup down, he spoke again.

"Have we met before?"

"No."

"You look awfully familiar."

"Your lines are more lame than your French."

He laughed, shaking his head. "I'm sorry. It wasn't intended as a line. I really do think you look familiar. But you are quite right about my French not being what it ought to be. I don't seem to be able to communicate at all with the locals. Is my pronunciation that bad?"

"Not so bad. They'll understand what they need to."

"So you say they're having a joke at my expense?"

"Most definitely."

He frowned in semiserious disapproval. "Not very friendly of them."

"They're not the most friendly lot."

"You talk as though you're not one of them."

"Not exactly."

He regarded her speculatively. "Your walking stick suggests a hiker, but despite your somewhat overstuffed shoulder bag, you're not dressed for hiking. And there's no car or bicycle parked by the curb in front of this, the only café in the village. The obvious conclusion is that you live here, or are at least visiting here for a prolonged stay."

"You're very inquisitive."

"Sorry. I don't mean to offend. As I tried to say before, I'm not quite used to this European custom of sharing tables with strangers. Where I come from, one shares tables with friends, and with friends a lively interest in their doings is usually considered positive. So if I've offended, please excuse me. I will consider myself rebuked. Perhaps we can find other things to talk about so that I can enjoy the good fortune brought to me by following the local custom of forced companionship."

His high-energy babble bemused her. It was a pleasant change from the clipped comments she had been getting from her neighbors. She decided that she'd let him divert her for a while. "What good fortune is that?"

"Why, yourself, of course. What better dining companion than a charming lady who has gifted me with the secret of the locals?"

"Hardly that."

"I must disagree. I find you most charming."

"I meant that I've hardly given you their secrets."

"Shh. Here comes one now."

He meant the waiter. He gave his order in his abysmal French, punctuating each request with a wink to Spae. "It should be entertaining to see what I get," he told her as soon as the waiter was out of earshot.

They talked about ordinary things like the weather and the pleasure of walking through the countryside. He seemed to take a delight in the outdoors that matched his deep tan. Despite her usual lack of interest in such matters, she found herself listening to him. He even got her talking about her college days, of all things; he laughed almost all the way through her story about Professor Wyngarde and the temporary librarian. He listened when she talked and he really seemed interested in her. Not what she could do, not what she knew—*her*. So interested that shortly after the waiter brought him his meal, he inadvertently poured half his bottle of mineral water into the flower vase. They both laughed over that. In the sparkle of his presence she forgot her problems, until her watch beeped and reminded her of other things.

Pushing away her cold coffee cup, she gathered up her things. He watched with an air of disappointment. She felt guilty leaving him so abruptly, but she really didn't have much choice. Then again, guilt was a little out of place; she didn't even know his name.

"It's been a pleasure, Mister . . . ?"

"David," he said, holding out his hand.

She took it, meeting a firm but not overpowering grip. She liked the way he demonstrated his strength without making a point of it. She hadn't felt so comfortable with anyone since . . . well, for a long time.

"It's been a pleasure, David, but I'm afraid I have to be going."

"Another date?"

For a second she thought he was asking for one, then she realized he was inquiring after her business again. With a personal interest this time? She didn't want to give him the wrong idea. "No, I have to see a doctor at St. Catherine's."

"Nothing wrong, I hope."

"It's not about me. It's just that it's taken me several days to get Kun's doctor to meet with me, and I don't want to miss a chance to convince him to let me in."

"To see Kun?" He seemed a little crestfallen. "Your husband?"

"Holger Kun? Hardly. He's a friend." David raised an eyebrow, prompting her to try another explanation. "A business acquaintance, actually. He's been ill."

"I'm sorry to hear that," he said, though he actually looked a little relieved. "I hope you won't be too disappointed."

That was an odd thing to say. "What do you mean?"

"Oh nothing. Just a hunch. This doesn't seem like a day for hospital visits."

"Well, it certainly won't be if I don't get there."

"Perhaps we can meet again."

"Perhaps."

Actually, when she thought about it, seeing David again sounded like a good idea. She wasn't ready to leave Chardonneville yet and she could use the diversion. He was a hiker, he wouldn't be around long. She could think of far less pleasant diversions. Assuming he was really interested; she hadn't had a lot of attention from men over the years. Then again, she hadn't really sought such attention, having been too busy with her work. Well, she didn't have any work at the moment; maybe it was time to give some thought to other matters. David had seemed really interested in her.

Was that so strange? She knew that she wasn't a *Fashion Forward*™ feature girl, but she wasn't a wrinkled old prune either. She'd heard that some men preferred their women more mature. David could be one of those men. She found herself hoping that he was.

But right now, she had business to attend to.

St. Catherine's Hospital was little more than a hospice, barely more than a small clinic—on the surface. Most of St.

Catherine's facilities were underground. Like everything else in Chardonneville, there was more going on beneath the facade.

The staff at St. Catherine's were no less surly than the general run of folks in the village, but it didn't bother her as much. Maybe it was just that surliness didn't seem so out of place in the hospital. The doctor was late, naturally. An emergency, naturally. She sat in the tiny waiting room and waited.

Eventually the doctor came through a door marked "office" that Spae guessed opened on the elevator to the lower levels. He was shorter than David but shared the dark, tanned look. He also didn't look old enough to be practicing medicine. God, what was she thinking? She was too busy noticing what men's ages were today. Spae was the only one in the waiting room, and the doctor came directly to her.

"Dr. Spae?"

She stood and took his offered hand.

"I'm Dr. Montague. Sorry I'm late. It was unavoidable. What was it you wanted to see me about?"

"How is he?"

Montague didn't bother to look confused. "Ah, Mr. Kun."

"That's right."

"Well." Montague sighed a practiced, professional sigh. "The news isn't all bad, Dr. Spae. Mr. Kun is stable. I'd say that he's doing as well as can be expected."

"Can I see him?"

"I don't think that would be advisable at this time. He is under heavy sedation. I'm afraid he wouldn't even know you were there."

"Meaning you're not going to let me in."

"As I said, I don't think that would be advisable."

"I see."

Abandoning the stern demeanor, Montague shifted to the helpful physician persona. "However, if you would care to record a message, I can assure you that he will see it as soon as he is able."

As soon as they were ready, he meant. Recordings could be frozen and duped, jiggered, and completely rearranged; they could even be manufactured. Hell, for all she knew they had already made their own "recording" of her to play for Kun. She wondered what they'd had her say. Would Kun have been thinking clearly enough to know he'd been duped? Or was she finding monsters and duplicity where there were none?

She might not know exactly what was going on, but she was sure that the truth wasn't what they said it was.

She was clearly not going to see Kun this way. She decided to stay polite and forced a smile. "Thank you, Doctor. I don't think so."

"Well, if there's any way I can be of help—"

"I'll be sure to ask." *So you can practice your Oh-so-very-sorries and your brick wall impression? I don't think so.*

She left St. Catherine's, another afternoon wasted. On her way home, she came across David leaning against a stone wall at the corner of Chardonneville's main street and the lane that led down to her cottage. A chance meeting? He had his head down, studying a map. His walking staff and sack leaned against the wall. To all appearances he was calculating his next ramble.

She thought about changing her path to avoid him, going across the fields to the back garden, but then she remembered that he'd said this wasn't a day for hospital visits. He'd been right, and she couldn't believe that it was just coincidence. What did he know that she didn't? If she didn't confront him now, he might be gone and she'd never know.

"Hello, David."

He looked up at the sound of her voice, already smiling. He was the only one who had shown any pleasure at seeing her recently, and the warmth that stirred in her almost made her forget her suspicions. His question, as honest sounding as it was, brought them back.

"How'd it go at St. Catherine's?"

"You knew I wouldn't get to see Kun. How?"

He flinched away from her earnest abruptness. "Because he's not there."

"If you knew he wasn't there, why didn't you just tell me?"

"Would you have believed me?"

"No!" Why did he have to seem so honest? "Yes." If he was honest, why hadn't he told her right out? "Well, maybe." Would she have believed him? "Hell, I don't know!"

"So they didn't tell you."

"Tell me what?"

"Look. I can see that there's some kind of trouble here, maybe it's best I don't get involved." He reached for his walking staff; she used her own stick to bat it out of his reach.

"You're not getting off that easily. I want to know why you lied to me. Why did you say you had a hunch that I wouldn't see Kun when you knew all along that he wasn't there?"

He looked her straight in the eye. "I didn't lie to you. I said I had a hunch, and I did. But I'm afraid I didn't express myself clearly either. My hunch was that you were Elizabeth Spae. When you mentioned Mr. Kun, I knew I was right and why you looked familiar."

He had known who she was all along. She wasn't ready to consider the implications of that and what it meant about all their innocent chat. How innocent had it been? She didn't want it all to have been a lie. To keep her head straight, she focused on what had started their conversation. "Well, since you knew Kun wasn't there, you must have some idea of where he is."

"The last information I had placed him at the Phillips Sanatorium, outside Southampton in England."

"England!"

"That's right."

How could he know and she not? "You seem to know an awful lot for a hiker who just happens to be passing through Chardonneville."

"I have some connections."

Connections, indeed. They'd have to be some kind of serious connections to get him information about an ECSS agent. "Just who are you?"

"David Beryle."

"And who is David Beryle?"

"A workingman."

"Working for whom?"

"Whoever pays the most," he said as if it were embarrassing. "Lord, did I just say that? I know what you must be thinking, but it's not— Well, you see, I'm something of a student of fringe—uh—unusual phenomena. I've written a few pieces for some magazines. I don't suppose you've read any of them."

"You suppose correctly." His discomfort made her feel uncomfortable herself. "So you're a reporter?"

"Not exactly. I write. The nonfiction pays the bills, but it's not my real work."

His explanation could cover how he might know about her. Barely. But Kun? "How do you know Kun?"

"I don't really. He's just a name to me. But I thought that you might know him because I came across his name in connection with the incident last year in New England." He interrupted himself to admit excitedly, "That's an affair that I'd like to ask you about sometime." Her frown damped his enthusiasm. "Anyway, I logged his name on a watch list with my clipping service—I've got a good one—and a week or so ago they posted me a note from a local net about an incident at the Phillips Sanitorium. There weren't any details, but there was a Holger Kun mentioned as a patient who had been injured. I wondered about it at the time; couldn't even be sure that it was the same guy. I had a feeling he was, though, so I poked around a little, but I didn't get very far; that sanatorium has got a pretty good data security system, the kind that places with V.I.P. patients have. Now, I'm wondering about other things. Is Mr. Kun part of Department M also?"

The alarm bells she'd been suppressing broke free. "What do you know about the Department?"

"I'll take your reaction as a yes."

He grinned as if he'd won a point, which he had, but he'd lost a few with her as well. "What's your interest in me?"

"Before today, I'd have said purely professional."

Before today? How long had he been secretly stalking her? It couldn't be like that! He wasn't like that! He couldn't be! Could he? How much did she really know about him? "What do you mean 'professional'?"

"I mean professional. I'm a writer, remember? I was doing some research for an article a couple of years ago and I came across your master's thesis. Interesting stuff. I wondered where your work had taken you, so I dug a little deeper, figuring that you'd have gone on and finished your doctorate. I wanted to see *that* thesis, see what conclusions you'd reached. When I found out that you had disappeared without ever turning your paper in, you became a mystery to sleuth down."

She wasn't sure how his explanation made her feel. "Should I be flattered?"

"I'm not sure. I hope you don't think I'm some sort of stalker freak. It's not like I made your career an obsession or something. I had your name and some associated keyword items on another watch list. I didn't get a lot and that surprised me. Remember, I said they're good; they've got connects with more than the usual databases. There was so much potential in what you were doing, that tantalizing hints only kept my interest up. I never really thought that I'd meet you."

It sounded plausible, and she had to admit that she was flattered that someone would be so dogged in following her work, but she couldn't let herself be blinded by the warm feeling his interest gave her. He sounded sincere and she wanted to believe him. "Why should I believe this cock-and-bull story?"

"Because it's true."

She wanted to believe that it was, but the Department had told her that they'd hidden her past. How could a mere magazine writer find what they had hidden? "You're awfully well informed. Who do you really work for, Mr. Beryle?"

"David, please."

"I think I'll keep it formal, *Mister* Beryle." For her own peace of mind; there were too many things that didn't add up.

David hung his head and sighed. "I was afraid this would happen."

"Apparently your fears are as reliable as your hunches."

"Please, Dr. Spae, let me explain."

"You've got a minute."

"That may not be enough."

"Try."

"This is not a good place."

She didn't really care. "You're wasting your time."

"We are being watched here."

"Really? By whom?"

"Agents of Department M, I presume. This is their town. If we speak here, they will know everything we say."

"Of course they will. *You're* part of the conversation."

He smiled and almost laughed. "You don't seriously think that I'm part of the Department, do you?"

"Aren't you?"

"If I were, would I be telling you how the Department's stonewalling you about Kun?"

"You might."

He almost answered immediately, but paused, presumably to think. "That's some very convoluted reasoning. Do you really think that's the case?"

She saw his point. "Jesus, I'm getting as paranoid as they are."

"If you're worried about that, there's still hope for you."

Hope, maybe. But that didn't mean she shouldn't wonder about him and where he came from. "How is it that you know so much about the Department? About me?"

"I told you. I'm a researcher. And I'm very good at what I do."

"My association with the Department is not on public record."

"Also, as I told you, I have connections."

It wasn't a very comfortable answer. "What brought you here?"

"Nothing brought me here. I'm on vacation. I was just passing through. Our meeting was pure coincidence. Not that I'm going to let that stop me from trying to help."

"I thought you didn't want to get involved."

"So did I, but now I don't see how I can't. You obviously need help."

Since her "resignation" she'd spent her nights in rituals designed to align forces in her favor. Was David the response? A magician couldn't always be sure how such positive forces would present themselves in her life. When the alignment was good, events often took on the appearance of useful coincidence, a coincidence like his appearance in Chardonneville. "What kind of help are you talking about?"

"Whatever I can provide. I know some people. Maybe I can get some strings pulled. What kind of help are you looking for?"

What kind, indeed? "Suppose I'm willing to listen to you."

"We could go to your cottage and see what we can figure out."

"Let's try somewhere a little more neutral."

"Still don't trust me, eh? How about down by the woods? Little chance we'll be overheard there."

She decided she was willing to trust him that far. She walked with him and let him talk, expounding on a plan that he was clearly making up as he went along. He had a way of speaking that made her just want to listen; so she did. He had her believing that the two of them could leave Chardonneville together. They parted when the sun touched the trees to the west and she promised to meet him again the next day.

But that evening, alone in her cottage, she began to have second thoughts. David's plan had sounded almost reasonable while he had been explaining it. Now it seemed a little farfetched, even full of holes. Chardonneville was the headquarters for a nest of spies backed up by the best magicians of the modern era. How were the two of them supposed to get away from that? David was just a writer. Sure, he'd had some experiences, but how did surviving a few brushes with the barely competent militaries of third-rate countries qualify him to deal with Magnus's agents? He was confident, and when she had looked into his eyes, she'd felt confident too.

Now that she'd had some time to think about it, she didn't feel so confident. How could they possibly manage it?

With her magic, of course.

It was their—*her*—greatest asset. Just the fact that Magnus hadn't made any overt moves against her demonstrated that they were afraid of her now. And why shouldn't they be? Hadn't she demonstrated a new facility with magic, beyond anything they'd yet cataloged?

And that idiot Dagastino didn't want to believe she'd been to the otherworld.

But their fear was based on ignorance. How fearful would they be if they knew how ignorant she was of her new abilities? There had been so little time for testing her new strengths, exploring the new sensations that she perceived, or analyzing her new insights. One thing she was sure of was that little in her improved repertoire of spells could match Magnus's hi-tech cloak-and-dagger toys. Worse, most of the magic she felt confident of required preparation, supplies, and equipment, and almost all of her supplies and equipment were still hostage in the underground labs.

And time was a factor as well. David couldn't remain in Chardonneville for long without attracting the attention of the Department's terriers. He might already be under scrutiny. If they hadn't noticed him talking to her in the café, they had surely marked the long walk he and she had taken through the orchards. If he left Chardonneville in the morning, they'd forget about him; he'd pass out of their calculations.

And out of her life.

She surprised herself at how that thought disturbed her. She wasn't the sort to fall for a pretty face. But she had fallen a little, hadn't she? He *was* attractive, but her response to him was based on more than that. Wasn't it? Could it be that her attraction to him came from the hope of escape from this mess that he represented? If only her problems with the Department weren't putting her in such turmoil, she'd be able to sort it out.

She got up and began to prowl the cottage. It was a small cottage, confining. As confining as her life with the Department. Before long she found herself back where she had started, sitting in the heavy padded chair in the main room, toying absently with the accumulated trash on the occasional table. She caught herself, put down the tarot deck she had been fingering, and chided herself. Such woolgathering was pointless and a waste of time, but she couldn't seem to focus her thoughts on anything in particular. Before long she realized that she had drifted again. She held something in her lap: the tarot deck.

Coincidence? Or was her unconscious mind pushing her toward something that might be useful? She'd studied the tarot, along with a number of other divinatory tools, but the cards had never been a friendly implement for her. So why was she turning to them now? It seemed that the otherworld had changed her. Had it made her able to handle the cards effectively?

She fanned the cards out and selected the Queen of Pentacles, her usual significator. If she *had* changed, was the Queen of Pentacles the right card for her anymore?

Dragging the table around in front of her, she swept a clear space amid the clutter and laid the Queen down in the center. Contemplating the card, she shuffled the deck.

Had she changed?

The cards seemed to think so; the first reading offered her lots of hints in that direction, but nothing conclusive. A second reading returned her to the same significator. Instead of being discouraged, she felt vaguely empowered. Each turn of a new card seemed to increase her awareness of the interplay of meanings and position among the cards. Each reading seemed more clear and focused. Change was a major component. Something had changed or was about to change in her life.

Was the change to come?

The cards pointed to her future, handing her the Wheel of Fortune in the last position. Change to come. She seized upon the card and laid it out as the significator for a new reading.

What, then, was her destiny?

As she shuffled the rest of the cards, they seemed to tingle in her hands as the pasteboard riffled against her palm. She felt a growing sense of assurance, of confidence. This would be a good reading, a powerful indicator. The cards were aligning themselves, shifting through the possible permutations until they reflected the forces bearing upon her future.

What was her future to be? She turned the first card and revealed the Last Judgment, a card of change, leading to a definite outcome. She wanted that, didn't she? But what sort of outcome?

What sort of obstacles faced her? The King of Wands, reversed. A dark man? Certainly not David; he'd been signified in the previous readings as the Knight of Wands, but this was a reading of change. Why would he be an obstacle? Or did the card signify another? Magnus, perhaps; he was certainly an obstacle to her present.

Another card, crowning the situation: the Five of Cups. A strange, ambiguous card of simultaneous gain and loss. At least it promised that something would remain in the end, even if it was not what she expected.

So what did she have to work with? The Magician. Herself? Her magic? Will over the vagaries of the world. That she could deal with.

Confidently, she turned the next card. Behind her was Justice, reversed. A familiar positioning and an easy read. The Department's treatment of her was anything but Justice. Was it time to leave all of that behind? And for what?

What was coming into play? The Knight of Wands. David.

She quickly turned the seventh card, the illuminator of her attitude. The Seven of Swords. Hope and confidence. She hadn't begun feeling that way, but she was coming more to believe in the solution before her.

Another card, the influence of those around her. The Knight of Cups, reversed. A messenger or invitation? David might be that as well. Or there might be another involved. Bennett? He was fair and graceful, but she would have thought other cards more suitable to the elf prince. Besides, that image didn't seem to fit, although there was a resonance when she thought of him. His son, the changeling, perhaps? Spae had no idea what had happened to the boy, but this was a reading on her future. Perhaps they would meet again.

The next card was supposed to reveal her hopes and fears. She turned it faceup. The Lovers. The obvious reading was, well, obvious. The card could also mean trials overcome. She felt hopeful and encouraged.

The last card would speak of what was to come, a key card in a reading aimed at the future. She uncovered the Hierophant. Was this the man to whom she had recourse? David again? One take on the card suggested that it spoke of marriage. Some said the card had a darker side, one hinting of captivity and servitude. Some—the same ones?—took marriage as a form of captivity.

With all the cards laid out, she had a sense of completeness and correctness. This felt like a good reading; the cards were aligned properly and in harmony.

But marriage?

She gathered in the cards and laid the Hierophant out as significator. Shuffling the deck, she did not sense the harmony of the cards; something was missing. Her next reading was confused. As was the one after that. She tried another half-dozen readings but none of them resolved into anything resembling sense. The clarity had slipped away.

If it had ever been there. She'd never been comfortable with the tarot.

But tonight had been different, hadn't it? How else to explain the rightness, the—dare she call it—power that she had felt? Or was it only the power of wishful thinking?

She laid down the deck and rubbed her face. She was tired, as tired as she might be from working a spell. She went into the bedroom and lay down. Almost immediately, she fell asleep. Her sleep didn't last long, though; she awoke feeling that her dreams had been chaotic. She thought about getting up or getting more properly ready for bed, but she couldn't bring herself to move. She stared at the ceiling, thinking about the readings. An insight, or a delusion? Had she sensed truth, or merely her desires and concerns, powerful factors in their own right? Her worrying faded into sleep.

All in all, she slept badly that night.

Charley Gordon's belt unit beeped right in the middle of the Hilton concierge's account of what he'd seen in room 746. Charley apologized for the interruption and took up the unit. He was ready to punch the file button when he saw the "requested notification" symbol lit. It'd be bad for his teamwork rating if he didn't answer it promptly.

From Manny's expression, he'd seen the light too. He knew what was coming and he didn't like it.

"I've got to take this call, sir," Charley said to the concierge. "Please go ahead with your story for Detective Salazar. I'll rejoin you as soon as possible."

Charley stepped away down the hall for a little privacy and pulled the message onto the screen.

>>21.10.11 * 05.24.12.56 * xxxxx.xxx
LOG #1012.67
AUTOROUTE
TO: GordonC@NECPOLNET*0004.13.00*874334
FROM: StanilausJ@NECPOLNET
    *0004.09.12*233487
RE: NOTIFY OFFICER REQUEST.
MESSAGE:
    CONCERNING UNREGISTERED, CRIMINAL MARABETH
LANCASTER. GENETIC ID MATCH WITH JANE DOE 12 *
45.23 * 211008.4. 98% CONFIDENCE.
***CRIM*LINKS: DNDLS3492//12*211011.4
                JD 12 * 45.23 * 211008.4 // ID
                JD 12 * 45.23 * 211008.4 // MD
                JUARZ7892//12*211011.4
                UNREG 11*5678238
***GORD*LINKS:KRAVATZ
                MODUS 112

Marabeth Lancaster?

For a moment the name meant nothing to him, then he linked it. Lancaster was Jimmy Kravatz's missing girlfriend. No surprise to have her turn up dead.

Charley approved the data transfer on the GORD*LINKS and logged a note to pass the word about her death to the ear. He'd get out to see Kravatz as soon as he got Captain Hancock off his ass about the Hilton report.

Part 2

A NECESSARY
DECEPTION

CHAPTER
8

"So what's this all about, Tall Jack?"

"You know as much as I do."

Frowning, Spillway Sue continued to prowl the room where Wilson had left them. It wasn't very big, only a little larger than John's old bedroom back in the rezcom, and the ceilings were so low that John could reach them without even straightening his arm. After attempting the door and finding it locked, Sue looked for an alternate exit. So far all her poking and prodding hadn't revealed any secret doors or escape hatches.

John waited until Spillway Sue was investigating the farthest corner of the room.

"Faye?" he whispered, hoping for an answer and afraid he'd get one. He hadn't sensed anything, but he'd felt dull and half-asleep since he'd gotten into Wilson's car; he might not have noticed her presence if she had disobeyed him and slipped aboard the car before the door closed. He called her name twice more, but even the third time wasn't the charm. No friendly voice whispered to him from the air. Faye wasn't here.

Wherever *here* was.

His memories of the trip were pretty vague. He remembered getting into the limousine, and Sue's frenetic searching for anything that looked like a control. She never found any that worked. At least John thought not; somewhere after the limousine started rolling, things got hazy. He remembered some motion that didn't seem right for a car, some steep banking and what felt like up-and-down movement, mostly down, but it might have been a dream; it had that sort of quality. The fuzziness of it all hadn't bothered him at the time, but now he began to suspect that Wilson had done something to them. Some kind of drug or sleeping gas, maybe?

He didn't like the thought of having been drugged. Wilson and his people, whoever they were, were not exactly acting like friends.

And who were these people? John didn't have the faintest clue.

He had a pretty clear memory of Wilson opening the door to the limousine and ushering John and Sue into a darkened corridor. They'd been quite tractable. More of the drug effect? He couldn't remember much about the corridor, no clues to tell him something about who their captors were or where they were.

The room wasn't any help either, with its strange amalgam of rustic primitive and chromium hi-tech. The floor was of packed earth, but the ceiling seemed to be a single seamless panel that glowed in circular patches with a soft reddish light, the only illumination in the room. The upper half of the walls was a similar material, without the glow spots, while the lower half was of a black stone so highly buffed and shiny that John thought it was plastic until he noticed the structure and tiny fossils within it. A band of thicker material marked the boundary between the two materials; John guessed it for some fine-grained dark wood because of the intricate carving on it. The fantastic interlaced shapes of coils, spirals, knots, and bizarrely elongated animals drew the eye in and spun it around.

There was a small couch against one wall and a circular table and three chairs in the center. All the furniture had bright chrome frames. There were soft deep cushions on the seating and the tabletop was a thick slab of highly polished wood. A perscomp with a swivel screen sat in the middle of the table. He sat down in one of the chairs and stared at the dark screen. He didn't think the 'comp would be connected to an outside line, and even if it were, whom would he call?

Maybe they wouldn't be here long. He hoped so; there weren't any sanitary facilities.

Having finished her fruitless search, Spillway Sue slumped into the chair opposite John.

"So who's this Arthur Bear guy? I don't know him."

Who did? "He's somebody I used to hang with."

"He corporate or fed?"

"What? Neither. He's just—" Just what? A man who'd magically slept for a dozen centuries. A killer. A gang leader. Supposed to be the real King Arthur. Had Spillway Sue even heard of the legend? If she had, would she believe that the man who had inspired it was living and breathing in the here and now? "He's just Bear. He's just a guy. That's all."

"Anybody with connections like these has gotta be corporate or fed. Big bucks or mega clout or both. This is some fancy shanty, and we didn't exactly get here on the public tranz."

"Do you have any idea how we *did* get here? Or where 'here' is?"

She started to answer, then stopped and thought a minute. "Ya know, I don't know how we got here. I musta fell asleep." She leaned forward accusingly. "Say, you didn't—"

"Didn't what?"

"You're asking. Ya didn't." She slumped back in the chair. Eyes roving around the room, she chewed on a hangnail. "Must've been good junk they used on us. Felt like I was flying a couple times."

"I don't remember leaving the car."

"Me neither. Pretty good trick, huh? These guys got real good toys. Ya know what they're playing at?"

"I don't think they're playing."

"Then what they want, huh? They came looking for *you*, not me. Me, I just got bused along for the ride. You're the one they laid this show on for. Gimme the prop. Who's boss and what's the deal?"

If only he knew. This was, however, an opportunity. "Maybe you'd be willing to trade. Roscoe and the Flake fingered you as the leader of the raid on my place. Who sent you after me and what do they want?"

"Them boys is just street muscle. Dumb boys with too much mouth."

"They said you had the connections. What connections are those?"

"That's biz confidential, ya know."

"I could say the same."

She gave him a hard, evaluating look. "Maybe ya could. But, ya know, I don't see we got a fair trade here. Ya been asking enough questions that I think maybe ya don't got any good idea what this scam's all about."

"I know about Bear."

"Ain't seen no Bear. Only seen this Wilson shrimp and the fine toys these guys got. Wilson says if I be quiet and don't make no trouble, that I don't get no trouble. Maybe I'll give Shorty a chance to show he's not touting the prop."

His bluff hadn't been much, but it had been worth a try. He could push some more, but his heart wasn't in it. Maybe the perscomp had some information; it wouldn't have a smart mouth. He slid his chair a little closer to the table. It was not like he was some whiz *CyberCowboy Chang*EM kind of decker, but he'd done a little fooling around. He might be able to get something out of the system.

Five minutes of trying every way he knew to get a response from the system got him nothing. Just when he was ready to quit, the perscomp beeped and the screen lit. Wilson's face appeared.

"Reddy?"

John didn't bother to answer; he felt sure that Wilson could see to whom he was talking.

"I know you're there and I know you can hear me. How are you feeling?"

"What's it matter to you?" Sue asked.

"I see the young woman has recovered. What about you, Reddy?"

"So you *did* drug us," John accused.

"You sound fine. Of course you were drugged. It was for your own safety," Wilson responded matter-of-factly. "If you want to leave here, it's best you not know where you are."

"And where are we?"

Wilson chuckled. "Beneath the mountain."

"That some kinda code word?" Sue asked.

John shushed her and spoke to the screen. "What do you want with us?"

"I want you to get ready for a meeting." A section of the wall opened, revealing another room. Through the door John could see little more than a bed. Clearly Spillway Sue saw it too.

"Hey, this ain't like some creepo breeding experiment!"

"Don't worry, young woman. There are separate accommodations for you." A second panel opened to a second bedroom. Sue shrugged to John and hauled herself out of the chair. She padded to the doorway and peered in. "Active! I could get used to a place like this."

John hoped they wouldn't have to. Well, that *he* wouldn't have to. Spillway Sue could go her own way.

Sue entered the room, neck craning back and forth. "So where's the— Never mind." John heard the quiet *shuff* of a panel closing.

"All right, Wilson. It's just us now. What's this meeting all about? Where's Bear?"

For an answer Wilson said, "Shower. Change. Compose yourself. I will come to get you at ten."

"How am I supposed to know when that is?"

Wilson's face was replaced by numbers on the screen. They read "9:11:43." The seconds started ticking off.

Wonderful.

Shower he could and would, if they'd provided the facilities. It had been a while since John had taken a good, long, hot shower. Change? Maybe. Again, if they provided; but if Wilson was sharing his clothes, John would be badly dressed for this meeting. Compose himself? Not likely, while he was so completely under their control.

Since they were in charge for the moment, there wasn't much he could do. He checked out the bedroom, and was relieved to see that the shower facilities were modern rather than rustic. He tried the water; it was hot. He shucked his clothes and took advantage of it, letting the steamy, humid, soapy sensations and the pounding water wash his mind free of his problems.

"Nine-fifty," a synthesized voice announced.

Reluctantly, John cut off the water. If his captors were this compulsive about time, he'd better go along; he didn't know enough about them to risk antagonizing them. Not yet.

As he emerged from the bathroom, a panel opened near the bed. A closet. Towel wrapped around his waist, he poked through the offerings. There was a suit—pure salaryman cut—complete with snap-collared shirt, string tie, and shiny black wingtips. They looked close to his size, but they weren't his style at all. He found some briefs and a tank top on the shelf and took those; the clean cotton felt good against his clean skin. But the concept of putting on the suit was too weird. He pulled his old pants back on and strapped into his boots. The old leather smell and soft suppleness of his jacket was familiar and comforting, reminding him of his days with the Dons; those had been good times, the best since leaving Worcester.

When he emerged into the central room, Wilson was already there, apparently dozing. He perked up as John reached the table.

"Ready?" Wilson asked.

"Almost," Spillway Sue answered from her room. John caught a glimpse of her bouncing across the room to snatch something from the bathroom, and had to catch his breath as well. She'd found herself an impressive selection of clothes; she looked ready to hit the clubs and set some trends. Her look didn't match well with his concept of her at all.

She headed for the door, still toweling her dark curls. As the panel started to slide shut in her face, she yelped and darted forward. She wasn't fast enough to make it through, but got a hand on the door's edge. The panel insisted on closing whether or not she had any extremities in the way. She managed to save her fingers. Sue's howl of protest was cut off as the panel sealed.

"Hey," John objected. "What's the idea?"

"She was not invited," said Wilson.

Divide and conquer was an old tactic. "I don't think I like the idea of leaving her here alone."

"She will not be harmed so long as she behaves herself."

"Like she can cause trouble locked in her bedroom?"

"It should minimize her opportunities."

Wilson pointed at the door, indicating that John should precede him out. The corridor was still dark, but not quite so bad as before. Had the dimness been a function of the drug? This time John noted that the walls were the same as in the waiting room, and so were the floors. Unfortunately, several of the archways they passed through were not as tall as the waiting room door; John bumped his head on the first, but the experience did teach him to duck for the rest. An experiment in using his greater stride to outdistance Wilson brought John to a halt in front of a sealed archway. Wilson, unhurried, rejoined him, and the panel opened. They continued on.

"Mind if I ask you something?"

"I'll answer if I can," Wilson replied.

"You're not holding Sue as hostage for my good behavior, are you?"

"Would it do any good?"

"No," John answered, trying to sound firm. He really wasn't so confident. His glimpse of Sue after she was cleaned up had made him rethink things. She didn't look at all like the streeter who had confronted him at his slump. What did he know about her anyway? One thing he knew for sure was that he was the reason Sue was here. He felt sort of responsible. He hoped Wilson wouldn't figure that out because he really didn't want to have to worry about being coerced by threats against someone who, when last left to her own devices, was threatening his life.

They came to a small chamber that looked remarkably like an elevator car. Wilson stepped in and turned around to face the doorway. John did the same and saw there were no controls.

"Wilson. Escorting Reddy."

The door closed and the car began to descend. The ride was smooth. Without a floor number telltale, John had no idea how far down they went. The car stopped with the slightest of jars and the door opened onto another dark corridor. Wilson led him out.

They came upon a short woman in a lab coat. She glanced back over her shoulder and immediately increased her speed. She stopped by a closed archway, laid her hand on the wall beside it, and disappeared through the doorway when the panel opened. It was closed again by the time John and Wilson reached it. John looked for the controls the woman had used, but didn't see any sign of them. Since Wilson kept walking, he didn't think it prudent to stop and make an examination.

They took a lot of turns, and walked through a lot more open arches and past many more closed ones. How many people had disappeared behind those doors just before John and Wilson rounded the corner? What sort of place was this? The anonymous walls and doors offered no clues, leaving John with plenty of room for wild speculation.

At last they came to a set of doors unlike the others he'd seen in their ramblings. They were great valves of dark wood, bound and garnished with golden metal wrought into exquisite relief. Rows of strange faces glared down at him like disapproving gargoyles. Wilson walked up to the doors, stamped his foot twice, and said something that John didn't quite catch. It must have been a code word because when he'd said it, the doors began to swing inward, revealing a larger space than John had yet encountered in the complex. John couldn't tell how huge it was, since it was wreathed in shadows and stygian darkness, but he sensed that it was vast.

Shoving John to get him moving, Wilson walked with him beneath the arch into the chamber.

Looming like the giant trees of a redwood forest, massive three-yard-thick columns of polished stone marched in parallel rows down either side of the chamber. The pillars reached up and out of sight into the deep gloom. Metallic flecks and veins made the material look exotic; the columns sparkled like cylinders of a night sky. The light reflecting from those mineral stars came from two beams spearing out of the over-head darkness to make ten-foot circles of brightness on the floor. One of the shafts fell on an empty expanse of the mosaic tiled floor, while the other, more distant one illuminated a raised area crammed with machines and consoles. In the midst of the hi-tech equipment sat a great chair of black stone, which faced the doors. A pair of carved dragons made the chair's arched back and writhed sinuously down its sides to meet nose to nose and form a footrest. Ivory teeth jutted up gleaming from the sculpted jaws, and red gemstones glittered beneath the hewn brow ridges. John found it difficult to tear his eyes from those of the dragons.

The shadows of the magnificent chamber were occupied. John estimated nearly two dozen people were moving about, coming and going in the darkness. Most wore gray or tan coveralls. A few wore long aprons or robes; it was hard to tell in the dim light. It seemed that every face he saw was bearded, many luxuriously so. But the most striking thing about the people gathered there was that the tallest came no higher than John's chest. Had they been at a hotel or conference center, John might have thought he'd wandered into a convention of little people. But that couldn't be the case here.

And Wilson—John looked at his escort—Wilson fitted right in. He was a little taller, and where John had thought him squat, he now looked slender compared to the denizens of this place. Who were these people?

John remembered the last time he had seen so many short, stocky people in one place: the Mitsutomo raid on the palace of the Lady of the Lakes. He hadn't thought it odd at the time; he supposed now that he should have, but so much had been odd in the otherworld. Were these people part of some kind of special Mitsutomo operation? Had Mitsutomo bred a genetic subspecies? If so, why? And what business did they have with him?

"Who are you people?"

Several of them whispered to their fellows, and someone John couldn't see laughed. Only Wilson responded directly to him.

"You're supposed to be bright, Reddy. Haven't you figured it out?"

"Are you Mitsutomo chimeras?"

More whispers. The laughter guffawed. Wilson chuckled. "Mitsutomo only wishes it had that kind of biotech capability."

Not Mitsutomo? John caught sight of one bushy-bearded male, almost as wide as he was tall. No, those people were neither ordinary little people nor genetic constructs. There was another answer. "Some of you look like dwarves. I mean, real dwarves, like in stories. Are we in the otherworld?"

Wilson looked up at him. "Can't you tell?"

"You *are* dwarves, aren't you? You're not human at all."

"No more than you, changeling," Wilson responded.

John's amazement shifted gears. "You know?"

"We're a pretty inquisitive people. We learn a lot of things we're not supposed to know." There was a stirring among the dwarves. Wilson noted it as well, lifting his head and staring avidly. He recovered himself and gave John an order. "Step forward into the light."

John balked. They had stopped short of the first empty circle of light. Now Wilson wanted him to step into it, apparently alone. There was something going on here. "Where's Bear?"

"You will see him shortly. First you have an audience."

"An audience? You mean like with a king?"

"Very like. Now, be quiet and step into the light."

He gave John a shove, forcing him forward. Stumbling into the illuminated area, John found that the light from above made it hard for him to see anything other than the small space around him and the other illuminated area with the dais. He might have been stranded on an island of light in a sea of darkness, staring out at another, unreachable, island. He felt the eyes of the assembled dwarves on him. Uncomfortable with the attention, he moved to the center of the circle; he'd have more time to react if anything came at him out of the dark.

Silence descended. Everyone seemed to be waiting for something.

Somewhere a drum sounded a deep and throbbing note, then another. In the darkness he heard the dwarves shuffling restlessly. Or maybe they jostled for better angles to view what was coming. Wilson emerged from the deep darkness to stand just inside the edge of John's circle. The dwarf was staring at the circle with the dragon chair, so John looked in that direction.

The drum rumbled a pair of notes as a rotund dwarf, with a snowy beard that fell nearly to the floor, stepped into the light and mounted the platform. Wilson bowed to the newcomer as though he was a king. Maybe he was. Although he didn't wear a crown, the dwarf did seem to be wearing some sort of formal robe and there was something regal in his slow, steady gait.

The king—if king he was—seated himself on the throne— if throne it was. He carefully set one foot on each of the dragon heads and fussed with the drapery of his robe until it veiled the glittering eyes. Seemingly satisfied, he placed his elbows on the arms of the chair and clasped his hands together, leaning forward until his hands masked his mouth. His great beak of a nose jutted out over his folded fingers. Under their shadowing brows, his eyes glittered as brightly as the dragons' gemstone orbs, black instead of red.

Under that glare John got a good idea of what a mouse must feel like when cornered by a cat. He started to take a step back.

"Stand where you are," Wilson whispered.

He stood. For five minutes he stood. No one said anything. No one moved. Was he supposed to do something? Wilson hadn't told him, and John had no idea what was appropriate. They'd brought him here. Shouldn't they start things?

The silence stretched on.

They'd said Bear wanted to see him, but John hadn't seen the first sign of Bear's presence. Was it all a scam?

"I want to see Bear," he said impulsively.

"You will make no demands here, changeling," the seated dwarf said in a thunderous, gravelly voice. "Were you to *ask,* such a request might be granted. Your kind is ever giving orders, demanding where they should make a polite request. I was wise to bring you here for judgment before you were taken to the sleeper."

Judgment? John didn't like the sound of that. In fact, he thought it downright presumptuous. "Judge me? Who the hell do you think you are?"

"You may call me Kranekin."

"I *may* call you a kidnapper. I mean, you have your flunky haul me off at gunpoint, drug me, and whisk me off God knows where, but wherever this is, I'll bet we went across state lines to get here, which makes it a federal crime. I'll just bet the feds would be interested in this place you've got here. And I'll be happy to—"

"Enough!" Kranekin thundered, pounding both fists on the arms of his chair. "Your protest is pointless. The humans have no succor for you. To their databases, you are dead. You are beyond the protection of that system of laws. Here you are under *my* law."

"Is that a threat?"

"As may be." Kranekin leaned back against the dragons. "You have your father's arrogance. Do you follow in his footsteps?"

"What do you know about my father?"

"You didn't answer my question."

"And you didn't answer mine."

"As I said, arrogant." Kranekin's tone shifted. "You wish to trade knowledge?"

The sudden change made John suspicious. "Maybe."

"We know many secrets."

"I'll just bet."

"More than you do, it seems."

"Maybe you'd like to share some of your secret knowledge with me."

"With nothing offered?" Kranekin shook his head. "Unlikely."

"I'm getting tired of this mystery trip routine."

"An odd attitude for one of your blood. Either you play your part better than I think you are capable, or you are truly lacking in your elven upbringing. What guarantee can you give me that you are not your father's tool?"

"Are you asking me if I work for Bennett?"

"Is Bennett the name he gave you?"

"You're the one supposed to know all the secrets."

"I would have your word. Are you his tool?"

"As far as I'm concerned, Bennett can dry up and blow away."

"He speaks from the heart," said a deep voice from the darkness.

"My own conclusion," Kranekin said. His mustache twitched as if somewhere beneath it lips were smiling. "I find your lack of filial devotion comforting."

Swell.

Kranekin continued. "Certain ones have suggested that you may be of help with the sleeper."

"If you're thinking of using me to coerce Bear, forget it. He won't bend that way."

"You obviously do not know his history very well."

"He knows the reborn man." It was that voice again.

John wished he could see past the blinding light; he wanted to see who was on his side. He'd have to be content with an invisible supporter. He'd grown up with an invisible friend; he should have been used to it.

"Perhaps he does know the man," Kranekin conceded. "Let us see if the reborn man knows him."

CHAPTER
9

Quetzal had experience dealing with strange, seemingly random environments and struggling with them until he could put them into order. Nakaguchi's computer environment was no more daunting than some of the astral dimensions with which he was familiar. As he had mastered moving in those dimensions, so he mastered finding his way through this dimension of data.

The thinkers of this current era knew astonishing things, the craftsmen were capable of awesome feats; but for all of their accumulated knowledge, for all of their wondrous artifacts, there was much that he knew that they did not. There was much more to reality than their philosophies admitted.

They denied many things which he knew as unalterable facts; yet much of what they professed, he didn't understand at all. He would not make their mistake; he would learn from them. A greater knowledge of the physical world could only improve his mastery of the spiritual.

And he would have mastery.

But he was not so foolish as to rush blindly forward when so much had changed. He would spy out the world around him and come to know it before venturing forth.

It was a more formidable task than he'd anticipated when he had laid his plans for his slumber. So much had changed! There were so many things to learn! Fortunately the computer enabled him to do so quickly. The speed with which information could be acquired and understood was dazzling; even more wondrous was the amount of information to be had. There was so much, so much.

He had so many questions. Many more than he felt comfortable in indulging at the moment. If all went well, there would be time for those intriguing questions. If his plans did not come to fruition, all questions would be irrelevant. Some of his questions demanded immediate answers, and to those he must turn his attention.

What had happened to the others? Was it truly the time? Perhaps most important of all, who stood ready to oppose him?

If Nakaguchi were a true follower, many of the answers lay within the archives he had prepared. But no matter how well prepared those files were, there would be some answers that Quetzal would have to seek elsewhere. For now, he would take what was to hand, wandering the landscape of the computer's world. He would find the mines of datafiles and delve into their records for the hidden diamonds of clues.

But his search was intruded on by sensations from the physical world: Joel Lee prodding his body, seeking his attention. Being under his thrall, Joel Lee had little in the way of independent thought; his action would be in response to Quetzal's orders. Reluctantly, Quetzal abandoned the hunt for answers. The return to the world outside the computer was accomplished swiftly and without the disorientation he had experienced at the end of his earliest excursions.

Through the glass partition to the next room, Quetzal saw the reason for his recall: Nakaguchi's security chief had come. Joel Lee had acted correctly. Still, Kurita's interruption was unwelcome.

"Let him in," Quetzal ordered.

Kurita was an Asian like his master Nakaguchi, though of a more precise and punctilious manner. The man walked briskly up to Quetzal and bowed.

"*Ojama shimasu,* Kendall-sama."

Quetzal stared at him while Joel Lee translated. "Kendall" would excuse the interruption only if it had more significance than the false name the security chief insisted he use.

"Speak English," Quetzal ordered. He had yet to absorb the Japanese language program. So much to do.

"As you wish, Kendall-sama. Nakaguchi-sama wishes to know if you find your new quarters satisfactory."

Quetzal didn't need to look around the suite to know that this location was better than the cold, barren place they called the medlab. He could feel it in the fiber of his being. Despite the machine-controlled environment, it was more alive. His time in cold barrenness was over.

"Nakaguchi chooses a strange messenger to inquire after my comforts."

"The *kansayaku* orders, I obey."

"Admirable," Quetzal observed honestly. "There are other matters, of course."

Kurita nodded. "I have the personal honor of reporting that security has been established on the Peruvian simulation chamber. The artifacts from Peru have been installed and all is as you requested. The chamber is ready for your inspection."

"Good." The chamber would serve as a meditation cell, and a workroom as well, at least until he'd had time to create a better.

"It would be an honor to have Kendall-sama inspect the chamber soon."

"Is that your wish or Nakaguchi's?"

Kurita's face was a rigid mask, hiding any emotion or reaction. "*Itachimashita.* Forgive me, Kendall-sama. I meant no disrespect. My team has worked very hard."

"And they are waiting to be sure there is no more work to be done."

"It is as you say."

"Dismiss them." He did not care to have anyone looking over his shoulder as he "inspected" the premises.

"But Kendall-sama—"

"If anything is unsatisfactory, we will deal with it later."

"Yes, Kendall-sama."

Kurita made no move to depart.

"What else?" Quetzal asked. He was growing weary with the interruption.

"I humbly remind Kendall-sama of the Cytronics Board of Directors meeting that is to take place today. Nakaguchi-sama suggests that it might be of interest to you. Nakaguchi-sama asks if the suit he sent is acceptable. If not, another can be provided."

"I will attend." Understanding the workings of these corporations was going to be vital in the new age. He already had ideas about how to manipulate them, but learning from the computer was like learning from a book; there was only so much to be gleaned. Real, practical experience was vital.

"Attendance will necessitate a short trip outside this facility."

"Give Joel Lee the details."

Kurita nodded sharply. "I would also humbly remind Kendall-sama of this morning's meeting."

"With William Jeffries. I remember."

"Mr. Jeffries is already in the building."

Conferring with Nakaguchi, no doubt.

There was still almost an hour before the scheduled starting time. Did they think him so adrift in time as to forget a meeting with this locale's highest ranking follower of the Path?

Sending the chief of security dignified the string of trivial messages, but they did not justify Kurita's presence. "These messages are insignificant."

"I am humbled by your insightfulness, Kendall-sama."

He had thought Persians indirect until he had encountered the Japanese. "Tell me why are you really here."

Kurita dropped his head in acceptance. "There is the matter of your recent unescorted departures from the secure perimeter."

"Which you find troubling." Quetzal found it troubling that he had been detected.

"The *kansayaku* has tasked me with your protection. I cannot protect you if you leave my agents behind."

"Their company is unwelcome."

"With all respect, Kendall-sama, such ventures are unhealthy."

"I find them most refreshing."

"To be blunt, Kendall-sama, your actions threaten the security of this operation."

That would not be Nakaguchi's chief concern; he would be worried by Quetzal's increased independence. "And have you informed Nakaguchi of this threat to the operation's security?"

Kurita took a moment before answering. "The reports are prepared."

But not sent.

A fortuitous moment. One to be seized. Quetzal took a step closer to Kurita. The security chief tensed, then moved with serpent quickness to block the hand Quetzal raised toward his face. Quetzal was impressed by Kurita's reaction speed, but it mattered little. Quetzal simply curled his fingers down to touch Kurita's hand. The flesh-to-flesh contact was all he needed to complete his intention.

He reached into Kurita's mind, seeking to encompass it. Kurita opposed him, actually fighting him. That was surprising; there was no sense of the adept about Kurita. But Quetzal had tasted his measure in the first moment: the security man's strength would be insufficient to resist; Kurita had strength, but his skill in the contest of wills was so small as to be nonexistent. The outcome was inevitable. Quetzal bore in. Kurita's body collapsed to its knees, still fighting. A strong will, indeed, but not strong enough. He closed his grip over the man's mind, feeling it squirm helplessly under his secure control. Satisfied, he released his physical grip. Kurita huddled in on himself.

The effort had been tiring, but it would repay.

"Tell Nakaguchi that I am content with your precautions," he ordered. "Tell him also that I shall rely on his bounty in the matter of my needs."

There would be no tiresome tattling to Nakaguchi. Kurita was his now; the security chief could conceal Quetzal's comings and goings from Nakaguchi while tracking the company man's own doings. Another step forward on what was going to be a long road to control.

For the moment, it was prudent that he travel that road in secrecy. Let Nakaguchi believe that he had a basis for his feelings of superiority. The man's impudence would reap its reward in time. For the moment, Quetzal was content to appear to be the ignorant visitor from an earlier time. When he was ready to expose his intentions, things would be diffcrent.

The worm would emerge from the darkness to take its place in the light.

Rearden's report held less uscful data than Pamela had hoped. Far less. Nakaguchi's databank had locks within locks, and so far the most promising files remained beyond Rearden's skill to open.

But the files Rearden *had* been able to access were intriguing. They offered insight into what Nakaguchi had prepared for the Quetzal creature. She recognized some of the programs from Cytronics's intensive education program; some of the simpler ones were to be among the Keiretsu's offerings at the spring electronics exposition. The datafiles serving the education program were mostly what one would expect for updating a man from another century—save for those dealing with the occult. Only those who knew what was happening to the world would include such information; only they would know that it was important.

Nakaguchi knew.

He was part of what was making it happen.

If only there were *something* in his databank that she could use to take him down, to disrupt his plans.

There was, of course, but the same information could damage her as well. Some of it could hurt the Keiretsu—and, by extension, her as well. There had to be *something!*

She sent Rearden an order to continue the search and busied herself studying what she had. She might have missed something.

"Hey, Gordon, you asleep, dead, or just off duty?"

"Dead," Charley replied without stirring.

"And here I was afraid you were off shift."

Johnston knew Charley was on; as desk sergeant, it was his job to know who was on and off, in and out. It wasn't his job to poke his nose into Charley's cubicle, but the fat old man was an officious bastard.

"You don't *look* like you're on shift," Johnston complained.

"I told you, I'm dead."

"You will be soon enough, and the captain'll be the one to do it to you. I'm getting a signal from Central that your buffer dump is full again. Your 'puter's started putting out refuse messages. And get your feet off the desk."

"Got it." Charley left his feet where they were.

"Do something about it."

"On it."

"*Now!*"

Reluctantly Charley pulled his feet down and set them on the floor. Damned stupid software. The secretary programs were supposed to be a blessing; the optimal throughput monitor was supposed to signal when a cop got overloaded, to let his supervisor know he needed help. Typical union blessing where something that was supposed to be a harmless aid turned into a career-torpedoing rat. Anybody who ever did any work in the Department knew a cop *always* carried more than his official caseload and that sometimes it took a while to get around to things. *Optimal throughput my ass!* If the programmers had ever put in any allowance for priorities, they hadn't protected it well enough. The way things worked a departmental memo about cleaning up the coffee area ended up as important as a "notify officer" request and the secretary programs dumped them all in your box and squalled when they couldn't cram any more in. The monitors gave people like Johnston something to use on people like Charley in trouble with people like the captain. Only thing to do now was to empty the buffer and avoid a reprimand, assuming one hadn't already been logged electronically.

"Computer, scan incoming. Sort, now. Send messages to subscreen 3, now. Subscreen 3, size up, now. Again."

That made the listing readable. He did his own scan of the incoming messages. If he had a good idea what they were about, he dumped them in a save file. The others, he read, saving the anonymous transmitter stack for last. Mostly junk as usual, but one caught his attention. Caspar again.

>>21.10.12 * 23.11.38.79 * xxxxx.xxx
LOG #1012.67
TO: GordonC@NECPOLNET*0004.13.00*874334
FROM:< UNKNOWN>
RE: Modus 112.
MESSAGE:
   The answer. Settawego Building lobby.
10.13.13.59. Pers. Atten.

Modus 112? Charley didn't remember what the reference number referred to. Whatever. Caspar was telling him that whoever was behind the case would be at the Settawego Building today, just before 1400.

What time was it? "Computer, time check, now."

"1322.58," the machine replied in its piecemeal voice. More than twenty-five years of voice-response tech and still the things sounded patched together. Maybe it was deliberate. Monkeyboy programmers again.

But programmers weren't the problem. Time was. It was less than an hour to Caspar's predicted revelation.

Where the hell was the Settawego Building? "Computer reference: location of Settawego Building, now."

"Define search parameters."

"Global."

After a pause, the machine came back with, "Denied. If you wish to pursue this search, please select more limited parameters."

Too expensive for the department's budget, probably. Available with proper authorization though, which he didn't have. Maybe he didn't need a global search. Wouldn't Caspar have said something if the dump was somewhere other than nearby?

"Computer, access file: Modus 1-1-2 and transfer all geographical references to subfile, now. Name subfile: Settawego, now."

"Complete."

"Good." That had been quick, the load must be light. Nice to have something fall his way. "Reference: location Settawego Building, now."

"Define search parameters."

"Reference subfile Settawego and search all sprawl districts listed therein. Send result to new subscreen, flasher, now."

"Acknowledged."

The code word for "sit there, sucker, and wait." Charley called up Modus 112 to refresh his memory.

Right.

A string of dead streeters. Caspar saw a pattern, which was more than Charley could. Dead streeters turned up all the time. What made these special? More important, what made Caspar think they were Charley's business?

The screen started flashing the address of the Settawego Building, and he put the questions aside. He just had time to make it, if the traffic wasn't too bad.

William Jeffries was an aged man with sparse hair as pale as his skin, a rattling collection of bone and worn-out sinew clothed in a baggy alabaster bodysuit. With his ankle-length white coat and trailing muffler of angora wool, he looked the part of a ghost, but Quetzal could sense the energy in him and knew at once from its taste how that energy was stoked. When Jeffries held his hand out in the greeting common to this place and age, Quetzal refused it. The man's decrepitude was repulsive.

Without intending to, Quetzal had scored a point in the interplay of status. Jeffries seemed to take his refusal to shake hands as an insistence on precedence. The man mumbled an apology for presumption.

Quetzal had expected an adept of greater magnitude. Was this man an imposter? No. He could not be. Jeffries followed all the forms of greeting, demonstrating that he knew the signs and words proper to an initiate of the inner circle of followers. Yet Quetzal sensed no real power surrounding Jeffries. A man of disturbing contradictions, an unfit cog for Quetzal's machine.

"I am most honored to meet you, Venerated One," Jefferies proclaimed fulsomely. "I have seen the signs and dreamed the dreams, but until this moment, I had not quite believed that the time had come."

An unfit cog, for truth. If Jeffries had not believed, why had he sent his acolyte to rouse Quetzal? Didn't the man know what a false awakening would cost Quetzal?

Quetzal listened to further pointless enthusing with growing impatience. He had assumed there was a point to the meeting other than to gratify an old man's desire for praise. There was a time and place for such things; praise was best given in a forum where others would be inspired by the accolades granted to those who served faithfully and energetically. If Jeffries needed such reinforcement, so be it. But not here and now; Quetzal wanted to make the best use of it. Besides, he needed to improve his contacts with the followers; he did not plan to remain coddled under the arm of the unknown and uninitiated Hiroto Mitsutomo for long.

"Arrange to gather your circle," he ordered.

"Tell us when you wish to grace them, Venerated One, and they shall be there," Jeffries said.

"As soon as may be."

"As you wish."

Nakaguchi gave Jeffries a sideways glance. "Venerated One, some of the circle will not be able to arrive quickly. They are scattered around the world, attending to your business."

"My business? I gave no orders." Yet.

"They work to prepare the way according to the ancient mandates."

"Yes," Jeffries said. "And they are zealous. Our understanding of the mysteries may be limited, but we know what must be done before the great hour. Lacking access to the higher arts, your followers use the lesser arts to sway men to the Path. We have been diligent. We use all means to hand to make the physical changes. Surely you've read the files. You have seen how far we have come in turning the world upon itself. It is pleasing, is it not?"

"I have read the files." But he would not believe that the reported desertification, pollution, and general environmental destruction were as widespread as those files claimed until he had seen for himself. If the followers had, for truth, been responsible for such things, they had taken great strides in preparing for the great change. "All appears to be in proper order."

Jeffries beamed satisfaction. "Then you know we have served well."

He *knew* nothing of the sort; he had only their word for what they had done. Perhaps they *had* been faithful; but perhaps they took credit for the unaided turning of the world. For one so little advanced in personal accomplishment, Jeffries pridefully claimed much credit. Almost certainly too much. "Much has been accomplished, but all is not yet in readiness. There is more to be done."

Jeffries was undaunted. "Command us, Venerated One. Set us on the Glittering Path. We have called you from the great dreamless sleep to lead us. Say the word and it shall be done, for we are eager to please. We have kept the faith, as you will see. Great shall be the rewards of the faithful."

"And justice come at last to the wronged," Nakaguchi said, completing the ritual phrase.

The two men before him had the fervor of true believers. They had ambitions for themselves, certainly, but that was no crime. Rather, it was the fuel to excellence, the strength of the Dragon. Their strength could be harnessed now that he was awake again.

"Gather the circle. I will choose companions."

"When the breath of the Dragon is upon the land, the Strong One will arise and lead the faithful," Jeffries intoned.

"He shall uncoil from his sleep and raise his head to the sun, who shall tremble and grow dim in the glory of his radiant plumage," Nakaguchi rejoined.

"Hail the Awaited One," they said together. "Hail the Lord of Change."

Quetzal basked in their belief, feeling the heat from their faith in the secret canon. He was sure that both of them believed that they would be among the chosen companions. Faith was a tool, an especially important one to a mage. He would use it and use it well, for he was a skilled craftsman. But knowing the temper of a tool was as important as knowing its proper use. A flawed tool could mar even the greatest craftsman's work.

"Go now. Do as I have bidden you."

Jeffries insisted on more burbling and more recitations from the secret canon, but Quetzal did not have to repeat the order to depart—barely. Once they were gone, he summoned Kurita. The security chief arrived almost immediately.

"Your desire, *tono?*"

Having taken Kurita as a bond servant, Quetzal had thought it wise to immediately increase his knowledge of the man's native language; words were the boundaries of thought. There had only been time for a brief lesson before the meeting with Jeffries, but he had learned the word "tono." It meant liege lord. How charming to have Kurita use the term without his ordering it.

"Bring today's offering immediately."

"Yes, *tono.*"

Kurita did not depart, clearly sensing that Quetzal had another matter on his mind. A good rapport. Quetzal's impulsive taking of Kurita had been an unforeseen wisdom; Kurita promised to be a good tool. Now it was time to test *his* temper.

"William Jeffries is an obstacle," he said.

"*Wakarimasu.*"

Do you truly understand? Unlikely. But Kurita did understand his role and that was sufficient. Most bond servants showed little initiative, but Kurita was so well versed in his role that he could be counted on to act within that role without Quetzal's constant attention. Kurita was the sort of man who had been good at his job, and his servitude would do little to affect that; the cold, precise mechanism of the security chief's mind promised admirable results. Quetzal could dismiss Jeffries from the picture.

"Wait until he has arranged the meeting I desire."

"*Wakarimasu.*"

Quetzal smiled. It was comforting to know that there *were* good servants to be had in this new age.

Nakaguchi returned from bidding good-bye to the doomed Jeffries just as Joel was removing the husk of the offering. Nakaguchi stepped out of the way, giving the burdened servant only the barest of glances. His attention was on Quetzal.

"This is a great day for the order," the man crowed.

"One for the annals," Quetzal agreed. "Is it not nearly time for the board meeting?"

Pamela kept being drawn back to the occult files. She noted that Quetzal had accessed them first, then ignored them. Why? Was it all old news to him? Probably. But how could Quetzal know five hundred years of occult theory if he had slept through it all? Could there be another reason he was ignoring the files?

Could they be flawed? Could Nakaguchi be working from a faulty base? Could that be why he was working with a monster like Quetzal?

Good questions, but she wanted answers.

She ran a comparison between Nakaguchi's occult history files and the ones she'd gathered in her database. The editor noted strong correlations, but highlighted some significant differences. She set the editor to sift for any common threads in data exclusive to Nakaguchi's files and got a large number of references and passages from a single source: a book called *The Hidden Splendour*. One of the passages proclaimed it a watershed work of occult philosophy.

She didn't recall the title.

The public library database responded to her request for a download with a "not available." There were no other works by the author, either. She checked her file of occult works, and though there was no copy, which was not surprising, there was a notation about it.

From Sörli. She understood why she didn't recognize the
title when she read Sörli's commentary. He dismissed the
book's author, W. E. J. Magus, as a lunatic and the book's
contents as the ravings of a madman. He must not have
thought the book important to her education in things arcane.
Why? So many of the occult references that Sörli had insisted
she read had seemed the ravings of madmen. What made this
one different?

On the theory that the author would be easier to find than a
single title, she consulted Gemmatics, one of the Keiretsu's
publishing companies. Among the variety of services Gemmatics offered was a database of pseudonyms; it was an ex-
tensive database. Her check revealed that the name "W. E. J.
Magus" belonged to William E. Jeffries. No date of death was
listed for Jeffries, suggesting that he was still alive.

She set a dossier trace on Jeffries and sat back to await the
results. She had a feeling she was getting close to something.
Knowing who Jeffries was, and learning more about his take
on the occult, would tell her things about Nakaguchi; the
hatchet man had clearly been a student of Jeffries and his occult worldview.

To know the student, learn about the teacher.

A madman, Sörli had said. Such a description might well
be applied to Nakaguchi. She needed to know more about the
sort of madness that was corrupting him and making a bid to
corrupt the Keiretsu.

Her perscomp announced departure time for the Cytronics
board meeting.

Jeffries would have to wait. She reconfigured the data
dump from on screen to her "immediate" file. The Keiretsu's
computers were the best in the world. She'd have what she
sought by the time she returned.

Charley made it to the Settawego Building with five minutes to spare. Good thing he'd been working out of the Need-
ham office to be nearer the ongoing investigation at the
Hilton. The building was a black rectangle thrust out of a
fringe of Sandcrete™, a not particularly noteworthy example

of early-century architecture, but he felt stupid when he realized it was his destination; the tower of the Norwood Hilton stood only a block away. He'd been back and forth past this place for a week.

The place was definitely corp, but like a lot of buildings of its vintage, it had no logo plastered on the upper stories to advertise the building's ownership. He didn't see any ownership marks until he walked up to the main entrance, where a discreet Mitsutomo Keiretsu logo was inlaid into the marble facing over the doors.

Hadn't Kravatz said somebody showing the Mitsutomo logo had 'napped Lancaster?

Mitsutomo was one of the biggest of the big; messing with them would make life miserable for him. He hoped that whatever Caspar thought was here was really connected to one of the remora clinging to the public floors of the corporate shark's building, rather than the shark itself. Charley wasn't big enough to survive getting stepped on by Mitsutomo.

As he entered the building, Charley slipped on his Tsurei Seeing Eyes™. The photosensitive glasses contained a fiber-optic camera and a short-range microphone that could transmit image and sound to his belt unit. Clean recordings were admissible in court and had helped put more than one rapist into psychochemic therapy. Not that he had a court order permitting him to record. And not that he'd be likely to get one for recording on corp property. But using the glasses for private purposes wasn't illegal; they made a great memory aid.

The lobby was the bottom of a yawning pit of an atrium, a six-story barn. A mezzanine made a second deck of public space and filled a small fraction of the vertical space. Stores and kiosks and restaurants made up most of the tenants, but there were a few small business offices too; most of those were on the mezzanine. Several banks of elevators to the corporate eyrie dominated the northern end, defended by a glassed-in security area. The transparent barrier extruded a tentacle to a private entrance; Charley saw several limousines waiting there. The rest of the place was open and lively and crowded with people.

Couldn't Caspar have been more specific?

Charley was still checking the layout when a full bank of elevators opened their doors with drill field precision. Computer-coordinated precision, more likely. A phalanx of suits flooded out of the elevator cars. Some formed up in a double row, an honor guard of sheep awaiting the vips of their flock. The rest bustled on down to the waiting limousines.

Big show.

Charley recognized the honcho when she emerged from the central elevator, Pamela Martinez. This wasn't the sort of turf the head of Mitsutomo NAG usually hung out in. Clearly something was up with the corp.

Business for the Special Investigations Unit? Charley hoped not.

The parade of suits got more interesting when he saw that Martinez wasn't the only one in her elevator car. Two guys exited after she did, a sharply dressed Japanese and a frail-looking Black with white hair. Etiquette among corps with Asian ancestry had the top dogs coming out last. Who were these guys, to outrank the head of Mitsutomo NAG? They were ciphers to Charley. He tapped the RECORD stud on his belt unit; if he was interested he could research them later.

The flunkies swarmed around the Mitsutomo bigwigs in the usual way, escorting them to the waiting vehicles. Nothing strange there. Although there were a few odd fish in the shoal; Charley noted a dwarf in the Japanese's wake, and a pair of suits with black leather medical bags tagging along behind the Black. Not typical suits, but not SIU strange.

After the limousines pulled away, the lobby seemed quieter, as if a storm had just blown through. Charley waited, keeping a lookout for whatever strangeness Caspar expected him to find. To blend in, he took a seat in the lounge near the elevator banks, where he had a good line of sight to the main entrance and a couple of the side ones as well. Occasionally he'd fake a call on the house phone as if he was trying to reach somebody upstairs. While he played his blend-in game, 1400 hours came and went. He gave it another ten, and then another, just because Caspar hadn't steered him wrong yet. He still didn't see anything that fit the spec for an SIU investigation.

Modus 112, huh?

The closest thing to a streeter he'd seen was an independent vendor checking in at the desk guarding the entrance to the Mitsutomo preserve. Her clothes were too offbeat to be corporate, but she was far too clean and well-heeled to be streetlife. No Unregistereds here. Especially no *dead* Unregistereds here.

The answer, huh?

Right.

What was Caspar thinking about?

CHAPTER

10

"He's not . . . well," Kranekin said in a warning tone as they stopped before a door no different than a dozen they'd passed.

John gave the dwarf a sharp look. "What do you mean?"

"Perhaps it's best that you see for yourself."

Kranekin nodded to Wilson, who placed his hand on the frame of the door. Silently, the door slid open to reveal a well-lit room that John immediately classified as a hospital room despite the stone and wood of the walls; it had that kind of smell. A scattering of odd machines gave an undertone to the lighting from their flickering readouts. Bear was in the center of the room, but he wasn't lying in bed. He was in some kind of fluid-filled tank like something out of *Stellar Wars*: *The Final Generation*[EM].

They had shaved Bear's beard to fit a respirator mask. The newly exposed skin showed an ashen color that was hidden by the darker tone of his tanned cheeks. He had lost enough weight that John wondered if he'd be able to stand. How long had he been in the tank?

John entered the room under Wilson's prodding. Neither of the dwarves said anything. They let John stare undisturbed.

Intermittently Bear's voice came from a speaker on the side of the tank. It was weak, his words strange. He was speaking in the tongue that John had heard him use when the crazy sorceress Nym had called him from his sleep. John still didn't understand a word of the babble.

John felt numb and confused. In deciding to accept the recorded invitation to meet with Bear, he hadn't really known what to expect; but this wasn't it. One thing was clear: Bear was in no shape for a conversation.

"He never made that disk, did he?" John turned on Kranekin. King or not, the white-haired dwarf seemed to be the one in charge around here. "He didn't send for me. You did."

"A necessary deception. We did not expect you would trust the word of our agent alone. Although the message was a construction to gain your confidence, the heart of the message remains true. Artos needs your help."

He certainly needed *somebody's* help. "What did you do to him?"

Wilson answered. "We were attempting to help him adjust to the present times, through the use of an accelerated learning process. Even though it's a new tech, we'd never had problems with it before. Unfortunately, there were some unexpected complications. Arthur has slipped into a delirium wherein he knows no fixed time or place. We had hoped that you might anchor him."

"He needs your help, John Reddy," Kranekin said.

"You mean *you* need my help."

Kranekin shrugged his massive shoulders, a motion that barely disturbed the flow of his hair and beard. "In this, it is the same thing. We are trying to help him."

"For your own ends."

"We have our concerns," the boss dwarf acknowledged. "However, in this matter we are obliged to do what we can to see him well."

"See him well? He wouldn't be like this if you hadn't messed with his mind."

"We acted with his consent and took all reasonable precautions. It remains unclear whether his condition is any fault of ours," Kranekin said gruffly.

"However, we did introduce him to the technology," Wilson said. "We understand our obligation and are acting to fulfill it, which is why we brought you here. Are you willing to help him?"

"Why? So you can control him?"

"He is of no use to anyone, including himself, like this. He would not abandon you in similar circumstances."

John wasn't so sure. Bear was fully capable of dumping people. He'd been ready to abandon Trashcan Harry when he and John had been in Mitsutomo's clutches. Of course, Bear had known that Harry was a goblin and had no use for him; he'd come to get John. In those days, John had enjoyed a somewhat dubious status as a *comes*, one of Bear's close companions, but that had been before Bear had learned of John's parentage.

Would he abandon John? Once John would have agreed with the dwarf and said no. But now? The last time he and Bear had seen each other, Bear had called John a traitor. Not a goodwill and boon companionship sort of attitude.

But John remembered other words as well, friendlier words. That was the Bear John preferred to remember. He looked at the tank and felt a little sick himself. The man in the tank didn't look like either of the Bears he remembered. Who could say how this man would see him? Where did these dwarves get off in making predictions about Bear's attitude?

"How do you know what he'd do?"

Kranekin took a moment before answering. "We have some experience of him."

What was that supposed to mean? This Kranekin looked as old as a fossil. Could it be—"You mean you knew him before, um, like, when he was king?"

Nodding solemnly, Kranekin said, "We knew Artos the king."

We? Was that the royal *we*? "*You* knew him *personally*?"

"Our history is not the question here. You are the question." Kranekin pointed at the tank. "Are you willing to help him?"

John stared at the frail figure floating in the tank. Unable to help himself, he had to ask, "How dangerous is it?"

Wilson surprised him. "For you or for him?"

John surprised himself by feeling as fearful for Bear's future as for his own. These dwarves were responsible for Bear's condition. What if Bear got worse? What if John ended up like that?

"For both of us."

"You will be in no danger," Kranekin assured him.

"What about Bear?"

"He can only be better off."

Some people said that being dead was better than being sick. John wasn't sure he believed that, though. Could he help Bear? God knew he needed help.

"Are you willing to try?" Kranekin asked.

John swallowed hard. "Yeah, I guess."

"Are you ready to try?"

"You mean here and now?"

"You got someplace else to be?" Wilson asked.

The sudden rush made John suspicious. "You haven't given me a lot of reason to trust you guys."

Wilson nodded. "For your own safety, in case you declined to help."

"You mean like, so I won't know much if you let me go?"

Kranekin nodded.

"You'd actually let me go?"

"Sure," said Wilson. "Why not?"

"Spillway Sue, too?"

"Again, why not? She's seen less than you have."

"I wish I could believe you."

"You can," Kranekin said. "You can go; you need only turn your back on Artos."

John didn't like the way the boss dwarf put it. Sure, he knew the price of leaving, but what was the price of staying and helping? The dwarves said it would be safe. They said

Bear needed him. But was any of it true? They'd used a lie to get him here. Were they lying now?

"What if I say that I want to go? What happens to Bear? What are you going to do to him?"

"You are not the only option," said Kranekin. "Perhaps not even the best."

"Most of our doctors favor a different course of treatment anyway," Wilson observed. "A radical course."

Pointing to the tank, Kranekin said, "You are wasting *his* time, Reddy. Possibly you are wasting his life."

Laying guilt wasn't the way to get John to agree to go along. *He* wasn't the one who'd gotten Bear screwed up. Let them fix their own mess. Why should he help them? They'd never done anything for him.

Still, John's eyes kept drifting back to the tank. Bear looked so helpless, so . . . what? John wasn't sure, but he knew something in him ached, seeing Bear this way. But what could he do? He wasn't a doc or a psych; he didn't have a degree in anything, let alone anything useful. He wasn't much of anything.

Bear had come for John when Mitsutomo kidnapped him. John had been Bear's *comes*. When Bear had made the offer, John had been thrilled. For a time John had considered himself squire to the greatest knight in the world, a knight who was a little tarnished and a lot outdated, but a knight nonetheless. It had been a dream come true. Sort of. Didn't he owe something to Bear? What if there was something he could do to help?

He'd given Caliburn back to Bear and saved Bear's life. And Bear hadn't even said thank-you. Hadn't that repaid Bear for his rescue of John? More than repaid him for the baseless accusation of treachery. He and Bear were quits, weren't they?

Staring at Bear's shrunken figure, John knew they weren't finished. Bear's accusation of treachery *had* been baseless. John had resented it, not just because there were no grounds for it, but because Bear had jumped to conclusions. Bear had believed John had betrayed him just because of *what* John was, not *who* he was. John wanted to show Bear just how wrong he was. But there had been no chance. Well, here was a chance.

A chance that, even if successful, might put both of them in more trouble than they'd been in before. He only had the dwarves' word that they wanted to help and that they were Bear's friends. They certainly didn't act like friends. But if John didn't cooperate with them, they would do something else to Bear. Maybe something worse. Knowing he would probably regret it, he asked, "What do you want me to do?"

Kranekin nodded brusquely and made some kind of signal with his hand. A moment later, a door that John hadn't noticed before opened and admitted a trio of dwarves wearing white lab coats that almost brushed along the floor. Their beards were close-cropped like Wilson's, but they were built more like Kranekin, almost as wide as they were tall and with big, solid guts; despite their conventional clothing and hairstyles, they would have stood out on the street as nonhuman.

One of the whitecoats carried a boxy helmet in one hand. John could see chips and wires embedded in the clear plastic surface of the lumpy thing. A pivot on either temple held a transparent half mask that would cover the wearer's eyes and nose. Kranekin took it and held it out to John.

"It is inelegant but functional," said the boss dwarf. He sounded a little embarrassed.

Inelegant? It was ugly. "Well it's not going to make the *Fashion Forward* list. What is it?"

Wilson answered him. "An interface device. It's your ticket to the virtual environment we've got set up."

Virtuality headgear? John hadn't seen anything like it at the mall; there it was all slick and rugged goggles and gloves and cockpits. While the idea of playing with some fancy virtual environment was exciting, the circumstances were something less than he'd have liked. At the very least, he wanted to know what sort of place they were going to toss his mind into. "What kind of environment are you taking about?"

"One familiar to him, at first. We need to reestablish his past before we work on his present."

And what about his future? John didn't think he ought to ask; he was a little afraid of the answer he might get. Was he going to be helping Bear, or just setting him up for Kranekin and his people? He took the helmet in his hands.

"Sit down first," Wilson suggested.

"Where?"

The dwarf pointed behind John. There was a padded chair that looked as if it had escaped from a passenger airliner. Where had *that* come from? It hadn't been there when they entered the room. Wilson smirked as John eyed the chair suspiciously.

"It's not magic," the dwarf said.

And John believed him. He wasn't sure why, but he did. But if not by magic, how had the chair appeared?

"Just a sufficiently advanced technology," Wilson said in answer to the unasked question.

Like the doors, he supposed. They appeared in seemingly solid walls. The chair must have come up through an opening in the floor. John looked for a crack in the floor and couldn't find one. He hadn't seen any sign of a door before the white-coats had entered either, but it had to have been there; even with their "sufficiently advanced technology," it seemed unlikely that the dwarves were manufacturing an aperture anytime they needed one. Most likely they just had a very good camouflaging gimmick. Holographic screening, maybe? Whatever the system was, Mitsutomo or one of the other megacorps could make a fortune marketing it.

"Put the helmet on and sit."

John did as he was told. The whitecoats busied themselves with something on the back of the chair. After several minutes one of them said, "Ready."

Another stepped around into John's view and said, "Close your eyes."

John did so.

"Open them."

For a moment John thought he was back in one of the forests of the otherworld. But only for a moment. It was different here; and at first John wasn't sure how he knew that. Then he listened. There were none of the strange sounds and the soft stirrings he had felt, as much as heard, while traveling in that other realm. This forest, for all its multitude of trees

and plants, its flitting small animals and birds, was dead. Or
rather, it had never been alive. It was a virtual forest, a computer representation of a landscape. John wondered how far it
extended. Was it manufactured anew as he changed his line of
sight, or were all the individual trees stored in discrete locations? Were the forest creatures random or did they run on
their own programs, living virtual lives in the virtual forest?
Did the little animals reproduce virtually, or did they just go
into reruns? However this virtual world worked, it was light-
years ahead of the best he'd seen in the malls. It was just sight
and sound there; here he could smell the leaf mold and feel
the breeze against his skin; that was Senzaround™ stuff like
in a theater.

He realized he was standing. He had no memory of getting
out of the chair. Try as he might, he was unable to feel any
sensation of his meat body sitting in the chair. Even better
than Senzaround.

He held a hand up. His, all right. Down to the scar by his
third knuckle that he'd gotten when he'd been three and tried
to punch out a bad guy on the vid set. He looked down at his
body. The shape was familiar, but the clothes weren't. He appeared to be wearing a baggy tunic, belted at the waist, and
sandals, an outfit out of a medieval costume drama, and one
of the better ones too; it looked like real clothes. He even had
a sword strapped to his side. Surprisingly, the outfit felt comfortable, all broken in and livable like an old T-shirt and
jeans. Even the weight of the sword on his hip felt comfortable. His old classmate Will Brenner would have been green
with envy. Or maybe Will wouldn't be; he hadn't ever had
much interest in virtuality, preferring his anachronisms to be
physical.

At the very least, Will would have gotten a thrill out of having a sword belted on; Will had never been able to afford one.
Thinking about the sword, John couldn't resist. He took hold
of the hilt and drew the blade. It was long, almost a meter, and
the balance was a little awkward. The blade was double-
edged and had a somewhat rounded point. Not much good for
thrusting; the sword was definitely tip heavy. The ridged grip
reminded him of something; the familiarity nagged at him.

When he saw the eagle cast into the crosspiece, things seemed to click into place. The sword was a Roman cavalry sword, a *spartha*; John had seen one at a traveling exhibition in the Woodman Armory Museum. This weapon looked just like that one.

He swung it a couple of times, just to get the feel of it. It moved as he imagined it might. It was not the sort of sword he preferred, but it would serve a horseman well. He imagined riding hard, charging toward a foeman, blade upraised. Then—

Then he put it away. He wasn't a horseman and he wasn't charging anybody. Wandering about with your sword out was what heroes in bad fantasy books did. Walking around with a drawn sword was a good way to get yourself shot or skewered by people who might otherwise be friendly. Although he supposed he really didn't have to worry about things like that; the dwarves were controlling this simulation, and they weren't expecting him to fight anybody.

Or were they? They'd given his virtual self the sword, hadn't they?

He looked around the forest glade. There was no one here to fight. Or to talk to. What was going on? Krunokin had said that the environment was supposed to be familiar to Bear, which John guessed a forest would be, but Bear wasn't here. What was John supposed to do? He tried asking the question aloud, assuming that the dwarves monitoring him could hear. He got no answer.

So, he was supposed to figure it out for himself, eh? For helpful friends, these dwarves weren't very helpful.

He looked around again. Off to his left the trees seemed to thin. There was a break in the brush that seemed to be a path.

Okay. I can take a hint.

He followed the path. After a couple of minutes it brought him to the edge of the woods. He stood overlooking a landscape of rolling, low hills dotted by trees, both individually and in small and large clumps. It looked like farming country, but he saw little sign of man's hand on the land, save for a handful of huts clustered near a stream. Smoke rose from all of the huts, but not from cookfires. The remaining straw and wattle were blackened. Several huts still poured forth smoke columns, broad and fitful.

John looked for people, live or otherwise. At first he saw none, but then a man emerged from behind one of the huts. The man walked about, inspecting the devastation. He was a burly fellow, a familiar fellow.

Bear.

John started walking toward him.

Bear looked more like himself, vital and strong, not the slack-faced hulk floating in the tank. He was wearing a red tunic with a skirt that hung almost to his knees. On his feet he had boot-sandals that wrapped and laced halfway up his calf. A broad leather belt, studded with metal, cinched the tunic at the waist. A half-dozen more studded straps dangled down from the center front over his crotch, while another strap ran from his right shoulder to his left hip and supported a scab-barded sword. With a shock, John recognized the hilt of Caliburn; the sword looked in a lot better shape than when he'd seen it in the otherworld.

"Artos!"

John recognized his own voice, but he hadn't spoken. He guessed the dwarves were opening their scenario.

Bear's head craned around; he was looking for the person who called his name. He saw John. Bear squinted and scratched at his beard as though trying to recall a half-remembered memory. There was no flash of recognition, but Bear put on his polite-for-company face and walked toward John. When he was a couple of meters away, he asked, "Do I know you?"

John was vaguely disappointed. This time, he spoke for himself. "Don't you?"

"I think not."

"This is John, Artos," Wilson said, having suddenly appeared at Bear's side.

John turned as Bear did. Where had the dwarf come from? And why was he dressed as Bear was?

"And who might you be?" Bear asked.

"I am the son of Will."

"In truth?" Bear cocked his head to one side and scrutinized the dwarf. "You do have his look about you."

Wilson smiled. "As my father served you, so am I come to serve you."

Bear nodded. "Will the Dwarf was one of my trusted men and stood high in my regard."

"I hope to deserve the same." Wilson and Bear shook hands—well, wrists actually; each man gripped the other's right wrist. When they were done Wilson grabbed John by the arm; his grip was painfully strong as he turned John to face Bear. "John here hopes to serve you as well. He is a stout and right brave fellow."

"Is he?" Bear gave John an appraising look. "Is it your wish to serve with me?"

"I guess so." John looked down at Wilson. "That's why we're here, isn't it?"

"It is," Wilson said.

"Well, I am in need of stout men. If the son of Will speaks for you and says that you are a worthy companion, then you may join my band." Artos turned and shouted. "Bedwyr! Pwyl! Look you here! The son of Will the Dwarf and young John have come to join the fight."

CHAPTER
11

Spae woke fully alert, quivering from a dream in which David, dressed as the Knight of Wands, had swept her up and ridden toward the sunset. She'd felt safe in his arms. He'd bent his head to her, his lips brushing her nose and sending a thrill of electricity through her. Then his lips had sought hers and she'd—awakened.

She felt a little like a schoolgirl again.

But schoolgirls weren't trained mages and covetously guarded by the Department. She was. And that was why she was awake now instead of dreamily lounging in Sir David's arms. Someone was probing her wards. She felt the touch as that someone tugged on her wards, testing them, and recognized the clumsy hand of Dagastino in the manipulations. She sent a charge through the field, repulsing him.

Take that, you prying bastard!

Had Magnus approved the probe?

Did it matter?

They didn't want her to leave and they weren't going to let her sulk forever in her cottage bastion. How long would it be before they sent in the bullyboys to drag her back for a real interrogation, with drugs and any other persuaders they thought necessary?

The cards had said that turmoil and distrust framed her present and immediate past. They'd pointed at David as the solution, and maybe he was. She just wished she could be sure. Sure of the truth of the reading, sure of her feelings toward David, sure of what she should do. Most of all, she wished she could be sure of getting away from Chardonneville and the Department.

The tarot had promised her a resolution and David was a part of that resolution.

The cards said change. David said get out. What bigger change could she make than getting out of the Department and leaving it all behind? She was getting nowhere here.

She grabbed her bag and stuffed a few more things in.

Either they'd manage the escape or they wouldn't, but at least they'd have tried.

She set out to meet David as they had arranged.

Chardonneville's café was nearly deserted, most of the locals having gone off to their underground work and most of the rest off to their aboveground deceptions. Granvie, the village's putative mayor, gave Spae a sour look as they passed at the entrance. The old man's attitude was a matter of the merest momentary concern, because almost immediately she saw David. He was seated at the table where they'd eaten together the day before. He looked bright and rested and hopeful as he waved her over. She went happily; just seeing him raised her spirits.

They chatted as chance-met acquaintances might, until the waiter took Spae's order; then David said, "We have to leave Chardonneville now."

"Now?" Spae had expected him to say as much, but she was suddenly unsure. There was so much she'd be leaving behind.

"Yes, now. They're onto us."

She didn't want to believe it. Maybe it was a mistake? "How do you know that?"

"Someone searched my room this morning while I was in the bathroom. I assume it wasn't the maid. Damned if I know what they were looking for. Incriminating evidence of my association with you, I suppose."

Guilt by association. Just talking with her had contaminated him in the Department's eyes, and they hadn't done anything more than talk. She hadn't decided to go along with David's plan. But they were pushing her. "Dagastino tried to probe my defenses this morning. I thought he might have been acting on his own."

"Unlikely. They're suspicious. It'll be more than probes soon."

She was afraid he was right. But surely there was a little more time. In her impulsive rush to cram things into her bag this morning, she'd missed a few things she didn't want to leave behind. She wasn't prepared. Neither was David; he didn't have his knapsack. They couldn't leave yet.

"We can't leave from here. I don't have everything I need and you need to get your things."

"We *have* to leave from here. We'll both have to get along with what we have, because if I go back to the B&B and you go back to your cottage, we'll be in trouble. Once we separate, they'll pick me up. They're not afraid of *me*."

"We could stay together. Go to your room and then out to my cottage."

"That would eliminate any doubt they might still have that I'm trying to help you. While we're packing, they'll be acting. It's no good; we've got to go right away. We'll have our best chance if we go now, before they get organized."

It all seemed so precipitous. David smiled and touched her arm. His grip was reassuring.

"It'll all work out. We're smarter than they are."

He didn't know Magnus. "How can you say that?"

"Easy. *I* never worked for the Department, and *you're* leaving."

She was, wasn't she?

David's hand left her arm, retreating to his side of the table as the waiter arrived with her breakfast. David pretended the hovering waiter wasn't there.

"It's such a wonderful morning," he said. "And the countryside is so lovely. Most of the folk around here haven't had the time of day for me, but you've been so nice. I was hoping I might prevail upon you to show a passing stranger one more kindness."

"And what would that be?" she asked, playing along.

"As I said, the morning is so nice, and I did come here to France to see the sights. Perhaps I could talk you into showing me some of the local points of interest. I'm particularly partial to anything from before the Revolution. Surely, there must be something ancient around here. Didn't I read somewhere that this village dated back to the Middle Ages?"

"The site goes back at least that far."

"Good enough," he said. The waiter disappeared inside and he took her hand, squeezing reassuringly. "Good enough, indeed. A sight-seeing walk will get us started on our way out of here."

She hoped so. "Think they'll believe we're just going for a walk?"

"We can only hope. If I leave my pack here, it'll help. Avoiding your cottage will help, too. But you must eat your breakfast, and I must finish my coffee, or they will be sure to be suspicious."

The waiter appeared again, fussing with the table settings on the empty tables near them. They talked about the region and the weather while Spae ate. David finished his coffee just as she finished her meal. They settled their account and departed; as they walked along the lane, he kept having to prompt her to point out the supposedly interesting sights. They were heading up the hill which offered the best overlook of the village when David announced, "We're being followed."

He told her where to look. It was Granvie. The mayor was inspecting the wooden footbridge they'd crossed to the path up the hill. Granvie looked innocent enough, if one didn't have reason to suspect him. But Spae knew he was Department.

"I guess they're onto us," she said.

"We can't be sure of that. They might be, they might not. There seems to be just one watcher, and we're out beyond where they've let you roam before. This fellow could just be ordinary surveillance."

They were farther from the village than she'd been since resigning. If the Department wasn't already coming down on them, maybe they didn't know she and David were intent on running away. Running away? What *was* she thinking; it sounded so childish. But childish or not, she *was* running away; or if the tarot was to be believed, running toward something. Yes, she liked that better. But whether running away from or toward something, she would soon be committed; the Department wouldn't let her go much farther without taking action.

"If we keep going, Granvie will call for help, and we won't get very far. They'll have vehicles. We won't be able to outrun them."

David's mouth grew taut. "Then we can't let him report."

"You don't mean . . ."

He looked surprised. "What? You didn't think I was talking about *killing* him, did you?"

Actually, for a moment, she had. She'd been around the bullyboys of the ECSS too long.

"I may be a lot of things, but I'm not some fictional action hero. Actually, I was hoping you'd have some magic trick to put him to sleep or something."

She knew the recipes for several sleeping potions, but she would hardly be able to get Granvie to drink one, even if she had one to hand. "I'm not a fictional magician either."

"Too bad. Isn't there any magic you might use?"

"I don't have a lot of field experience." Except for her blowup in the interrogation room, her successes with her improved ability had all been in the laboratory. She was fairly confident that her emotional level had contributed to the strength of that magic. Here, now, could she do anything effective? It seemed unlikely; she didn't have anything of Granvie's to focus any spell she might attempt.

"Could you distract him?" David asked. "Or make him think we're going in the opposite direction?"

She shook her head. "A moving illusion would be impossible to maintain."

"What about a stationary one, then? Something to get him looking the wrong way."

"It wouldn't work for long."

"Then you *can* do it."

"Maybe. But I think I just got a better idea. Sit down, as if you're tired."

A questioning look on his face, David did as he was told. She walked a short way down the sparsely wooded hill, looking about. She spotted some stray branches. There were clumps of tall grasses and a goodly number of old leaves caught under the bushes. All to the good. She spotted a stand of small willows growing near a hollow in the ground. As she ambled past, she looked back up the hill. David was still sitting there, looking back at the village.

There might be something she could do.

"Now lie down," she called softly up the hill. "And go to sleep."

She poked about a bit more, then wandered back up the hill to where David lay. He opened one eye as she sat down. "Stay still," she whispered, and he didn't stir. Good. Granvie wouldn't see the open eye from his distance, but he'd notice if David moved.

She closed her own eyes and concentrated. Granvie was still by the bridge, leaning on the rail and pretending to watch the stream. She knew he was pretending because in her heightened state of awareness she could *feel* the intensity of his attention on them.

What would be best? Something that would attract his attention, yet be believable; they'd need a bit of time. What would motivate the skulking mayor to abandon his post and investigate? Another skulker, perhaps.

She concentrated on the image of a man dressed in black— no, camouflage—creeping through the woods by the bridge. She paid special attention to the sounds such a man might make. Sounds would be easier to maintain. Holding the image firmly in her mind, she cast her thoughts outward, forming the image in the trees beyond the bridge. She willed the sounds to begin, to be real.

She turned her head toward the village, but shifted her eyes to watch Granvie. The mayor seemed unaware of her efforts.

She envisioned the nonexistent skulker brushing through the leaves, each leaf scraping softly along the fabric of his clothes. The lurker was stealthy but not utterly silent; she made her phantom man step on a dry stick. A crack! Soft but carrying.

Granvie's head turned toward the wood.

It was working!

Granvie cast a look up the hill. Spae held herself still, pretending to be unaware of the mayor. Granvie got to his feet, looking first into the woods, then back up at the hill. Stealthily, he slipped into the bushes.

Spae moved her phantom man away from the bridge. She kept him going for several minutes before letting go of the spell. It would take Granvie some time to return; they needed to use that time.

She leaped to her feet. "Come on, David. We've got work to do."

Following her directions, he helped her haul branches and rip up grass and drag leaves. Hurriedly they bundled the forest debris into vaguely human-shaped lumps. She was unsatisfied with their handiwork, but there wasn't time to do anything better. She fumbled in her bag, looking for something she could bear to abandon. Her wristwatch snagged on something. It would do. She stripped it off.

"David, give me something of yours."

"Like what?"

"Anything. A pen, a handkerchief. Anything."

He pulled a handkerchief from his pocket. She snatched it and tucked it into one of the piles they had made and her watch into the other. Grabbing David's hand, she dragged him down the hill, heading for the spot she had selected on her ramble. They tumbled the last few meters and lay in the hollow near the willows. She shushed him when he tried to ask questions.

She needed to concentrate.

If only there was enough time.

Concentrate, she told herself. *Concentrate!*

She formed the seeming, focusing her mind until the image stabilized. Then she relaxed. She'd done what she could. Either it would work or it wouldn't.

"What have you done?" David whispered.

God, couldn't he see it? Hadn't it worked? "I think I've cast a glamour on the stuff on the top of the hill. It's supposed to look like we're taking a nap. Can't you see it?"

"I—yes, I think I can," he said. He didn't sound sure.

Was it that bad? She looked for herself. All she could see was leaves and grass and sticks. Oh, hell!

There wasn't time to try again.

From their vantage point, they watched Granvie emerge from the brush near the bridge and look up the hill. He didn't shout. He didn't go running back to the village. He just looked up the hill.

Was it working?

Apparently satisfied that his quarry hadn't moved, the mayor found himself a place in the shade of an old oak and sat down with his back against the ancient bole. He seemed to be settling in for a long, boring watch.

Her ploy had worked.

Her *magic* had worked!

With a sudden surge of confidence, she felt sure that their escape would work, too. She gave David a hug. Using the willows to shield them from Granvie, they started down the far side of the hill. David led. When they reached the bottom, he took a moment to get his bearings. She asked, "Where do we go now?"

"Cross-country for a bit. I think I saw a car rental office in a town a few miles to the west. We'll get a car and head toward Dijon. That ought to be far enough out of the escape paths they're likely to check first. There's an airport there that'll do. The best thing we can do is get out of the Community."

"But I don't have a passport. The Department canceled it."

"Hmm. Well, that complicates things." He was silent for a bit. "Maybe Lebeau."

"Lebeau?"

"Someone I met in Paris. But if we have to, I guess we can manage it. Going to Paris will make it a little trickier."

She was sure of that. "Who is this Lebeau?"

David answered cautiously. "A person who's got connections with some people who might be able to help."

"In the government?"

David chuckled. "Not exactly."

Spae wasn't pleased with his evasion. "I've had enough of people who are 'not exactly' the government."

"Don't worry; it's not like that." He chuckled again. "If anything, these people are less fond of the government and its legitimate and semilegitimate arms than you are."

"Are they criminals, then?"

David gave her a sideways glance. "We can't afford to be too picky about who helps us just now."

"I don't know, David."

"Of course, you could just cast a spell and magic us out of the Community."

"No, I can't."

"Then it seems we have no other recourse. But we're not going to get anywhere standing around."

They started walking. He was in much better shape for it than she was, but he didn't seem to begrudge her the rest breaks she needed with all the up-and-downing they were doing as they crossed the wooded countryside.

While they traveled, Spae considered what she was getting herself into with this escape. She wasn't committed to dealing with criminals yet—if David's friends even *were* criminals. She hadn't met them yet; she shouldn't judge them. And, well, if they were criminals, there was still time to come up with another plan. She and David could find another way to leave the continent, or maybe they wouldn't have to leave the Community. Where would they go anyway?

"Are you sure we have to leave the Community?" she asked during one of their rest breaks.

"I think it would be best that we get you somewhere that the ECSS isn't quite so influential."

That made sense. Magnus wouldn't like losing his only mage who had been to the otherworld. But the arm of the ECSS was long. "Where would we go?"

"Back to the States would be the best bet. I know lots of people there who'll be more than happy to help us out."

"More criminals?"

"Not exactly," he said, with an infectious smile. She smiled back. "Now, come on. We'd best keep moving. Old Granvie's not going to watch those sleeping leaves forever."

CHAPTER 12

When John returned to the room where Wilson had first left him, Spillway Sue was in the central area. Obviously Wilson had arranged to let her out of the bedroom after he'd taken John away. She looked surprised to see him. And a little relieved.

"Where ya been?" she blurted out as she bounced out of her chair. "Whaddid they do ta ya?"

"They took me to see Bear." He didn't really want to explain that just now.

"Bear? He's really here? Wherever here is. Where is here, anyway?"

John's head hurt from all the virtuality exercise it had gotten. He was tired. Too tired to deal with Sue's frenetic energy. "I don't know."

"Whaddaya mean, ya don't know? You're the only one been outta this room."

"I *mean* I don't know."

"Whaddo ya know?" She looked at him scornfully, hands on her hips.

He sighed. She wasn't going to leave him alone until he told her something, so he told her what he'd seen on the way to the audience chamber. His account of the darkened, empty corridors didn't impress her, so he told her how everyone he'd seen so far was a dwarf, and about the audience chamber and meeting Kranekin. She started pacing the room toward the end of John's recitation.

"And this Kranekin's in charge of this op?"

"Seems to be."

"So what ya got I don't? How come I ain't seen the boss?"

"Wilson came looking for me, remember? You just came along for the ride."

"Not by choice, Jack. Not by choice. And what do I get?" She waved her arms around to encompass the sitting room. "I get canned in this sleaze hole that looks like a Motel Twelve™ for androids." She kicked at the dirt floor. "Android *far*mers.

"Nobody even comes by to roust me for data. Closest thing I get to seeing somebody is a voice from nowhere saying they've got a selection of entertainment for me on the damn console. Enter—bleeding—tainment!" She kicked the table, jostling the perscomp. "Entertainment for proles and dodes, maybe. A bunch of vid games, old network shit, last year's— last *year's*, can you believe it!—music vids, and nothing, *nothing* live. No news. No connect with the net. Nothing *useful!* Do these half-liter size 'nappers come from another dimension or something? Ain't they got no idea that ya can go moonhowling in a can like this? Or ya could if there was a moon ta howl at. How come I get cramped up here while you—you get to go wandering around and meet their goddamn boss? What makes *you* a zoomer with a bullet?"

She took a breath, giving John a chance to get in a word.

"Look," John said, dragging himself up from his seat. He headed for his bedroom. "Can we talk about this in the morning? I'm whipped out."

"Morning? There *ain't* no morning in this can." She followed right behind him. "There ain't no light. Ain't no windows."

He stopped at the door and she plowed into him. She backed away, continuing her tirade. "This place is a real geek-out palace! I hate it, hate it, hate it!"

John's bedroom door had a control on the inside frame that hadn't been there when he had left. He was happy to see it. He used it to close the panel and cut off her noise. Barely managing the few steps to the bed, he let himself fall toward it. The muffled pounding on the door chased him into sleep.

John stumbled out of the shower. His head was still aching, but he was getting a bigger complaint from his stomach. How long had it been since he'd eaten? A while, obviously. How long? He hadn't been eating all that well at his slump, and so far his captors hadn't bothered to feed him.

As if on cue, Wilson's voice came over the hidden speaker. "Breakfast in ten minutes."

John's stomach growled eagerly.

While dressing, he thought about what calling the meal breakfast might mean. It had been night when Wilson had picked him up. An unknown amount of time had passed while he had been traveling to this place in a drugged stupor, then there had been the session with Bear that had lasted for another unmeasured period, then he'd slept. Could this only be the morning after? He tried several ways of fitting the pieces of time together but couldn't come up with any that crammed everything that had happened into such a short space of time. So if it had been longer, why wasn't he more hungry? *Hungry enough,* his stomach growled. John bent over to grab his jacket and used the motion to lift one leg and extend his toe to tap the door control. He swung upright and was through the door before it finished sliding open.

Wilson was waiting in the sitting room, seated at the table. In place of the perscomp on the table was a spread of dishes and covered platters. Upon seeing John emerge, Wilson lifted a bright silver carafe and poured some of the contents into the cup of the single place setting. The coffee's aroma slapped John in the olfactory nerves, and his stomach urged an instant assault on the table.

John held back. There was only a single place setting. He might have expected Wilson to have eaten, but what about

Sue? The door to Sue's room was closed, and Sue was nowhere in sight.

"Where's Sue?"

"Still asleep in her room. I thought you'd appreciate a quiet breakfast," Wilson said cheerily.

John always appreciated a quiet breakfast. And he hadn't wanted to face more of Sue's questions; he had a lot of his own, and with her at the table he'd never get the chance to ask Wilson any of them. Still, he found himself a little disturbed by her apparently enforced absence.

"I got some questions I want answered," he told the dwarf as he sat down.

"I'm sure." Wilson quirked up one side of his mouth as John's stomach growled out its impatience. "Ought to eat first. The coffee'll get cold." The smell *was* appetizing. Wilson lifted the lid on one of the platters, revealing a stack of flapjacks. "Dig in."

John did, deciding he could ask his questions while he ate.

It took a while to check out each of the platters. He took a little of everything, nibbling as he went; it all looked, and tasted, so good. Once his plate was jammed, he dug in earnestly. As it turned out, he got so busy stuffing his face that Wilson asked the first question.

"You think this Spillway Sue is trustworthy?"

John hadn't really thought about it and said so. "Why do you want to know?"

"Now that we know you'll help, I can make other arrangements for her." His hand indicated the room. "If you wish, that is."

Wilson was awfully accommodating all of a sudden. Maybe he could take advantage of the change in attitude. "You mean leave? That's what she wants to do."

"That's not advisable yet."

"As you said, I've agreed to help—and you came looking for me, after all, not her. Want to tell me why she can't go?"

"No."

"Right." So much for a more positive and cooperative attitude. "You think you've got something for her to do that'll keep her happy, or at least quiet?"

"Nothing will keep her quiet," Wilson replied, with a confidential wink. "You want separate quarters?"

John almost said yes. Sue wasn't taking her confinement well at all; if she were separated from John, the only other nondwarf in the place, her cabin fever might get violent. They hadn't met under very friendly circumstances, but they were in the same predicament. She might not be the best of company, but she was the closest thing to an ally he had at the moment. And, when it came down to it, *he* didn't want to be alone among the dwarves. So he said, "Nah, we'll get along."

Wilson nodded, smirking. "Like a dragon with a panther."

"What do you mean by that?"

"Think of a cat and dog crammed into a small box." A chime sounded. "Time for another session with Bear."

John had barely started his breakfast. Was there time for a few more bites? He looked down at his empty plate; he'd hoovered it all down.

Wilson beckoned to him from the door. "You can have more later. Never seen an elf put so much away so fast. You trying to look like one of us?"

John stood, feeling the heaviness in his belly. "I'm too tall."

"Got that right. Let's go. Bear's waiting."

Bear looked down the line of his men, nodding to each as he met their eyes. When Bear's eyes met John's, the king smiled slightly. John found himself smiling back.

So far, the Saxons in the camp below had shown no sign of noticing their approach. That was the way Bear had wanted it. They readied their weapons while business in the camp went on as usual.

This wasn't exactly the sort of thing John had imagined when he'd dreamed of being a dashing warrior and serving a king, but it was more like it than the time he and Bear had spent on the streets. It was dirtier and a lot less glamorous than John's childhood dreams of knighthood, but there hadn't been real knights in Bear's historical time. There'd been real warriors, though, and in this sim he was one of them.

The sim had such conviction that he sometimes had trouble remembering that he *was* in a simulation. It felt and looked and sounded—smelled—so real. This dwarf sim was light-years better than any adventure in the arcades. John didn't think even milspec-training sims were this detailed.

Staring down at the unwitting Saxons below them, he wondered if the dwarves used magic to enhance the computer effects, but knew as the question formed in his mind that it wasn't so. He wasn't sure how he could be so confident that there was no magic present, but he was. This was tech, pure tech—magical, but absolutely techno-magical.

Bear raised Caliburn and brought it down in a slash. Roaring, John and the others swept over the rise and poured down on the surprised Saxons.

Jessie grabbed a selection of Nuke 'Em™ meals from the freezer case of the convenience store. She didn't pay a lot of attention to what meals she grabbed so long as they didn't include any peas. Her friends didn't like peas.

She still remembered the morning she'd woken to find the casting she'd needed to complete for the Greyshelda Prototypes contract all finished. She hadn't done the work; she had no idea who had. But she couldn't afford spurning the gift; it had allowed her to get the piece in by deadline. By the time she'd returned home from the delivery, though, she'd been creeped out from thinking about somebody using her tools and equipment and working in her shop while she slept. She'd spent the next few nights with a friend, too afraid to stay in her apartment.

Now she thought she'd been pretty silly to be afraid. There was nothing to be afraid of; her friends weren't scary. She'd never been a believer in good fairies, but she had always accepted what her senses told her. A finished piece was a finished piece. And if it was magic that made it happen, then there was magic in the world. Cheap magic it was, that could be bought with a few Nuke 'Em meals.

Jessie knew a bargain when she saw one.

She 'waved the meals just before going to bed, and left them on her worktable beside the models and enough molding and casting material for the three copies the new contract specified. Her delivery meeting was at ten in the morning. She went to sleep confident that the copies would be ready.

They were sitting on the table when she awoke.

Jessie sang as she showered. It was going to be a good day.

CHAPTER
13

Nakaguchi didn't stand when Pamela entered his office. The breach of etiquette didn't bode well. Before she was halfway across the room, he spoke.

"Is this about your budget?"

"It is." He had changed her allocations, forwarding the document to Keiretsu headquarters without bothering to inform her of his meddling.

"I thought as much. I am very busy just now, Ms. Martinez. If you have something to say that wasn't in your memo, say it and be brief."

"You've read the memo." She wanted him to say it for the record.

"Yes."

"And?"

"And no, your discretionary budget will not be restored to its former level. I have better things to do with that money."

She hadn't expected to get the funds back.

"And?"

"And what, Ms. Martinez? Your objections are noted, and your requests for changes under consideration. Your accusations are irrelevant."

"Not to Mitsutomo-sama."

"To whoever I decide will hear them."

"Mitsutomo-sama will say otherwise."

"Are you so sure? Have you forgotten that I am Mitsutomo-sama's voice?"

She had not forgotten; she just wasn't sure Mitsutomo-sama knew what his "voice" was saying. "You're making a mistake."

"Is that a threat, Ms. Martinez?"

"It is a warning. Your fascination with Quetzal is dangerous. That monster is dangerous. You are imperiling the Keiretsu."

"*So ka*. I think perhaps you are the one making a mistake."

"Mitsutomo-sama will not approve what you are doing with that monster."

"An incorrect assumption."

Did Nakaguchi have the old man's permission to nurture that abomination? Mitsutomo-sama was ruthless in business, but he was no murderer of innocents.

"I think you are acting on your own. Somehow you found out about my Charybdis Project, and now you're trying to take over the project for yourself. You're poaching."

"Really? The old man sent me here, didn't he?"

Nakaguchi seemed so sure of himself, so confident. Rearden had said he had upper management approval of his private data security locks. Could she be mistaken about Nakaguchi's being on his own? "Mitsutomo-sama knows of the Project?"

"Of course, he does. Did you think yourself so clever as to keep it hidden?"

Actually, she had.

"Why did you think I came here? To investigate some minor budgetary discrepancies? Mitsutomo-sama knows about your pet program, but he has become impatient with your plodding progress. Now that Charybdis is under the control of a responsible and properly aggressive administrator, he is much happier. He is inspired by the possibilities and is talking about a new company, possibly a whole new group, to take advantage of our ground-breaking discoveries."

"What discoveries?"

"You *are* out of the loop, aren't you?"

She knew she was. She also knew he was baiting her, trying to anger her. He had succeeded.

"I am the *head* of North American Group. The project is under my purview."

"For only a while longer. There is a small matter of some previous budgetary discrepancies. And possibly certain other matters having to do with civil infractions. The Keiretsu cannot countenance a senior executive being involved in illegal activities."

"Getting caught in them, you mean."

"Even so. By the way, how is Mr. McAlister? Have you seen a compensation claim from him regarding your reckless endangerment of his life?"

McAlister was loyal to her; she wouldn't let Nakaguchi plant a seed of doubt. "If there is, I'll know where the advice to start it came from."

Nakaguchi smiled unctuously. "Ms. Martinez, I find myself shaken by your belligerent attitude. Such hostility is not in keeping with the harmony, for which all within the Keiretsu strive. Could it be that you are no longer happy in our corporate family?"

"I am loyal to Mitsutomo-sama."

"I am pleased to hear that, which is to say the old man is pleased, since I am Mitsutomo-sama's ear as well as his voice." He leaned back in his chair. "It would be unfortunate if I heard a disgruntled member of the Keiretsu threaten to disrupt the harmony of the family. Such misplaced anger could easily sway a person to foolish acts, acts which would have unfortunate consequences."

Now *that* was a threat. Pamela sat quietly, biting down on her anger. He would get to the price of continued harmony momentarily. She wondered if she would be able to pay it.

"I can be a generous man, Ms. Martinez. Go back to your office. Tend to the ordinary matters of North American Group. Forget Charybdis. Forget Quetzal. Stick with things that are more familiar to you and there may be no need for drastic action. The Keiretsu is big enough to harmonize many divergent paths."

What? Was that all?

"Don't look so shocked, Ms. Martinez. I don't want your position."

What do you want? She almost asked it aloud.

Nakaguchi smiled indulgently. "Consider the advantages of working together."

She'd rather work with a pit viper. "I will."

"Good. Now, I really do have a lot of work."

She stood shakily and left his office. She was still confused. The revelation that Mitsutomo-sama knew everything had gutted her plan, trashing her threat of exposing Nakaguchi's independent ambitions. For a few moments she had thought she had lost more than her plan; she had thought she had lost it all, but Nakaguchi had confounded her again. She hated the way he was one step ahead of her. Even more she hated the way he displayed his superiority. There had to be some way of taking him down a few pegs.

"Ms. Martinez."

It was Hagen, one of Nakaguchi's creatures. Or was he? The rest of the bastard's toadies were icing her out. What drove the little man to break ranks? She remembered his arguments for destroying the Quetzal thing while it was still in the cave, and his muttered comments when Nakaguchi had fed the thing its first victim. In the matter of the sleeper, at least, Hagen stood apart from Nakaguchi. Far enough apart to be of use?

She stopped and looked down at the little man. "Yes?"

"A moment of your time, please." He seemed anxious, worried. "Not long. A profitable moment."

Intrigued, she responded, "I think I have a moment free."

Hagen led Pamela to his office, refusing to speak until the door closed behind them—and then all he did was direct her to a seat. Hagen activated his perscomp and spent some time calling up routines and studying the monitor. Her angle allowed her an oblique view of the screen, not enough to read it but enough to recognize some of the displays; they were security programs, anti-eavesdropping routines, and control displays. Hagen's concern might be genuine or he might just be putting on a show. Even if he was keeping their meeting private from others, he might be running recording devices for his own security, a not unreasonable precaution. She waited patiently, curious enough to allow him some latitude; his interaction with the computer went on for some time. At last he seemed satisfied, but even then he spoke hesitantly.

"Ms. Martinez, can I trust you?"

"To do what, Mr. Hagen?"

"For the moment, simply to listen with an open mind. And to keep what passes between us strictly confidential."

As long as confidentiality was in his interests. She had her own interests to protect. "Do you intend to threaten the health of the Keiretsu?"

"You and I both know that a threat already exists."

"Meaning?"

"First, do I have your word?"

"I would be happy to work with you in any matter to the benefit of the Keiretsu."

"A cautious answer, Ms. Martinez. I approve of it. You may be assured that I am not trying to trap you into betraying the Keiretsu. We both know that someone else is already betraying the Keiretsu."

"And who would that be?"

"Only who? I would think you would be as interested in *how* this fool is endangering everything you hold dear."

She was beginning to lose patience with Hagen's evasive attitude. "Just what is it you fear, Mr. Hagen?"

"First, your word of confidentiality."

"Very well." *Within limits.* "As long as my silence will not endanger the Keiretsu, I will keep whatever secrets you want to share."

"Your word?"

"My word."

"I will hold you to that bond."

Will you? Only if he was making a recording, which, given his attitude, she was beginning to doubt. "Now that we've settled that, what is this danger you fear?"

"The greater danger, I believe you know. As to the more immediate one, you have seen it. You were there when he uncovered it in the preservation chamber."

"Quetzal."

"Not just Quetzal but the corruption surrounding him."

There was nothing surrounding Quetzal but Nakaguchi and his circle, of which Hagen was supposed to be a part. "Are you suggesting that your superior is a danger to the Keiretsu?"

"Nakaguchi is a danger," he said, nodding slowly. "Before you decide that I am an ungrateful traitor, let us speak of a related matter."

An ungrateful traitor to Nakaguchi might be just the tool she needed; there might be something here for her after all. "What matter is that?"

Hagen gave her a quick smile, something halfway between friendly and conspiratorial. "For some years, you had a person by the name of Sörli in your employ. He worked his way onto your staff, advising you in many matters, including the original setup of your clandestine Charybdis Project. Ultimately, he became your principal agent in matters concerning Charybdis. Did you trust him?"

The question was unexpected. Trust Sörli? What did Hagen know that she didn't? What kind of time bomb had Sörli left behind? She elected what she hoped would be a noncommittal answer that would keep Hagen talking. "He was very secretive."

"Yes, he was, wasn't he?" Hagen replied, sounding a little far away, as if he were remembering personal dealings with the departed Sörli. After a moment, he added, "Necessarily so, I'm afraid. Or so we believed at the time."

Necessarily? *We*? Sörli *had* been secretive, and Hagen was apparently one of his secrets. Pamela needed to know more. The little man apparently wanted to talk. Who was she to stop him? "And now times have changed?"

"Indeed they have. If we are to work together to avert the threat that hovers over us, you will have to trust me as you trusted him."

"He always asked me to take a lot on faith, while offering little in the way of hard data. I was never very happy about that arrangement. Now, as you say, times have changed. I am not inclined to be so readily trusting, and you have yet to give me any reason to rely on you."

"A fair point. However, I am not at liberty to give you the sort of proof you prefer. I can offer no hard evidence that we are trustworthy."

There was that "we" again, and this time without any apparent connection to Sörli. "That is the second time you have said 'we.' Perhaps you'd like to explain yourself."

"So you may trust me?"

"It would be a start."

"To explain my use of 'we' would make you privy to a secret known to few of your race."

Her *race*? What did race have to do with it? What was the little man talking about? Pamela's train of thought jumped tracks. Little man? Sörli had been a "little man," too. She remembered his insistence that small people were necessary for the intrusion into the otherworld. Of a sudden, there were too many little men in this business. "Are you suggesting that it is no coincidence that you and Sörli are both . . . similar?"

Hagen nodded gravely. "We are of the same stock."

"Not . . . human stock?" Pamela managed to ask.

"A different race."

Pamela could feel the sweat trickling Icily down her sides. "Are you some sort of otherworld being?"

"Not at all." Hagen's somber mien vanished, replaced by a strange amusement. Disconcertingly, he chuckled. "Not in the least. The farthest thing from it.

"Sörli and I are both part of an organization, a cabal, if you will, dedicated to working against the machinations of such beings. We oppose the irrationality of magic. Always have. It is our goal to put an end to things like Quetzal, for we know them of old. More than once we have been the victims of their deviltry. We dwarves have not always been able to be as effective as we would like, but we have very long memories and are very patient."

Dwarves? She looked at Hagen, at his broad shoulders, his full beard, his beaky nose. Put him in a Robin Hood costume and he would look like something out of a fairy story. But dwarves were mythical.

"You don't believe me," Hagen said.

"You're surprised? You just told me you are a fairy-tale creature."

"You believed in goblins when Sörli brought you the boggle's head from the Museum."

How had he found out about that? "You hacked into my files."

"No, not me. Sörli did that. He also reported on his association with you. I know everything he did while in your employ. The two of you made a good team. Considering."

Considering what? That Sörli had lied to her, manipulated her? And this creature wanted her to trust him as she had trusted Sörli. She hadn't trusted Sörli, not as far as she could see him. She had worked with the little man, the—God, could it be true?—dwarf, even come to believe in the otherworld and the elves Sörli wanted to fight, but she had never trusted him. She had only feared what he had feared. *The enemy of my enemy is my friend*, the old saw claimed, but "my ally" would be more appropriate. She'd had more than enough experience in her life to know that a smart person only trusted an ally so far; only a fool believed everything an ally told her. So what should she believe here?

She drew in a breath to steady herself. "Why should I believe what you're telling me?"

"Because you can feel the truth of what I say. Because you have seen that there is more to the world than your race's skeptical scientists would have you believe. Because you know we have common cause here. Or perhaps for some other reason. You are having some trouble assimilating what I have said, but I am sure that you will come to believe its truth. You can reach no other conclusion.

"We are natural allies, you and I. Our races are allies as well. My kind was born of this earth and of this reality as was yours, and we have shared this world in harmony for longer than you can know. Our races are not like the soulless creatures of the otherworld.

"In times past our races have worked together. Throughout the centuries, your kind has received much good aid and advice from mine, although your histories record little of it. You tall folk are very self-important. But this is hardly the time to air old complaints. As I said, we knew harmony in the past; we can again know such pleasant times, but only if we act to forestall the dangers before us. The otherworld threatens our harmony. Once again your kind and mine must stand together against a mutual foe. We have a common cause. We have a joint interest in eliminating the influence of the unnatural creatures of that other reality."

"Creatures like Quetzal?"

"Unfortunately, Quetzal is one of your own kind. Seduced by and given over to the lure of chaos, but human. Originally, anyway."

"How can you say that? I saw how it sucked the life out of Doctor Hasukawa and the others. This Quetzal isn't human. It is some kind of monstrous vampire creature from the otherworld."

"Quetzal is neither from the otherworld nor a vampire. Well, in some senses, he is a vampire, but I'm used to that word applying to a different sort of monster. Even if Quetzal were a vampire, that would not change his genetics. Your legends say that a vampire was once a normal, mortal man—or woman—so there is no escaping your kinship to him. But genetics are mostly irrelevant here. What is important in this case is that Quetzal has surrendered to evil, that he has fallen into the false faith, and that he has embraced the chaos. He has been deluded. If unopposed, he will drag others to a similar doom. The chaos is seductive, but its promises are those of a poxed whore. In the end there is a far greater payment than one bargains for. There is no hope of redemption for the fallen."

Pamela felt dizzy. She'd accepted Sörli's tales of the otherworld and magic. She'd even acted as though it all was real. By God, she knew it *was* real! But it had all been different when Sörli had told it; the threat had come from outside, from elsewhere. Magic and its irrationality had been from somewhere else, somewhere that could be walled off. People couldn't be a part of it; they were safe from the madness.

The power leaking into the real world from the magical otherworld had the potential to remake the universe. She'd feared that change and had worked to stop it. Now it appeared she had been fighting a battle without understanding the stakes, without understanding the opposition she was facing. People could use the chaos, seizing the magic and bending it to their will. There would be people—people like Quetzal?—who would embrace such power, no matter what the personal cost. They would only see the power. Power was seductive; she knew that well enough. Men—men like Nakaguchi?—would seize upon this new avenue to power and rip apart the sanity of the world. Then where would she be?

Hagen had to be wrong; Quetzal had to be something from the otherworld.

"I can't believe it," she said.

"You mean you don't want to believe it. I fear you must. Quetzal is evil incarnated into a walking being."

"But Sörli never mentioned anything like Quetzal. All the magical creatures were from elsewhere. They weren't human."

"Did he not speak to you of sleepers and the danger that they posed?"

"He told me that the awakening of the sleepers would release magic. I feared the chaos that would bring, and that was more than enough to fear. Sörli never hinted that the sleepers were things like Quetzal."

"They are not all like Quetzal. Quetzal is the immediate danger against whom we must unite. Hourly this creature's hold on Nakaguchi's imagination grows. Soon Quetzal may command more than his interest."

Though she suspected she already knew the answer, she asked, "Just what are you suggesting?"

"Quetzal must be destroyed," Hagen said quickly.

Sörli had been bloody-minded, too. A dwarvish trait? "As in murdered?"

"One does not murder a rabid dog."

One has it put down. Just as one puts down any memories of how much a part of a family the dog might once have been; one had to think about the safety of the family, about stopping the harm from growing further. But euphemisms did not change the nature of the act; killing was killing. Was killing the answer here?

"Nakaguchi will oppose any such action."

Hagen nodded. "His opposition must be avoided."

How far was Hagen prepared to go? "Or overcome?"

"If necessary."

So bloody-minded. Was she any different? Hagen's suggestions were not wholly unattractive. If Hagen eliminated Nakaguchi, Nakaguchi's threat to her position would die along with him. She would be in control again.

She lifted her eyes to meet Hagen's. "I suppose you have a plan."

"Several, actually."

"For contingencies."

"Exactly so."

"I think it could be interesting to work together with you on a project, Mr. Hagen."

"My feelings exactly, Ms. Martinez."

CHAPTER
14

The world was so much bigger than it used to be. While the view from Quetzal's suite took in only a small part of that wide world, even that sometimes overwhelmed him.

Buildings, buildings as far as the eye could see and beyond. Each twinkled with a constellation of lights, which from a distance appeared to be stars. Those man-made stars were poor replacements for the real stars. How deplorable that the imitations masked the real.

There were few stars to be seen by looking up in this new age. The glow of the man-blight called the sprawl ate them and even dimmed the light of the moon's great globe. For truth, there were still lights to be seen in the sky: aircraft lights. The multicolored lights moving with deliberate speed across the night sky were another of mankind's mockeries of the celestial glory.

He had liked the night—when he had been able to see and talk to the stars. Nights were different now. Very different. His nights were his days now, as his sensitivity to the sun's light was increasing.

He did not like the constraint, but he had little choice; the antagonism of the sun was an unavoidable side effect of the magic he'd used to take himself into this new age. Full day-light was actually painful to him now. How ironic that his re-newed life tied him to the darkness. Imhotep would have smiled with wry amusement to see him in this state.

He hoped the old bastard's bones had long ago turned to dust and joined the desert sands to shift restlessly forever in the Saharan winds.

A nocturnal existence was a limitation. He hated limita-tions. He resolved to find a way around it. He would find the answer. With sufficient power there was always an answer. At worst, he would have to wait until the Glittering Path was opened; after that, all was possible.

Unfortunately, that time was not as near as he had hoped.

The gathering of the followers had been a disappointment to him, even though he stepped without the slightest problem into the void left by Jeffries's unfortunate demise. For truth, they had welcomed him as their new leader, saying that it was only proper that the old die to make way for the new order. He had taught, he had praised, he had warned, and they had drunk it all in like the finest of wines. He had drunk deeply of their adulation, buoyed by their belief in his puissance.

But he had expected to be working with mages. None of their paltry number, not even the members of the inner circle, showed more than an adept's mastery of the mysteries. Much potential, for truth, but little actuality. He could change that in time, but for now it was his expectations that he must change.

His ship of dreams was running afoul of the strangest of rocks.

Why were the followers so stunted? It was not as though there was no magic for them. He could feel it all around. There was more energy than there had been when he entered the dreaming chamber, much more. He could feel the crea-tures of the otherworld scampering about in the shadows. How long had it been since there had been so many of them? As the magic had been drained from the world, they had re-treated to the otherworld. Clearly, that retreat was over.

So, then, where were the wizards, the sorcerers, the en-chantresses, and the shamans? The necessary energies for powerful spells were available. Why was no one using them?

Was there some factor at work that he did not understand? Had the opposition become so skilled as to be able to hide from him? The thought did not bear thinking; its consequences were too great for the opening of the Glittering Path.

Folly! What the sages of this age would call paranoia. It could not be so!

And in his heart he knew that it was not so. There were manipulators of the mysteries in this new age. They were not as puissant as he expected; and they were so few. But then, had they ever been numerous? Certainly the true masters had never numbered many.

One, he knew, was approaching. He'd sensed her last night when he drifted the astral, contemplating the sorry state of the followers. His contact with her had been fleeting, the lightest of touches. There had been much of the fuzziness that pervaded the higher planes in this age, but the contact had been enough for him to confirm her existence and to gain a taste of her power. She was in the sky, over the ocean, a clear confirmation of that power. The shade of her aura told him that she was not dedicated to the Wyrm. Was she opposed—or did she cling to the false hope of neutrality? In either case, he would have to confront her.

But not yet.

He was still too weak to contemplate a duel with a master. When he was better prepared, he would confront her. Perhaps he'd offer her a chance to join the followers; her skills would be an asset. Did she imagine the power that could be hers?

If she was so dull as to refuse him, he would crush her, or take her as a bond servant. Better still, he could drain her of her essence, adding her vitality to his. What would a mage's soul taste like? Intoxicating, for truth. The thought of it wakened his hunger.

He summoned Nakaguchi to bring him the evening's offering.

The Asian was satisfactorily prompt, but draining the wretch he brought sparked Quetzal's appetite rather than sating it. The pitiful things Nakaguchi acquired had already lost so much of what he wanted.

"I crave more."

"It would be unwise." There was the faintest hint of disapproval in the Asian's manner.

"What is unwise is the miserable dole of offerings you provide."

Nakaguchi acted oblivious to the warning Quetzal was giving him. "We must be cautious," he said. "Too many disappearances and our work will be noticed. There will be questions asked. "You already risk exposure with your outings. Mitsutomo—"

"Mitsutomo! Where is your loyalty, Nakaguchi?"

"I follow the Glittering Path."

"You follow the path of your own ambition. Beware that you do not stray from the true Path. Those who await the opening of the Glittering Path accept only unswerving loyalty. There is no place for those with dual masters. Forget Mitsutomo."

Nakaguchi was uncowed. "That also would be unwise."

The man's impudence uncapped the raging frustration that boiled within Quetzal. He backhanded the fool, knocking him against the wall.

Did he think he was dealing with mortals?

"Unwise? Unwise! What do you know of wisdom? What *can* you know? You are an ephemeral creature. Had you lived as long as I, your words might have weight. Your words are those of a blind child."

Ashen, the Asian regained his feet, gripping the arm Quetzal had struck. Without a word, he backed away. Quetzal sneered at the fear glimmering in Nakaguchi's eyes; the dog had taken the blow without reply. The Asian fled, leaving Quetzal alone in his suite.

In his cage.

But not helpless. He had made contact with the followers' inner circle now. He had recourse beyond Mitsutomo's control now. And only this morning Nakaguchi had reported that the resonators he'd ordered built had all been delivered to auspicious locations, ready to be activated. Quetzal was still not ready to activate them, lacking several crucial pieces of information. The major work for which he needed Nakaguchi was done; no longer need he rely on the two-faced Asian.

For truth, he need no longer remain chained.

It was time to put new plans into motion.

He turned to the broad window that made up the outer wall of his suite. His view of the world. A great tower stood just to the northwest of the building. Letters of red light proclaimed it "Hilton." It was a place where travelers stayed, a hostelry of insane size; an entire town could live in the one building. From the windows of the tower, its inhabitants could stare down at the streets below them like gods. Once such lofty viewpoints had been the exclusive purview of mages.

Did they think to pretend to power?

Fools and dogs, all of them!

He *was* power.

With a sweep of his hand he shattered the window and sent the shards spewing out into the night. The wind howled in, far more chill than Mitsutomo's controlled air. He walked into it, stepping into the night.

Let them do *this* with their machines!

Lowering himself along the etherometric lines, he floated to the ground.

The glass that had preceded him had skewered a half-dozen unlucky pedestrians. One was dead, but the others writhed and screamed in varying degrees of agony. He strolled among the wounded, touching them one by one. One by one their screams stopped, as did their breathing. Their pain gave a tang to their essence, and he grew giddy with the new strength they gave him.

High above, the red signature of arrogance gleamed.

No longer.

At his command, the letters flared and sparked and died. The tower went dark with them.

"Let darkness be the dawn of the coming age!" he screamed aloud.

He would show them all. He stalked away from the Settawego Building, his cage. Where he passed, the lights on the poles and storefront buildings flickered and died.

Mitchell Benton was not the sort of man who got involved in things that didn't offer a substantial return, so he didn't do

anything when he heard the woman's first terrified squawk.
He was on a job—for which he was receiving big bucks—and
his paymasters wouldn't care to have him involved in anything that might involve the police. Molested women were
prime cop attractors. Not that there were many cops in this
stretch of open country, which he supposed had motivated
whoever was bothering the woman.

It wasn't his business.

She squalled again—a full-throated scream—just as he
reached his truck. He looked around; his truck and her motor-
cycle were the only vehicles in sight. This stretch of prairie
was awfully desolate for some pervert to wander in and set up
a woman trap in the rest house. Maybe she was having a bad
reaction to something she had pumped into her body. That
was cop bait of a different kind, but a kind he had even less
interest in being involved with.

He unlocked the truck. A woman cruising through these
parts on her own had best be expecting to deal with any problems she encountered on her own. His orders had him chasing
phantoms, but they were the phantoms his bosses wanted him
chasing. Dragons he was supposed to kill and cart back, but
damsel rescuing wasn't on the agenda. Nowhere did his contract say he should spend any time pretending to be Sir Gala-
had. And since they paid the freight, he had their interests to
consider. He slid behind the wheel.

The rest house blew apart in a fireball that lit the night.
Benton's eyes shuttered against the flare, but the sound
dampers didn't cut in; there wasn't any bang. Benton didn't
understand; the explosion was big enough for a couple of
kilograms of C8, but there was no noise.

"Be alert for the unusual," his boss had said. "Especially at
night."

This was sure as hell unusual.

It got a lot more unusual when the woman came running
out of the smoking wreck of the rest house chased by something the size, shape, and shagginess of a bear that was running on two legs.

Bears didn't run that way, which meant that whatever was
chasing the woman was no bear.

The woman was headed for Benton's truck, which meant the whatever-it-was was headed in the same direction. Which meant Benton was about to be involved.

He reached behind his head and snatched the gun off the rack. The weapon looked like a Remington Hawkeye™ hunting rifle, the Marcus Preiss signature model, but it was something completely different. Benton was confident that it would do the job. He scrolled through the settings readout and made his selection as he exited the truck.

His shot took the shaggy thing in the chest, rocking it back on its heels. He could see the bloody cavitation that the explosive round had made in the thing's pectoral muscles. Benton had intended to take it in its forward-hunched shoulder, but he misjudged its speed—it didn't run quite like anything he'd ever seen. Not that placement mattered; shock from a wound that large would kill even the largest animal. The thing toppled over backward.

The woman stumbled into him, panting and winded. He moved her over to the truck, where she could lean against it. She wasn't as good-looking as he'd first thought when she passed him on her way into the rest house. In fact, she looked pretty travel worn. He'd rescued her, but she didn't fit his idea of a damsel.

"You okay?" he asked.

"I'll be all right." Her voice quavered. "Is it dead?"

"God, I hope so."

She was looking at the hairy thing's corpse and shivering. She might be on the edge of going into shock. He didn't need her doing that. She needed to be thinking of less bloody things. He put his arm around her shoulder and turned her away from the corpse.

"My name's Johnson," he said. "What's your name, lady?"

"Nym," she said, still trying to get a look at the carcass. "It moved."

Benton let her go and spun, weapon ready. *Shit!* The thing *was* moving!

He put another round into it. But he'd fired without aiming properly, and the round only took a divot out of the thing's leg. The beast groaned in pain, but continued to rise to its feet.

The awful wounds it had taken were only slowing it down. It should be dead.

Benton was spooked. This wasn't natural. The hell with orders; he wanted it ended. Taking aim at the beast's muzzle, he squeezed the trigger.

The monster lurched as Benton fired. The round took it in its burly neck. Blood and flesh and shards of bone gouted. It slumped forward, its head bounding free of its shoulders as it crashed to the ground.

This time Benton watched until the blood stopped pulsing out of the shattered arteries. He wanted to be sure the thing was dead.

When he turned back to see how the woman was doing, she was gone—like she'd vanished. Maybe she had. A scan of the area didn't pick up any thermal signatures big enough to be human.

Weird.

But over.

Surely this episode fit his boss's definition of "unusual."

There might be some decent profit in it. He hadn't destroyed the thing's head as he intended; and heads were high on his boss's list. "Heads are very identifiable," his boss had said. Looked like his boss was going to get one that would need identifying.

Benton went into the back of the truck and got out one of the small preservation bags. The big ones wouldn't be large enough for the whole carcass, so he'd have to be selective. He bagged the snouted head. Seen up close the mix of animal and human features unnerved him, but those disturbing features also told him that he was doing the right thing collecting it.

His boss had said to be sure any specimens were bagged and sealed before dawn. He hadn't said why. What difference did dawn make?

Well, dawn wasn't that far away.

He stowed the head in one of the refrigerated bins, and closed up the truck before walking back to the cab. He could report in and be ordered to head to a pickup point at once or he could wait awhile. He decided to wait. Leaning against the front fender he settled down to wait. He kept the pseudo-Hawkeye near to hand.

When the first rays of sunlight touched the carcass, it began to smoke. In a matter of minutes it was nothing but fine ash blowing away on the morning breeze.

Benton began to wonder if he was being paid enough.

CHAPTER 15

Spillway Sue's head snapped up as the door slid open. She relaxed when she saw John was alone; Wilson had allowed him to find his own way back to his rooms, which he had managed pretty well. His sense of well-being evaporated when he saw what she was up to. Sue had the perscomp pried open and several components scattered around on the table. As the door closed behind John, she went back to poking around in the computer's interior.

He shook his head. "They're not going to like that."

"Their problem," her muffled voice returned.

"I'm surprised someone hasn't been here already."

"Been here already." She hoisted a thumb over her shoulder, directing John's attention to a smear of something dark and greasy-looking on the wall behind her. John noted three other smears, one on each wall of the room. "They didn't like what I did ta their vid pickups, so they came ta check it out. I told 'em *I* didn't like being watched all the time."

"And they said you could tear their equipment apart?" Wilson had said they'd find something for her to do. Letting her tear up their perscomp seemed a strange sort of hospitality. "Didn't they tell you to stop when they came?"

"I wasn't doing nothin' then. Just sitting. Told 'em, they wanted ta watch, they could do it here. They declined." A loud snap wrenched a curse out of her. John smelled ozone. Sue pulled her head and hands out of the casing. She slumped into a chair and sucked her finger, staring disconsolately at the guts of the computer. "Damn! I don't know enough about this shit."

John picked up a circuit board. He knew a little about computers, but this was not quite like anything he'd ever seen before. "Can you put it back together?"

"Sure."

He was certain that she was lying, but he didn't say anything. "Wilson said he'd be down in a little while with some food. He won't be happy with you if he finds the console like this."

"What's he gonna do, lock me up?"

"Have you been locked up here all day again?" John was sure he wouldn't have been able to stand it. No wonder she'd taken to trashing the cage.

"Nah. They let me outta the cell today."

"That's good. Maybe they're beginning to trust you." Though what she'd done to the perscomp would reverse that.

"Trust me? What a guffer. They opened the door. Stupid, I thought. Good for me, though. Leastwise that's what I thought till I went walkabout. All they got around here is corridors and more corridors. Most of them ain't got any doors on 'em, but sometimes their interior decorator goes wild and tosses in a couple of doors that ain't got no handles, buzzers, pads, or nothin'. All ya can do is go where they want ya ta go. This whole damned place's like a low-mem vid maze."

John had felt like that himself on his first excursion. Today he'd been too anxious to get to Bear in the morning to notice, and too tired tonight to be interested. Thinking about it, he realized that, except for the audience room, he still hadn't seen anything more than corridors between here and the place where they kept Bear.

Sue was still talking. "And ya know what? You were right, Jack. This place is full of half-liter gene-lacks."

"They're dwarves."

"What I said. Mein freund, they are shor-ort! Ain't seen no-body wasn't a midget like Wilson. It was nerco, absolutely creeping. Made me feel like some sort of giant freak type."

So Sue had seen some of the dwarves. Maybe that explained why she wasn't acting stir-crazy as she had yesterday. "Wilson said they were going to find something more interesting for you today."

She snorted. "They did. Oh, they did. If ya call lunch at a cafeteria and a workout in a gym *fun*. Course, there's fun and there's fun." She slipped a short metal rod out of her pants pocket. "Left one too many bars lying around the weight room." She hefted the heavy rod and made a tentative swing with it. "Got a good feel."

"They won't let you keep it."

"Let 'em try and take it away." She swung it again in a snapping blow, bringing the follow-through around and thrusting with a jab. "Just let 'em try."

"Dinner in ten minutes," the speaker announced.

Sue started scrambling to repack the computer parts into the console. Seeing her fumbling in her haste, John helped her. She gave him a sidelong look when he picked up the first circuit board and handed it to her, but she didn't say anything. Just as they managed to get the casing closed, John heard the faint click of the door's lock mechanism. They both slid into seats and tried to look nonchalant.

It was a wasted effort.

The door opened on a cart. No attendant, just a cart. The laden dinnercart rolled forward under its own power and stopped just short of the table. "Please return all glasses, tableware, and crockery to the cart," it said. "Soiled linen may be placed in the slot on the port side." A green bulb glowed to clarify which of the cart's sides was "port." "Please press down on the handlebar to indicate that the cart is loaded and ready for return to the kitchen."

"Where do we put the tip?" John asked.

The green light switched off, but the cart didn't answer him.

They ate, Sue demonstrating that she had little in the way of table manners. They didn't talk much during the meal.

When she finished, she fiddled with the perscomp and, to John's surprise, brought up the video player. John finished his meal to the raucous laugh track of *The Trials and Tribulations of Martin A. Felloe*[EM], a long-running, early-century sitcom about a software geek who had become a billionaire with his first program. John had heard of the show but never seen it; he wasn't really seeing it now because Sue turned the screen to face her. He was left to assume the humor was visual; none of the jokes were funny. Sue didn't lift a hand to help John pile the debris from their meal onto the cart. He supposed she wasn't used to having to clean up after herself, so he didn't complain. If they were going to be here for a while, though, she'd have to learn. He sent the cart on its way and turned to find that Sue had abandoned her position in front of the monitor and lay sprawled on the couch, staring at the ceiling. Martin A. Felloe's predicament continued to draw guffaws from the digital audience.

Sue looked different somehow; he wasn't quite sure why or how. Maybe it was the lighting, but she looked calmer than she had. John could have pictured her cruising the mall at Rezcom 5 or studying in a lounge at the university. She could have been just an ordinary girl. Except for one thing: Sue had her stolen weight bar out again and was idly smacking it into her hand. That wasn't the sort of thing a mainline straightline girl would be doing.

"Ya know what I want?" she asked wistfully. She didn't wait for him to respond. "I wanna see sunlight. The sky, ya know? I wanna be back on the streets, out where there's people. People, for God's sake, instead of these damn munchkins."

"They're dwarves."

"I don't care if they're Martians! I want out."

It wasn't as if John could open a door and send her on her way. "Talk to Wilson."

She heaved herself up and slipped the rod back into her jeans. Her demeanor shifted once she was on her feet, got softer. Her voice got softer, too. "Ya know, I really don't like it here and that Wilson guy, he don't like me much. I can tell. But at least he's talked ta me. Them other munchkins, they just stare. They don't want me here. I can tell. So why don't they just let me go?"

"I don't know. Ask Wilson."

"We both know Wilson ain't calling any shots around here. I don't know anybody else here. This were the streets, I could go to a fixer, ya know, and find out what I gotta do ta make things straight. I don't know nobody here, don't got no connections."

John looked into her dark eyes and found himself wanting to help her. "You want me to talk to Wilson?"

She smiled, showing surprising bright teeth. "Like I was thinking ya could talk ta whuz hiz name, ya know, their boss guy."

"Kranekin."

"Yeah, whatever. Him." She had closed the distance between them as she talked. Now she laid her hand on John's arm. "I'd be grateful."

There was a promise in that statement. John knew what it would mean on the streets; he was sure she did, too. From what little he knew of her rep on the streets, it wasn't the sort of promise she made often. It wasn't the sort of thing he took lightly, either; he didn't much like the feeling that he had bought someone's affection. Surprisingly, he found that he didn't want to disappoint her.

"I'll ask," he said.

"Would ya really?"

Sure. All Kranekin could do was say no. What did he have to lose? He felt the heat of her palm through the fabric of his shirt. And he might have something to gain.

The next day he did as he said he would, asking Kranekin before he began his next session with Bear, but all Kranekin would say about releasing Spillway Sue was, "In time." It wasn't much of an answer, but Kranekin made it clear that it was all the answer John was going to get for the moment. Later, John passed the word on to Spillway Sue and she took it stony-faced.

"Ya asked like ya said ya would," was all she said before retreating to her bedroom and shutting the door. She didn't come out to eat when the dinnercart arrived. John ate alone.

When he was finished, he put his dirty things back on the cart, but he left her untouched stuff on the table; she might be hungry later. He sent the cart off and retired to his room.

His head was still buzzing from the sim, and he was tired; not as much as he had been after the first sessions, but enough to make crashing out sound really attractive. He let his clothes fall where he stripped them off, used the toilet, and headed for the soft embrace of the bed. He realized that he had forgotten to close his door when Sue spoke from the doorway.

"Not a bad bod, if ya like 'em pale."

John started, turning at her voice before recollecting that he was naked. He glanced around frantically for something snatchable. He grabbed a pillow from the bed to hold in front of himself.

"And shy, too. Chill down, mein freund. Ya ain't got nothin' I ain't seen before."

She sauntered into the room, running her eyes up and down his body in a frankly evaluating way. He backed away from her until his calves came up against the bed. She came into the room, straight toward him. Her hands lifted and began unbuttoning her shirt. That done, she slid her arms back and sent the shirt to the floor with a shrug. She stood before him naked from the waist up. Her body was lean, sleek with toned muscle. Her breasts were small but well-shaped globes and their nipples were crinkling to hardness. John swallowed hard. Swallowing wasn't the only thing that was hard; he felt the pillow resisting his rising interest. She was very close.

It might have been a dream, but he could smell her. Then again, in a dream, she would have been smiling.

This wasn't right.

"I didn't get you what you wanted," he managed to say. "You don't have to do this."

"I don't do nothin' I don't wanna," she said with a shrug.

The movement drew John's eyes to her breasts. He felt hot.

She finally smiled, but it was an ironic one. "Ya didn't say ya'd get me out. Most guys woulda. Ya just said ya'd ask, and ya did what ya said, and I appreciate that."

And now she was here to pay off. John's hardness slipped a little. "You don't have to show your appreciation this way."

"A deal's a deal." She popped the top fastening on her jeans and started slowly sliding the zipper down. John could see the top of her panties in the crack; they were deep blue and shiny. He caught a new whiff of her scent. "Only got one commodity here ta trade with."

"Pretty high price when you don't get what you want."

"It ain't worth as much as yer making out."

She started to peel the denim down over the flare of her hips. The situation was really strange; John had dreamed of beautiful women making this kind of come-on to him, but the reality was different. The reality *was* different; this wasn't right. He hadn't done anything to deserve her giving herself to him.

"It's worth as much as you want it to be," he said.

She froze, halting her undressing. She looked up at his face and there was puzzlement in her eyes. "Ya saying ya don't want ta hump me?"

"No—I mean, yes—I mean, it's not that I don't—ah, I don't think we should—"

Words failed him and he stood there, openmouthed and feeling stupid. She looked at him, clearly calculating. But what? She broke the stalemate by reaching down and picking up her shirt. Throwing it over one shoulder, she turned and walked away. She looked back when she reached the door.

"You're a strange one, Tall Jack."

Who was he to argue?

Shaking her head, she disappeared into the common room. A few seconds later, he heard her door slide shut. John padded across his room and shut his own door. Tossing the pillow ahead of him, he threw himself on the bed. He had a hard time getting to sleep that night.

There was no mention of the previous night's episode at breakfast the next morning. Sue was quiet, subdued. She even refrained from making any surly remarks when Wilson arrived to escort John to see Bear.

Over the next couple of days, they settled into a sort of routine. Breakfast together, then John would go off for a session with Bear, to return in time for dinner. They talked some, about this and that, nothing close or personal. Sue seemed friendlier, less and less the hard streeter. He liked this Sue a lot better than the smart-mouthed punk who had confronted him in the factory. He began to think that she was coming to trust him.

Each night she left her door open when she retired after their talks, but he couldn't bring himself to go in there. He didn't want her to sleep with him just because she owed him something, or because they were stuck here together, or because there was nothing more interesting to do. He didn't want himself doing it for any of those reasons, either. Still, their proximity and her availability made it harder every day to deny the growing attraction. But was it a real attraction, and not just two lonely people clutching at each other because there was no one else? Their togetherness was artificial, thrust on them by the dwarves. Their interest in each other could just as easily be a product of this enforced intimacy.

He left his own door open as well, fearing that shutting it would offend her, but also a little afraid that she might accept what could be construed as an offer. After a few days, despite his misgivings, he found himself almost hoping she *would* accept the offer.

He continued to sleep alone.

Each day the dwarves interrogated him about details of Bear's modern life; they said they needed the information to construct the reintegration sims. John answered all their questions, watching as they input data and developed visuals and sim personas. He corrected details and helped them adjust the sims; a couple of times they even let him use the construction software. He didn't feel as though he was betraying anyone. It wasn't as though there were any real secrets. At least not any secrets that he *knew* he should be keeping; the dwarves already knew about Nym and Bennett and Faye and the magical otherworld. The last was the one area he would have refused to tell them about, but they never pressed him for details about it.

Every day the sessions with Bear were all the same. For a week, the same. The meeting, the admittance into his choice

band of fighters, the raid on the Saxon camp, the party after-
ward. An endless round of hairy-chested bonding stuff. Each
time it seemed to be a new experience for Bear, but John remembered that everything had happened before. Did Bear?
Why was everything being repeated?

"Baseline familiarity," Wilson said.

It became *very* familiar. The awesome detail and realism of
the dwarf sim became old hat. John grew tired of it; the lack
of change and challenge stifled him. Did anything he was
doing matter? What would happen if he didn't bother to fight
in the next attack sequence? Would it make a difference? Did
he dare try?

The dwarves' assurances that progress was being made
grew thin. And not just for him. As the week wore on, Sue's
newfound calm grew more ragged, and more and more her
frustration at being cooped up came to dominate their conver-
sations. Her agitation infected John. Like her, he began to
wonder if there would ever be an end to their strange impris-
onment.

He was ready to tell Wilson that he wasn't going to bother
fighting the Saxons next time, but the dwarf had his own surprise announcement when John came out of the sim.

"Things are looking good. We'll start the next phase tomorrow."

When John told Sue the news, she exploded.

"*Next* phase? Ya mean this is gonna keep goin' on? We're
gonna be here forever!"

"Only till Bear's better."

"That's what they tell ya?"

"Well, they haven't said so in so many words."

"And they ain't gonna. They're gonna keep us cooped in
this can forever."

"Kranekin said he'd let you go in time."

"In time? What? A *life*time? His or mine?" She glared at
him. "Ya believe them munchkins too much, Jack."

The dinnercart arrived and they ate in a tense silence. John
reloaded the cart and Sue helped. They still didn't say anything to each other, but the silence seemed more companion-
able than it had.

When the cart left, Sue said, "I been thinking about this situation real hard, Jack. And, ya know, it keeps comin' down ta one thing. Ya owe me, Jack. Major league. 'Cause if it wasn't for you, I wouldn't be here."

That was true, after a fashion. "Seems to me that when we received our invitation from the dwarves, you were talking about getting a good price for my eyes."

"That weren't nothing. Fight talk, ya know. Ta spook ya. It don't mean nothin'."

It had seemed to mean something at the time. She still hadn't told him what had brought her to the factory looking for him. "Were you really going to cut my eyes out and sell them?"

"Nah. I told ya, it didn't mean nothin'."

"So why were you looking for me? It seems that might have a bearing on whether I owe you or not."

"It was a job. Nothin' personal, like. Some suits wanted ta dump the place you wás living. Wanted you ee-victed."

"Well, that's done." John was gone, but the factory might not be empty; Faye might still be there. Was she waiting for him there as she had at the rezcom? Guiltily, he realized he hadn't been thinking about her.

"Seems like we both got evicted pretty good," Sue said. "Left behind everybody we knew."

That wasn't exactly true. Bear was here. But Faye wasn't.

"Ya think the munchkins wiped the guys?"

"No." Whatever else they were, the dwarves didn't seem to be cold-blooded killers. Sue's guys hadn't represented a threat to anyone when Wilson had shown up.

"I think ya might be right. If Wilson wanted ta wipe 'em, he didn't have any need not to do it while we was there." She smiled to herself. "Good thing the suits didn't know who I'd picked ta get ya; they'd be on the guys like melting polycarb. The guys don't know nothin', but the suits wouldn't believe that. They'd wipe 'em just for saying 'I don't know where she went.'"

"These suits sound pretty heinous. Why'd you agree to work for them?"

"Monetary units. What else? Girl's gotta get along."

What else, indeed. "And they wanted me?"

She hesitated. Maybe she sensed how angry being a target made him. "They wanted ya out of your slump. That's all."

"And the eye thing, that was just entrepreneurial spirit?"

"I told ya, that didn't mean nothin'!"

Her indignation was real. Lord knew, John wanted to believe her. "So they just wanted me out of there?"

"Getting out can be bright. Like getting outta here, ya know? I gotta get outta here, Tall Jack. I'm dying in this can. You oughta leave, too. We both gotta get outta here."

"Bear needs my help. I can't leave now."

"Best help ya could give him would be ta get him away from these munchkins."

"He can't be moved."

"That's what they're telling ya."

That *was* what they were telling them. Could she be right that it was only a ploy?

"If you're not bright enough ta get out yourself, at least help me get out."

"I can't get involved in some half–thought-out escape plan, right now. They're going to start the next phase tomorrow, and Bear needs me. I owe him."

"What about me? Ya owe *me*, too."

All the rational arguments said that he wasn't responsible; her situation was happenstance. So why wasn't he able to feel comfortable with those arguments? Did he really owe her, or did he just not want her to feel as if he did? Was the difference important?

"Let me sleep on it," he said.

To his surprise, she was willing to do that. To his even greater surprise, she didn't say anything more about it over breakfast. She even wished him good luck with the day's sim runs. Her cheerfulness made him a little suspicious, but it also made him feel good. He liked seeing her smile.

His attitude continued its upswing when he saw that Bear was out of the tank. However, the new arrangement made him almost as uncomfortable. The dwarves had Bear suited up in some sort of bulky bodysuit studded with shiny silver lumps at all the joints. Fiber-optic cables trailed from the lumps and disappeared under the bed.

"Progressive resistance sheath," Wilson said. "We may have to release some of the neuro locks on his motor control. The PRS will prevent him from hurting himself if he starts thrashing."

At least Bear no longer had to wear the respirator mask.

"He looks different without his beard," John observed.

"An embarrassing necessity," Wilson said. "We've already done a growth stim on the hair follicles. If everything goes smoothly, he'll have his beard back before he has to face the public."

"And if it doesn't go smoothly?"

"He'll have his beard back in any case. Now, come on. Get in the chair and get the helmet on."

John did as he was told. This was to be a replay of Bear's awakening by the mad sorceress Nym, the first step in bringing Bear up to date by helping restore his memory. John wasn't sure how it was supposed to work, but the dwarves seemed confident. He supposed that they had been confident when they had first messed with Bear's mind, but he tried to convince himself that they knew better now. And that seemed to be the case; nothing had gone wrong with the earlier sims.

"We're going to start now," Wilson announced. "We'll set you in first so you can get accustomed to the sim frame. Speak out if there are any anomalies."

John nodded and then he was back in the Woodman Armory Museum wearing his new night watchman's uniform. The flashlight in his hand sent its beam roving across the silent armor and weapons. The hall wasn't silent, though; scrabblings and chitterings echoed from the darkness. Then he'd thought the noises had come from rats; he knew better now.

The setting was real enough that John could have believed that he was back in the museum. But the setting was the easy part. He heard the crash in the special exhibit gallery and walked in that direction. This time he knew what he would find, but he felt the edge of uncertainty and fear he'd felt that night because the sim was feeding him an analog of those emotions as part of the replay.

Nym was there, moving about the case, preparing her spells. The dwarf sim masters had gotten some of the details of the magic stuff wrong. Not that it mattered; Bear had been unconscious for that part.

"Come, Lord. Waken. 'Tis time," the sim Nym said.

Naked as the day he was reborn, Bear appeared in a nimbus of magic. He had his beard; his face, though now familiar to John, brought the analog feelings of awe and wonderment.

"You would probably call him Arthur," the sim Nym told him.

Bear is what he prefers, John thought. Wilson had said that Bear's auditory input would be active before his other senses, so in the sim John said what he had said that night. "As in King Arthur?"

The sim Nym nodded. "Rise, O King. The fight is to be fought."

Bennett appeared. "I see I'm too late for the show."

In John's sim arms, Bear started to struggle. In the reconstructed museum, Nym and Bennett began their battle. Bear opened his eyes, allowing John to see the terror there, and started to thrash. It hadn't happened that way. Bear began to cuss; some of the words John knew, some were in the old tongue that Bear spoke. It hadn't happened that way.

Wilson cut off the simulation.

John's head spun with the abrupt cutout. For a moment he was in two places at once, then only one. The dwarven medlab. In the sim chair. Under the helmet. He opened his eyes, still a little confused by the whirling spots overlying everything.

Bear's body lay still in the PRS, but his facial muscles were rigid as though he was making an intense effort of some kind. The dwarf behind the monitor board watched closely and tapped at his keyboard. John didn't know what the dwarf was doing, but it seemed to have some effect. Bear's jaw unlocked and the furrow in his brow softened. After a few minutes, he looked as though he were sleeping.

The whitecoats huddled by their consoles, talking worriedly.

Wilson looked up and said, "Hang on, John. We need to steady him."

The medlab whirled away and was replaced by a forest. John recognized it at once. They were playing the Saxon raid again. John went along. At the conclusion of the sim run, John found Wilson at his side.

"You okay?"

"Yeah."

"Up for another run?"

"I'm sick of Saxons."

"No Saxons. We're going to try another update run. Something less traumatic, where he's in control. Something from the spring. Sound okay?"

"I guess so."

"Want something to drink before we start?"

"Some water?"

"You got it."

They spun up MaxMix Manor, from the early days after Bear had dethroned Ferdy and become leader of the Dons. Everyone was there, and John was surprised to find himself feeling nostalgic. Maybe it was because Bear recognized him right away, and called him Jack without prompting. Everything was simple again, better than it had been. The camaraderie with Bear reminded him of why he was involved with helping the dwarves restore him.

It all fell apart when the dwarves introduced Trashcan Harry into the sim. Bear freaked, talking in the old tongue again.

Wilson said that they had managed half an hour of sim time, and that it was a good sign. John wasn't as optimistic.

They went back to the Saxons for the last run of the day.

John was whipped out and depressed when he got back to his room. Sue was waiting for him with more guilt to lay down; she didn't wait for the dinnercart, but started right in.

"I got people missing me, ya know. Hell, by now they prob'ly think I'm dead. Ain't ya got no family, Jack?"

Did he have a family anymore? It was not exactly an easy question to answer. His head hurt, and he didn't want to deal with her and her problems right now. "Look, I understand your position, but I don't think there's anything I can do about it."

"That's where you're wrong, Jack. I been looking around, doing the snoop, ya know. There's this door, see, out by where they let me exercise. I seen them open it once in a while. I'm telling ya, there's daylight the other side of that door. All we gotta do is nip on through and we're outta here."

"If it's so easy, why are you still here?"

"I ain't got the key."

"I see. Who does?"

"*You* can get it real easy, Jack. Real easy. We could be gone outta this place."

John wasn't surprised; everybody wanted him to do their work for them. "Bear still needs my help."

"Ain't ya glimmered that they're just using ya?"

And you aren't? "Maybe they are, but I've got to help Bear if I can. Look, what if I help you get away? What then?"

She grinned. "Life'd be deucey. Eternal gratitude ta ya."

The same kind of gratitude you offered last time? he wanted to ask. She must have figured out what he was thinking, because her smile started to fade. He had enough to deal with and didn't want to add the sexual tension between them to the list just now. He shifted gears. "You'll dump the contract on my eyes?"

"How many times I gotta tell ya, that weren't nothin'."

He'd hit the right button to distract her. "Okay. What about the suits?"

"You're outta your slump, ain't ya?"

"So that contract's over?"

"Don't see how it can be anything but."

"Okay." He couldn't think of any other objections to stall with. "Okay. Tell me what you got in mind."

CHAPTER
16

Spae opened her eyes, half expecting to see the shadowy figure looming over her. There was no dark man standing before her. How could there be? She was still jammed into the cramped confines of her seat; airline seating arrangements didn't leave anyone room to stand in front of a seated passenger.

A blanket that had not been there before covered her; David, asleep in the seat next to her, no longer had his. Could his action of covering her have intruded on her dream?

No. She still felt chilled by the dark man's regard. David could not have inspired such dread in her. There had been no concern for her welfare in the shadow man's icy stare.

She reached out to touch David, to reassure herself that she was free from her dream. He didn't stir, still asleep, undisturbed by whatever it was that had intruded on her rest. How did he manage to sleep so deeply?

She had been surprised by David's announcement that he was going to sleep, impressed by the speed with which he had surrendered himself to it. She hadn't felt able to close her eyes; she had been too excited, too anxious. The noise level in the cabin had been too loud. Obviously, she had surmounted those obstacles. She didn't remember falling asleep, and she didn't remember what she had been dreaming about, but she knew what had awakened her.

Did she really? All she really had was a sense of presence, a feeling of being observed. And the dark, shadowy image of a man.

No, not just a man. A mage.

She had thought it amazingly good luck that they had not run afoul of the Department in their escape. Up until the time the 9767 left the runway, she'd been expecting agents to board the craft and haul her back. But they hadn't. The Shabrique Airways jet had taken off and headed over the Atlantic unmolested. They had escaped the Department.

Or had they?

She couldn't keep her concern bottled up. Only days ago, she wouldn't have had any other option but to keep it to herself. Things had changed, and she was glad that they had. She nudged David, calling his name softly and trusting to the pervasive roar of the engines to keep her voice from waking any of the nearby passengers. David came slowly awake at her prodding.

"What is it?" he asked sleepily.

"I think they know where I am."

He sat up straight, fully awake now. "How?"

"Someone touched me in a dream."

"I thought you said none of them could do that sort of thing."

"I didn't think they could."

"But now you've changed your mind." His brows were furrowed in concern. "Did you recognize who it was?"

"No."

"Then how do you know it was someone from the Department?"

"I don't, really."

"Are you sure it wasn't just a dream? We've been moving pretty hard and we're tired. Having the Department catch up to us has been preying on both our minds. You said you were dreaming. Maybe that's all it was. Fears have a way of taking over your dreams."

And dreams had a way of putting you in touch with mystic realities. But he was right; she was tired, and she had been very much concerned that the Department would try to locate her magically when more mundane methods failed. Had they finally made such an attempt, or was David right? Had her fear made the dream seem real? Surely she would have recognized the touch of any of the Department's magicians.

They talked some more and finally she came to realize that David's was the most reasonable explanation.

But, just in case, she didn't go back to sleep.

Pamela watched Nakaguchi go raving through the assembled Yamabennin guards. This was the other side of his reputation, the fiery tirades to balance the legendary cool. He was breaking careers in the security force, dooming good corporate men and women.

He was pitiful.

He was clearly distraught. In kindness, she might have attributed his faulty judgment to a pain-clouded mind, but if he was in such agony from his broken arm, he should have had the doctors give him a better painkiller. She knew where his rage originated. He was distraught by the loss of his pet monster.

Hagen appeared at her side. "It is as I feared. Kurita is under Quetzal's control."

She realized then that Nakaguchi's personal security thug was not present. "Where is he?"

"Gone."

"What about Joel Lee?"

"He was not so wary. I arranged for his collection."

At least they'd retained one of the monster's minions. If he wouldn't tell them where the creature had run off to, he might be useful in other ways. She inclined her head toward the raving Nakaguchi. "Does *he* know you have Lee?"

"No."

"Good. Move Lee to the Brookfield facility as soon as feasible."

"The police and the press will be here soon," observed Hagen.

"Tsuroboru from Relations is on it. She's good and the local police owe us a few. The lid should stay on." Unlike some people, she'd had enough presence of mind to start damage control instead of wasting her time looking for a scapegoat, as Nakaguchi was doing.

Any further discussions with Hagen would have to wait; Nakaguchi had noticed them and was on his way. All the haranguing he had been doing had left him a little short of breath. As he drew in a new gulp of air, she jumped in.

"Mitsutomo-sama will not be happy to learn that your monster has escaped."

Nakaguchi's eyes narrowed. "You will not tell him." He stated it like an order.

"No. I will not." *Not until your monster has done enough to discredit you. Not until I have disassociated myself from your fiasco.* "But he will learn nonetheless."

"It is unavoidable," Hagen echoed.

Nakaguchi glowered down at him, then turned back to Pamela. "Something must be done to conceal the truth of what has happened tonight."

"It is already being done," she said.

"So I see." A dismissive glance at Hagen. He looked eyes with her. "Striking already?"

"Serving the Keiretsu," she told him. "As we all should."

"I am Mitsutomo-sama's voice. My word is the word of the Keiretsu."

"I do all that the Keiretsu lawfully asks of me."

"Tread carefully, Martinez. I know better than you the ways of the gnawing worm within," Nakaguchi warned. "This is not over yet."

"Indeed not. With perseverance we will weather this storm. Does the voice of Mitsutomo-sama have orders for me?"

"We must recover Quetzal. I will expect preliminary action plans on my console within the hour."

She bowed to his back.

"We must destroy Quetzal," Hagen said.

"Those are the plans we must make," she agreed.

*   *   *

Again Spae awoke with the feeling of another presence nearby. This time, however, there was no fear, no sense of dread, just a slow languorous blending of dream and reality. David. She could feel the heat of his body where it lay under the covers.

So near.

Her thoughts drifted warmly back to their arrival at the hotel room. They'd been exhausted. She'd invited him to stay, expressing her very real concern that he was too tired to drive safely to his friends' place; it was a wide bed, after all. She'd been intending to sleep, just that. Or so she had told him. And herself as well. Then, as she was starting to drift away, he had shifted and his arm had touched hers. She had stroked that arm, feeling the strength of the muscles beneath the skin and the feather touch of his hair. She rolled over to find his deep, deep eyes staring at her. His hand had reached out to smooth her hair back away from her cheek before pulling her head closer to his. Their lips had met and, for a time, there had been no thought of sleep. And when sleep came at last, it found them in each other's arms.

She burrowed under the sheet and across the bed to snuggle up to him. Her hand slid over the curve of his hip.

"Looking for something?" he asked sleepily.

"Found it," she said. Not all of him was sleepy. He rolled over, but she kept her grip. Though not for long. She soon had him in another grip. She locked her ankles to keep him safely there. Their lovemaking was even better than that of the night before; he had already found several of her buttons.

When they finished, she stayed in bed while he rose to shower. He'd made her remember that she was more than a mage. How could she have forgotten? On the bed of her reawakening, she vowed, as she had once before, not to let the Art consume her. This time she'd keep the vow; she wouldn't ever give David that excuse. She thought about joining him in the shower and decided against it. A little private time was a good thing for the moment; they were still very new to each other and she was already assuming that they were a pair.

But weren't they?

It seemed that way to her. But what about him?

She took her turn in the shower and came out to find him signing off of the room's perscomp. She hadn't heard the tone for an incoming call.

"Who were you calling?"

"My friends. They've got an interview lined up for you this afternoon."

"Already?"

"Why should you be surprised? You're a special commodity, my dear."

"With whom?"

"With me."

Though she was pleased to hear it, it wasn't the answer she was seeking. "No, I meant with whom is this interview?"

"Lowenstein Ryder Priestly and Associates."

"Who are?"

"A concepts development firm. They're a division of Metadynamics."

"THE Metadynamics."

"If somebody else is using the name, they're in for a fast lawsuit."

She sat down on the bed. "I don't know, David. From what I've seen, the megacorps are as bad to work for as the governments. Worse in some cases."

"Look, it won't hurt to talk to these people. You never know what they might offer. It's not like you've got any visible means of support and Lebeau's patched-together ID package isn't going to hold up to any serious checks. You're an illegal alien. You won't be able to stay in the country without at least a work license."

"I thought the US had a law that said a foreigner could stay if she married an American citizen," she said. She wasn't sure how serious she was.

"I think my keen investigative sense detects a ploy," David said. His tone suggested that he wasn't taking her seriously.

"You wouldn't be trying to take advantage of me, would you?"

"This is all going very fast, David."

He joined her on the bed, putting a comforting arm around her. "If it's going too fast, we'll slow it down."

"Maybe I don't want it slowed down."

"What *do* you want, Elizabeth?"

"I'm not sure, but I do know that I don't want to trap you. I don't want to have you thinking you're trapped. Anything between us, I want to be pure and uncontrived."

"I want that too. To that end I think it would be best for both of us if you have an honest means of staying in America."

Honest? Sneak in under an assumed name, then seek an honest way to stay? But then, there were lots of meanings to the word *honest*. Could David be thinking of the one she had just remembered? "Don't you Americans have a saying that marriage makes an honest woman out of the bride?"

"Are you saying you're *not* an honest woman?" He drew away from her in mock horror. "Gads, I've been taken! Used! Taken advantage of!"

She gave him a shove and he sprawled on the bed.

"Now physical abuse," he complained.

His silliness showed her just how maudlin she was becoming. She'd had enough worry. Playing into his silliness, she pounced on him. Striking for the ticklish spot she had found in his ribs, she cried, "I'll show you physical abuse!"

Charley's in box had a new message from Caspar, adding another five to the list of deaders to Modus 112. Only this time they weren't all streeters. It was the highest number of additions Caspar had ever made at once, which caught Charley's attention. Almost immediately he noticed another oddity: all five had the same case number, a new one dated last night.

He called up the case, and his stomach knotted when he saw the location. The Settawego Building. He hated coincidences.

It had to be a coincidence, didn't it?

He wished. SIU's job was to find the reasonable explanations for cases where the circumstances were unreasonable. Sometimes they couldn't. Those cases were the real ones, the ones that gave Charley the nightmares, the ones they closed up as quietly as possible. All in all there were more Baskerville Hounds among SIU cases than Barrington Slashers, but every so often they ran into a Slasher. Nightmare time. It was so much tidier when there was a reasonable explanation.

He kept reading, looking for that explanation. Vuong and Falerio had reviewed the case for SIU, and signed off on it as not being unit business. Their report cited the prelim investigation conclusion: explosion of suspicious origin, six accidental deaths resulting. The investigation was ongoing.

Caspar didn't agree with Vuong and Falerio that the deaths weren't SIU business. Why? What did Caspar know that they didn't? What was there about the six deaths that Caspar was seeing and the SIU detectives were missing?

Six deaths?

Charley checked the subscreen where Caspar's message was still displayed. Caspar only said five. Vuong and Falerio's report had six morgue refs, so there were six bodies.

The morgue refs gave the Cause of Death on five of the six as traumatic blood loss resulting from injury by falling glass. The shards must have cut them up pretty badly. One stiff's CoD was undeniable: the head had been severed. He'd probably been the lucky one; death had been instantaneous. The others had bled pretty badly before they'd died. The coroner hadn't looked any farther than their wounds for a CoD. But then, why should he? There might be technical differences in the cessation of bodily functions, but the proximate cause was clear. Clear enough for insurance investigators, anyway.

It was the last one on the list that made Charley reach for his pet jar of antacid tabs. The report said injuries from the glass were minor, incapacitating but not life threatening. Cause of Death: myocardial infarction. Heart failure. Some morgue wit had appended, "Must have been looking up and seen it coming."

Modus 112 was a list of heart failure cases.

Charley checked the five body tags that Caspar had included in his message. Five of the accident victims matched Caspar's five; Caspar hadn't listed the decap. One of the five already had a 112 sort of CoD. Would an autopsy show that each of the other four had died of heart failure, too? Officially they had died from massive blood loss as a result of multiple traumatic injuries. Open and shut, right? The cause of death was obvious, wasn't it? Why bother with a full autopsy? When a man went through a meat grinder, who would check to see if his heart stopped halfway through? Certainly not an overworked coroner's office.

Charley popped another antacid. He had a bad feeling that Modus 112 was going to be one of the real ones.

David's smile was the only reassuring thing she had seen since the cab dropped them at the main entrance of what was the tallest skyscraper in downtown Hartford. The plush lobby had been bad enough, with rich natural woods and polished brass and uniformed door attendants, but the richness of the reception area for Lowenstein Ryder Priestly and Associates made the downstairs lobby look like a subway station.

Spae felt as nervous as she had when she'd first met Magnus. She had the same "I don't belong here" feeling. The clothes David's friends had sent over might be a better fit than she could have hoped, but they were casual business attire at best. And the shoes were too tight and had heels that made her wobble. The opinion she'd reached before they left the hotel that she had made herself at least presentable foundered in the face of the rich surroundings.

She didn't have long to suffer her pangs of inadequacy. David introduced them to the receptionist—who Spae was sure she had seen once on the cover of *Fashion Forward*—and they were immediately ushered into Hershall Ryder's palatial office.

Ryder turned out to be an affable man in his late fifties, well dressed and distinguished looking but in a friendly, avuncular way. Even in his Sarmondi silk suit, he seemed a little at odds with the hard-edged corporate decor of the room.

If he thought Spae unsuitably dressed, he gave no sign. Ushering them to chairs, he apologized for Mr. Priestly's absence; Mr. Priestly, it seemed, was out of the country.

"What about Lowenstein?" David asked.

Spae thought David's question forward, but Ryder didn't seem to mind.

"Been dead for nearly fifteen years." Adding with a conspiratorial wink, "Name still brings in business, though, so we keep it on the door."

"I have to confess that I'm a little confused, Mr. Ryder," Spae said.

"You're wondering why we're interested in you."

"Frankly, yes."

Ryder smiled expansively.

"All one has to do is read the scansheets or bring up any of the tabloid channels to know that the strange and mysterious is on the public's mind. That sort of thing used to be totally a freak show, but that seems to be changing. Catch the last *Supernova*EM report, the one on McKutchen Wood? Real Bermuda Triangle stuff, and they covered it all, without an explanation. A show like *Supernova* has got a reputation for serious scientific subject matter. You know the producers had to be concerned that they didn't have a scientific answer, but they aired it anyway. There's a lot more of that going on these days. There are a lot of eyebrows raised, a lot of people wondering what's next. The climate's changing. Some people—and not people given to wild exaggeration, I can assure you—have suggested that there is a whole new world ahead.

"*Evolve or die* is our motto, Dr. Spae. We don't intend to die, so evolve we must. We at LRP are always looking to the future. And when we look forward we see that we may not have all that it takes to find our way in this changing world. We need people with special talents, people who have an unusual—dare I say visionary—slant to their worldview. You would seem to be exactly the sort of person we're looking for. Mr. Beryle has painted a picture of you as some sort of new Darwin."

What *had* David been telling them? He wouldn't meet her eyes.

"I think that perhaps you've been misinformed." She started to rise. "I'm sorry that we've wasted your time."

"Please, Doctor, stay. If the comparison is inept, it's my fault. Too many early years spent in advertising. Always looking for the phrase that will light the right fire. Seems I misjudged this one. Forgive me if I offended."

She hadn't been offended, just spooked by Ryder's hyperbolic enthusiasm. "There's nothing to forgive. I think you may have been misled as to my abilities and interests."

"Doctor, I like you already. But to think that we don't know what is going on is to belittle Mr. Beryle and his friends. I may speak broadly and overdramatically at times, but I am quite sure I am not mistaken about you. Rest assured that I have a realistic understanding of what you can do."

"And just what do you think that is?"

"I refer, of course, to your arcane knowledge and skills. Such ability is just what we are looking for. We're putting together a program involving people like yourself. So far, we're still in the formative stages, so there's plenty of room for a knowledgeable, ambitious person like yourself to make her mark. You'd be getting in on the ground floor, so to speak. A rare opportunity. Your credentials with Department M—oh yes, we know about them—suggest that you would be the perfect person to direct this new effort. We can make you a home here at LRP. With substantial compensation, of course. Yes, a very happy home."

The last thing she wanted was be part of another Department, but the thought of being out on her own was a bit frightening. It had been so long, and she had grown used to the resources an organization could provide. And she did need some way to make a living. She probably would need some kind of protection from the Department as well. "I don't know . . ."

"How does Head of Esoteric Research sound?"

He went on to describe a facility and a program almost exactly like the arrangement she had always dreamed of. She looked to David. He nodded his encouragement to accept. How could she refuse? It sounded so wonderful. But there would be strings attached, and she had only just cut one set of strings.

Ryder wasn't giving her a lot of time to ponder. "I'm probably tipping my hand unnecessarily here, but your experience is highly valuable to us. We are willing to make concessions in order to secure your talents."

"I really appreciate what you're offering, Mr. Ryder. It's just that I'm not really sure that I want to be a part of any organization at the moment."

"I can respect that. I truly can. And I must admit that I am not surprised to hear it from you. Not surprised at all. As I said, we are willing to make concessions. If you don't want to work with us just yet, I can understand. I expect you'll change your mind over time. But one does have to live in the present, doesn't one. Perhaps we could set up an interim arrangement, give you a chance to get to know us. How does that sound? Perhaps we could put you under retainer? You would still have access to our facilities, of course, and we *would* expect that you'll be participating in developing those facilities. And, of course, we *would* expect to have first call upon your services."

David interrupted the pitch. "If she's not working directly for you, there is the matter of a work license."

"Ah, yes. Didn't I mention it? It's already arranged. Consider it a sign of our sincerity, and a mark of our gratitude that you have chosen to speak with us first. You may pick up the paperwork from my assistant on your way out."

"Thank you," Spae said. She felt a little overwhelmed. She had heard that Americans could be very openhanded, but this was—overwhelming. She had to wonder if there was a string attached.

Ryder frowned. "You don't seem very happy, Dr. Spae."

She made herself smile. Ryder smiled back. "It's just that—well, I just hadn't expected such generosity. I don't know what to say."

"Try thank you," David suggested.

"Yes, well, thank you."

Ryder beamed at her. "I'm sure you can find a better way to express your gratitude, Doctor. Why, for example, you might consider putting your new license to use. I would like to suggest a trial arrangement. Would your gratitude extend to consenting to work with us on a current matter? With full compensation, of course. What do you say? It would give you something to do and it would give us a chance to demonstrate our desire to create a fulfilling and mutually profitable relationship."

That seemed the least she could do.

David chose this moment to be suspicious, asking, "What sort of matter? And for what compensation?"

Ryder directed his answer to her. "We would like your advice, your expert advice, with regard to a recent incident. Now I know there is no precedent establishing pay scales for persons of your expertise, so let's use our own pay scale as a guideline. Say, two thousand a day? Naturally, we will cover any expenses you might incur in your investigations. Travel mostly, I would expect. The situation is mostly a matter requiring observation and forethought, I expect. Of course, there may be the odd test or two, that sort of thing. What do you say? Are you willing to give it a shot?"

For that kind of money, she'd be a fool to refuse; the Department had frozen her accounts and she didn't want to live on David's charity. To do so would destroy her resolve to make their relationship a free one.

"All right," she said.

"Excellent, excellent." Ryder raised a bushy white eyebrow. "Now, I would guess from your circumstances that you don't have any other pressing appointments just now. Am I right? I thought so. What do you say to starting at once?"

It wasn't what she had expected, but how could she refuse? "All right."

"Excellent, excellent. This particular matter into which we'd like you to look occurred just last night in Norwood."

"Norwood?" Spae asked. She didn't know local geography, if Norwood was local.

"Just southwest of Boston," David explained.

Boston she knew. If Norwood was south and west of there, it was less than two hundred kilometers away. How much less she couldn't guess, but she supposed it wasn't important. "What happened?"

"Yes, well, that is the question. It seems that there was an unexplained power surge in the grid, resulting in a progressive loss of service to several locations. At approximately the same time, there was a very mysterious explosion in the penthouse suite of a nearby building."

"There was nothing about an explosion on the news this morning," she said.

"And there won't be."

"Now *you* are being mysterious," David accused.

"Sorry. That dramatic flair, you know. The reason that you have heard nothing is that the building belongs to Mitsutomo Keiretsu, and they're quashing the story. They say that there was no explosion. They say the glass that fell from the penthouse was the result of a structural failure. And—and this is all without fanfare, mind you—they are compensating the survivors of those killed in the incident without recourse to an insurance investigation."

"That's odd," David said. "I would think they'd want whoever built the building to take the rap."

"Frankly, we expected the same thing. You see, that building was built by Carenellicorp, a company that just happens to be part of our own corporate family."

"All the more reason to hang it around your necks," David said.

"Curious, isn't it?"

Spae shook her head. "I don't see where this involves me. I'm not a structural engineer, or an insurance investigator."

"Well, Dr. Spae, there is more to this situation than structural engineering. I think I can say with some assurance that there was no structural problem. The building was soundly built. This morning, Carenellicorp had crews out to survey the damage and test the rest of the building; from the outside, of course, since Mitsutomo is letting no one inside. The tests show nothing wrong with the structure; it is as sound as the day it was completed."

"Then there *was* an explosion?"

"Well, that's the mystery. Our survey team was unable to discern any sort of damage inside the penthouse suite, yet the entire wall, three centimeters of structural monoacrylic, was entirely gone, not a shard remaining in the frame."

"And you think it was done by magic," David said.

"We would like to know if it was," Ryder said. "Can you ascertain that, Dr. Spae?"

"Maybe. But I can't tell you from here. I'll need to see the site. Walking it would be better."

"I'm afraid a visit is not possible: Mitsutomo security, you know. But I can most certainly arrange a viewing. One of our corporate family maintains a nearby high-rise hotel with an excellent view of the Settawego Building." Ryder came around his desk, hand out. Spae rose and shook his hand; he had a firm grip that did not overpower. "I am most pleased to have you aboard, Dr. Spae. I am sure we will have a most rewarding relationship."

CHAPTER
17

Spillway Sue gave John a broad smile when the control panel emerged from the wall at his touch.

"Deucey," she crowed. "See, your access is good enough ta get us through. We're outta here."

"Don't be so sure." The panel's indicator lights showed that the door was locked.

"Six-three-two-seven-seven-star-two-three," she said, still smiling.

He punched the numbers into the keyboard.

"Out and free," Sue said as the indicator switched to unlocked. As the door started to slide open, she brushed past him and walked without hesitation into the glare flooding in from beyond the open door.

John's eyes had grown accustomed to the dim light of the dwarven halls, and the bright light was blinding. Shading his eyes and squinting, he could barely make out the slim shadow that he knew was Sue; she had stopped just over the threshold.

"Shit!"

Spillway Sue's voice was filled with anger, but there was disappointment, too. Somehow her plan for escape had fallen apart. But how? John's eyes were adjusting rapidly; he stepped through the door to see for himself.

A wildwood stood before him across a narrow verge of gravel. Daylight flooded down on him, but though he smelled earth and growing things and felt the moisture in the air, he had no sense of being outside. It was very strange.

He looked up, searching for the sun, but the light was soft, as though diffused by clouds, but it was far brighter than any overcast day in John's memory. By shading his eyes, he could make out faint lines of darkness crisscrossing the sky. The thickest lines formed a gridwork of rectangles. The thinner lines swooped across between the thicker ones, sometimes turning, sometimes stopping in the middle. Beams defining panels of light while pipes and conduits crossed beneath them.

There was a ceiling above their heads!

The light came through the rectangular panels, but those panels weren't transparent; it was impossible to tell if they were frosted windows to the outside world or if the light came from bulbs hidden behind the milky whiteness. The evenness of the illumination suggested the latter.

A ceiling! John could hardly believe it. If there was a ceiling, they had to be in a chamber, a chamber bigger than anything John had ever seen bounded by walls!

The only wall he could see was the one at his back. Everything in front of him was forest. Could you call it a forest if it had a roof? There was greenery in extravagant profusion as far as the eye could see, a veritable jungle of plants. There were shade trees and bushes and fruit trees and low ground cover and shrubs and grasses and pine trees and ferns, all growing in a riot that beggared the finest corporate arboretum he'd ever seen. It was the sort of growth he could imagine the legendary untouched rain forests to boast.

And they were still inside the dwarves' realm!

They stood on a three-meter-wide path of gravel that ran along the wall they had come through. A narrow path in front of them led into the verdure. Looking down that shadowed aisle, John could see that it forked not very far in. A glance in either direction along the edge of the wood revealed what appeared to be other paths leading into the trees from the perimeter path as well.

John found this place the most congenial he'd visited in the dwarves' domain. It was alive, full of energy! Totally unlike the stony coldness he'd felt everywhere else.

Why had the dwarves constructed such a place? Was it a park, or a farm, or an arboretum, or something else entirely? What purpose could a captive forest have for the dwarves? As he stared in wonderment, the door slid shut behind him.

Sue tensed, giving the panel a dirty look. She looked around suspiciously. When nothing happened, she relaxed.

"No alarms. I guess we're okay for now."

It was almost as if someone was urging them to go on.

The perimeter path ran straight for a long distance in either direction. It was hard to tell for sure, but it looked like the forest eventually curved out to press against the wall. Or maybe the wall curved away from the trees and the forest followed it. They could walk in one direction or the other and find out, but somehow the path in front of them seemed a more inviting avenue for exploration, even though it was cloaked in the shadow of the trees whose branches arched over it and the gloom gathered under the leaves shaded everything to a dark mystery.

Sue took a step toward the path into the forest. "Come on. There's gotta be an exit somewhere."

The forest might be the most inviting place John had seen in the dwarves' realm, but he hesitated to enter. "I only agreed to help you get through the door to this place. I can't leave Bear yet."

"Oh, no. You're not shimmying out on me. We ain't out yet. Come on. The outside's gotta be on the other side of the trees."

It sounded like wishful thinking to John, but he *had* promised to help her escape, even though they had taken different views of what a completed "escape" would mean. How bad could it be? Once they'd found the door to the outside, he'd come back and make sure the dwarves got Bear back on his feet. And having helped Sue escape, he'd know the way out himself.

He followed Sue under the cool and pleasant cover of the leaves. The air was full of forest smell, flavored with the scent of a bewildering variety of wildflowers and other blooming plants. Insects buzzed and moaned through the air, and crawled and scurried through the leaf mold and along the branches and stems of the plants. John found the filtered light easier on his eyes than the harsh glare that beat down on the perimeter path. The environment made for pleasant and serene walking, quite unlike the city.

They took the left-hand fork and hadn't gone more than a couple of dozen meters before the path forked again. Sue took the left branch again. She ignored each of the lesser paths that occasionally intersected the one they traveled on. Before long, John became convinced that they were paralleling the wall through which they had entered. How long before they encountered another wall?

Sue stopped and crouched low, listening. After a moment, she whispered, "Somebody's comin'," and dived into the greenery beside the path. Catching the faint sound of dwarvish voices, John followed, just fast enough to see that she was cutting through the underbrush, heading toward where he thought the wall lay. Being smaller than he, she made better time sliding through the tangle and was soon out of sight. He pressed on, thinking they would have been better off hiding in one place and trying his best to move quietly. He came upon a narrow path and could hear the voices of the approaching dwarves; they sounded close and were getting closer. Thinking that they must be using the path he'd just found, John crossed it and kept to the untracked brush. He hoped Sue had not taken the path; if the dwarves *were* using it, they'd surely catch her.

Before long, John discerned a lightness through the leaves and brush. The wall. Staying within the cover of the brush, he stopped and scanned the perimeter path. Sue was nowhere in sight. He could hear the dwarves more clearly now; they were definitely coming closer. If he called out to Sue, they would hear him. He silently wished that she would stay low and out of sight. He kept silent himself, crouching down and trying to make himself as small as possible.

Too bad Faye wasn't here; her invisibility trick would be useful.

As it turned out, he didn't need Faye's trick. Three dwarves emerged from the brush. The trio crunched down the gravel path, headed toward the door. And John—John thought inconspicuous thoughts, wanting to go unnoticed. Talking in a language John didn't comprehend, the three dwarves strolled by his hiding place. They gave no sign that they noticed him crouching in the shadows of the plants.

He was vaguely surprised that the dwarves didn't seem to be searching. He was sure the alarm must have gone up even if he hadn't heard anything. Maybe the dwarves were searching elsewhere and just didn't think John and Sue would have come here.

He waited until the trio went through the door and were gone, then waited some more before stepping out on the path. He looked around, hoping Sue would see him and emerge from the brush to join him. She didn't.

Softly, he called her name.

She didn't respond. Had she abandoned him?

He didn't think she'd take off on her own until she was sure that her way to the outside world was clear.

So where was she?

He stepped back into the shelter of the brush. There was no sense standing around in the open.

Should he wait for her to come back or should he go looking for her? If she was coming back, where would she come back to? They hadn't made any plans for a rendezvous. He'd have to go looking. But this place was huge; they could both stumble around for hours without running into each other. He didn't dare shout to her and she wouldn't dare either; there might be other dwarves about.

There had to be some way he could locate her without bringing down every dwarf in the place. If only he had some thermal goggles, he might spot her hiding place in the greenery by scanning for her body heat. But he didn't have thermal goggles and wishing for them wouldn't get him a pair; he might as well wish he could summon her by magic.

Then again, maybe he could. He hadn't been able to replicate the magic he'd done in the otherworld. Even though he had not gotten any effects, he'd almost always had a sense that *something* was happening when he tried. He remembered the feeling of vibrancy he'd had when he first returned to the mundane world; there was something of that sense here. He hadn't felt it anywhere else in the dwarves' halls, but he felt it here. Maybe a spell would work here.

If he knew one.

Which he didn't.

He felt useless. Was there anything he could try? Sometimes in fantasy stories, a magician could find someone just by thinking about them. A piece of clothing helped, a nail paring or lock of hair was even better; something with a psychic link to the person. John didn't have any of those things, but he could try anyway. All he could do was fail.

Crouched in the brush, he concentrated on Spillway Sue. He tried not to think about how foolish he'd look if Sue or a dwarf walked up on him. He tried to think only of Sue, picturing her as well as he could. He saw her standing in front of him, bare-chested and pants open. A hint of blue panties drew his eyes down. This wasn't the sort of picture magicians got in fantasy vids.

A vague sense of presence impinged on his embarrassment. He opened his eyes and looked guiltily to his right.

No one was there.

This was stupid.

He'd just look and listen for her; sooner or later she'd show herself. The perimeter path stayed deserted. Slowly, with nothing to disturb them, the insects returned to their workaday chorus around him. John waited, growing more fretful. Had he made a mistake in deciding to wait?

The line of his gaze kept drifting off to the right. Waiting was getting him nowhere. He stood slowly to stretch his cramped muscles and started moving through the brush at the edge of the woods, following the perimeter path. Without understanding why, he found himself scanning the wall rather than the forest. The stretch of panels, grilles, and pipes didn't look any different than the wall he'd been staring at from where he had hidden until he noticed that the colored strips tied on one of the vent grilles weren't moving; when there was air flowing, the strips fluttered with its passage. What was different here?

John emerged from the woods and crossed the path to examine the vent. The opening was covered by a grille about two feet across. The top of the vent was about head height for a dwarf; John had to crouch to squint in between the slats. The inside was pitch-black and he couldn't see anything. Moving his hand across the surface of the grille, he discovered that there was a slight airflow, but only in the corners.

Something was blocking the vent.

"Sue, come on out. They're gone."

She didn't answer.

Was she in there, or was he just making a fool of himself?

He found the latch. It was an automatic closure type and hadn't quite caught. He popped it open and the grille swung wide on its hinge without any urging from him.

The increase in light slanting into the duct was enough for him to make out a huddled form. He recognized the running shoes. She didn't respond when he called her name, so he reached in and grabbed her ankle. Her other leg stirred in a weak attempt to kick his hand away from her. He just hung on tighter and grabbed her other ankle.

He pulled her out. She was a deadweight. What was wrong? He felt better when she began to struggle feebly against his attempts to get her away from the vent.

"Take it easy," he told her. "It's just me."

"Jack?"

She sounded as orbital as a tapvid junkie, but she stopped struggling. Her knees were too rubbery to support her, so he helped her sit down. John didn't like the look of her reddened skin. Her breathing was uneven, too. She was sick, or something.

"Got sleepy," she mumbled. "Not real bright ta sleep."

"You're going to be okay." He hoped he wasn't lying.

"Was gonna hide. Couldn't stay awake."

"You just sit here a minute."

"Okay," she agreed lethargically.

John went back and stuck his head in the vent. The air in the duct was moving freely again; he could feel it on his face. There was a faint odor of old sweat and rotting food. He had a vision of a locker room inside a trash bin and realized that he was getting a little light-headed. Not much oxygen. He pulled his head out of the airflow.

A little woozy, he sat down beside Sue. She leaned over and laid her head on his arm.

"Wha' happened?" she asked in a voice that sounded a little more normal.

"You crawled into that vent to hide?"

"Only place I could see ta hide."

"You passed out in there."

"Passed out? I thought I was falling asleep."

"I think it's some kind of gas vent. Maybe carbon dioxide for the plants. It's sure not normal air. You're lucky I figured out where you went."

"Ya got me out?"

"Yeah."

She didn't say anything for a while. "Ya coulda left me there."

"Why would I do that?"

"Why not? I don't mean nothing to ya. Ya coulda gone back ta Bear and pretended nothing had happened."

Her hand slipped across his rib cage and she gave him a brief one-armed hug.

"We gotta get going," she said. "They're gonna come looking for us soon. We gotta get outta here 'fore that."

"You're not in very good shape," he protested. Though she was breathing and talking almost normally, he was still worried about her color.

Using the wall as a brace, she pushed herself up onto her feet. "I'll survive."

"I think we should go back. Maybe they haven't missed us. We could try another day."

"Got this far." She took a couple of wobbly steps before putting out an arm to hold up the wall. "I ain't gonna give up yet."

He hadn't really thought she would. "Try the main path again?"

"Sounds good."

She started back toward the path, but stayed near the wall, using it to steady herself. John caught up with her and put his arm around her shoulder.

She looked up at him, an unreadable expression on her face. She slipped her arm around his waist.

"Let's go," she said.

They had almost reached the opening in the greenery when the door in the perimeter wall opened. There were two dwarves on the other side. The dwarves looked surprised to see John and Sue; John was certainly surprised to scc the dwarves.

"It's Reddy," the blond dwarf said. "Grab him!"

His dark-haired companion lunged through the doorway. John disentangled himself from Sue. The dwarf ignored the staggering girl and came at John. Sue stuck out a leg and tripped him, but it cost her her balance. Both of them went down, the dwarf pitching toward John. John swung his fist at the dwarf's head as he fell forward. The shock of contact burst through his hand as he connected. The dwarf hit the ground and sprawled limply. The blond dwarf came forward more cautiously, moving around the fallen Sue.

Something in Sue's hand reflected light: her stolen weight bar. With a sprawling lunge, she swung her weapon and managed to catch the dwarf in the shin. He howled and began to dance, hopping on one leg. John shoved him and sent him tumbling back through the doorway. Sue scrambled to her feet and started slapping at the wall in a vain attempt to activate the door mechanism. John stepped up beside her and ran his hand along the frame; he couldn't always find a door's hidden control panel. This time he did. He triggered it. The door slid shut, cutting off the dwarf's angry shouts.

They still had one opponent on their side of the door. Sue gave the fallen dwarf a nudge with her foot. He groaned, but made no effort to move.

"You're in it now, Tall Jack." She tugged on John's arm. "We're both going now, or staying forever."

John let himself be dragged into the forest. He kept looking back at the fallen dwarf, hoping the guy wasn't totally concussed. Sue let go of his arm and with a "Come on!" started trotting down the path. John couldn't bring himself to go. He stood in the shadows of the trees, staring at the dwarf he had taken down.

The door opened again, revealing three dwarves this time, the blond one and two new guys in gray coveralls. All were grim-faced, and all had pistols in their hands. Eyes roving, they came through the doorway. They did not seem to spot John standing still in the forest gloom. The three stopped by their fallen comrade and holstered their weapons. The two newcomers kept watch while the blond stooped over and examined the prone dwarf.

"Good thing Corey has a thick skull," the blond said.

"Gesham, you figure they went into the arbor?" one of the standing dwarves asked.

"Where else?" Gesham said. "You and Lorenkin go get them."

The two dwarves in gray nodded and started for the path, toward John. They had deadly grim expressions on their faces.

The dwarves hesitated at the edge of the path, as if reluctant to step under the arms of the trees. When Lorenkin started forward, the other stopped him with a touch on his arm, whispering something that sounded like, "Don't spook him." Lorenkin gave him a look, then squinted in John's general direction.

John felt as if he were in the petrified forest hunt scene from *Stellar Wars*, but at least Zan had had a tranq gun to take out the guys chasing him.

"I don't see anything," Lorenkin whispered.

"I do," the other said. He pulled something from his belt and pointed it toward John. There was a sharp crack and something pocked the tree next to John.

A bullet! That was a bullet!

Muscles frozen, John stared at the splintered wound in the tree.

They were shooting bullets at him. Real bullets! No tranq guns here.

He stumbled a step backward. Lorenkin clearly caught the motion; he reached for his weapon. The other dwarf fired again. Chips of bark pattered on John as another wound appeared in the tree.

Why were they shooting at him?

John didn't think it wise to hang around and ask. He turned tail and ran, taking the path to run faster. Behind him he heard the dwarves start after him. With his longer legs he was by far the faster runner. He increased the distance between them easily.

But where was he going?

He turned a corner and found Sue standing in the path.

"I thought I heard shots," she said.

"You did." He reached out and spun her around as he passed her. "Run!"

She started after him, too.

When he came to a fork in the path, he didn't stop to ponder which might be the better way; he took whichever looked to offer a better path for running. He slowed his speed a little so that Sue could keep up, but he didn't stop running until he took a turn and nearly overran a figure standing in the middle of the path.

All he could do was stare.

Sue came around the turn at full speed and ran right into John.

"Jesus, what'd ya stop for! Ya crazy—"

Her words stopped as she saw why John had stopped. She stared openmouthed at the figure who stood in their way. His appearance alone would have been a shock, even without the shifting multicolored glow that surrounded him.

He was dressed flamboyantly and looked every inch the part of a fairy-tale elven prince, from his features to his clothes. The pointy ears, flowing silver hair, and slanted, opalescent eyes were familiar, but John had never seen the glittering mail, green thigh boots, and flowing cape. The tall elf bowed in an out-of-place, courtly way to Sue.

"Bennett is the name," he said. "In time to be of service, I trust."

John couldn't believe it. He'd never seen Bennett dressed so oddly, but he had no trouble recognizing him. But the outfit? The elf might have stepped out of a bad fantasy vid, except that Bennett was not an actor, and the swirling colors behind him were no Hollywood special effect.

Nor was the hulking gray thing that emerged from the rainbow vortex and stood behind him. Sue grabbed onto John and made sure he was between her and it. The monster looked like an unholy crossbreed between a lizard and an ape. Gray scaly skin covered its wedge-shaped, reptilian head and burly anthropoid body, with arms longer than its legs. Judging by the wings that sprouted from its shoulder blades, there was a bat in the gene mix somewhere, too.

"Toold you dwaarves toook heem," it grated.

Sue squeaked when the creature spoke, but Bennett ignored it and spoke to John.

"I'm glad to see you finally got this far, Jack, although it took you rather longer than I'd hoped. I had begun to think I'd never hear from you again."

"I'd been hoping the same thing." Why did this feel like leaving the frying pan for the fire? "What are you doing here?"

"I'm here to help you escape, of course."

"Ya hear that, Jack?" Sue said, emerging from behind John. She gave the lizard-ape a wary glance, then beamed a megawatt smile at Bennett. "Look, mister, I don't know who ya are, but if ya got a way outta here, we're going your way."

"Who's your charming companion, Jack?"

"Spillway Sue's the handle," she answered for herself. "Look, mister, we got some truly pissed hardcases on our asses. We gotta move. So, like, where's the exit?"

"There's no need to be in such a hurry. Your pursuers have taken a wrong path."

"Your doing?" John asked.

"A trifle. Nothing you won't be able to do, with training."

"Dwaarves," the creature said, crouching low. It stared down the trail behind John with the intensity of a cat waiting at a mouse hole.

John thought he could hear the faint sounds of running feet. So much for the dwarves having taken the wrong path. Despite the danger, he was pleased the elf's spells weren't working the way he'd expected them to. "Your trifling spell doesn't seem to be working too well for you."

"Surely you've noticed things are a bit more difficult in this domain."

John didn't know enough about magic to tell hard from easy. Just to annoy Bennett, he said, "Not really."

Bennett raised an eyebrow, but whether in disbelief or acknowledgment John didn't know.

"I will set the matter to rights," the elf said, closing his eyes and beginning to hum softly.

John thought about running. With Bennett concentrating on fixing his spell, and the lizard-ape totally absorbed in watching the path, they might slip past. Sue tugged on John's arm, pulling him down to whisper in his ear.

"Where do ya know this Bennett guy from?"

"Let's just say that he and I have met before."

"So like, who is he?"

"He's a lying, murdering bastard," John replied, not bothering to whisper.

"Now, Jack," Bennett said in a hurt tone. Apparently he had finished retuning his spell; John could no longer hear the dwarves coming closer, and the batwinged monster had relaxed. "Is that any way to talk about your father?"

CHAPTER
18

Charley pulled over in front of the Settawego Building, stopping at the edge of the police line. As expected, Manny asked, "How come you're parking over here?"

"I'll just be a minute," Charley told him.

"This ain't the Hilton. We're supposed to be at the Hilton."

"I just want to look."

"The locals aren't gonna like it," Manny warned unnecessarily. "Especially after Vuong and Falerio signed off on it."

"I won't get in their way."

"That's what you said last time."

As it turned out, Charley was right; he didn't get in the way of the local investigating officers, because they weren't around. But then, he didn't learn anything either. The scene looked like hundreds of other violent crime scenes: yellow tape, body marks, the vid security monitor, the stains that wouldn't go away fast enough. Somebody had already cleaned up most of the glass. Charley was careful to stay out of the monitor's line of sight.

Caspar claimed that this was related to Modus 112.

Charley looked up at the hole in the Settawego Building's facade. It was too easy to see the reasonable explanation here.

Explosion, the prelim said. Scuttlebutt had it that a major suit had been killed, too major to make the news as a victim of violence. Betting at the station said that the exec would be "dead" within a week; opinion was split on whether it would be from a medical situation or a sporting accident. Nothing weird here. Just more collateral victims of the megacorps playing their games.

God, he hated the corps.

"You gonna stand here all day?" Manny wasn't happy. The day hadn't warmed up as predicted, and he was shivering in his light overcoat. Manny didn't like cold weather even when he was dressed for it. Charley didn't understand how the man could have grown up in New England without learning how to be prepared for the weather.

"You could've waited in the car."

"I coulda waited in the lobby of the Hilton if you'd parked where we were supposed to go. I coulda been doing what we're supposed to be doing. Something you might consider showing some interest in. I coulda already been done talking to the tight-assed manager at the tight-assed Hilton. I coulda already started logging our report on the damn tight-assed polterghosties. I coulda—"

"All right, all right. Let's go get it over with."

"The captain'll be so pleased."

"Hancock can suck rocks."

The manager kept them waiting once they got to the Hilton. They helped themselves to the office coffeepot. The manager finally got around to them, and they started the interview in a quiet corner of the lobby; Charley set his belt unit on RECORD. It was all pretty tiresome and it all could have been done over the lines, but Captain Hancock's "face-to-face" policy sent him and Manny here for the interview. In among the manager's repetitive complaints was the information that the hotel desk had recorded a new high in numbers of guests and staff complaints about poltergeist events in the last twenty-four hours. However, the only real crimes were a couple of petty larcenies; the hotel's insurance would cover them if anyone decided to ignore the "not responsible" signs and pressed a suit. There hadn't been any new reports for the last six. It sounded like the incident had played out—a conclusion they could have reached by phone. The trip was pointless and aggravating, actually. If Captain Hancock's policy hadn't been Captain Hancock's policy, Charley would have thought that the old fart had sent him and Manny here to suffer.

Hancock could suck rocks.

Traffic noise burst in on them, overriding the hubbub from the lobby. Charley felt a gust of cold air.

"Jesus, who's the damn fool who opened the door?" Manny's tone promised mayhem for the "damn fool" if Manny caught him.

"Check it out," Charley suggested. More to get Manny out of earshot of the manager than anything else. Under the circumstances, it was the best he could do to protect Hancock's "professional image" policy. Charley watched out of the corner of his eye to make sure Manny didn't start more trouble than he ended.

Manny's "damn fool" wasn't one, but half a dozen: six guys wrestling four heavily laden carts in through the open doors. The huffers weren't using hotel luggage carts, and they weren't in hotel livery. When Manny began harassing the workmen, threatening to cite them for violations of the Urban Environmental Resources Conservation Act, Charley asked the manager, "What's up?"

The man took a little too long to give his answer. "A private party. They must be with the band."

They didn't look like roadies. "What band?"

"I don't recall the name. Ah, excuse me, I have to take that call."

The perscomp on the desk had been buzzing, but it had buzzed unanswered several times before. The manager had ignored it then, preferring to continue complaining about the department's lack of results in resolving his problems. He hadn't found any "need" to take any of those other calls. Judging by where he went, he needed to take the call in his private office.

Made a person wonder.

Charley gave the boxes another look. Metal, with locks and reinforcements, the kind of cases electronics got moved around in. From the way the guys were straining, the stuff was heavy. Charley watched them roll the carts to the elevator banks. One of the huffers punched for a car from the bank that went up to the guest floors. Not the activity rooms? After they muscled their loads aboard, Charley watched the board. The elevator stopped at the forty-second floor.

Manny came back. "Tight-ass run outta steam?"

"Found something more important to do with his time."

"Good. Let's go back to the station house."

"I think I'd like to take a look upstairs first." He started for the elevators.

"Not so good." Manny clumped up beside him. "Don't tell me there's some meat this time."

There was a car waiting in one of the shafts. Charley and Manny boarded.

"Okay," Charley said. "I won't tell you."

"Floor, please," the car asked.

"Forty-two," Charley told it.

The car let them out on the requested floor. Manny had been silent during the ride, but when the doors closed behind them he asked, "What are we looking for?"

"I want to poke around."

"You've got that look."

"I just want to poke a little, okay?"

"Should I call for backup now?"

"What you should *do* is shut up."

"Come on, Charley. What are we doing up here? There ain't been any reports of polterghosties up this high."

"Maybe there will be."

Manny wasn't buying. "Highest floor with a complaint is twenty."

"Call it a hunch."

"Maybe I *should* call for backup."

"Funny. Why don't you take a look around the north wing, and I'll take the south." The carpet leading to the south wing still showed ruts depressed by the passage of heavily laden wheels.

"You think we oughta split up?"

"This isn't a horror vid."

"Light up your belt anyway," Manny demanded.

The belt units could be set by partners to monitor each other's position and, at a code word, transmit vid-aud of their surroundings. The video didn't do much good while you were walking around yourself, but with the audio you could listen to your partner's progress if you wanted. A potential lifesaver if there was trouble in the offing. It was an unnecessary precaution here in the Hilton, but when Manny got it in his head to be a hen, there was no point in arguing. Maybe that was the way Manny felt about Charley's hunches. Charley popped the compartment that held the ear receiver and felt the custom-molded piece fall into his hand. He snugged it in his left ear and ostentatiously set up the belt unit.

"Okay? Feel better?"

"Much," Manny said. "Now you can go get yourself shot, and I won't get my ass up before a board."

They split up to walk the floor. As Charley walked around the first corner, he caught a glimpse of a man wearing a leather bush jacket entering a room halfway down the hall. There were two empty carts in the hall near that door.

Charley hadn't gotten a good look at the guy's face, but something about him fired some memory circuits. He'd seen the guy somewhere before. More than once. Then he remembered who wore a jacket like the one he'd seen: David Beryle.

If Beryle was here, maybe there was something of interest.

The door to the room was still open. Charley walked down the hall, deliberately taking his time maneuvering around the carts so that he could check out the room. The occupants were all busy, giving Charley a chance to get a good look before somebody spotted him. There was some sort of apparatus set up near the window. Two guys in gray coveralls were fussing over it. Two more were unpacking one of the metal crates, taking out more electronics.

A woman, mid-forties Charley guessed, was looking out the window. Though she wore a business suit and had her hair pulled back in a no-nonsense arrangement, she didn't look straightline corp. Odd. Odder still that the huffer who walked up to her didn't act particularly deferential. Maybe he wasn't a huffer? Whoever he was, he launched into a soft-voiced monologue that Charley couldn't make out and started pointing out the window. Charley shifted position, trying to see what the man was pointing at. He couldn't quite get the angle, but just before the doorway cut off his view, he got a glimpse of the dark hole in the Settawego Building's face.

Were these people connected with that business?

How was Beryle connected?

Beryle played the odd stuff, fanning the fires that SIU was supposed to put out. The reporter's presence suggested that this might not be just intercorp rivalry. Vuong and Falerio might have been hasty. Caspar thought so.

Maybe it was a good thing that Charley had decided to be nosy.

On the other hand, Vuong and Falerio wouldn't like having the Settawego incident pulled into an SIU investigation after they'd signed off on it.

The next door down opened and Beryle emerged. There must have been a connecting door. Charley had been standing flat-footed; it was too late for him to pretend that he was just walking down the corridor, so he decided to take the offensive.

"Well, well. If it isn't 'News from the Edge' Beryle. Found any good alien ax murderers lately?"

"Hello, Gordon. Didn't expect to see you here. Where's your shadow?"

"Manny's around."

"Didn't know there was a donut shop on this floor."

"Old joke. Been guesting on the *Nostalgia Comedy Channel*EM again?"

"Not since you hosted it. What are you doing here, Gordon?"

"Was going to ask you the same thing."

"Beat you to it."

"You asking professionally?"

"Yeah, sure. Why not?"

"No comment."

Beryle looked like he was sucking rocks, which suited Charley.

"David, who are you talking to?" The woman emerged from the room to collect her answer personally. She had a stern stare that evaluated Charley; he was startled to note that she had mismatched eyes, one green and one blue.

"This is—still just a detective?" Beryle asked. Charley nodded. "This is Detective Gordon, one of the more distinguished members of the Cooperative's Spook Squad."

Charley hated that nickname. "Special Investigations Unit, ma'am." Beryle seemed satisfied with a one-way introduction; Charley wasn't. "And you are?"

"Elizabeth Spae."

"*Doctor* Elizabeth Spae," Beryle clarified. "She's an authority in certain obscure matters."

Dr. Spae furrowed her brow at his description of her area of expertise, making Charley wonder what she considered herself to be an authority on.

"Pleased to meet you, Doctor. I must say you're a step up from the usual 'authorities' Beryle drags around with him."

The doctor looked even more puzzled. "Thank you, I think."

Beryle edged his shoulder between them. "So what *are* you doing here, Gordon?"

"Just poking around."

"The poltergeist thing?"

"You know about that?"

"My business, remember? That shouldn't get you up here. There have only been incidents on the first twenty floors."

He was well informed. "You know me, I like to be thorough. Can I look around your suite?"

"Got an investigation warrant?"

"Do I need one?"

"Yeah. This time I think so."

Charley's turn to suck rocks. He gave Beryle a tight smile. "I'll remember."

Beryle ushered Dr. Spae back into the suite. This time he shut the door. Charley headed back toward the elevators, wondering where the connections were.

* * *

Anton Van Dieman of the inner circle provided the vehicle. He called it a LeRoyale™, describing it as the finest limousine in the world. The car was not as large or elaborate as the Mitsutomo limousines, but it was sufficient for Quetzal's needs. The ambience of the vehicle was far less important than its ability to carry him from place to place. There was only one amenity that he found indispensable: the darkened windows that shielded him from the burning sun.

Soon it would be night again and he would not need the shield.

Van Dieman sat beside him, answering his questions as to the followers' activities and resources. Oblique questioning revealed that Nakaguchi had yet to take action to disrupt Quetzal's plans. The Asian had it in his power to arrest certain operations. Quetzal hoped the man understood what any such delays would ultimately cost him.

When the Glittering Path opened, great would be the suffering of any who hindered those who would walk the Path.

Until that time there were steps which could be taken to minimize the difficulties.

"Nakaguchi is unreliable," he told Van Dieman. "He is no longer to be considered an intimate of the inner circle."

"But Master Jeffries trusted him implicitly."

"Jeffries did not understand the division in Nakaguchi's loyalties. I do. You must as well. As long as his actions are in our favor, he may live; but we must be vigilant. He *will* betray us. His heart is not truly on the Glittering Path."

"He shall be watched carefully, Venerated One."

Quetzal liked Van Dieman's attitude much better than Nakaguchi's. This man would have a place in the new order.

Outside the limousine darkness was gathering.

His departure from Mitsutomo's imprisoning palace had tired him more than he expected. The energy he'd taken from those at the foot of the tower had dissipated more quickly than he had expected. He had a hunger that the limousine's stock of delicacies could not assuage.

"Is the driver discreet?"

Proudly, Van Dieman said, "She is an initiate of the eighth circle."

"Good. Have her take us to the place where bodies are sold for money on the street."

Van Dieman was clearly surprised by the order. He spoke hesitantly. "Venerated One, if you wish a woman, there are many of the followers who would—"

"No, there are *not* many. The followers are too few, and that is why I must seek alternatives."

The followers would give, but he could not yet afford to take from them; they were too important. Believers were too few, and too necessary for other uses.

Van Dieman gave the orders.

The surroundings and language and dress of the participants might change, but the interaction remained remarkably constant. He selected a spot and had Van Dieman direct the driver to stop there.

They waited.

Van Dieman was nervous, continually glancing out the windows. Twice he told the driver to keep a careful watch of something called the proximity sensor. Quetzal simply sat back and watched, confident that opportunity would present itself.

In time, it did.

Half a block away a car pulled over to the sidewalk and stopped. A woman crowned with blond tresses got out. After the car pulled away, a man walked up to her, and she handed him something. He smiled, slapped her on the buttocks, and vanished back into the darkness of the alley from which he'd come. She straightened her short skirt, tugging it down over a tear in her stocking, before taking her place by the graffiti-covered, shattered shell of a bus stop. Despite the cold of the evening, she tossed her coat back on her shoulders, the better to display her body wantonly.

She would do.

"Move the car forward. Stop by the blond woman." Van Dieman relayed his orders to the driver.

He watched the whore follow the slow approach of the limousine. When it stopped beside the ramshackle shelter, she stood in what Quetzal supposed was intended to be an alluring fashion; her actions were awkward, too harsh and stilted to actually be sexy. When he opened the door, she smiled invitingly.

She put one hand on the car roof and leaned down to look in the opening. Her eyes widened at what she apparently thought was abundant luxury.

"Watcha looking for, mein freunds?"

Quetzal answered. "What else other than what you offer?"

She cocked her head, suddenly skittish. Where had the hostility and suspicion come from? Van Dieman whispered in his ear that she feared entrapment by the police, that he must be more direct to eliminate her fears.

"We are not police," Van Dieman said. "My friend wishes to buy your services."

"Who said I'm selling?"

"The Franklin brothers," said Van Dieman, displaying three hundred-dollar bills. "What's your name?"

"Kandi. With a K and an I." Eyeing the money avidly, she added, "That's a short trip."

"Will that be satisfactory?" Van Dieman asked him.

"Yes, I believe so." To the whore, he said, "Come, join me."

But she still did not enter the car, saying, "I count two of you. And I don't do no two-fer-one specials, but I can be more'n enough woman fer both of ya, if ya catch me. For the right incentive, I mean."

Van Dieman doubled the visible incentive.

She came of her own free will. She had her expectations of his desires; it mattered little that they were incorrect. She would say, in the phrasing of the age, that he "wanted" her. For truth, he did, but not in the way she thought. He would "take" her; again, not in the way she thought. Her consent gave him the opening he needed.

He pursued the charade, saying the pointless words she expected. For her part, she cooed and flattered him. They both played roles, actors in two different plays that only appeared to be the same.

He turned her, bending her back over his lap and masking his intentions with kisses. Drawing back, he unfastened the flimsiness of her shirt and likewise the shiny wisp of a bra that shimmered beneath the translucent fabric. There was a moment of awkwardness while she shrugged out of the garment, then she lay back again, arching her back and offering her bared breasts.

He smiled down at her, touching her hardened nipples with a feather-light caress. She quivered.

She played the part well. But beneath the surface was an honest truth; she had consented to him. For payment, of course; she would receive a payment of sorts, a payment that others had believed the greatest reward possible.

"Are you ready to give yourself to me?"

"I'm hot, baby. I'm ready."

He stroked her cheek, willing relaxation into her limbs, cooling her heat. It was a mercy, he supposed, but an unintentional one, a mere side effect. It would not do to have her squirm away and withdraw the consent.

The soft mounds of her breasts sagged to either side of her chest. He struck between them, cracking the sternum.

"Hey, not so rough," she protested.

Her tone was not serious, though, for she could not feel what he had done to her; he had taken that sensation from her. Her hands fumbled at the catches of her skirt. The consent remained.

Time to consummate the act.

He willed his fingers to granite hardness, his fingernails to obsidian sharpness. He slashed once, slicing through skin, muscle, and bone. He plunged his hand in. He pried up the ribs. His fingers probed into her flesh. Deeper. Deeper, until they slid around her pulsing heart.

He ripped it free.

The blood sprayed, as it always did, spattering everywhere in the close confines of the limousine. The blood was very red against the ashen hue of Van Dieman's face. Quetzal believed that the man had not been expecting this.

Laughing, he raised the pulsing heart to his lips.

He ate the whore's life as he consumed the muscle that had powered it. With each bite, he stripped away that which made her a person, consigning it to oblivion. He swallowed her life energy as a snake swallows a lizard. Her essence was his, all his.

It had been too long since he had tasted the heart's blood.

As an afterthought he offered the last bit of the whore's heart to Van Dieman. The faithful should be rewarded. Van Dieman took the morsel, more from fear than from desire. He swallowed without chewing. Then his eyes changed, when he understood what he was receiving.

Quetzal laughed again.

The limousine had not been an altar, ritually configured to focus the release of the life energy. The wanton had not been a completely willing victim, knowingly giving of her essence. But the sacrifice had still been good. He felt renewed, stronger than he had since the end of his long sleep.

He was empowered!

In this impoverished age, there were none to oppose him. His will would be the Law.

CHAPTER
19

"I'm not leaving without Bear."

John expected that the declaration would get a reaction from Bennett, but the elf's expression didn't change.

"Artos is here, then," he said. "I'd been wondering where he'd hidden himself. Yet I suppose I should not be surprised to find him here. Where is he, by the way?"

"He's in the, uh, infirmary."

"Injured?"

Was that real concern in Bennett's voice? Unlikely, considering. John didn't think it wise to reveal Bear's real condition; he probably shouldn't have said anything in the first place. But now he had to give some sort of explanation.

"He's been sick."

"I would offer my sympathy; but you probably wouldn't believe there was any sincerity in it." He didn't sound very sympathetic. "I must say that I am surprised the two of you are still talking."

"No thanks to you."

Bennett sighed. "I only have your best interests at heart, Jack."

"Why don't I believe you?"

"An interesting question, Jack. *Why* don't you believe me?"

Because you're a liar. Because you killed Trashcan Harry. Because you almost killed Faye. Because you tried to kill me. Because. Because. Because.

But this wasn't the time to get into any of those things.

"You said you were here to help."

Bennett nodded. "To help you escape this place, yes."

"Why?" John wanted to know.

"Who *cares* why, Jack?" Sue asked. "He's our ticket outta here. Let's go with him."

"*I* care why."

Innocently, Bennett asked, "Isn't being your father reason enough to want to help you?"

"For you? I don't think so."

"You wound me," Bennett said, actually managing to sound hurt.

John wasn't impressed. "I doubt it."

"So callous. You have been brought up badly," Bennett said.

John snapped back, "What do you know about how I was brought up?"

"Shit, John! Keep yer voice down," Sue cautioned.

John knew that she was right; the dwarves were out there searching for them. Shouting could draw their attention; it wouldn't improve the situation.

"We have limited time here, Jack," Bennett said. "The dwarves are drawing closer. If we are to go, we must be about it."

"I said that I'm not going without Bear. I'm also not going anywhere with you until I know the real reason you came. What is it you want?"

"Well, there is a matter on the horizon in which I thought you would have some interest."

"So you *do* have another reason. You want my help in one of your plots."

"You phrase it so coldly."

"But correctly, apparently. Well, if you want my help, you'll have to give me the kind of help I want."

Bennett raised an eyebrow. "You wish to strike a bargain?"

"I want to get Bear out of here."

"And me," Sue prompted. "Don't forget about me."

"And Sue. All of us. Out of here."

"And if Artos doesn't want my help?" Bennett asked.

All too likely. "You get him out anyway."

"He won't like that."

"He'll survive."

Bennett smiled. "An excellent attitude."

John didn't care for the elf's approval. "Is it a deal?"

"Are you willing to pay my price?"

"I haven't got any money."

"Not all prices are paid in money."

"I'll pay your damned price," John said—adding quickly, "as long as it doesn't involve killing someone."

"You have my promise that I will not set your hand to killing anyone in this matter. Now, there are witnesses here, Jack. Do you say, in front of them, that you will pay my asking price for this aid?"

"You can get all of us out of here?"

"Of course," Bennett said. "A foregone conclusion."

"Safely?"

"Do you doubt me?"

"You didn't say you'd get us all out safely."

"Yes, safely," Bennett said in a clipped fashion. "Answer. Will you pay the price?"

"Get us out and I will."

Bennett's snippy attitude vanished. He smiled warmly. "Then the deal is done."

Turning, he whispered something to his creature. The lizard-ape's alien features scrunched up into an expression that John couldn't read, then it nodded. Bennett was all business when he turned back to John.

"Gorshin will remain here to continue distracting the dwarves. Ms. Sue will stay with him while you and I go to fetch Artos."

"Jack?" Sue clutched his arm in a vise grip. Her eyes were wide as she stared at the creature Bennett had called Gorshin.

"Sue stays with me," John said.

"Thanks, Jack," she whispered.

"She will be safer in Gorshin's care," Bennett suggested. "She is an added complication if she goes with us."

"I said she stays with me."

Bennett bowed concession. "Lead us to Artos, then, and let us gather him into our stealthy band."

Finding his way back to the edge of the woods was harder than John expected; he'd taken some turns without noticing while he had been running from the dwarves. From time to time, they stopped and hid to the side of the trail while a party of dwarves clomped by. Sometimes they'd hear dwarves, and hide, but then not see anyone.

During one of those halts, Sue whispered to him, "Is Bennett really your father, Jack?"

"I don't want to talk about it," John whispered back.

"Ya don't look much alike."

"I *said* I *don't* want to *talk* about it."

Sue wouldn't let go. "Hey, Jack, ya ain't the only one here, ya know. I wanna know, can he be trusted?"

"No. But I don't see much other choice."

That was clearly not the answer she wanted. She fretted for a bit. Her next question showed that she was catching on to the fact that Bennett's word couldn't be trusted in anything. "How do we know he can get us outta here?"

"He got in, didn't he?"

"That's all we got ta go with?" She sounded upset by the concept.

"That's all."

"All clear," Bennett said in a voice only slightly louder than the whispers John and Sue had been exchanging.

They moved on.

There was a guard at the door connecting the forest chamber to the rest of the dwarven complex. Bennett said, "I'll take care of that," and made a gesture. Almost immediately there was a ruckus among the bushes off to their right. The dwarf ran to investigate. John, Sue, and Bennett ran across the perimeter path and entered the spare halls of the dwarves' domain.

The corridors were deserted. Where were all the dwarves? Could they all be searching the woods? John had heard a lot of them crashing through the brush and tramping down the paths, and John had never seen many of the little people.

He decided to hope that they were all out looking.

They reached the medlab without running into anyone. John opened the door and led the others in. Bear was alone in the room, lying in the bed. Nothing had changed except the level in the intravenous drip bottle.

"That's the guy in Wilson's vid?" Sue sounded surprised. "He looks like shit. What's with the diver suit?"

"It's not a diver's suit," John told her. "It's a progressive resistance sheath. It keeps him from hurting himself when they run the sims."

"He is not conscious, Jack," Bennett observed. "Are you planning on carrying him?"

"If necessary," John replied, but he didn't think that it would be bright just to unhook Bear from the machines and drag him away.

John hadn't thought this out. What to do? Run the reawakening sim again and hope it worked this time?

The dwarves' program hadn't succeeded in bringing Bear's mind back to the present. While they had gotten the main parts of Bear's awakening right, including the magical battle between Nym and Bennett, Bear had reacted as predicted. Instead of going with the sim in its attempt to reinforce his memories, he'd freaked. He hadn't done much better with the MaxMix Manor sequence.

What could John do that would improve on what the dwarven docs and psychs had done?

There had to be something, something different.

John's goal was different from that of the dwarves; maybe their chance lay in the differences. Getting Bear up and moving was more important than bringing him up to speed with the twenty-first century. Bear had done all right by himself before. John had faith that Bear could do it again; if the guy was anything at all, he was a survivor. But how to give him a jump-start? What could John try that was different?

Bear had freaked when the bad stuff had started happening in the sims. Maybe feeding Bear's brain a reawakening that didn't have all the trauma of the real one would help him to handle it.

"Well, Jack?" Bennett asked. "We can't stay here all night."

What to do? John couldn't think of anything else to try. "Give me a couple of minutes."

John sat at the control console and called up the main sim in editing mode. He jiggered the program a little, most significantly by editing out Bennett, a curiously enjoyable action. He concocted a new plot, making the awakening go as he thought it might have gone if Bennett hadn't shown up. He made up some loopy parting lines for Nym and added some real clothes for Bear instead of the ragged costume robe that he'd actually worn while escaping the museum. Would the changes be enough? He hoped so. He switched the program from editing to interaction mode.

John slipped on the helmet and started the sim, cutting in just as he discovered Nym. The false history played, and Bear, upon awakening, played into it. Nym gave her speech. John led Bear through the museum. The break-in by the fake feds started and John had a few tense minutes as Bear's personality fluttered, but Bear finally went with the flow. The night was still cold when he and Bear ran out into the streets. Bear made it through the sim to the safe getaway John had preset. The interface went into its preset fade down to sleep for Bear.

The sim melted into the medlab for John.

Had it worked?

"Jack?"

Bear's voice was weak, creaky, but he'd called John's name. Tearing off the helmet, John went to the bed. Bear's eyes were open, and he seemed to be at home behind them for the first time since John had been here.

"I'm here, Bear."

"Jack, what's going on? I can't move my arms."

"Take it easy. You've been sick."

Bear nodded, accepting. "I'm glad to see you, Jack."

Glad, eh? John would think about *that* later. "We'll talk later. Right now, we've got to get you out of here."

"But I can't move."

"Don't struggle. You're okay. It's just the suit. We're going to help you get out of it." God, he *hoped* it was just the resistance suit. Bear had been laid up for a long time. How weak would he be? Peeling Bear out of the thing wasn't a one-man job.

"Give me a hand here," he said to the others.

Sue pitched in at once, and with her help John got Bear out of the PRS. Bennett never lifted a finger, standing aloof in the corner and watching.

Bear's eyes narrowed when he saw the elf; clearly he hadn't realized Bennett was there. How much did Bear remember about Bennett from after the reawakening? John felt him tense. He also felt the tremor in Bear's muscles—Bear was in no shape to take on the elf. Clearly, Bear knew it too; he relaxed. A little.

"What are *you* doing here?" he growled at Bennett.

"I'm here to help, too." He held up a hand from which dangled clothes that he must have conjured; there hadn't been any in the room before. "Can't wander about naked. Not in front of the lady."

Bear hadn't shown any concern about his nakedness. "I don't want any gifts from you."

"Then don't accept them." Bennett opened his hand and the clothes dropped to the floor. "If I were you, Jack, i'd convince him to put them on. He'll be very conspicuous without them."

As if they weren't already conspicuous; Sue, the shortest among them, was head and shoulders taller than any of the dwarves. Still, once they got out—*if* they got out—Bear would need clothes. It was still fall out there.

"Bear," John started.

"I do not wish to owe anything to an elf," Bear said firmly.

"For this you owe nothing to me," Bennett said. "I am here at Jack's request. He is the one who is buying your freedom."

Bear turned his stare to John. "Is that true, Jack?"

"I said we'll talk later. First we get out of here, and that means getting dressed."

Bear was too wobbly to manage by himself; he let John and Sue help him into the clothes Bennett had provided. The fit was perfect. John turned to Bennett.

"Where do we go from here?"

"We go back to green," Bennett said.

"The forest? Is that the way out?" Sue asked.

"It will be our way out."

They retraced their path back to the great chamber and its forest. As before, their journey was miraculously devoid of encounters with dwarves. Were they that lucky, or were the dwarves letting them think so? Or did it have something to do with Bennett's magic? John was more interested in getting out than in getting answers.

They got into the woods without incident and returned to the spot where they'd left Gorshin. The lizard-ape wasn't there waiting, but it soon appeared, moving nearly silently through the brush. Bear stiffened when he saw the thing, but to John's relief he neither tried to fight it nor relapsed into catatonia.

"Dwaarves steel serr'chh," Gorshin announced.

"Any nearby?" Bennett asked.

"Naht neecr."

"We've been more fortunate than we deserve, Jack," Bennett said.

"A trap?" Bear and Sue both asked simultaneously.

The question had come to John's mind as well.

"I think not," Bennett said. "But there will be trouble enough if we dally."

"Then let's not dally," John said.

"The path is hard to see," Bennett announced. "I will lead."

Bear shook off John's supporting arm. "I will walk by myself now."

"You sure?" John asked. Bear looked as if he was about to fall over.

Bear's answer was a glare.

Bennett set out, moving more slowly than John had expected. Was he actually showing some concern for Bear's weakness? Bear walked almost at Bennett's shoulder. John and Sue fell in behind him. Gorshin followed.

"Stay close, everyone," Bennett warned. "For your own safety."

To John's surprise Bear kept the pace, staying close to Bennett as he had been told. John tried to stay close to Bear, ready to catch him if he stumbled. Sue was right at John's side. Bennett's warning seemed unnecessary; with fanged and clawed Gorshin taking up the rear, there was little likelihood that anyone would want to straggle.

The character of the forest changed as they walked. John felt his skin begin to tingle. The leaves around them seemed tinged with blue fire, and light reflected from them in rainbow sparks. The shafts of white glare penetrating from the ceiling panels grew grayer, darkening with a suddenness surpassing that of a summer dusk. The air chilled.

Sue shivered and stepped closer to John. He put his arm around her, and she wrapped her arm around his waist so that they had to walk in step. Her free hand reached up and grasped the hand he'd put on her shoulder, tugging it down to her chest. Restlessly, her head swiveled back and forth as she tried to catch each new sparkle, to seek out the source of each odd sound. This was all very strange to her.

No surprise there. John remembered what it had been like for him the first time. For that matter, he still found the experience pretty strange. Hell, who was he kidding? The otherworld was still wondrous, utterly amazing to him.

How much stranger must it be for Sue, who didn't know that she was walking into the Faery realm.

Part 3

—— — —

TOO
DANGEROUS

CHAPTER

20

On the other side, Bennett provided elven steeds for all of them, except Gorshin. They came out of the fog in a clamor of hooves and stood pawing the ground and snorting. Bear, to John's surprise, mounted one of the beasts without a word. Sue refused to go near her mount despite Bennett's assurances that the beast would not harm her.

"It looks hungry," she protested.

It took a lot of arguing, but finally she agreed to share John's beast. She clung tightly to him as soon as he pulled her aboard behind him. Bennett leading, they galloped away.

They saw little of the otherworld beyond the grass beneath their feet because they rode through a dense mist, which Bennett claimed to have summoned "for your protection."

Although the fog made it hard to tell how fast they were moving, it seemed to John that the steeds ran faster than any earthly horse ever could. Not that he had much experience with horses, any experience really. He was surprised that he managed to keep his seat. But with Sue clinging to him, he didn't dare to lose it.

Time, he knew, was strange in the otherworld, so he never knew how long they rode. They moved in silence, the only sound the drumming of the steed's hooves against the ground. When Bennett finally reined in, Bear was reeling in his saddle and Sue seemed to have worn a groove around John's waist. They dismounted, Bear almost collapsing; John rushed to steady him, ignoring his protests that he was all right—he clearly was not and his inability to fend off John's aid confirmed it. Gorshin, having flown away into the fog, rejoined them in a tumult of flapping bat wings while Bennett gathered the steeds in a circle around him. He spoke to them in what could only have been Elvish, then sent them away with a word.

"From here we walk to the sunlit world," Bennett announced.

Walk they did, the elf leading them into the fog which became iridescent. Bear insisted on walking unaided and managed to summon the strength from somewhere to do so. Sue clung to John, seeking comfort amid the strangeness. He didn't mind. In fact, he liked it. Her closeness and human warmth made him feel better. Hugging each other tightly, they hiked through the fog. The rainbow scintillation increased with each step.

After only a couple of dozen paces, John noticed that the colors swirling around them were becoming a shade less intense. Though the magical fog still hid all around them, the tinctures began to fade, diminishing in intensity with each stride, and the shifting swirl began to slow. John realized where they were emerging even before his vision had fully adjusted to the brightness of the real world. He recognized the tall windows shedding light into the cavernous enclosure and sending wide shadows across the hardwood floor from the massive metal constructions. The dust and rust and old oil smelled very familiar.

They had arrived in the factory he had adopted as his slump.

He looked around. Nothing had changed, as far as he could see; but where before the walls had seemed grim and dull, now, after his stay in the dwarven halls, the place seemed brighter and more alive. Maybe he still had dust from the otherworld in his eyes.

Or maybe he was home.

Home or not, being here meant—

Faye!

He felt her presence all around him, warm like a summer breeze but caressing him with a concern that no breeze could ever provide. Her attention didn't have the palpability or heat of the arm Spillway Sue had around his waist, but Faye was no less real to him.

"John! Are you all right? Did they hurt you?"

"I'm fine." Better, now that he knew she was all right.

"Artos doesn't look well."

Artos? John had expected that she would be curious about Sue. After all he and Sue were still standing with arms around each other. He and Sue. Embarrassed, he said, "Bear's had a hard time."

"Will he be staying with us?"

Us? Sue stirred, rubbing her hip against John's thigh. Which *us*?

"John? Is Artos staying?"

"For now at least."

"Jack?" Sue disentangled herself from him and looked at him as if she thought him crazy. "Who are ya talking to, Jack?"

"F—" He caught himself. Faye was invisible even to him. Though he heard her voice and felt her presence more clearly now, she was still nonexistent to ordinary people. Spillway Sue was a material girl, in more ways than one. Recently she'd been introduced to a lot of things that weren't part of her world, and she hadn't taken them well. Despite all the strangeness she'd seen of late, how could she believe in John's invisible friend? Faye would understand John's pretending she didn't exist; she was used to it.

"Just thinking out loud," he said.

Sue looked at him thoughtfully, but didn't say anything. Her scrutiny made him uncomfortable.

The mist that had accompanied them from the otherworld had dissipated completely now. Bear stared at the hulking, silent machines. In some ways this place would be stranger to him than Faery. He stumbled, and John lunged to catch him. With Sue's help, he lowered the exhausted Bear to the floor.

Sue looked. "Are we where I think we are?"

John nodded. Sue kept looking, her mouth slightly open and her eyes wide. Faye giggled. John shushed her; when he drew Sue's attention, he pretended that he was fussing over Bear. Faye's amusement increased, only to vanish as Bennett stepped to John's side. John felt her back away.

"Mortal flesh is so feeble," the elf said, looking down at Bear.

"He's had a hard time," John said defensively.

Bear seemed to become aware that there were people around him. He opened his eyes and looked at John.

"Where have we come?" he asked.

"Home," John said without thinking.

Bear nodded. "I feared that the elf would deceive us. They are deceitful creatures."

Sue looked up at Bennett nervously, then caught John's eye. Her expression was worried. She didn't even know the history between the two. John looked at Bennett; the elf had the slightest of smirks on his face. John turned back to Bear.

"Do you remember when you are?" What he really wanted to ask was whether Bear remembered that John was also an elf.

Bear looked puzzled. "What kind of question is that?"

The twenty-first-century Bear would have known it was a valid question.

"I'm so tired," Bear announced. His eyes slid closed.

"Feeble," Bennett said. "See to him. There is still a little time. I will wait."

John roused Bear enough to get him on his feet. Sue helped without being asked. Together they managed to get Bear to the stairwell and up to the first landing. Bear was too weary to climb all the way to the top and too much of a burden to carry; John abandoned his intention to put Bear on his own mattress. They got him into the nearest room. It had been an office and had been furnished with a long couch. The couch's frame was broken now and the cushions moldy. Sue dragged the battered cushions into a line on the floor while John helped Bear over to them. Bear was conscious enough to stretch himself out.

"Where's Caliburn?" he asked. "Do you have it?"

John had last seen the sword in Bear's hand. He'd put it there himself. "Don't you remember recovering it?"

"Recover?"

"At the Lady's palace."

"The Lady." He smiled weakly. "You were there."

"So you do remember?" *How much? Do you remember calling me a traitor?*

"Perhaps I do. Everything's so confusing. Some of my memories seem different from others. I see myself in places and sometimes I do one thing, sometimes another. The people with me change. It is strange. Some of my memories must be real and some just dreams, but I cannot tell one from another. Cei would know. I must ask him."

"You can't ask Cei."

"Has he left for Camulodunum?"

Camulodunum was an old name for Camelot. Bear didn't have it together at all. Had John jumbled something in his brain?

"Cei's gone."

Bear nodded knowingly. "Not to Camulodunum. Not anymore."

"That's right."

"This is a different time."

"That's right, too. Do you remember the museum? Do you remember Nym?"

"Is she with the Dons? Hector's girl?"

Carla had been Hector's girl, and the Dons were a part of Bear's reawakened life. Bear was all screwed up. What was John going to do? What could he do?

"You need to get some sleep," he told Bear. "We'll sort things out after you've rested."

Bear nodded slowly and lay down. He seemed to drop instantly into sleep. John started to rise, but Bear's hand shot out and grabbed his arm. Bear stared earnestly into his eyes.

"Then you don't have Caliburn?"

"No. The last time I saw, I had just given it to you."

"The Lady," Bear mumbled.

"Did you give it back to her?"

"I don't know. I think I did, but I don't know if it was a dream."

Bear released John's arm. This time John waited until he was sure Bear was asleep. Sue was waiting at the doorway.

"Them dwarves unzip him, or is he always like this?"

John looked back at the sleeping Bear. He didn't want to think that it might not have been the dwarves that had unzipped Bear. It was going to work out. It had to. "He'll be okay. He'll be better after he's gotten some sleep."

"He's not the only one." She took his hand. "Come on. You sack upstairs, right?"

Had he told her that? Whether he had or not, she knew the way. Not that there was much opportunity to get lost; the only thing at the top of the stairs was the uppermost floor, the chamber that he had made his own.

She only looked around long enough to spot the mattress that was his bed. It was in the same disarray that he'd left it in. She towed him across to the foot of the mattress and stopped, turning to face him. Her shove took him by surprise and, thanks to the ankle she hooked behind his knee, he collapsed sideways, flopping down. The mattress jounced as she plopped next to him.

He started to get up, but she grabbed him and pulled him down on top of her. He felt her lips on his chin, then they slid up to his lips. She kissed him hard. Surprised, but pleased, he responded.

After several breathless moments, he broke the kiss and levered himself up on one arm to look down at her. Her hair wasn't long, like Faye's had been in the otherworld, nor was it as fine; and it was dark, night to Faye's starshine. Still, it suited her, framing a face that held a softer expression than he had ever seen upon it. She wasn't a perfect beauty like Faye, for her skin was marked with her humanity and the strains of making a living in a hostile world.

Faye wasn't here, and—for the moment—he was just as glad.

What good was beauty you couldn't see?

"Well?" she asked.

She was here in his bed, such as it was. She was solid, real.

He bent down and kissed her. Her lips were warm and alive. *She* was warm and alive. Real. Solid. Warm. Her arms reached up and encircled his head. She pulled him down to her.

"Thank you," she said when they'd finished their lovemaking. He wasn't sure what to say, so he just hugged her hard. She hugged back. They lay quietly in each other's arms. For all his tiredness, John couldn't sleep. Sue was not so burdened; it wasn't long before she was drawing the deep breaths of a restful slumber. In frustration, John opened his eyes.

Gorshin crouched at the foot of the mattress.

For a moment he locked eyes with the batwinged creature. How long had it been there? What did it want? Granite-hued lips wrinkled up, revealing sharp teeth. Was that a snarl, or a smile?

"Hee waants taaw'k you," Gorshin grated.

John didn't need to ask who the "he" was.

Talking with Bennett wasn't the first thing in his queue, but he wasn't sleeping anyway.

Slipping his arm from under Sue's head without waking her, John rose from the bed. Gorshin's eyes glittered in the gathering dusk. The lizard-ape's stare was unremitting; John grabbed one of the ratty blankets and covered Sue. Gorshin didn't bat an eyelid; it continued to watch patiently as he scavenged up his clothes. At least, John guessed that the lizard-ape was patient; its expression remained still and it didn't fidget.

Bennett was sitting on a low rail that ran along the side of one of the machines. He no longer wore his elf-prince garb; instead he was dressed much as he had been when John had first met him: a trench coat over a standard business suit. He even wore his human guise.

Bennett rose as John approached; his nostrils flared once as if taking in a scent. A half smile curled on his lips. "Enjoy yourself?"

What business was it of his? "You wanted to talk to me. I'd assumed it wasn't about my personal business."

"If your business wasn't personal, what would make it your business?"

"I'm not in the mood for your riddles." John didn't like having Bennett here, and wanted him gone. "Didn't you say that you needed me for some sort of pressing problem?"

"There is a danger to someone you know."

"My mother?"

"Marianne Reddy, you mean."

"You know who I mean."

"If she is in danger, I know nothing of it."

"I'm getting tired of this. Why don't you just tell me what you want?"

"First tell me how you came to be in the dwarves' domain."

What did that have to do with anything? "They came here and got me."

"Did they demonstrate that they knew who you were?"

"Wilson knew my name, if that's what you mean."

"This Wilson knew your name, and came here, and just asked, and you went? Voluntarily?"

"He did have a message from Bear, asking me to go with him."

Bennett shook his head. "And you naturally assumed that Artos had really sent him."

"It seemed reasonable."

"After what happened when last you saw him? I think not."

John was surprised at how much Bennett's scorn hurt. What did he care what the damned elf thought? "All right, so I thought it was odd. What difference does it make?"

"Much. And none." Bennett shrugged. "I know that you are woefully undereducated in matters of your heritage, but I had thought you more intelligent."

"Look, let's get one thing straight," John snapped. "I don't care what you think!"

Bennett looked at John out of the corners of his eyes. "Don't you?"

"No."

"Very well, Jack. If you say so."

"What do you care why I went with Wilson? Since when did it matter to you why I did *anything*?"

"I am your father, Jack."

"So you say. It's not what my *mother* says."

"Forget Marianne Reddy. She is no longer a part of your life."

"What do you mean by that?" What did he know?

"I mean that now that you know your true heritage, you have no need to rely on the fiction in which you were reared. Living in the past can be very dangerous, especially to elves. I'd rather not see you fall into that trap."

"Oh? What sort of trap would you want me to fall into? Yours?"

"I am not trying to trap you. But I had begun to fear that the dwarves had. They are not your friends, Jack. They are, in fact, long-standing enemies of our blood. It's always been that way. Remember how they tortured Harry, and put a transmitter on him to follow us to the otherworld?"

That wasn't how John remembered it. "I thought that was Mitsutomo's doing."

"So did Mitsutomo. Oh, to be sure, there were those in the corporation who were willing partners in the venture; but they were dupes, as well. In the end, it was the dwarves who instigated the attempts to kill Artos."

"Don't be ridiculous. The dwarves have an old friendship with Bear. They want to help him."

"You think they were helping him? Not to disparage your facility with electronics, but why do you think that it was so easy for you to rouse Artos, once they weren't around to *help*?"

"Why? What did they have to gain?"

"Caliburn, perhaps."

"But only Bear can use it."

"Don't believe everything you read," Bennett said warningly. "But they need not be able to use the talisman, to desire it. Their purpose might simply be to keep Caliburn from the hands of those who *can* use it. The dwarves are driven in ways you and I will never understand. They are magic-dead; that is a fact. They don't want anyone to have magic."

"Why's that a problem? Lots of people want some things and don't want other things. If they don't want magic, that's okay. They don't have to have any."

"They are not a tolerant folk. They have a tendency to make their problems into other people's problems."

John tried to dismiss Bennett's bigotry with a wave of his hand.

"You can't dismiss the problem so easily," the elf insisted. "The dwarves couldn't have magic if they wanted it. It is a flaw in their kind that has warped their view of the way things should be. They have always striven to keep the magic bottled up. Nothing would make them happier than to see our realm permanently separated from the sunlit world."

"Might not be such a bad idea."

"You're very wrong, Jack. Magic is the hope of the world. Both worlds. The dwarves are too stupid to see the truth."

"Maybe they don't think it is the truth."

"I'm quite sure they don't. However, no amount of thought or desire can change the truth, Jack. Just as no amount of self-delusion can change the fact that they were using you for their own purposes."

"Like nobody's ever done *that* before," John said, staring accusingly at Bennett.

"Jack, I didn't come to get you for selfish reasons."

"I'll just bet."

"I understand your hostility. There's so much you don't understand, and there isn't time right now to explain it all to you."

That riff again. "Will there ever be a right time?"

Bennett ignored his question. "Do you remember that I said there was a danger?"

"So we're finally getting around to what you want. Took you long enough. Just remember something I said—I'm not going to kill anyone for you."

"I am quite content to let you make the decision as to whether there will be any killing." A pause. "Do you recall Dr. Elizabeth Spae?"

Of course he did. She was one of the two foreign secret service agents who had gone with them to the otherworld. She'd been a little standoffish, but okay for an old lady. John had kind of liked her.

"The danger that is loose in the sunlit world threatens her. A thing, a deadly creature, has set its sights on her. She's in danger, and she needs your help."

"Is this a real threat or did you set it up?"

"This abomination is nothing of my doing," Bennett said earnestly.

John believed him; there was a loathing in the elf's tone that was too deep to be faked. "What can I do about it that you can't? Or her, for that matter? Isn't she a mage? I have trouble lighting a candle with magic." Another thought occurred to him. "If you know all about this threat, why don't you go help her yourself?"

"Artos has poisoned her against me. I fear that she will not believe what I tell her."

"I guess some people aren't too stupid to see the truth."

"Your attitude is not helpful, Jack. I had hoped that you would be concerned enough for her to tell her of the danger. She will trust you. She will believe you, and she will accept your help."

"I don't even know what this danger is."

"I will tell you."

"I don't know . . ."

"Are you going to turn aside and allow her to be killed?"

Against John's better judgment, Bennett's "responsibility" trip was getting to him. But there were so many questions. "How do you know about this? How do you know this whatever-it-is is going after Dr. Spae?"

"Will you let her die, knowing that you could have warned her?"

"You didn't answer my questions."

"There may not be enough time to save her if you continue to dither."

There had to be deceit somewhere in what Bennett was doing, but John didn't have enough data even to guess at what. "Why are you doing this?"

"Whether you believe it or not, I like Dr. Spae," Bennett said evenly. "I would not like to see her hurt."

It sounded honest, real. With Bennett momentarily vulnerable, John couldn't resist the shot. "Got a use for her in mind?"

"Jack, I don't use everyone I meet."

"No? I guess you just save your manipulations for family." Bennett looked stern. "Will you warn her?"

"How? I don't have any idea where she is."

"I do."

"Then *you* warn her."

"She won't believe me. Will you let her die?"

Could taking a warning to the doctor be a bad thing? At the very least Bennett would stop pestering him about it. If the threat was real, he might actually save Dr. Spae.

"All right," he said, resolving to tell the doctor exactly where the information came from. He'd let her decide whether or not to believe it.

"You've made a good decision, Jack." The air behind Bennett began to sparkle with a rainbow shine. Bennett held out his hand. "Come. I will take you to her."

"Now?"

"Now. Time grows short. I'll tell you about Quetzal on the way."

John took the offered hand. The tingle of the transition to the otherworld was beginning to feel familiar.

CHAPTER
21

Quetzal floated among the stars, basking in their radiance. They were magnificent in their multitudes, uplifting in their brilliance. Would that he could see them as easily with his bodily eyes as with his astral vision. He hadn't expected that the conditions necessary to the opening of the way would rob him of the stars.

Things would be different after the change.

There were stars below him as well. Not real stars, dimmer than real stars, but sparkling nonetheless. The apparent stars were flickerings of power, signs that magic was loose upon the earth.

Most of the false, earthbound stars marked where some human stood upon the land and touched the cosmic energies. The intensity of the light varied according to how the power was being manipulated as well as the general ability of the individual. The strongest manipulators were always visible, to some degree, to the trained astral eye; mastery of the mysteries marked the master as a beacon does a distant coast.

It was a sparse starscape.

He noted the presence of the local followers. There were other practitioners as well, but Quetzal observed only a single significant point: the mage he'd first sensed as she flew over the ocean. The magical unsophistication of the new age was disappointing; where was the pleasure at being the most accomplished among such a sorry lot?

There were other luminaries among the lamps of the earth. The largest of them marked places of power, convergences of thaumaturgic energy and the etherometric lines. Such places were called *lucernae* by this era's students of the Great Art closest to his own tradition. Quetzal knew the energy loci under many names, preferring some of the others to the Latin name; he would refer to them as *lucernae* from now on, as an exercise in commonality. Commonality was one of Luciferius's favorite magical laws—unsurprising given his love for words; the law stated that the magic of naming and compulsion worked better when those involved shared a language—quite similar to the principle behind True Names and, as he had often argued with Luciferius, possibly making Commonality merely a corollary of *that* law. But this was a time for harmony, not argument; and under Commonality, Quetzal's harmony with the current era would be improved by using Latin. A not insignificant side effect would be an increase in his relative power with regard to the followers— other magicians descended from his tradition as well.

Such considerations were best undertaken at other times; the astral state tended to lead one into a wandering state of mind. He returned his thoughts to his purpose and fell again to observing energies of the astral landscape.

There were minor lights dotting that landscape, dimmer by far than the diffuse regional glows of the *lucernae*. Such lights showed where objects of power reposed. It was one of those objects, a *telesmon*, that he sought in this excursion.

The easiest objects for him to perceive were the resonators. To him, they were the brightest by far of their kind, more visible due to his connection to them. He could not see all of the resonators—even astral vision had its limitations—but all those within his range of sight remained where he had ordered them set. When linked, they would form a glowing web of a theurgic geometry that would be pleasing to the stars.

The gateway.

And *he* had achieved its placement!

Understanding the form was an old achievement for him; he had understood the form for centuries before he'd taken the deep dreaming sleep. Creating the resonators had been a comparatively minor accomplishment. Arranging for their placement had been trivial; the followers of the Path had been prepared by the secret canon and they had been ready to set the devices in place.

But the gateway was worthless without the Key, and *that* remained elusive.

The prophecies claimed that the nature of the Key would be revealed in the time of the Opening. They also said that the Seeker would find without knowing, but in finding would know. Knowing, the Seeker would open the gateway to the Glittering Path.

By all the signs, the time was now.

He would be the Seeker.

The Key was waiting to be found. He sought it, not knowing its form or nature, but holding its purpose in his mind. He must not doubt that he would recognize his prize when he found it.

It, or a clue to its hidden location.

Over and over his attention was drawn to a particular *lucerna* among the scattered places of power. Power gathered to power. He turned his attention to it. The region glowed softly with solid coils of thaumaturgic energy; flashes of activity flickered fitfully across its breadth. Only when he devoted his full attention to the *lucerna* did he perceive that one of its interior sparkles did not fade and did not move. It was not a magician, or a spirit, but a *something* hedged by power.

Could it be what he sought?

He felt compelled to peer beyond the energies enwrapping the *thing*. Cautiously, he examined the compulsion and found that it was not laid upon him in any way he understood.

The starshine warmed him, filling him with preternatural wisdom. Soft, sibilant voices whispered in his head, promising the fulfillment of all his dreams and urging him to act. He understood what he was seeing, knowing it with a clarity usually reserved for things seen under the full light of the sun he could no longer face.

This *lucerna* held a key to the Key.

His unique place in the scheme of things was clear. He was the greatest mage. His was to be the glory.

He *was* the Seeker of the prophecy!

His essence drifted higher toward the loving embrace of the stars.

It would all be his!

Yet there was another nearby who might use the key. Her strength was less than his, but sufficient nonetheless.

The mage who flew.

Below him shimmered the spark that was she.

Did she know how close they were to the time of the Opening? Was she aware of him and his intentions? He did not sense the aura of the opposition about her, but she need not be one of them to oppose him. Unaligned forces had ruined his plans before. And obtaining the key to the Key might expose him. He could not afford to act without knowing her side in the great struggle, because she was close enough to present a danger were she to operate against him.

On the other hand, if she was truly unaligned, she might be convinced to join him. Her power would be useful. Not necessary, of course, but useful.

And if she offered a threat, he would dispose of her. He was stronger now, more awake. He was confident that she would fall before him if they dueled.

He returned to his fleshly shell, eager to take the next steps on destiny's road.

Spae was tired, having spent a long day studying the readouts from the machines monitoring the Settawego Building and trying to match the data with her own impressions. There were still half a dozen output files to get through, but she decided that she had probably done enough for the day. She picked at the remains of her room service meal, deciding that she had definitely had enough of it. She sat back and looked around her.

The room Mr. Ryder had arranged for her in the Hartford Nikko was much fancier than the one where she and David had spent their first night together. It was actually a suite, with four bedrooms and a common area, that occupied one whole floor of the hotel's northwest tower. Two of the bedrooms were unoccupied. Three, actually, with David off at some editorial meeting; not that he slept there anyway. The suite was more spacious than her cottage in Chardonneville. She was sure the rental fee was outrageous and was glad that the suite was part of the "expenses" in her arrangement with LRP and Associates.

But while well-appointed, spacious, and comfortable, it lacked something, as all hotel rooms seemed to. She felt an emptiness about it. And not just because David was out. Hotels always gave her the feeling that she was on display.

It was vaguely like the feeling she'd gotten in her last weeks at Chardonneville.

Which made her feel even less like getting back to work.

She went to her room and took a long, hot shower. Feeling better, she pulled on her new nightshirt—one of David's T-shirts—and wandered back into the common room, intending to wait up for him. She considered calling up some entertainment on the room's perscomp and decided against it. Quiet had its virtues. She stretched out on the couch, thinking she'd give some thought to her future, but couldn't manage to keep her thoughts on any one track. She must be more tired than she thought. To hell with it; there was always tomorrow to worry. She needed rest. She let herself go and was soon drowsily drifting into sleep. She really did need some rest.

She really did need . . .

She really . . .

She . . .

She opened her eyes to find a man standing before her. He was tall, with coal-dark skin and snowy hair. Although his skin was unlined and shone with youth, his eyes were old with wisdom. Those eyes told her he was a wizard.

Recognizing that, she saw that he was dressed as the Hierophant. Long robes swathed his body, draping elegantly from his raised right arm, which he held as if preparing to give her a benediction. In his other hand he held a crosier glittering with gems and shining with power. A multitiered crown sat on his head, but unlike the crown in her tarot deck, made of gold and gems, his was of iridescent feathers that sprouted in three tiers from a band of jade, tourmaline, and turquoise.

In the distance behind him, a flickering image caught her attention. Faintly she could see a pale outline running toward her. "David," she called—but it wasn't David; David was not so pale. The Hierophant stood between her and the pale man; she tried to see past him, tried to see who the pale man was since he wasn't David. For a moment, the Hierophant vanished and the pale man stood before her. With a courtly bow, he offered her a cup. She reached out to take it, but when she closed her hand upon the stem, there was nothing there. The pale man frowned and turned upside down. Although he appeared to be running in her direction, he got farther away rather than closer.

The Hierophant returned to stand before her, flat as his pasteboard representation. No. It couldn't be. She could feel the power cloaking the man; he was real. With that, the Hierophant's robes and accoutrements dissolved away, paper eaten by a sudden fire. Behind the facade was a more believable image, a gaunt, white-haired Black man in an elegant Italian silk suit. Despite his appearance of African ancestry, there was something in his face that made her think of Central America.

The Black wizard floated serenely in the air outside the window of the common room.

Floating outside the window?

"*Iacé,*" he commanded.

She shouldn't have been able to hear him through the window, but she did. She shouldn't have been able to see him either; she had closed the curtains before lying down on the couch. It had to be a dream. To prove it, she opened her eyes—just as the curtains finished parting.

The man *was* floating in the air outside her window.

Not a dream.

If it wasn't a dream, she should be able to leap up as she wanted to; but she couldn't move. The wizard's command to lie still had force to hold her.

With an audible snap, a pock appeared in the surface of the window. Spidery cracks radiated out from it, tracing a mad grid of jittery lines across the pane. Pieces of window began to fall, but not just down. Some moved to the sides, some straight up along the plane of the window. The shards moved in slow motion, but not far, until the opening was big enough for him to pass through. Chill air and the sounds of the outside world intruded on the suite.

The man floated to the sill and settled there. With finicky grace, he stepped down into the room. Behind him, the shattered fragments of the window crawled back together, fusing into a whole again.

He walked across the room and stood looking down at her. Spae wanted to writhe under his intense stare. Feeling like the proverbial bird under the stare of the serpent, she found that she couldn't even look away. Her mind seemed as paralyzed as her body. Time crawled by. At last, he spoke.

"Do you know the Glittering Path?"

Glittering Path? The name was vaguely familiar. Hadn't there been an American insurgency movement called that? This man—this wizard—was not the insurgent type. He must be referring to something else, most likely something arcane. Her brain raced, skidding to a halt when she remembered an incomplete grimoire known as *Callis Luxorum Dubiaria*.

"*Dicé*," he commanded.

She heard herself say, "*Callis Luxorum Dubiaria?*"

He gave the sort of nod a person does upon having suspicions confirmed. "So you know Luciferius."

"I've read the *Callis*," she admitted. Of the author, clearly pseudonymous, she had no knowledge.

"And do you believe the words of Luciferius?"

"There are a lot of symbols I don't understand." Actually, the writing was just plain confused. "It's not all there." Luciferius had promised that all would be revealed in his third volume. "The third book is missing."

"Luciferius never wrote the third book," the man said matter-of-factly. "Tell me, do you see that the time he wrote of, the time of the man-blight, is upon the world?"

True, the world wasn't in the best of shapes. True, a lot of it was mankind's fault, what with urban sprawl, deforestation, and continued pollution. But Luciferius's apocalyptic man-blight? Well . . . maybe.

The mage smiled. "Yes, I see that you do. Is that why you study the Great Art?"

She hadn't thought about *why* for years. The Art was everything to her; that was just the way she was. She couldn't *not* study it.

"Do you hate the blight?" he asked. "Do you wish to heal the world?"

Hate the blight? Who wouldn't? But heal it? She hadn't thought about things in that light. Sure, the world was in awful shape, but what was one person supposed to do about it?

"I hadn't thought about it that way," she said.

"And if you saw a way to stop the blight? What would you do? *Cogitá et dicè.*"

There was a lot to be considered, but there really wasn't much of a decision. If there was something she could do to materially improve the state of the world, or to stop or even to slow its deterioration, she'd do it. Who wouldn't?

"So," the man said, frowning at her. "We are to be enemies."

Suddenly she felt icy claws ripping at her brain. She screamed. Breaking the paralysis that had held her, she scrunched into a fetal ball. Screaming.

The claws dug for her, shredding Spae the consultant, ripping through Spae the thaumaturgic doctor, tearing toward Spae the magician, trying to reach her innermost self.

"No!" she pleaded.

The Hierophant bent over her. His claws tore jagged rents in the robes of the Queen of Pentacles. The Queen was knocked from her throne, and the throne shattered, causing the creatures of the woodland around her to flee for their lives. Her crown rolled away in the mud.

The Hierophant's crosier metamorphosed into a pair of black iron manacles connected by a length of gleaming chain. He opened the fetters.

"No!" she screamed, understanding at last what he was doing to her. "NO!"

Knowledge became her power.

A golden disk emblazoned with the pentacle appeared between her and the Hierophant. He balked. She struck out in a frenzy, slapping the manacles away.

The iron links writhed like a serpent as they struck the ground. Angry orange rust spread along their length. All around them, the woodland creatures peered from their hiding places to watch the thrashing fetters. The Queen of Pentacles rose from the mud to stand tall again.

"*Abitá*," she said.

The manacles crumbled into flakes of rust. The Hierophant was gone, but the Black wizard remained. He glared at her.

"If I cannot possess you, I must destroy you."

Her world became fire.

CHAPTER
22

John and Bennett emerged from the otherworld in the small parklike promenade. Despite all the greenery around them and the pond before them, they were not at ground level; John could tell that from looking at the neighboring buildings. They stood in a multiacre park bounded by yard-high concrete walls. In front of them, four towers rose into the sky. A smaller, glassed-in structure stood in the center of the square demarked by the towers. Through the windows of the central building, John could see a lounge or lobby of some kind and the top of an escalator system. The whole arrangement was a little disorienting; they'd been on the crest of a small hill in the otherworld.

The towers and lobby arrangement were, he supposed, their destination, the Hartford Nikko Hotel.

"The northwest tower," said Bennett, pointing out the one he meant.

There was an elevator car ascending through the tube on the lobby side of the tower. The bottom of the tube joined an enclosed gallery connecting the tower and the glassed-in structure containing the lobby. There was a door to the garden in the gallery. Bennett led him toward it.

"The elevator opens directly to the common room of her suite on 42," Bennett said as they entered the gallery; it was deserted, not surprising given the hour. "The access code is 42 pause 7723. Not very imaginative. 42—S-P-A-E."

"How do you know the code?"

"I have connections." Bennett pointed at the elevator. "Hurry, there's little time."

That had been Bennett's refrain for the entire trip here. John punched the call button and turned to try—once more—to convince Bennett to come along. The elf was gone, vanished.

Leaving John to do the dirty work?

The door—a transparent cylinder operating within the transparent cylinder sandwich of the car—rotated open, and John entered the car.

"Welcome to the Nikko," it said in a pleasant, feminine voice. "What floor do you wish to visit, please?"

"Forty-two."

"I'm sorry," it said with no real emotion. The door cylinder rotated shut, sealing him in a glass jar. "There is no visitor acceptance on file for forty-two. Please state your name and the name of the guest you wish to visit and I will confer with the desk."

And call the cops, too, he expected. There was probably an intruder light flashing in the security office already. John didn't really want to meet hotel security, and he wasn't about to state his name. He punched the "open door" button without effect. No good. He punched Bennett's code into the control panel, hoping it would override the expert system controlling the elevator.

"Thank you," the elevator said.

John was thankful himself, thankful that whoever had designed the Nikko software hadn't been a paranoid.

The car rose slowly. His first thought was that he hadn't fooled it after all and it was just going slowly to give security time to get ready for him, but then he remembered that the car had been moving slowly when he'd seen it from the outside. To give the guests a good view of the city, he supposed. It was too slow for him; he wanted to get this over with. After an interminable time, the elevator announced, "Forty-two."

The building side of the car was a mirror, reflecting the sky and cityscape behind him and giving a momentary sense of floating in space. The mirror parted as the car's door cylinder began to rotate open, revealing an entryway.

John heard the screaming at once.

He shoved at the cylinder, trying to make it open faster.

It jammed.

He shoved harder, but it didn't give. There was only a narrow opening, but he pressed himself through it. It was a tight scrape but he squeezed through, thankful that he was so slim.

When he saw what was going on in the suite, he had second thoughts about being thankful.

It was Dr. Spae's suite, all right. She was here, writhing on the floor. She was the one doing the screaming.

Standing above Dr. Spae like some kind of human vulture was a tall guy in a weird robe. The robe looked as if it was made of translucent feathers, strengthening the vulture image. Rustling dryly with every move the guy made, the robe draped from his shoulders to the floor, flaring out in a circle that shadowed the doctor. Not that he moved much; he seemed intent on Dr. Spae's struggles.

"Hey!" John yelled. "Let her go!"

The vulture man raised his head and looked in John's direction. His face was a serene and vacant mask of gold, its placidity totally alien to the violent emotions roiling through the room. The man said nothing and returned his attention to Dr. Spae, apparently dismissing John's presence as irrelevant.

John didn't care to be dismissed. The guy was tall, but not as tall as John. He had a little weight on John, maybe, but he was standing still. John charged forward, planning on knocking the guy away from the doctor.

He hit what felt like a wall. But it was a wall with teeth; his nerves screamed as he hit, for a moment adding his anguish to the emotions flooding the room. The next thing he knew he was sitting on the floor, ten feet away.

Some kind of magic jolt.

If John had been a mage, he could have tossed a fireball or fried Dr. Spae's attacker with a lightning bolt. Really taken care of the guy. But John didn't have real power despite what the elven knight had said, and even if the knight had been right about John's being able to do magic, John wasn't trained; he didn't know any spells.

John had to do something. Distract the guy at least. Then maybe he could get past the wall, or Dr. Spae could help herself, or something. If Bennett had been here, he could have done something. Even the elven knight could have—

Magic! The knight! The knight had shown him how to make a flame. It wasn't much, but it could be a distraction. The vulture guy's robe looked awfully flammable. It would be a distraction. In that moment when he'd been in contact with the doctor's attacker, John had sensed that Dr. Spae was fighting him. A distraction might buy her a chance.

John tried to remember what the knight had told him. It wasn't hard; he had repeated the scene many times in his mind since he'd returned from his first trip to the otherworld. He hadn't had much success in conjuring a flame before, but there was magic here. Maybe here—

He pictured the flame. Felt the heat. Smelled the burning. That part was easy, the room already smelled scorched. Light, heat, odor. *Flame.*

There was fire.

John pictured it nibbling on the edge of the vulture man's feathers. The tiny flame nearly died.

No!

Fire! Burn! Eat the cloak!

The flame rallied, growing. With a startling suddenness, it flared, engulfing the feathered cloak. The vulture man howled.

He sounded more surprised and angry than hurt.

The feathered robe was gone. The golden mask, too. Vanished. But the vulture man was still there, only he wasn't a vulture man anymore. He was a Black guy in a slick suit who fitted Bennett's description of Quetzal, the guy John was supposed to be warning Dr. Spae against. John couldn't imagine it was a coincidence.

Quetzal looked pissed.

It was one thing to jump from the pan into the fire, but when you'd set the fire yourself . . .

John felt more than a little queasy with Quetzal looking in his direction. This time there was no dismissal of his presence. Quetzal came toward him.

"What do you want, meddler? Who are you?"

John didn't want to give the guy his name. He kept his mouth shut.

Quetzal reached down and grabbed John's shoulder. It was a light grip, but it kept him from scuttling away as he wanted to. Quetzal's hand might have been hot iron, the way it burned. John could only squirm under its heat.

"How do you hide from my sight?" Quetzal demanded.

What was the guy talking about? It was plain he could see John.

"*Dicé,*" Quetzal said commandingly.

John didn't want to talk, but he could see Dr. Spae starting to gather herself back together. He had to buy her time; she was their only chance. If he could keep Quetzal talking, the guy might forget about the doctor until it was too late.

"Hey, I'm not hiding. I'm right here."

Pain shocked through John.

Quetzal sneered at him. "I am in no mood for insolence. Speak, and I may only make you a slave."

"Maybe I'd rather take another option," John said. He thought he was ready for the pain this time, but it still took his breath away and left him sobbing.

"I would call you a fool, if I did not know you were hiding something. Perhaps you *are* a fool. I intend to know."

The pain stabbed into John's brain this time.

Before he could scream, it was gone. Gone, too, was the burning in his shoulder. Quetzal had released his physical grip. John could move, but only slowly and with great effort.

"A soulless one!" the mage exclaimed with loathing. "What brings you into this, elf?"

Without the subtle mental push to cooperate, John wasn't about to tell Quetzal anything. At least not anything useful. But he needed to keep the guy's attention; Dr. Spae still wasn't up.

Quetzal seemed to know he was an elf. Maybe he could use that.

"We order you to leave Dr. Spae alone!"

"Order?' Quetzal laughed.

Well, that *wasn't it.*

The mage reached for him again. The memory of the pain gave John the strength to shift to his left. The movement surprised Quetzal. He hesitated. When he did, the thick, heavy air around John relaxed. John surged against it, gaining his knees. His shoulder drove into Quetzal's hip. The mage stumbled back a step and fell, landing hard.

John got to his feet, wanting to run, but knowing there was no place to go.

Quetzal rose, rage in his eyes. Energy crackled around him, sparking in tongues of flame around his hands.

John swallowed hard.

Wrong move again.

"Hey, shithead!" Dr. Spae shouted at Quetzal. She was finally on her feet. She held her walking stick like a quarterstaff; the metal ends sparked blue lightning like static generators. "I'm not half-asleep now."

She raised her staff as Quetzal turned to her.

The lightning crackled from the ends of her staff, joining into a single bolt that arced toward Quetzal. He raised his hand defensively as the bolt struck. A flash! A thunderous crack boomed. John smelled ozone.

When John could see again, the dark-skinned mage was running for the window. The pane shattered outward as he neared it. He leaped to the sill and turned to face them.

"I have marked you," he screamed as he stepped into the air. "I have marked you both!"

"Mark this!" Dr. Spae yelled back at him.

Another bolt leaped toward him. Again the flash dazzled John, and the thunder assaulted his ears. This time, when he could see again, Quetzal was gone.

Dr. Spae approached the window cautiously, peering up and down and to both sides before stepping close. She repeated the scan when she reached the sill.

"He's gone," she announced.

John joined her at the window. He looked down. There was no body sprawled in the garden below. Had she vaporized Quetzal? John wasn't about to ask.

Dr. Spae was shivering; not surprising given the cold air and the light weight of her nightshirt. She left the window and went into the kitchenette. From one of the cabinets she took a bottle of liquor, and from another, a pair of glasses. The glasses rang in her hands. The doctor tried to pour herself a drink, but her hands were shaking too hard; she poured most of the liquid onto the counter.

John took the bottle from her and poured an inch or so into one of the glasses.

"What the hell are you doing here, Reddy?" she asked.

Handing her the glass, he said, "I came to warn you about Quetzal."

"You're a little late."

"Maybe you'd rather I never showed up."

She drained her glass and held it out for him to refill. "How the hell did you find out about him?"

"Bennett told me."

"Bennett, huh?"

He nodded.

"Something tells me that we've got a lot of catching up to do."

CHAPTER
23

Going after the mage Spae had been a mistake. Had he left her alone, he would not have suffered such an ignominy. But retreat had been wise. For truth, in the light of intervention by the soulless ones, retreat was the only prudent course at the time.

At least neither the mage nor the elf knew of his immediate intentions. He knew for a certainty now that Spae's sympathies lay with the opposition, though she was not a sworn member of that fraternity. Her enmity would be a matter to deal with at another time; he could hope that she would not strike before the Path was opened. If she waited until then, he would deal with her as a handful of sand blown to the wind.

The soulless one was another matter, a deeper and more disturbing puzzle. Normally he would have noticed an elf of such power, but he hadn't. How had that come to pass? He had been unaware of the elf's approach until it was almost upon him, and when it first appeared, he had thought the soulless one to be a human, and a powerless one at that. How had it hidden its nature from him?

A question to ponder.

He arranged the brazier, lighting the fire with a thought. He cast frankincense into the dish. The aroma rose to fill the room, a pure, heady scent. He added the rest of the herbs and sat in the great chair, sinking into its leathery embrace.

He was roused briefly from his trance to silence the computer's complaints about the smoke, ordering it to disable the fire sensors and to cease disturbing him. He could not fail to notice if the building were threatened by fire.

Thus he was unaware of the intruders until they entered his sanctum. Then, for truth, he knew them at once.

"Nakaguchi." He swiveled the chair to face them. "And Bwaatu. Van Dieman said that you belonged to the Asian."

"I am loyal to the Circle," Bwaatu protested. "Van Dieman is a font of lies. Having fallen under your sway, he no longer walks the true Path."

Bwaatu's skin was as dark as Quetzal's own, but there the resemblance ended. Bwaatu was a pawn. Quetzal gave his attention to Nakaguchi.

"I hadn't expected you to have the skill to find me."

"A subcutaneous transmitter," the Asian said. "It was placed beneath your skin during one of the medical examinations."

"Ah, that. I was wondering what its purpose was."

"You knew about it?"

"Of course. How could I not know that you had placed something within me? For truth, you do not understand the measure of difference between me and all you have known."

"And you fail to understand the nature of the age into which you have come," the Asian retorted. "I could as easily have had a bomb implanted. Perhaps I should have."

"It would have availed you nothing. I would have recognized the threat and countered it."

"You did not counter the threat of the tracer."

"It was no threat."

"That's where you are wrong, Quetzal."

Quetzal did not care for the Asian's familiarity; he understood what motivated it too well. "I see no threat."

"No?" Nakaguchi reached under his jacket with his left hand and withdrew a small black pistol.

The time had come to end the farce.

"By your vows, I bind you," Quetzal said, the command of Art in his voice. "By your oaths, I still your hand. The Circle encompasses you. The Circle binds you. Once, twice, and thrice, you are bound. Your bodies are as stone. Move not."

Nakaguchi and Bwaatu struggled, internally as well as externally, but they were bound. As they realized their situation, their struggles ceased. Bwaatu's eyes were wide with the knowledge of what happens to the faithful who lose their faith. Nakaguchi remained defiant.

"You should have bound our tongues as well," the Asian said. "*Tasukeru!*"

The Asian's shout for assistance brought two men to the door. Soldiers. They wore the armor of the modern age, ballistic corselets and dark-visored helmets of composite plastics. Each man had a military grade assault rifle pointed at Quetzal; he felt the touch of their laser sights upon his chest.

"They are neither followers nor members of the Circle," Nakaguchi told him. "They have protections. You will not bind them easily, and before you succeed, you will be dead."

"So you think to kill me."

"You are too dangerous."

"In that, you are correct." But, unlike Nakaguchi, not always in the obvious ways. "Should you succeed in killing me, who will open the Path? None among the followers, yourself included, has the knowledge or the skill or the power."

"There are others still waiting to wake."

The Asian was confident despite his magical bonds. Overconfident. "You may find them less pleasant than I."

"At this point, I see no other alternative. I think that one among them will better understand the problems we face. In the future, the education will be better structured to render a more tractable mage. I will not make the same mistake twice. You've come to the end of your long road, Quetzal."

"In that, you are mistaken."

Nakaguchi sensed something of the shift in his position. His voice sharp, he asked, "What do you mean?"

"Kurita," was all Quetzal felt the need to say.

The security man had arrived undetected. He struck mercilessly.

The first soldier received Kurita's foot in his back. He slammed into one of the tables, doubling over. The second reacted, but too slowly. As he turned, Kurita swept away the muzzle of his weapon with one hand and slammed the other against the man's chest. The blow stunned him. Kurita knocked the soldier's feet from under him, knelt, and drove three rapid blows into his chest. The soldier lay near death; Quetzal could sense the irregular beat of his heart.

Kurita turned his attention to the first soldier. The man was still dazed from his collision with the furniture. He offered almost no resistance as Kurita threw him to the floor and dealt with him as he had with the other.

But with Quetzal's attention focused on his servant's display of martial prowess, Nakaguchi had taken his chance and slipped free of the mystic bonds, proving himself stronger than Quetzal had given him credit for. He proved himself stupider at the same time; he turned to face Kurita.

"Kurita," Quetzal said warningly.

The security man looked up and immediately started for his former master.

Nakaguchi didn't give him a chance. He fired his weapon, shooting Kurita in the gut.

Bad choice or bad aim? Nakaguchi was not using his primary arm, so it could conceivably have been the latter. He should have known better.

Kurita was made of stern stuff, stern enough to finish Nakaguchi even after such a wound. Even so, Quetzal extended strength to his servant. He had underestimated Nakaguchi once already tonight; he was not about to do so again.

Nakaguchi fired again. Kurita took the shot and kept coming. Panicking, Nakaguchi fired three shots in quick succession. Like a fool, he continued to target the torso. One of his shots missed all the same.

Kurita began to weave, but came on.

Finally, Nakaguchi raised his aim. Unfortunately for him, his shot missed. Kurita was nearly close enough to launch a kick, and shifted his weight to do so.

Nakaguchi's next shot blew away Kurita's jaw. The following shot entered his left eye.

There was no more that Quetzal could do to keep the man moving.

Kurita collapsed at Nakaguchi's feet.

Nakaguchi's shoulders slumped in relief. He took a deep breath before turning to point the gun at Quetzal.

"Your turn," he said, and pulled the trigger.

Nothing happened.

He looked down to see what Quetzal had already seen. The slide of his semi-automatic pistol was cocked back; there were no more shells in the clip. Nakaguchi had been too rattled to notice that he had expended all of his ammunition.

Quetzal laughed at him.

"Not *my* turn." He stood and stepped up to the Asian, taking him by the throat. "Yours."

"You can't," Nakaguchi protested. "I am a follower of the Path!"

"Ever faithful?"

"I bow before the Wyrm."

"For which you expect reward?"

The goggle-eyed Asian tried to nod.

"Fool! I know you. You never understood me or your place. Your protection was never more than what I wished to grant."

Quetzal drank Nakaguchi's life and let the husk fall to the floor.

Bwontu, the pawn, had remained bound through the whole vignette. He found his voice at the last and used it to beg for mercy as Quetzal drained him. He took the soldiers, too. This situation had been dealt with; it was time to get on to important things.

CHAPTER
24

"Nakaguchi's dead," Hagen said.

There was no hint of emotion in the dwarf's voice, no trace of victory in his face that Pamela could see. She allowed herself a brief smile. And why not? She was free of the *kansayaku* and his interference at last. However, it was not yet time to celebrate; his demise probably only meant a change in her problems, not the end of them. "And the creature?"

"Still free."

And still one of her problems. "The transmitter?"

"Dead as Nakaguchi."

"Was the thing any more discreet than when it left Settawego?"

"Considerably. It made no public display of its power. However, we do have five corpses."

"Five?"

"It appears that Kurita was present for the confrontation."

One less problem. "What happened?"

"It appears that Nakaguchi gunned down his former security chief. Quetzal killed the others." Hagen shook his head. "The details are scanty. The damage control party from Rela-

312

tions is already working with the police. Given the location—not a Keiretsu property—and the clear evidence of hostility between two Keiretsu members we have the basis for a plausible story of intercorporation rivalry and subversion. It seems that Mr. Kurita was seduced by an unknown rival corporation and tasked with eliminating his former master. He sought to poison Mr. Nakaguchi; the others died to conceal the specific target. Unfortunately for Kurita, Nakaguchi did not die until he had taken his revenge." Hagen shrugged. "It's not an airtight story, but it should be sufficient. We may get some tabloid exposure, but it looks as if we will be able to keep Special Investigations out of it."

Hagen's arrangement of the cover-up was commendable, but he had taken a lot for granted. He should have told her of the strategy earlier. This was too delicate a situation for her not to know exactly what was happening when it was happening. Most likely she would have proceeded as he had, but perhaps not. The whole mess surrounding Quetzal had alerted her that her previous course of action might no longer be valid. It might be time for new solutions.

"Perhaps we should not keep the police out of it. We could let them deal with the monster."

Hagen looked at her sternly. "That would not be wise."

Once, she would have agreed wholeheartedly. Now, she wanted to hear his reasons. "Explain."

"Firstly, they would learn of Quetzal's nature if they deal with it. I cannot believe that someone among the police has not already starting linking together some of Quetzal's other killings. If nothing else, they would surely recognize that Nakaguchi and the others did not die of poison and become suspicious.

"Secondly, they would learn of Mitsutomo's role in unleashing the monster. The tabloid publicity for a sensational multiple murder is unfortunate; the revelation that the Keiretsu has unearthed and unleashed a monster would be disastrous."

"But it wasn't the Keiretsu who unleashed the monster; it was Nakaguchi."

"That would be difficult to prove. Even if it is established, there would be those who would not believe the Keiretsu was not responsible."

"There are always those ready to believe the worst about Mitsutomo, or any corporation, for that matter. We have dealt successfully with their kind in the past."

"Times are changing."

"Indeed they are, Mr. Hagen. New times demand new solutions. I find myself wondering about your approach to this problem, noting—as I must—the order in which you state your objections to involving the police. You do not place the health of the Keiretsu *first* in your thinking."

Hagen sat back, eyes narrowing as he looked at her. She had just changed the focus of their conversation. She let him have some time to consider the implications. She wanted to see which way he would jump.

At length he said, "Ms. Martinez, you already know that my primary loyalties lie elsewhere. I hope you understand that this does not make me, in any way, stand in opposition to the Keiretsu and its interests in this matter. Your Charybdis Project has had admirable success in confining and suppressing the instrusions of things unnatural. I see no reasons to alter the policies that you have endorsed, and many reasons to maintain them. This is not the time to go public; publicity would only inhibit the further success of Charybdis."

"Nakaguchi has already altered Charybdis," she pointed out.

"Nakaguchi is gone. You are in charge again."

"Exactly, Mr. Hagen."

He met her gaze. "I see."

"I hope so, Mr. Hagen."

"What is it you wish done?"

"I believe that we need to cut our losses. We need to minimize the Keiretsu's exposure in this affair, but the monster must be eliminated. Given the proper spin on the backstory, I believe we can disassociate the Keiretsu from responsibility for the monster and dump this problem on the police."

"If that is the way you wish to deal with it, I cannot stop you."

"That is the way I wish to deal with it, Mr. Hagen."

Hagen nodded slowly. "In that case, I have a suggestion that may minimize the damage."

She liked this dwarf much better than Sörli. He was more manageable. She listened with interest to his suggestion.

Charley broke his usual pattern of reading his morning E-mail by going straight to the anonymous transmitters. He'd had a feeling he'd have one from Caspar waiting, and he was right.

>>21.10.19 * 13.02.13.79 * xxxxx.xxx
LOG #1019.49
TO: GordonC@NECPOLNET*0004.13.00*874334
FROM:<UNKNOWN>
RE: Modus 112.
MESSAGE:
Add crime file 33*1018*F103

He asked the computer to pull the file and got, "Stored as preliminary report only."

"Pull it anyway," he ordered. Being a detective had some privileges; when he was a street cop, he would have had to wait until the final was filed.

He added the file to the 112 dossier, scanning it as it went through on fast feed. One of the flashing datapics caught his eye. He froze the scan and backed it up. The morgue pic showed a Japanese who had died shit-faced scared. There was something about the guy that was familiar, but from where?

The prelim listed the guy's name as Ryota Nakaguchi and his corp as Mitsutomo. He was from the home office according to the lapel pin listed in the property section of the prelim. The report said he was a junior level exec, but that didn't seem right.

Charley scanned the property list more closely. All quality stuff, expensive stuff. Too fancy for a junior suit. Nakaguchi wasn't what the prelim said he was.

How come the investigating officers hadn't caught that?

While Charley was pondering that, Manny came into the cubicle they shared. He made a sour face at his empty coffee mug. "You're slacking off, Gordon."

"Johnston didn't have the pot on when I got here," Charley lied. He was trying to remember where he'd seen Nakaguchi's face before, and didn't want to argue about coffee.

"Sure, blame your sins on someone else. You want some?"

"Okay." What he *wanted* was to know who Nakaguchi really was.

As Manny left, Charley's memory flashed him a vision of Nakaguchi's face—not hardened into a rictus of fear, but stony and self-important. Same suit, same pin. There was a Mitsutomo logo behind his head.

That logo was in the lobby of the Settawego Building, and Nakaguchi had been the guy who'd come out of the elevator behind Pamela Martinez the day that Caspar had sent Charley to the Settawego Building. The late Mr. Nakaguchi was not a junior suit at all, if he ranked the head of Mitsutomo NAG.

So who was he?

A simple request to Mitsutomo public relations got him an answer that fit Nakaguchi's position in that elevator. According to public record, Ryota Nakaguchi was a *kansayaku*, an auditor, currently on assignment to Mitsutomo North American Group. *Kansayaku* was a fancy *Nihongo* name for a corporate hatchet man. Not a junior position at all.

Heart failure, huh? Nakaguchi was the kind of guy who *gave* heart attacks.

Either the corp PR hacks had gotten overconfident or Charley had managed to slip in before they'd finished painting over the stain.

Manny brought the coffee and Charley did the usual chatty partner things, but his mind was on Nakaguchi, his connection to Modus 112, and the *kansayaku*'s sudden death. "Hey, Manny, you know anybody down in thirty-three?"

"Thirty-three?" Manny had to think about it. "Yeah. I know somebody down there."

"Put me onto him, will you?"

"You're not gonna get us in trouble again?"

"Nah. I just got a question on a report from down there."

"What's up?"

"Tell you if it turns out to be anything."

Manny's somebody was able to put Charley onto somebody else who knew somebody else who got Ramierez onto the line. Ramierez was investigating officer on 33*1018*F103. He wasn't happy to find out that Charley was from SIU.

"What do you want, Mr. Spook? Ain't no need for ya to come messing around in this."

Charley tried to keep it friendly. "I just read your prelim and I thought it looked kind of odd, you know. Four heart cases and not a one over forty."

"Look, this ain't none of your business."

"Sounds pretty special to me."

"We got it covered."

One more try. "I just thought you might need some help."

Ramierez's face scrunched together like he'd just been told his wife was screwing around. "How much ya want?"

Now the misidentification of Nakaguchi made sense; there was a cover-up in progress. "Look, I was just wondering if there might be a connection between this multiple and something I'm working on. I'm not looking for a piece of anything that might be floating around. Just trying to do some police work."

"We ain't got nothing spooky here, got it? We got us a bunch of nuts been playing rough with each other and too dumb to do it on their own turf. Corp wants it shut up, is all. There's not a lot in this, so don't get greedy."

Charley wasn't looking for a piece of the hush money. "Forget it."

Ramierez got suspicious. "What's your angle, Gordon? I swear, if you're with Internal Affairs, I'll eat your guts for supper."

"Relax, Ramierez. I'm not IA, and I'm not doing them a favor. I'm just doing my job. Do me a favor and send me a copy of the final report."

"Pull it yourself," Ramierez said, and cut the connection.

Fine. Charley set the computer to pull a copy.

Corp cover-up, huh? Made sense for a junior involved in some messy stuff, but Mr. Junior Suit Nakaguchi wasn't really a junior. There had to be more to this than a simple corp shadow affair.

He wondered what Pamela Martinez would have to say about her auditor turning up dead in District 33. Or was she the one arranging the cover-up?

The comp buzzed with an incoming call. He checked the caller ID. There was definitely something spooky going on, because the computer said that the caller was Pamela Martinez.

It was the sort of thing that could make a person believe in magic.

CHAPTER
25

A guy named David Beryle showed up, all worried and anxious, about an hour after the brawl with Quetzal. When Beryle first got out of the elevator John thought that he might be Dr. Spae's partner, like Holger Kun had been, but her greeting made it plain that she was involved with the guy. For a few awkward minutes, John was left standing there feeling more than a little embarrassed.

At least he and Sue had done their clinging in private.

After breaking their clinch, Beryle insisted on being told everything about the incident with Quetzal. John had never met this guy before and wasn't sure he liked him, but Dr. Spae seemed to trust him; she certainly didn't hold anything back from him. John went along, telling them about how the warning bit was Bennett's idea. When Dr. Spae started asking detailed questions to try and figure out what had been going on between John and Quetzal, Beryle bowed out of the conversation, claiming he was going to bed.

Shortly thereafter, Spae's questioning veered off into the "catching up" she'd said they had to do. Their talking took them well into the night. Before disappearing into her room—

the same one Beryle had entered hours ago—she pointed John
at one of the suite's other bedrooms.

The room was luxurious by his current standards, even by
his old standards, but it was a cold bed. He should have been
elsewhere, but knew he didn't have any way to get back to the
slump before morning. Maybe he could have gotten back if he
had been able to enter the otherworld by himself and whistle
up an elven steed, but that was a trick Bennett kept to himself.

In the morning the doctor insisted on seeing Bear right
away. She wanted to see Bennett, too. John couldn't do anything about the second—she'd see Bennett if Bennett wanted
to be seen. He could, however, take her to see Bear, despite
some misgivings about her working for the ECSS—for
which, naturally, she said she no longer worked. He decided
to take her; he wasn't sure he was going to be able to get Bear
straightened out and living in the twenty-first century by himself, and he didn't know anyone else to turn to.

When Beryle heard the doctor's decision, he jumped in
with both feet.

"So when do we leave?" he asked.

John frowned at him. He didn't care for the way Beryle just
assumed he'd be going along to see Bear. "We?"

"Yeah. When do we leave?"

"It was the doctor I asked," John said.

"If she's going, I'm going," Beryle announced.

The doctor didn't agree or disagree; she just watched John,
a neutral expression on her face. What was he supposed to
say? He was already committed to taking Dr. Spae back to the
slump. Was this some sort of test?

"That true, Doctor?"

"I think it would be a good idea," she said. "I'd be more
comfortable."

"Fine," Beryle said as if that had settled everything. "I'll
rent a car."

John had assumed they'd take pub tranz. "And what are
you going to do with it when we get there?"

"Is the parking bad?"

Beryle was clearly not as slick as Kun; the doctor's previous associate would have gotten the message right off. "Not too many rental cars around there."

"I think it's the neighborhood that's bad, David," the doctor said.

Beryle nodded. "I'll arrange something that won't attract too much attention."

John decided that maybe Beryle wasn't a total loss when he saw the junker that the guy had gotten for the trip. The vintage Hernando™ was all mismatched paint and bare Meshglaz™ patches; John had seen lots of its relatives near the slump. Somehow Beryle had even been lucky enough to get one with Rhode Island plates.

Or had it been luck? The ECSS had connections in the States; John had learned that from Kun.

It took three hours to drive the distance that John and Bennett had covered in less than an hour on elven steeds. Beryle parked where John directed, and grumbled about it for the last three of the four blocks of their walk to the factory. John ignored his complaints; the Hernando might look like it belonged in the neighborhood, but he still didn't want it parked in front of his slump.

Faye met them at the loading dock with a warm greeting for John. As he sometimes did when there were other people around and he wanted to talk to her, John turned his head away from them and mouthed his hello.

"Boar's been asking for you, but he's asleep right now. Gorshin's watching him. Bear hasn't been awake much; I hope he's all right," Faye said. "I'm glad you're back. He said you'd be coming back with company. These are sunlit folk. Should Gorshin hide?"

Her question went right by John; he was stuck a little farther back. "Wait a minute," he said aloud. "*Who* said I'd be back with company?"

"Bennett."

Who else? He should have known.

"Hello, Faye," Dr. Spae said.

John's mouth dropped open in astonishment.

"Hello, Doctor," Faye said tentatively.

"You can hear her?" John asked.

"Certainly," the doctor said. "I'd hardly be talking to her otherwise."

John wasn't sure how he felt about this new development; Faye had been his private friend. He felt a little cheated, somehow; as if a confidence had been violated.

"Can you see her?" Dr. Spae asked.

When John admitted that he could not, she hmm'ed meditatively.

"What are you two talking about?" Beryle asked.

Dr. Spae looked at him curiously. "Oh, of course. You can't hear her at all, can you, David?"

"Hear who?"

"This is really very interesting. It raises a number of questions. I wonder if—" Dr. Spae paused for a moment, clearly thinking about something. "Faye, I'd like to try some experiments. Would you be willing to work with me? I would like to—"

"Elizabeth!" Beryle didn't sound amused. "We didn't come here to conduct experiments."

The doctor gave Beryle a hot look. John knew from previous experience that she didn't like to be interrupted. To cool things down, John said, "Bear's upstairs."

He led them to the office that had become Bear's room.

The morning sunlight slanted in through the room's grimy window, making little impression in the gloom. It would get brighter later in the day, but not by much. Bear lay on the couch, asleep. Someone had covered him with a blanket. Faye had said that Gorshin was watching Bear, but John thought the batwinged lizard-ape had abandoned its post, until he spotted a lumpy form huddled in the darkest corner of the room. He ignored Gorshin and started across the room to check on Bear. He'd only gotten halfway there when Dr. Spae shouted.

"David, no!"

The doctor's exclamation brought John around in a crouch. He didn't know what he was expecting, but it wasn't seeing Beryle pointing a boxy pistol at Gorshin's corner. Gorshin had come out of its corner and was hunched in an aggressive stance, wings half-unfurled. Dr. Spae was quietly pleading with Beryle to put up the weapon, but he wasn't listening. He kept his weapon pointed at the lizard-ape. Gorshin started to growl.

"What is it?" Beryle asked. His voice was unsteady, but his weapon hand remained unwavering.

"One of Bennett's pets," John told him.

"Gorshin," Faye said.

"Where'd you get the gun?" John asked Beryle.

"Is it dangerous?" Beryle asked no one in particular.

"Are you a gargoyle?" Dr. Spae asked Gorshin.

All the babble brought a response from Bear.

"Hold it down, compadres, or I'll do some booting," he said, chastising them as he had the noisy Dons at MaxMix Manor.

Beryle spared a second from his staring contest with Gorshin to look at Bear. "Arthur?"

"Artos," Bear said.

"How are you, Artos?" Dr. Spae asked.

"Been better, Doctor."

"So you remember me?"

"I know we've met. Or at least I think we have."

"I was hoping Dr. Spae might be able to help you," John said.

"No leeches," Bear said firmly.

John was afraid Bear had slipped his frame of reference again until he saw the twinkle in the man's eye. "Maybe you don't need a doctor."

"Maybe," Bear agreed. His shakiness when he tried to sit up belied that. He was naked under the blanket, but that didn't seem to bother him until he noticed the doctor's sudden stiffness. Without reference to the situation or apology, he pulled the blanket around himself. "I seem to recall that Dr. Spae is not that kind of a doctor anyway. Is that right?"

"I do have some medical training," the doctor said. "But I'm not leech qualified, unless you count having worked for some."

The ease with which the bitter irony came to Dr. Spae's lips made John think, for the first time, that she really had left the

ECSS behind. That thought raised other questions, but he already had too many questions. Not the least of which was: where was Spillway Sue? She should have come down by now to see what was going on.

Dr. Spae started doing her "catching up" routine again, this time with Bear as the target of her questions. Beryle kept eyeing Gorshin, but the gargoyle subsided and returned to squat in his corner once again. John wasn't exactly needed here; he already knew more than he wanted to about Quetzal. He took the opportunity to head upstairs.

Sue wasn't there.

There wasn't a note. Nothing left behind. But then, she hadn't had anything to leave behind. He stared at the mattress that was his bed.

She'd felt something, hadn't she? He'd thought she had. Certainly he had.

The rumpled bedclothes on the empty mattress made him feel a little disarrayed himself. He went to the window and stared out. She was out there somewhere. Doing what? Every few minutes he'd turn around and stare at the empty bed.

Had it just been payment, after all?

He didn't want to believe that. He couldn't believe it. Their closeness, as sudden as it was, hadn't felt like that.

So why wasn't she here?

The room was suddenly too empty. He went back down to where there were people, but instead of entering the room he hung back in the hall. Faye came to him.

"She's gone, John," she told him.

He didn't need to be told that. Faye wasn't the one to ask, but who else did he have? "Did she say anything before she left?"

"She doesn't hear me, and she's afraid of Gorshin."

Was that all there was to it? Sue could have left a message, at least; she could have written a note, there was paper and a pen in John's room. Then again, maybe she couldn't. John didn't know whether she could read or write. Just one more thing among many that John didn't know about Spillway Sue.

John felt like an idiot, standing in the doorway of Bear's room. He should either go in or leave. But where would he go?

After Sue?

He knew in general where she hung out, but he didn't know where she slumped. She'd grown up around here, and he was a newcomer; if she didn't want to be found, he doubted he could find her.

If Bennett hadn't hauled him off to save Dr. Spae, she would still be here. But Dr. Spae might not. Was that a fair trade? Fair or not, it was another thing to add to the list of what Bennett had cost him.

"Where's Bennett?"

Faye hesitated. "He's not here either."

"But he's coming back, isn't he? He must be, he left his pet behind."

"Gorshin's not a pet, John."

"Yeah? Then maybe he knows." John stalked over to the gargoyle. "So where's Bennett?"

"Gaawn."

"If he's gone, what are you still doing here?" he demanded.

"Lii'k theez playzz," Gorshin croaked. "Staaay."

Wonderful.

"Jack!" It was Bear. "Get me some clothes. Bennett's gifts have the staying power of his promises."

"You're in no shape to do anything," Dr. Spae told Bear.

"Somebody has to do something. Jack, the doctor believes that the wizard is still on the loose."

The idea gave John chills, but he tried to sound unconcerned. "So?"

"He's a wyrm lover," Bear said. "Something's got to be done about him."

"We can tell the police," John said. He'd had more than enough to do with Quetzal. Dr. Spae had been saved from him. Wasn't that enough?

"The police won't be able to handle him," Dr. Spae said.

If they couldn't, what was Bear—especially a weakened Bear—supposed to do? "You're in no shape to fight anyone, Bear."

"But Artos is right," the doctor said. "Something's got to be done."

Why don't you do it, Doctor? "You chased him away before."

"With your help, John."

"You're the one who blasted him."

Dr. Spae shrugged away her efforts. "There was a tremendous sense of tentativeness about Quetzal. I'm fairly sure that he was holding back. At the very least, he was dividing his attention between us."

"We could use Caliburn now," Bear said. "It has a certain efficacy against such as he."

"Well, we don't have it," Dr. Spae said firmly. "We've been over this, Artos. You're in no shape to fight anything."

"You probably couldn't shoot straight, let alone use a sword," John added, thankful that the doctor was being reasonable about at least one aspect of the situation. "You're still confused, Bear, and your coordination's shot."

Bear looked to be on the verge of rebellion. "The serpent lover must be stopped. The doctor needs help."

"So she'll find help somewhere else," John said. "She's got connections."

"You will help, Jack."

Who was Bear to decide for John?

"I don't think I'm strong enough to defeat Quetzal by myself," the doctor said. "We'll need your help."

"Quetzal's a mage," John pointed out. "You need magical help, and I don't do magic."

"You may not be trained, but you have talent," Beryle said.

What did he know about it?

"You do have a strong natural talent," Spae agreed.

Faye joined in. "It's in your blood, John."

Oh, thank you, Faye. Why are you siding with them?

"I've had some experience in teaching," Dr. Spae continued. "I believe that you'd be a quick learner."

Why was he resisting a chance to learn magic? His shoulder twinged in memory of Quetzal's burning hand. Because whoever went along with Dr. Spae was going to be facing Quetzal, that was why.

Was he afraid?

What kind of a question was that? Of course he was afraid. But of what?

Quetzal was the easy answer. And an honest one.

But John suspected there was more to his reluctance. What if he wasn't very good at magic? What if he didn't live up to his blood? He wouldn't be an elven prince if he turned out to be incapable of more than the simplest magics. His heritage was all he had to hold on to since he had rejected Bennett's version of an idyllic life in the otherworld. What if John's dreams turned out to be as much smoke and air as Bennett's promises?

He needed a more concrete—and less personally damning—excuse to use in front of Bear. He grabbed at the first one to come to mind. "How long did it take you to use magic effectively, Doctor?"

"We're not talking about me; we're talking about you. You have certain natural advantages."

"You mean because I'm—" John stopped himself before he said "an elf." So far, Bear had apparently not remembered that John was an elf. John recalled how Bear had reacted; he didn't want to deal with that rejection all over again. He'd had enough rejection today, already. Lamely, he finished, "because I've already had some experience?"

"Experience helps," Dr. Spae said. "But there are some things I think you can handle right away."

She sounded confident enough for both of them. Could she really teach him to harness the magic?

"Listen to her, Jack," Bear urged.

Could she teach him? Could he learn?

Even if he did learn—"What good will it do? We don't even know where Quetzal hangs out. Are you going to scry him out?"

"That'll be one of the first things we work on," Dr. Spae said.

We? John hadn't agreed yet, but the doctor was assuming he had. "I don't know."

"Come on, Reddy. You can't let Elizabeth go up against this wizard by herself."

"That wouldn't be chivalrous, John," Faye said.

She knew him better than all of them.

"I suppose we have to try," he said.

"Good lad, Jack," Bear said. "Cei will be proud when he hears."

John tried to ignore Bear's slip.

Dr. Spae gave him a slap on his shoulder. "There may not be a lot of time. We'll have to get started at once."

CHAPTER

26

For the second night in a row, Spae didn't sleep after she'd sent John Reddy off to bed. It wasn't that she wasn't tired; she was. To the bone. She'd forgotten how tiring it was to work someone through basic exercises. But she couldn't afford sleep just yet. She took out the packet of Wake-EZ™ pills she'd had David get when he'd gone out for food and stared at it. There was a lot to be done and no time to do it in. Drugs were chancy things for a magician, even mild ones like these. If only she felt she had time to get some rest; she would be considerably fresher, able to think more clearly, after she got some sleep.

And *he* might find her again while she slept.

She popped the pill. With luck the side effects would be minor. She lay on the inflatable mattress, which David had also brought, until she felt the buzz start to kick in.

She slipped off the mattress without disturbing David, and rummaged in his case until she found her computer. It was one of the few things she'd taken with her from Chardonneville, and it contained her research files and her library. Tucking it under her arm, she left the room and sought out another, where she could work without waking David, or being disturbed by his occasional bouts of restless tossing.

Her machine, an old Sonymac Romer™, had a virtual keyboard setup; she'd never gotten used to optical boards. She slipped on the gloves and started it up. The first thing she did was disable the vocal circuits; she didn't want to disturb anyone. Voices in the night would draw in anyone who was awake in this dump—she'd seen that the gargoyle was still prowling—and she wanted to be left alone while she worked.

The portable didn't have the power of the perscomp back at the hotel, but it let her use the mobile phone circuits to tap into that computer. Tapping in via airwaves didn't make for the cleanest data flows: some of the files she recovered had been turned to garbage. But she got more than enough to keep her busy for hours—the programs she had left running had been doing their work.

She had remembered the *Callis Luxorum Dubiaria* as being the only known work by Luciferius, and it looked as though she was right; the search hadn't uncovered any others. Failing to find any other works, the programs had defaulted to her alternate search parameters, and had been slogging through occult databanks, of general and limited access, trying to assemble as much of the *Callis* as possible. In college, she had learned that very little of the grimoire was digitized. If anything, the situation had gotten worse than she remembered; the file she'd set up to collect the results of the search held only a dozen entries. She could tell from their sizes that none of them could cover more than ten pages.

As she had told Quetzal, she had read the *Callis* once, but that had been years ago. She had found it on a shelf in Joseph Wyngarde's study during a visit. She'd been surprised to find that the volume was a hand-copied version; the professor's own translation from the Latin, of course. It had been a new book to her, clearly a major arcane work, and she'd been excited. When she'd asked to read it, Joseph had surprised her by refusing, the first time he refused any of her requests for access to occult knowledge. Naturally, she had immediately started searching for the *Callis* on the library net, where she had only been able to collect fragments. When she'd started to discuss them with Joseph, he'd relented, insisting that she read his copy—but imposing the condition that she do all her reading in his study. After all the fuss and bother she'd been disappointed, finding the book obtuse and frustrating. She had put the denial-work-reward routine down to a training gimmick on Joseph's part.

Although she still didn't understand Joseph's take on the matter, she now knew there was more to the *Callis* than a joke or gimmick.

There was no indication of the order of any of the fragments within the *Callis*, so she started with the longest. It was in the original Latin; not a problem as it had been in college when she was still weak in the language. She'd forgotten how unsettling and upsetting she had found the imagery. As she worked her way through the pieces, her agitation only increased in light of Bear's references to Quetzal as a serpent lover and wyrm follower; thoughts along those lines opened interpretations that she had missed before. John's description of the psychic imagery he'd seen around the mage fitted too, disturbingly.

"The pinioned serpent who shone like the light through a prism."

The more she read, the more she worried. Luciferius's pinioned serpent was supposed to change the world and bring the dawn of a new age. Luciferius urged his readers to "follow the Path of Light to the new age."

The Path of Light? A mistranslation for the Glittering Path perhaps?

Quetzal had asked her what she knew of the Glittering Path. The title by which the work was known, *Callis Luxorum Dubiaria*, could be translated as the Gleaming or Shining Path. Admittedly the title was not used by Luciferius. According to Joseph, the mysterious author had left his work untitled; the name had been appended to a twelfth century version. Nonetheless, the associations were too close.

Association was a law of magic. One could touch an entity by touching something once associated with it. Associations worked for research too.

Failing to find satisfaction in the little of the *Callis* that she could access, she turned to the spin-off files, the bulk of what her programs had collected. They'd been set to uncover anything associated with the book or its author. There were a lot of files, but most of them were third and fourth degree connections. Tenuous stuff. She started in on them.

The name Luciferius turned up as a spirit worshiped by several obscure cults; Spae had never heard of any of them, suggesting that they were truly obscure. Most researchers examining the cults dismissed the name as a variation of Lucifer, but one author stated categorically that the name referred to someone other than the devil. That author had been writing of an English cult whose members had fled Puritan persecution, and prosecution, for the New World, only to be exterminated right here in Providence before the end of the seventeenth century.

Associations.

She ran a check to cross-reference the files with Providence.

Spae was amused to find that the first citation the programs turned up carried David's byline. The cut was from an article in a series called "Strange Witch Cults of New England," recounting the tale of a sect who had called themselves the Glittering Dawn, also associated with Providence. David cited an old newspaper archive, with an account of the police breaking up a "black mass" on the East Side of the city almost a hundred years ago.

Associations.

Providence.

Providence was another name for God, especially used in connection with His care or guidance.

Luciferius had written something about special guidance from "beyond time." John reported Bennett claimed that Quetzal was from an earlier time, in a sense from "beyond time."

The "beyond time" phrase had been in one of the fragments she'd read earlier. She decided to reread that passage. She called it up, but the computer flashed a warning box, complaining of suspicious activity and asking for instructions. Before she could give it any, the message box blinked out; it appeared again and began to blink on and off, rapidly. When it stopped blinking, only portions of the screen graphic were visible; it looked as if it had been chewed on.

Spae tried activating the Romer's virus defense, but the keyboard was frozen. She checked the connections on her gloves; fine. Battery; fine. She tried all the standard tricks and got nowhere. She gave up and went for a restart; the keyboard worked when the computer came back up. She looked for the file again and got a "not found" message. Checking the file where she had ordered her programs to dump the fragments of the *Callis,* she found it empty. The backup program claimed nothing had ever been there.

This work was seriously fancy techno-sabotage. Somehow she didn't think Quetzal had made the time to acquire such skills. But someone out there didn't want her reading the work of Luciferius.

Duncan Middleton was Pamela Martinez's personal assistant. So Charley knew that he wasn't dealing with a joke when the smiling Middleton met him at the security desk. Middleton had arrived so quickly that he had to have been waiting for Charley to show up.

Charley wasn't sure whether or not that was a good sign. He wondered if he should have logged his coming here as an official visit despite Martinez's advice against it.

After the requisite polite chitchat, Middleton escorted him upstairs. Instead of taking Charley to meet Martinez, Middleton led him to an empty office. The lights in the room were down, set at optimal level for viewing the wallscreen. There was a file box on the screen with Charley's name on it.

"Ms. Martinez will see you shortly," Middleton said. "The computer has been sensitized to your voice. You may use it as you would your own. After you have read the material, simply state that you are done, and I will be back to escort you to Ms. Martinez."

With a corporate bow and a corporate smile, Middleton was gone and Charley was alone, his name flashing on the wall.

Pamela positioned herself by the one-way window in response to Duncan's message that he was on his way with Detective Gordon. While she waited, she watched Joel Lee. The man had been manic since sometime last night, babbling about his master needing him. Even now, he paced and prowled the confines of his room and mumbled to himself. Pamela ordered the computer to depolarize the window in Lee's room. As the light level increased, the man glanced about frantically. He began to rush back and forth in mindless, frenetic haste. He ran to the door and pounded on it. No one responded; his keepers had already learned to ignore him. The backs of his hands began to blister. Pamela was impressed by the speed with which the sunlight had affected him. Lee screamed as if he were in agony. He   ed to the floor by the side of his bed, the only piece of furniture in the room, and cowered in the meager shade it provided, cradling his hands and muttering.

Observing Joel Lee was educational. The change coming upon the world was as inevitable as the rising of the sun. She knew that now; Nakaguchi and his monster had made her realize that it couldn't be stopped. She could be like Lee and try to hide from that which she feared to face. She could run, searching fruitlessly for a place to hide, or she could make pitiable attempts to stop the inevitable. The sun would rise and, with seemingly equal inevitability, magic would infest the world. The chaos would come. She could not stop it from coming.

She had no intention of becoming a pawn as Lee had become.

She would not let fear rule her. She had not let the chaos of her youth rule her; she had risen above it by taking control of her life. She would just have to take control again.

Nakaguchi's tenure bequeathed her more than his runaway monster. The most immediate benefit was learning that Nakaguchi had misled her about Mitsutomo-sama's involvement; it was clear from Nakaguchi's files that the *kansayaku* had been acting without Mitsutomo-sama's approval. Without fear of angering the master of the Keiretsu, Rearden had been able to rampage through Nakaguchi's databank. The preliminary survey of the files suggested much that was promising, especially with her new focus.

If the mob is storming the gates, open those gates and lead them to the palace.

She would continue Nakaguchi's efforts to develop an arm of the Keiretsu to deal with the new order of the world. Thaumatechnics was the name he'd been service-marking. She'd keep the name, not just because of the financial economy, but because it would remind her of the importance of taking what came one's way. In her fear of chaos, she'd forgotten that when she set up the Charybdis Project.

Sometimes it was good to be afraid of what one ruled: it kept one alert. And rule she would. She would make Thaumatechnics a force to be reckoned with, and in doing so assure herself of a secure place in the world. She would recapture her empire within the Keiretsu. Improve it, even.

She would not cower, hiding from the inevitable.

The door to the observation room opened and Pamela turned to face it. Duncan ushered Detective Gordon in. She didn't bother to introduce herself; he knew who she was.

"You reviewed the file that Mr. Middleton showed you?"

Gordon searched her face, apparently trying to gauge how he was supposed to respond. "Pretty farfetched stuff."

"Suitable for the Special Investigations Unit?"

"I was under the impression that Mitsutomo doesn't want us involved."

"What gave you that impression, Detective?"

"Something I heard from somebody."

Although she had a good idea, she would confirm what and who after the interview. "What you have heard is not quite true. Though I have little doubt that whoever you heard it from believes it. What Mitsutomo wishes—what I wish—is that justice be done and the law enforced. Mitsutomo wishes to aid in such efforts, but declines public involvement."

"I would say that the Keiretsu is already involved."

"I could suggest that such a view is limited. Perhaps you didn't examine the data closely enough."

"Give me a copy and I'll take it home with me. I promise I'll study it real hard."

He reminded her a little of McAlister in the way that he exuded confidence. Gordon's manner was a bit rougher than the special operative's, but she had to admire the man's initiative. But then, Gordon's initiative was why he was here. Still, too much misdirected initiative could be troublesome; she would just have to make sure he was directed properly.

"Surely you can see that only certain individuals are involved. The Keiretsu has been manipulated in this matter. It is a shameful situation. But exposure would result in an even greater shame. I would rather not see that. You understand, of course."

"Let's pretend I'm really stupid, Ms. Martinez. What is it you have in mind? You didn't call me here to spill the beans and then tell me to hush it up."

"Cooperation is the word of the day, Detective."

"Cooperation, huh?" He gave her a lopsided smile. "The department is always happy to have civic-minded people cooperate, Ms. Martinez. Personally, I'm particularly gratified when a megacorp acts as a civic-minded corporate person."

She thought his sarcasm uncalled for, but kept a pleasant expression on her face. "Mitsutomo Keiretsu has always been civic-minded."

He started a retort, but clearly had second thoughts. He said, "We still haven't established what you want with me."

"Look here, Detective." She indicated the room beyond the window. "The man you see before you is Joel Lee. He was once considered an exemplar of loyalty and dedication. He was one of the first to come in contact with Quetzal. Now, through no fault of his own, he is a traitor."

"He looks like a pretty unhappy traitor."

"His distress is directly related to his relationship with Quetzal, whom he calls master. Yes, master. The unfortunate Mr. Lee is no longer what you and I would call rational."

"That's no reason to torture him."

"His hands, you mean? That is a reaction to sunlight. A psychosomatic condition. We have not mistreated Mr. Lee, and his detention is entirely legal under the Corporate Security Act of 2015."

"Would you mind if I verified the circumstances of that?"

Yes, she would mind. "Duncan, arrange for the detective to see Mr. Lee's file before he leaves."

Gordon continued to stare through the observation window. "If the light's a problem for him, can't you cut it down?"

"Certainly." She ordered the windows repolarized. "Mr. Lee's aversion to sunlight is a sympathetic reaction, a reflection of the condition of his master, who suffers a similar affliction. It is the relationship between the two of them that will make Mr. Lee useful to you."

Gordon turned his head and looked at her, but he didn't say anything.

"When you hunt Quetzal down," she added.

"What?"

"We intend to release Mr. Lee. He will be allowed to gather clothes and certain other items which will include a pair of dark sunglasses. The glasses will incorporate the Tsurei Seeing Eyes system. With it, you will be able see what he sees and hear what he hears."

"I'm familiar with the system."

"Then you understand how you can use the system to monitor whoever Mr. Lee contacts. You will see where he finds Quetzal. Then you can go there and destroy it."

"I can't go along with this," Gordon said abruptly.

"You don't agree the monster must be destroyed."

"I'm not a jury."

"This is an extraordinary situation. Quetzal is beyond ordinary law. Surely you see that."

"I see that he needs to be stopped."

"At least we agree there."

"But I can't go around breaking the law myself every time I stop a criminal."

"Quetzal is more than an ordinary criminal."

"Well, lady, *I'm* just an ordinary cop."

His resistance was unexpected. Had Hagen been right about him? She'd see; there were still more cards to play. "Even an ordinary cop is still expected to protect the innocent, is he not?"

The suspicious look he gave her was answer enough.

"What happens if you discover a crime in progress, Detective? Do you go to a judge and ask for a warrant to arrest the criminal?"

"You know the answer to that," he said sullenly.

"Even off duty?"

"Yeah, yeah. Even off duty. What's your point? Putting an illegal Seeing Eyes monitor on this guy and busting him when he steps over the line ain't gonna last a minute in court."

"I did tell you that we do not wish to be involved in this. You need not mention the Seeing Eyes. You need only be in the right place at the right time. Mitsutosmo security personnel seeking the escaped Mr. Lee can be present, providing you the backup you will need to deal with Quetzal. The right place and time, Detective. It will save lives."

"I can't involve civilians in this," he objected.

"All field-grade employees of Mitsutomo's Yamabennin Security Services are fully licensed constabulary operatives. Section 232 of Yamabennin's incorporation papers states that, in case of a civil disturbance, all personnel are expected to operate under the command of duly authorized personnel. A police officer in the performance of his duty is a duly authorized person. There is in fact a precedent of a police officer in Paris leading a squad of Yamabennin troopers in the storming of a barricade in the '03 riots. The principle is sound."

"You're quite the boardroom lawyer, Ms. Martinez."

"I respect the law, Detective."

"Which is why you're working so hard to get around its letter, no doubt."

"I am working to see that the community is saved from a very dangerous threat without causing unnecessary panic. I was given to understand that such a goal was not dissimilar to the mandate for the Special Investigations Unit."

"Our mandate doesn't include murder."

"Killing Quetzal is not murder, but justice. The monster is a killer. So far the number of victims is small."

"Small?" Gordon sounded appropriately appalled. "According to your file, he's killed twenty-five people!"

"Quetzal is capable of far greater crimes; so far, the number of his victims is small, but the death toll will grow soon. Quetzal is planning something . . . greater." So Nakaguchi had believed. "The monster must be stopped soon."

"You got proof of whatever it is that Quetzal is going to do?"

"No."

"Then I can't help you."

Last card. "Did you have proof of the Barrington Slasher's plan?"

He looked at her through narrowed eyes. "What do you know about that?"

"Enough."

"I don't like to be pushed, Ms. Martinez."

"We are *all* being pushed, Detective. I like it even less than you. But the monster will kill again. I am offering you a way to stop it."

Gordon stared into Joel Lee's room for a long time without saying anything. Pamela knew she had him even before he turned and said, "When are you letting this guy go?"

"Mr. Hagen will act as liaison for me. He will arrange things."

Charley left Martinez's presence a lot more unhappy than he had gone in. A lot more worried too. Martinez's Quetzal had been the third person in the elevator car; Charley knew now that *he* was Caspar's "answer" to Modus 112.

Whatever Mitsutomo had been up to, it had gone sour. The computers wouldn't show it, but Martinez was in this up to her armpits. Now that things had started to stink, she wanted it cleaned up, and she'd picked Charley to be her janitor.

He wanted to let her stew in it, but if she was right about Quetzal's planning something . . .

He couldn't stand by and let the bastard kill any more people.

And he didn't have anything substantial enough to bring in the Department. Not yet anyway.

They took him to security central for their Brookfield operation; the place was going to serve as the command center for the cleanup. He sat in the back of the room, too busy trying to figure the angles to watch the techs do their work. He left that to Hagen; like a lot of short guys he seemed to need to prove he was in charge.

The wallscreen came to life. Joel Lee had left the Brookfield facility.

"We're running," Hagen announced.

On the fast track to hell, Charley thought.

"Dr. Spae?"

Faye's voice was faint, almost a thought, but it startled Spae; she'd been half-asleep. On the verge of bad dreams.

The Faery girl sounded worried. What did her kind worry about? Spae tried to sound kindly and concerned, rather than clinical.

"What is it, Faye?"

"You sounded disturbed."

Sounded? Had she been talking in her half-awake state? She must have been. "What did I say?"

"You're worried about the darkling mage."

"Quetzal?"

Spae sensed affirmation.

"Yes, I'm worried about how we're going to deal with him."

"Do you know where he is?" Faye asked.

"I wish. I was going to try a scrying with John tomorrow."

"Tomorrow may be too late."

Too late? What did she know? "What do you mean? Do you have some source of knowledge, some kind of elven sense?"

"I—I'm not an elf, Doctor." She sounded embarrassed. "I know I'm not important, so you don't really want to talk to me, but I just have a feeling that there will be trouble. Soon. I think you should look for the darkling mage *now*."

"Why now?"

"I don't know."

Spae didn't like the fear she heard in Faye's voice. A creature of Faery would have to have senses people didn't; Faye might not understand what she was feeling, but the feeling couldn't be discounted because of that. There was little that was coincidental when magic was involved.

"All right. I'll go wake John and we'll get started."

As she started to stand, Spae felt the lightest of touches on her arm, little more than a breeze plucking at her shirt sleeve.

"John's not a seeker, Dr. Spae. He won't be much help. Besides, he needs his sleep. Please, Doctor, do not disturb him. I will help you."

A thousand questions tumbled through Spae's brain, but the ones that fell out were, "Can you do that? Are *you* a seeker?" Whatever a seeker was.

"I think I can help once you are in trance," Faye said.

"All right. Let's give it a try." Remembering to be polite, she added, "Thank you."

"You are a good person, Dr. Spae."

What brought that on?

Faye started to croon a song, so softly that Spae couldn't make out any of the words. Still, she had a sense that they were not English nor any other language Spae knew. The song was soothing, relaxing, almost soporific. Spae drifted into it.

She sat down, too unsteady on her feet to remain standing. The song went on. Spae noted distantly that she had unconsciously adopted a full lotus position. Faye was still singing, more clearly now, but the words remained elusive. Spae followed the melody, slipping into trance state.

Faye became a somewhat more palpable presence. Spae could see her as a gossamer image of smoke. Spae, a glowing image herself, stood. They joined hands and flew into the sky to search for the darkling mage.

CHAPTER
27

Quetzal stood at the corner of Hopkins and Benefit Streets, contemplating the house there. A bronze plaque proclaimed it to have been the residence of one Stephen Hopkins, a man of some historic import locally. The white clapboard colonial structure was considered old for the city, and the city itself was old for this continent. He had slept through almost all of their existence.

He continued up the hill, taking George Street. After a block he was walking along the great black iron fence that separated him from his goal. He passed four of the great brick pillars into which the iron was set before stopping to gaze at his destination.

Headlights swept over him. He flinched before he realized that the light contained little to disturb him. The light's influence was fleeting in any case. A local resident, a student, a visiting family member, a campus patrol? No matter. None of them had any interest in him. He was just a pedestrian, coated and hatted against the wind and cold. No one of consequence.

He let the car pass.

The well-tended green on the other side of the fence sloped up to a row of buildings. Most were old—for this city—but not so venerable as the Hopkins house. He only had eyes for one of them, the nearest, a small, pseudoclassical monstrosity of concrete. Van Dieman had provided him with much information about this building, its history, the city in which it resided, and *its* history. Useful information. He was about to use some of that information.

He lifted himself over the fence on the etherometric lines. It would have been easier to walk to the gate and open it, but he had no desire to; not when he was so near. He walked up the slope.

The building had a door facing toward the city, which was situated on the river plain below, even though the building's principal door was on the far side, facing the main college green, where the students would pass. The student traffic on this side went only down the hill and through the gate, to the great library and other less important facilities outside the fence.

That principal door might still be unlocked—the graduate students here were supposed to be forgetful—but again he had no desire to deviate from the most direct route. He placed his hand on the lock. It was more complicated than those with which he was familiar, but no more an obstacle; still less the heavy bolts securing the top and bottom of the door.

He entered the building.

The hallway ran straight to the front door. Despite the darkness, his mage sight allowed him to see that the door's locking mechanism was engaged. Faint light leaked around the curve of the stairway to the upper floor. Someone was up there. No matter. He was interested in the basement, not the upper floor. He took the stairway down.

The lower hallway was as narrow as the upper but more cramped, because of the boxes and crates and loose specimens shoved haphazardly against the walls. This building had once been the home of the geological sciences department of this university. For truth, it still belonged to the department, but the center of activity had moved away to the more spacious and modern facility on the eastern side of the campus. Unlike some of the other departments, geological sciences understood time and tradition; chairman after chairman had refused to part with the old hall even when it was clear there was little use for it. Offices that had once housed eminent professors were now shared by groups of lowly teaching assistants. The building was now a repository of the unimportant and the neglected.

Neglected, yes, but unimportant?

Not if what Quetzal suspected remained here was truly here.

He found the room he sought, knowing it by the feel of the air. Only a mage would have known that this office was different from any other.

There had been a writer of fiction who had once lived in this city, a man who had known much that he should not have known. For truth, he'd had a part in exposing some of the followers. But mostly the writer had hidden the terrifying truths under the cloak of his tall tales. One of the things that the writer had so disguised was the history of a university expedition, a trek to the south polar wastes. Much had been discovered in those frigid wastes that the university's rational scientists could not understand. Someone had whispered of those things to the writer. Afraid to speak the truth, the writer had couched what he had learned in a fictioneer's lies, going so far as to invent a fictional university to sponsor the fictional expedition.

But the expedition had been real. What they found had been real. And this room—this room had once been the office of a young professor who had gone on that expedition and was still carried on the university's rolls as a Professor Emeritus. The young professor had made wise investments and grown rich—rich enough to endow a chair at the university. The holder of the chair was supposed to maintain this office as his own. Dust on the furniture and books said that the current holder did not take his responsibilities seriously.

The false wall behind which the young professor had hidden his secret things would have fooled any ordinary visitor, but Quetzal was no ordinary visitor. What would be hidden from a mortal eye could not escape his magesight. It took but a few minutes to clear a space so that he could open the hiding place.

The compartment was small, no more than a closet, and filled with shelves. Quetzal looked over their contents. One shelf held an assortment of ritual implements, suggesting that the young professor had been a student of more than geology. The rest of the shelves held objects of carven stone, wood, bone, and ivory. Most were irrelevant, mere fetishes, born of superstition rather than knowledge. A handful were something more. Sharing the shelf with those objects were a linen-wrapped book and another object—wrapped in dried rawhide, and bound with strips of hide whose loose ends were gathered and embedded in a hardened clay seal. The signs and sigils of the opposition had been cut into the clay of the seal while it had been still wet.

What had drawn Quetzal here lay beneath those wrappings and bindings. The seal had masked the object well enough to hide it from the followers, but not so well that Quetzal had missed it. He could feel the power in it.

He took it up. It was weighty, doubtless of stone. Eagerly, he smashed the seal. The latent power of the piece bloomed. Breathless, he clawed at the rawhide bindings until the last strand released its grip and fell to the floor. He pried back the wrappings.

He knew that the object was what he sought even before he uncovered it, but even so he felt a thrill upon first seeing it. It was a *telesmon* of vermetid form. It had been made from a dark but translucent stone, each coil shaped in sinuous curves and cut with cunning facets that made strange angles where hidden surfaces were visible through the smoky stone. Had there been light, it would have flashed reflections around the room more wildly than a hundred prisms. Its beauty took his breath away.

Faint, so faint that touch could not discern their presence, he saw marks on the surfaces of the *telesmon*. He recognized some of the sigils at once. This was not just a thing of power, but a thing dedicated to the power he followed.

The key to the Key.

Had they not fallen farther than the followers, the opposition would have mobilized all their forces to bar Quetzal from this treasure. They had not. They had failed their self-avowed duty.

He was elated.

He placed the unwrapped *telesmon* back on the shelf and, heedless of the dust, sat in the chair to admire it. The key to the Key! This was what he had sought, what he had wanted— the heart to the web of resonators. With this *telesmon* he could open the Glittering Path.

Had they known, they would have destroyed it.

Or had they, in their pride, thought they need not destroy it, that they could hide it away forever?

He took down the linen-wrapped book; it would be the professor's diary. He did not have to read much to ascertain that the young man and his cronies had not understood what they had found. They had known that the *telesmon* was powerful, hence the masking, but they had not had the slightest clue to its true importance.

But Quetzal understood.

He tucked the diary away in his coat and fell to staring at the *telesmon*, dreaming of the new age he would begin.

CHAPTER
28

John woke from a dream in which the world was shaking itself to pieces, to find himself still being shaken. Dr. Spae had a grip on his shoulder and was making like a terrier.

"Come on, John. Wake up!"

He felt as if he'd hardly gotten to sleep. It was still dark; he couldn't have been asleep long. His head still hurt from the exercises Dr. Spae had made him practice over and over. The doctor had said she'd let him sleep till morning. So why was she here yelling at him to get up? He mumbled a protest.

"We've run out of time. He's here."

John's head was still out of focus. "Who's here?"

"Quetzal."

His sleepiness left him, his mind hitting racing speed from a dead stop. "What?" Had he heard right? Quetzal was here? "How?" Had he tracked them through astral space or something? Shouldn't they be doing something? "Where?" If Quetzal was here, what was the doctor doing standing around? "We've got to do something!"

"Exactly."

"Why are you standing around? What's he doing? Where is he? You said he was here."

"Calm down, John. I meant here in the city," Dr. Spae said. "Which is bad enough. Faye and I discovered him on the East Side. He's found something terrible."

John barely heard her last statement. "Faye? Where is she? Is she all right?"

"As far as I know. I left her to watch—"

"You didn't leave her to face Quetzal alone?"

"She's not a child, John. She'll stay out of his way." Dr. Spae bent down, picked up John's pants, and tossed them to him. "But we can't leave her holding the fort alone. Get dressed."

"What are we going to do?" John asked as he dragged the pants under his blanket.

"What we have to do. We'll talk about it on the way."

"But you haven't shown me any combat spells." He struggled to pull his pants on underneath the covers. "How can we fight him?"

"I've shown you how to link. It'll have to be enough."

"Car's out front," Beryle said breathlessly as he appeared in the doorway. He gave John a disgusted look. "Jesus, kid, aren't you ready?"

"Let's go!" John tossed off the blanket and leaped up. His flashy move was undermined by his unfastened zipper; his pants started to slip.

Beryle shook his head. "You sure we need this kid, Elizabeth?"

"Leave him alone, David. He'll be fine."

Embarrassed, John snatched up his shirt. His boots. His jacket, too; it was going to be cold out.

Beryle led the way down the stairs. He started past the landing on Bear's floor. John stopped.

"What about Bear?"

"Gorshin will watch him," said Dr. Spae.

"You haven't told him?"

"He's in no shape to fight." Beryle was staring up at John. He looked annoyed. "He'll be a liability if we have to watch out for his ass as well as our own. Better he stay here."

"He won't like being left out," John said. "We may need his help."

"Not tonight, John," the doctor said. "The world may have a greater need of him if we fail tonight."

She started down the stairs. John looked down the hall to Bear's room. They were right about Bear not being in any shape for a fight. Besides, what could he do against a mage? So why didn't John feel good about leaving Bear behind?

John caught up to Beryle and the doctor as they reached the ground floor.

Dr. Spae explained her plan as Beryle careened through the streets toward the East Side. They were going to wait outside the building where Quetzal was. She was confident that he wouldn't be staying there, because she thought that he'd want to get back to wherever he made his lair before dawn. If so, he'd have to leave soon; there was less than two hours till sunrise.

They would ambush him when he came out. For the ambush Dr. Spae, John, and Faye would link, sharing their thaumaturgic power. The doctor would anchor the ritual chain, directing their combined power in an effort to draw out and envelop Quetzal. The doctor showed John a cord woven of her own hair.

"You will hold one end and I'll hold the other," she told him. "We will use this instead of holding hands as our physical link, it'll be less obvious that we're linking. We'll have a better chance if he thinks we're operating separately, since he's already beaten us that way before."

It was an awfully slim thread to hang a victory on.

"Almost there," Beryle announced.

The Hernando labored up College Street with such difficulty that John wasn't sure that the junker would make it to the top. Apparently Beryle wasn't sure either; he cut down Benefit Street and tried the less steep slope up George Street. He turned onto Magee and pulled over.

"I don't think we ought to take the car closer," he said.

"Where are we going?" John asked.

Dr. Spae pointed out the back window toward the first building inside the university's fence. It wasn't big, just two stories, and it wasn't fancy. What did it have that would attract an ancient wizard?

Beryle was already out of the car. "Don't close the doors all the way. Just in case we're in a hurry when we get back."

The three of them walked quickly back to George Street and crossed it. The tall fence stood between them and the building. The nearest gate was shut.

"How do we get past the fence?" John asked. "I'll bet all the gates are locked at this hour."

"Faculty card," Beryle said, holding up a thin rectangle of plastic. How had he gotten that? Beryle slipped the card into the slot by the gate. The lock released and he waved them through. He came through and closed the gate behind him.

"Why not leave that open, too?" John asked.

"Security timer."

Though insufficient, it was all the answer John got. Beryle headed toward the building that Dr. Spae had pointed out. The doctor took John's arm and directed him toward the open lawn in front of the building. About forty feet from the door, she pulled him down. The grass was wet and cold, but because of the slope of the ground, they were mostly concealed from the door.

Not that anyone seemed to be looking for them. The building was dark, apparently deserted for the night.

"Why isn't Beryle out here with us?" John asked.

"He needs to stay out of the line of fire."

Not a comforting answer.

Dr. Spae spoke to the air. "Faye?"

"Here," Faye answered. "It has been very quiet. Someone left, but it wasn't he."

"Are you sure?"

"Very."

"Then he's still in there," John said.

"Probably," the doctor agreed. She didn't sound convinced. "Faye, would you check?"

"You can't ask her to go in there alone," John said.

"It's all right, John," Faye said. "I'll be careful."

And she was gone. Dr. Spae began to build preliminary astral constructs for her spell. Faye was back in less than a minute.

"I'm afraid that he knew I was there."

"He saw you?" John didn't think that was possible.

"Not exactly. It doesn't really matter. He's coming."

"Let's get ready," Dr. Spae said. She handed John his end of the cord. "Let Faye do whatever she can do that's the equivalent of holding your hand. I'll need both of you."

John felt Faye's presence settle beside him. He held his hand out. She couldn't actually hold his hand, but the gesture seemed important. He tried to calm himself, to leave himself open to the link. He became more aware of Faye, to the point of knowing that she stood beside him, her slender, intangible hand in his. He could tell that she was nervous, but whether that certainty came from the link or from his long experience with her, he didn't know.

He got a little dizzy when Dr. Spae asserted herself over the link. He spent a moment awhirl in disorienting sensations, trying to sort them out, but he had to shut his eyes to cut down on some of the confusion. Even with his eyes closed, he retained an impression of vision, kind of like a bad copy of a video from the last century. He knew that the view was what Dr. Spae saw; as the controller of the linkage, hers were the dominant senses and emotions.

The doctor was watching the building in tense anticipation. She was more confident than John had expected. In fact, he felt something that he interpreted as satisfaction as the door began to open. Annoyance rose when Quetzal appeared in the doorway, but did not leave the building.

"Stay down," Dr. Spae whispered.

Quetzal looked in her direction when she spoke. Already discovered, she stood.

"Come out of there," she ordered Quetzal.

"Spae?" Quetzal gave a good-humored chuckle. "I should have expected that you'd sense the *telesmon* and come running. I was right to consider you a threat."

"And wrong not to finish me when you had the chance."

The mage shrugged. "Unwise greed for a good servant on my part. I've had so little luck with them of late. Perhaps tonight my luck will change."

"*Tonight* your luck ends."

Dr. Spae began to feed power into her spell constructs. John let her draw on him to energize the spell. Almost at once, he felt as if he'd been running hard for half an hour.

Quetzal knew that the doctor was working. John could feel the darkling mage's touch as he examined the structures of Spae's spell. Unfortunately for the doctor's plan, Quetzal remained inside the building; the spell construct wasn't designed to deal with the building's disruptive influence.

"Come on, you bastard," Spae shouted. "Come out and fight!"

"I thought it prudent to wait until the odds were a little more even."

What did he mean by that? John didn't have time to ponder. In three quick strides, Quetzal left the building. Calling out in a loud voice, he raised his hands. At once, John felt immense pressure squeezing him.

Quetzal was resisting the spell. Spae poured their strength into her construct. John gasped from the strain.

"Now," Dr. Spae said under her breath. "Do it now."

Do what? John felt her anxiety through their link; the emotion threatened to upset her control of the magic.

Quetzal upped the pressure.

John cried out in pain as Dr. Spae drew on him. At his side Faye swooned.

"David?" This time Dr. Spae spoke loudly.

Despite their combined strength, the doctor's spell structure shrilled under the load Quetzal was bringing to bear. Faye's departure from the linkage hadn't helped.

"David!"

There was no response to the doctor's desperate call. John felt her attention waver from the spell.

"No!" she screamed.

John saw what she saw.

Beryle lay sprawled on the ground near the corner of the building. A man stood over him, more like a scavenger than like a victorious warrior. Beryle's assailant was dressed like a mid-rank executive out for an evening stroll. The man wore a set of visor glasses that looked like a virtual reality feed, but he didn't move like a VR addict when he reached down and picked something up. Beryle's gun.

The spell form rippled and started to crumble as Dr. Spae abandoned her control. The sudden shift left John blinded and dazed.

He heard a shot.

And Quetzal's voice saying, "You should have selected a more alert assassin, Spae."

John recovered enough of his wits to realize that his blindness was due to his eyes being closed. He opened them in time to see a bolt of pure power leap from Dr Spae's staff. Unlike the blasts she had unleashed in her hotel suite, this one wasn't aimed at the darkling mage. Her target was Beryle's attacker.

He was no mage. He had no protection. The energy blast lifted him, flailing, into the air. He crashed into the top of one of the fence's supporting brick pillars and rolled off onto the iron bars. Pointed iron pierced his body and tented the back of his coat. Beryle's gun fell from his limp hand and smacked against the sidewalk.

Quetzal avenged the loss of his henchman by launching his own bolt. The blast tossed John and the doctor in different directions and ripped a crater in the lawn. John landed somewhat downhill of where he'd lain, battered and winded, but conscious. The doctor must still be conscious too; he could feel the interplay of energies as Quetzal struggled to complete another blasting spell. Someone—it had to be Dr. Spae because it wasn't John—fought against him.

Away! Get away!

The struggle between the two sorcerers was beyond John's competence. All he could think about was getting out of range of another arcane blast. He didn't think he could survive another. He started crawling away from the danger.

He had to get away!

The night sky seemed shot with lightning as the magicians fought their battle. Tired and dizzy, John crawled on. His head was spinning and multicolored lights danced before his eyes. Sounds seemed to come from very far away.

There was someone lying in his path. A girl, apparently unconscious. Someone else hurt in tonight's disaster.

He crawled toward her. He hadn't done much good tonight. Maybe he could get her away from the danger. The least he could do.

The girl was Faye.

Away! his brain shrieked at him.

Yes! He had to get them both away. John forced himself to his knees, then to his feet. He got a grip on her wrists and started to drag her after him. His head spun with the effort, but he persevered. If they were to be safe, they had to be elsewhere.

At least the lightning had stopped. The air was clear. There was no storm here.

Here?

Dropping Faye's arms, he looked up. Despite a distant diffuse flashing on the horizon, the sky was lit by billions of brilliant stars. They twinkled and danced and swirled. They spun John around, and he crashed to the ground.

The dank, cold darkness was everywhere.

CHAPTER
29

Spae felt as if she were coming apart at the seams. When she'd seen Quetzal's slave standing over David, she'd gone a little over the edge. She'd blasted the slave, but at what cost? She'd lost the link with Reddy and Faye. She'd lost control of the entrapment spell. She'd lost David.

Lost it all.

Quetzal's power beat down on her. She fought back. As long as she prevented him from forming a coherent spell structure, she would live. But what was the point?

They had failed.

David had died, shot in the back while he lay helpless.

The Faery kids, the material Reddy and immaterial Faye, were gone, vaporized by Quetzal's blast.

Only she was left. For the moment.

She was abandoned.

Alone.

It was only a matter of time.

Quetzal created structure after structure around her. She tore them down. He made new ones, each harder to destroy than the last. She knew the despair was undermining her ability to resist Quetzal. What did it matter? She couldn't beat him. She'd run out of tricks to try on him. He knew them all.

Still, she fought.

But he was strong, stronger than anyone she had ever tested her power against. She couldn't beat him. His spell forms came closer and closer to completion. She was going to die. The wind started to roar in her ears. Maybe she was already dying. Well, that was better than living as Quetzal's slave. Infinitely better.

He loomed over her, as he had once loomed over her in a dream. He was darkness, all shadow and sinister dread. Her defenses were slowing, she was weak.

Dying.

A light blossomed in the sky behind Quetzal's head, a brilliant, dazzling white light. Some people said that you saw a great, shining light as you passed from life to death.

Did angels have running lights?

John was lying on his back, staring—once he'd opened his eyes—at the sky. Stars! Billions of them! He knew those stars; they lived in the sky of the otherworld.

He was in the otherworld!

And he had come here by himself!

But not alone. Faye? "Faye!"

He found her a few yards away, lying on the ground, her arms stretched over her head where he'd dropped them. Was she all right? He couldn't tell if she was breathing. He knelt beside her. She was, she *was* breathing! He'd been afraid she was—

Her eyes fluttered open when his tears fell upon her cheek.

"John?" Her voice was weak, but there was strength in her arms when she pulled his head down and kissed him.

"I'm so glad you're alive," she exclaimed. "When the darkling mage struck, I thought you'd— I thought we'd— I thought— I don't know what I thought. His spells were so powerful. How's Dr. Spae?"

Her question crushed his happiness. He had abandoned the doctor. He looked back in the direction he thought they had come from. There were no buildings, just a few trees that looked familiar, and a lot more that didn't. Diffuse flashes of light reflected from the dark leaves, but John couldn't make out a source.

"I guess she's still fighting him," he said softly.

"She needs help, John. She can't defeat him alone."

"What am I supposed to do? I can't beat him either. It's hopeless to try to link with the doctor while she's in combat with Quetzal. If I knew more about magic, I might be able to *do* something. Elf princes are supposed to be great magicians, aren't they? Why am I such a wuss? You know why? *I* know why. It's because I'm a frigging changeling. You know what a changeling is? I'll tell you! A changeling is a frigging elven orphan. I might have known enough to do something, if my *father* had ever bothered to teach me anything. What little I've learned, I've learned without any help from *him!*"

His tirade ran down into sobs.

"He's strong, John," Faye said gently. "He could help her. I think he would help her, if you asked. I could find him for you."

How could she consider being beholden to *him* after what *he* had done to her? "I can't."

"Dr. Spae needs help, John. She'll die."

"Don't you know any other elves?"

She dropped her eyes, and said in a small voice, "I'm not their kind."

"Forget it, then." It was for the best. It had to be. Besides, if she went to Bennett, he might not listen; and even if he did, there might not be time for him to do anything. "Maybe there's something we can do ourselves. I got us here; maybe I can go back and get her."

"If she's dueling with the darkling mage, you'll never get near enough to open the way."

Then they had to find somebody to help them. "Do you know where we are?"

She looked surprised at his question. "Home."

"You live near here?" If she did, she would know people. Maybe someone who could help.

"Only in the sunlit world," she replied.

Only in the— His hopes sagged. To her, the otherworld was home, all of it. "You don't know this neighborhood at all, do you?"

"Only in the sunlit world. Like you, John."

Wonderful.

He couldn't stand by and let Quetzal kill Dr. Spae.

"We need help, and I don't know my way around, and I certainly don't know anyone to ask." He hated himself for it, but he asked, "You can find Bennett?"

She nodded.

"All right, then. Go get him."

"What about you, John?"

"I'm going to stay here and see if I can come up with something."

"But John—"

"Go! You're wasting time!"

She pouted at him, but he glared back. She turned and ran away, vanishing into the mist that, in the strange way of the otherworld, always seemed near at hand.

John turned back to the place where the light flashed. When he squinted hard and thought about the real world, he could make out faint, fleeting outlines of the fence and the building where Quetzal had hidden. It was as if the flashes illuminated them somehow. In a way he was not able to put into words, he felt the presence of both Quetzal and Dr. Spae. He seemed to understand where they were located.

He could go back. At least he thought he could.

But what would he do once he was there?

The tension in the Brookfield security center shot up when Joel Lee's point of view swept across a building front and revealed a man standing in a doorway. Charley didn't recognize the guy, but Hagen did.

"Quetzal," he said, as if he were naming a poisonous snake.

To Charley's surprise, Lee didn't go straight to his so-called master. He circled around a block, coming back toward the building from another direction. There was a big iron fence in Lee's way and he went over it, displaying more agility than any desk jockey Charley had ever seen. Lee's point of view moved slowly after that, as if he were stalking something.

It turned out he was. The point-of-view revealed a man crouched next to the building that Quetzal had been standing in front of. It wasn't Quetzal. Charley spotted the gun in the man's hand; he recognized the tenseness in the man's crouch, too—the guy was waiting in ambush.

For Quetzal?

Whoever he was waiting for, he was about to be bush-whacked himself.

"There's got to be something we can do," Charley said.

Hagen ordered a launch.

The last thing Charley had expected when he had agreed to work with Martinez and her clandestine crew was to be crammed into the number two seat of an Omni Dynamics MRVWC-7 Mamba™. The variable-wing aircraft—known as a verrie to just about anyone who flew one—looked a lot like a dragonfly. The Mambas might look like dragonflies, but bugs didn't have stubby airfoils with weapon hardpoints like the Mambas. When Charley objected to using milspec verries, Hagen said, "These are *civilian* ships."

He pointed out that the only thing affixed to the wing mounts was a pair of directed-beam actinic lights, and that the lower chin turret was not carrying the usual 25mm rotary cannon. "The night sights and targeting systems," he allowed, "are still installed."

Civilian ships or not, a flight of five Mambas was not standard equipment for a corp office block like the Brookfield facility; nor were the other eight crewmen. They all wore Yamabennin flight suits, which Charley had expected; it was the guys themselves that took him by surprise. None of them was taller than Hagen, and that guy was what in a less sensitive age would be called a dwarf. Charley knew that smaller pilots were preferred for a lot of reasons, but Yamabennin was carrying the maxim to an extreme with these shrimps.

The rush to launch didn't leave Charley time to pay attention to anything other than the clipped—and no doubt incomplete—briefing the ground crew gave him while they crammed a helmet on his head and stuffed him into the verrie. He missed most of what they said, their words lost in the undampened howl of the warming engines. Charley had been in combat verries before, but never in a gunship. He was already sure that he wouldn't like the experience any better. Hagen put the ship into the air as soon as the cockpit dome was locked down.

The verries lifted with their wings vertical for launch and tilted them down for full forward flight. The craft were fast and they made good time, flying low and illegal. Charley didn't complain.

Charley wasn't as confident as Hagen that they would get to Providence before things started happening.

As they crossed the Seekonk River, the last before their destination, Hagen slowed their Mamba and reconverted to hover configuration. The verrie slowed further when he cut in the stealth baffles on the engines.

They had covered the thirty-odd miles in under eight minutes. Staring at his helmet's projection of what the Mamba's night sight saw, Charley knew that they hadn't gotten there fast enough.

As they closed on the building, Charley saw that Lee had reached his man. The guy was sprawled and still. Lee was still, too, spitted on the spikes of the university's iron fence.

One of the other pilots asked for instructions, but Charley missed most of it; there was some sort of crackling interference. It had to be all over the e-m bands, to defeat the automatic frequency shifters.

"Hold on," Hagen's voice said in his ears. The internal circuit was clear, at least. "I'm going to take us over the top."

As they cleared the roof, the first thing Charley saw was the crater. It looked as if somebody had dropped a bomb on the lawn. The second thing he saw was the woman, leaning against a tree and waving her arms as if she were chasing away bees. The third was Quetzal, slowly advancing on the woman. Neither the woman nor Quetzal reacted to the verrie's approach.

"Morning's coming early today, abomination," Hagen said. "Now, Gordon! Hit the lights!"

Charley stabbed the trigger button on his virtual console, sending twin beams spearing down to impale the tableau. Like a bug hit with insecticide, Quetzal began to writhe.

The flashes were shifting, changing their nature in some way. Something significant was happening back in the mundane world. The color John saw less frequently, which he had come to associate with Dr. Spae's magic, came less frequently still. He suspected that Dr. Spae's battle against Quetzal was going badly. Suspected? Hell, he *knew*.

And Faye had not returned.

The doctor didn't have a lot of time left.

He had to do something.

Maybe he could reenter the real world behind Quetzal. Sneak up on him. Surprise him and distract him. Distracting him had worked before.

It wasn't much of a plan, but John didn't think there was time to come up with anything better.

He ran toward the building, or at least where he thought the building ought to be. Standing where he guessed the door to be, he turned to face in what he hoped was Quetzal's direction.

Now, how to walk between the worlds?

He didn't know.

How had he done it before?

He had needed to get away, get anywhere, and he had. But now he needed to get to somewhere, and a very particular somewhere.

He stared at the flickering light, feeling helpless. It had been a long time since he'd seen a flash of Dr. Spae's color.

She needed him.

He needed to get to her.

The air around him began to sparkle.

He needed—

Rainbow colors glistened.

He needed!

Dimly, he perceived the shadowy shape of Quetzal; the wizard had backed the doctor up against a tree. John could see the tree clearly. *She needed him*. John ran forward, holding with as tight a will as he could to the fact that he needed to be in the sunlit world.

The ground changed beneath his feet as he ran. The shift shocked him and he stumbled, sprawling face-first on the ground. His ears roared.

What a putz!

He struggled to sit up. A windstorm had blown up while he'd been away; maybe it was a side effect of the magic—he didn't care. He was back in the sunlit world! There was light all around, bright and piercing. He'd done it!

Now he needed to get off his ass and help Dr. Spae.

Or did he?

The doctor was slumped at the base of the tree, but Quetzal no longer menaced her. Instead he writhed as if he were in agony, and flung uncontrolled bolts of magical energy at the sky.

What in hell was going on?

Screaming, Quetzal ran across the green. Shafts of light from the sky tracked him as he headed toward the great gates. John expected him to stop, or try to climb, but the darkling mage ran straight at the gates. There was a flash and a clap of sound like thunder. When John could see again, he saw a jagged hole in the gates. The edges of the iron pieces glowed a dull red.

Quetzal was gone.

CHAPTER
30

"Keep the lights on him! Keep the lights on him!"

Charley didn't know if the other crew still chasing Quetzal heard him. Their erratic success suggested that they did not, but maybe they were having the same troubles that Hagen was having. Something Quetzal was doing was screwing up the electronics.

The Mamba banked hard, just missing a church steeple. Charley could've counted the cracks in each slab of roof slate. Scraping a building had already sent one of the verries limping away to find a safe landing zone.

"Watch where you're flying," he said.

"You run the lights," Hagen snapped back. "I'll fly the verrie."

Two verries should have been more than enough to stay on Quetzal's trail, but for a guy who wasn't supposed to know about being hunted by aircraft he was very good at taking advantage of every bit of cover the city provided.

"We're down on the university grounds." It was the pilot of one of the two verries that had landed. "No sign of the guy who popped out of the air or the woman. Lee's dead. The other guy's got a bullet in his torso. You want an evac?"

"Negative," Hagen replied.

"Call 911," Charley ordered. "Tell them you've got a man down with a gunshot wound." The radio was silent for a moment. "Do it!"

Another moment of silence. "Is that a confirm?"

"Confirm," Hagen said. "Get your butts back in the air first."

"Wilco."

Hagen banked hard again. Charley was learning that the Mambas had more than a visual resemblance to dragonflies—at least when Hagen was in the pilot's seat. The verrie danced through the sky like a dragonfly, all zigs and zags and swoops and dives. It was a good thing Charley wasn't prone to motion sickness.

They had lost Quetzal again and until they had the other two verries back in the air, they didn't have enough eyes in the sky to keep the wily bastard in sight.

Hagen put their Mamba into a widening spiral centered on the last place they'd seen the fugitive. The other verrie kept station over that point. Run or stay, they'd be ready for him. Charley killed the lights, relying on the night sight. With luck, Quetzal might think he'd lost them and emerge where they could nail him again.

"There!"

Hagen slaved Charley's night sight long enough to point it in the right direction. Quetzal was scampering down a steep bank. Hagen turned the verrie in pursuit, calling the other Mamba to join him. They were low, coming in on the fugitive, when Charley saw where Quetzal was heading.

"Shit! What's that wall?"

"Railroad tunnel," Hagen said.

"Tunnel?"

"Check the console map."

"How do I get it?"

The map appeared. Hagen must have done something; Charley certainly hadn't. It took him a few seconds to spot the tunnel. "But it's sealed."

"Only to vehicles," Hagen said. "He can get in."

Hagen sounded sure. "Not good. It comes out the other side of the hill, near the river. Your other birds back in the air?"

A moment. "Roger."

"Send them over there. We'll have him trapped."

"We got civilians down there." It was one of the other pilots.

"Where?" Charley demanded.

"Closing on the mouth of the tunnel."

Shit! There were two ragged figures, a man and a woman, making their way along the wall toward the tunnel. They looked like streeters; they probably had their slumps in the tunnel. "You got a horn on this thing, Hagen?"

"A what?"

"A loudspeaker."

"Affirmative."

"Patch me into it. We've got to get them out of there. They have no idea what they're getting into."

John and Dr. Spae ignored the echoing voice from the hovering verrie demanding that they turn around and leave the area. It said it was the police, but John didn't believe it; the police didn't fly milspec verries like that Mamba. He tuned out the noise as he helped Dr. Spae toward the slit at the edge of the wall. Once they were under the roof, the voice shut up, which was fine by John. They kept moving until they reached a point where the tunnel turned, cutting off most of the light leaking in from the sprawl glow.

"What is this place?"

"Railroad tunnel. Goes through. The hill." Spae was panting, nearly out of breath. "Give me a minute. I'll be okay. In a minute."

John looked back at the bend in the tunnel. There was a paler patch, deep gray against the jet of the dark tunnel. The tunnel was broader than he would have expected, ten yards across at least. There were two sets of tracks, huddled on one side of the tunnel. Half of the right-of-way was not set up for trains at all. The place smelled vile, and trash and litter almost covered the gravel that crunched underfoot. Dr. Spae had insisted that Quetzal would head here. Now that they had stopped running for a moment, he had a chance to ask, "How do you know that this is where he'll come?"

"He needed to get away from the searchlights. They weren't ordinary lights."

"I know. I saw. But why come down here? Wouldn't any building do?"

"To escape the lights, yes, but the men in the verries would have seen which he chose. They could wait him out. Down here, he has a surprise for them."

"A trap?" John didn't like the idea of following Quetzal into a trap.

"An escape route," the doctor said. She was getting her wind back. "One of the cults associated with his Glittering Path had a sect here in Providence. They had a house up on the hill and were supposed to hold rituals down here. It's been speculated that the cult had dug a connection down to the tunnel. It seems likely; it fits the facts. A passageway leading from here to a house on top would have let the cultists travel unseen to their ritual site. This railroad tunnel gives Quetzal the same protection from the lights that it gave the cultists from prying eyes. Their passageway will be his escape route from the verries. Once he gets to it, the men up there will have no idea where he's vanished to. They couldn't possibly know where he'd emerge."

"And we do?"

"No, but we can follow him. Can't you feel him?"

John wasn't sure. There was something about the place. He had a sense of space, stretching vastly before him. He could almost feel the weight of the earth pressing down from above. Deeper in the tunnel there was a glimmer where no light should be.

"You ready, John?"

He wasn't. "Sure."

They stayed near the wall, using it to keep their orientation in the dark. Even John's excellent night vision was stymied here. But the longer they remained, the better it got. He began to see things by the faintest reflection of light leaking down the length of the tunnel.

There were people living down here. Streeters. John and the doctor passed several carefully arranged piles of debris and trash. To someone without anything better, those trash heaps were home.

They came across two of the tenants.

The bodies were sprawled, limp and lifeless. John didn't need to look closely to know that Quetzal had drained them. There was a stink on the air that wasn't natural, a stink he could now associate with the darkling mage.

Quetzal had come this way.

Dr. Spae was the one who found the entrance to the secret passageway. It was hidden in the back of an alcove in the wall. A pivoting panel opened on a rotting black curtain, behind which was a small chamber lit by the feeble glow of an ancient incandescent bulb. An angled shaft led up into the hill. Somewhere up above, another faint light glowed.

John insisted on going first.

"Be careful," Dr. Spae advised.

It was a bit of doctor's advice he intended to follow scrupulously.

The shaft was steep enough that to ascend, he needed to use the rusty iron rungs driven into the wall. After twenty feet or so, it opened into another chamber. This one was very irregular, a strange place where in the dim light a shadow might be an opening leading away into darker realms, or just a smudge on the rockface. It gave the place a feeling of a hall of mirrors, where you could not tell the real passages from the reflections. John discovered another shaft leading up, from which faint sounds emanated.

Quetzal, making his escape.

Dr. Spae joined him and listened. She agreed that the noise they could hear was Quetzal, but she disagreed about which direction the wizard was going.

"He's coming back."

It wasn't what John wanted to hear. "Why? The men in the verries couldn't have cut him off. You said they wouldn't know what house he was headed for."

"Maybe he can't get through. Maybe the tunnel up there has collapsed. It's been a long time."

"Maybe he's coming back because he knows we're here."

Spae shrugged. "His reasons don't matter."

"What will we do?"

"Fight him."

"That didn't work before."

"Then we bring the roof down on his head."

The earth above them felt very, very weighty. "We'll die, too."

"Then we'll die."

John didn't want to die under tons of dirt. "It's that important?"

"Did you get any sense of the *telesmon* he'd uncovered?"

John didn't know what a *telesmon* was, but he had gotten a sense from the object Quetzal had been carrying. He hadn't liked it at all. It had felt . . . evil. "Yeah."

"Then you *know* it's that important."

"Can't you just collapse it on him, and not on us?"

"I don't think I can be that selective, especially with him fighting me."

"Try, Doctor."

"I'll do what I can, John. Now give me your hand; we need to link."

As the doctor built her spell construct, shadows began to play against the floor of the chamber. Quetzal was coming closer. Dr. Spae pronounced herself as satisfied as could be expected. Quetzal's foot emerged from the shaft.

Why didn't Dr. Spae *do* something?

His other foot. His legs. This would be a good time.

Do it! Bury him!

The doctor must have sensed John's distress. "He has to be in the right place," she whispered.

Quetzal stood upon the floor of the chamber. He turned and saw them. Smiling grimly, he said, "I see I was not the only one to know of this passage."

The doctor didn't respond, so John was silent as well.

"What brings you and your shy elf puppet here, Spae? Didn't you get enough last time?"

"We came to stop you," the doctor said.

"I've already been stopped. Time and the earth have beaten you to it. The passage is blocked, and the only way out is the way we came in."

"You have no way out," Dr. Spae told him.

"A duel here would be dangerous. The deep earth likes not our kind. If you insist upon having your death at my hand, let us do it outside. In here, the walls could collapse."

"I'll help them."

Quetzal shook his head. "You won't. You'll be trapped here as well."

"I'm willing."

John felt her release energy into her spell construct. A sound like thunder miles off echoed through the rock. Quetzal's eyes darted wildly about for a moment, then he set to disrupting the doctor's spell. Through his rapport with Dr. Spae, John could feel the doctor working the spell on the earth around them, calling it to close. He felt, too, the props she had placed to shield them; they seemed terribly flimsy.

The play of magics in the chamber sent shadows scampering crazily about the rockface. The arcane light illuminated a dark spot on the wall; a spot that seemed to be a shadow, but was not an ordinary one. If the interplay of arcane forces hadn't heightened his senses, he wouldn't have recognized it for what it was.

The earth moaned around them, bending closer. Dust shifted from the walls, and clods of dirt and small stones dribbled down from the roof.

Dr. Spae's construct was achieving reality. The roof would fall soon.

John tightened his grip on her hand and tugged her back toward the shadow that wasn't exactly a shadow. She let out a wordless howl of protest as Quetzal reacted to her broken concentration. Through the link with Dr. Spae, John felt Quetzal wrest control of the magic. The groaning stopped, and so did the fall of rocks. Quetzal laughed and stepped forward.

John didn't care.

"John, let go of me!"

John didn't. He intended to hold her where he wanted her. "Stand still, Doctor! Let me have the spell."

"But you don't—"

"Now! There's no time to argue!" He was betting that the rapport they shared would help her to trust him. He tried to be calm. And why not? They were only staking their lives.

"You've made a mistake, elf. I have the spell now."

"We'll see," John told him.

He ripped at the lattice the doctor had set to try and save them.

"No, John! You're wrecking it!"

He knew. But by destroying their back door, the spell would be reenergized.

Quetzal recognized what John was doing. The darkling mage scrambled to take control of the astral props. John let him have the lesser ones without a fight, concentrating his effort on wiping out the mainstay over the spot where Spae had been standing. Where Quetzal now stood.

John willed the earth above to join the earth below.

The stone moaned its longing to become whole and seal the hollow in its midst.

"You should have been buried long ago," John said, as he felt the last of the prop evaporate into nothingness. He forgot the spell, forgot the rock, forgot the earth closing in on them and gave his will to *need*, the *need* to be elsewhere. He took himself and the doctor sideways into the shadow.

Behind them, the trickle of falling stone became a torrent. Looking over his shoulder, John saw Quetzal raise both hands in a fending gesture, dropping his precious *telesmon*. The artifact rang like a gong as it hit and bounced. The small sound was lost in the clamor of the rockfall.

Even Quetzal didn't have the power to stop the earth in its motion. His screams were buried with him under tons of dirt and earth and rock.

John tugged harder on Spae. They could not afford to tarry; they might still be caught. She stumbled; only his hand in hers kept her upright. John felt something bang off his shin; it clattered away in the darkness. Coughing from the dust, they staggered on.

When John thought they had gotten far enough to be safe, he kept going for another dozen yards. He listened. The rock was silent. It was safe to stop. He leaned against the tunnel wall and slowly slid to a sitting position.

Dr. Spae sat beside him. "What happened? Why aren't we buried?"

"We're in the otherworld, Doctor."

She looked around, though they were in near darkness and there was little to see. Her mouth was open as if she might taste a difference in the air. "You brought us here?"

He nodded. "I seem to have discovered the trick."

They rested for a while in silence.

John broke the quiet by saying, "I'm sorry about Mr. Beryle." The doctor didn't respond. Maybe it had been the wrong thing to say. After another while he tried, "We had probably best get out of here."

Dr. Spae nodded. "Can we stay in Faery awhile? I'm not sure I'm ready to go back to the real world."

"Sure. I guess so. The tunnel still seems to go in the right direction."

They followed the tunnel. For some reason, John found it easier to see in the dark of this Faery tunnel than he had in the railroad tunnel. The doctor seemed to have the same advantage; they walked along in the center of the broad passage.

"Why is this passage here?" Dr. Spae asked suddenly.

"I don't know."

"But we're under the hill, aren't we? The natural landforms are supposed to be the same in the two dimensions. Since they don't have trains in the otherworld, this should be a solid hill in Faery."

John hadn't considered that. If he had, he might not have tried what he had done, and they might have been buried with Quetzal. He didn't want to think about that. "I guess that there are tunnelers in the otherworld, too. I didn't create the place, Doctor. I just found it and walked us here."

"But what would need a tunnel this size? It's big enough for an eleph—"

She stopped abruptly and stood staring, wide-eyed. John felt his own eyes go wide when he saw what she was staring at.

The tunnel before them was filled with massive, scaly haunches and a spined tail. A great wedge of a head rested on the tail. The creature's skull was crowned with a pair of spiral horns. Many lesser horns formed a row from the base of each of the greater pair that joined at the eye ridge and marched down the long muzzle to meet a prominent nose horn. Teeth of varying sizes jutted from the closed jaws, and faint wisps of steam rose from its flaring nostrils.

There could be little doubt what this Faery creature was.

"A dragon," breathed Dr. Spae. "This is a dragon's lair."

The beast was curled up like a cat sleeping. Its slablike flanks heaved up and down, undisturbed by the doctor's voice. John hoped it would stay that way.

He pointed to a narrow space between the wall of the tunnel and the slumbering dragon. As silently as they could, they tiptoed past the beast. To their unspoken relief, it didn't stir. To their even greater relief, the stars of the otherworld soon appeared, framed by the tunnel's mouth. They hurried out of the hill.

They hadn't gotten more than ten meters when Faye appeared out of the brush. Without a word, she grabbed their hands and tugged them back the way she had come. She waited until she'd dragged them among the trees before speaking.

"Dr. Spae, you look terrible. Are you all right?"

The doctor gave her a weak smile. "I'm just tired, dear. I'll survive. I always have before."

Faye smiled encouragement and support, then turned to John. "Why did you take her in there, John? Don't you know what's in there?"

How was he supposed to know? This wasn't exactly his native turf. This was his father's turf. Speaking of whom . . . "Where's Bennett?"

"He couldn't come, John. I have help, though. Lesser folk, mostly, but willing to fight."

John didn't see anyone but Faye. "So where is this help?"

"They were afraid to come closer to Urre'shk."

"Who?"

"The dragon," said an elf, who might have appeared out of thin air. The newcomer was as tall as John, but dark where he was fair.

"Who are you?" John asked him.

"You haven't earned my name, changeling. I came to fight the wyrm lover."

"So did we!" chorused a medley of voices. Shining eyes peered from beneath bushes and around trees. Noses, some long and pointed, some stubby and shiny, others entirely more human, poked from hiding places among the greenery. The vegetation hid dozens of Faery folk, but John couldn't see all of any of them. A shy folk—but, to judge from the glints on teeth and claws and unsheathed weapons, a fierce folk as well. Even if they were afraid of dragons. The largest of all the folk gathered around them lurked where it was almost completely hidden from sight; John caught a glimpse of a bright red hat and heard the clink of metal on metal. From the hidden skulker, a deep voice rumbled, "We're ready to fight now."

"Quite the army," the elf remarked. "Are you ready to be the general?"

"There won't be any fighting," John said. "The battle's over."

The dark-haired elf said nothing; he turned and walked away. A rustling in the brush announced the departure of many of the other Faery folk as well. But some remained, their eyes glittering in the darkness under the leafy hiding places, their faces appearing fleetingly from behind the trees.

"Is it true, John? Quetzal is destroyed?"

"Buried beneath the mountain."

Faye threw her arms around him and hugged him hard. Shrill, piping voices and froggy croaking raised a ragged cheer.

Conscious of Dr. Spae's presence, John hugged Faye back, but only for a short while. "Pretend I'm not here," the doctor said, but John couldn't do that. They had to go back. Besides, there were better places to celebrate than the middle of the woods with who knew how many Faery folk hanging about, watching.

Dr. Spae was right about the landforms being similar in the otherworld and in the sunlit world. John knew the hill was the hill, which meant that his slump was . . .

He turned to find Faye already pointing in the correct direction.

She was smiling at him, and he had to smile back. They laughed.

John helped Dr. Spae up, but she refused his assistance beyond that, saying, "I'm not that—what's the current phrase? Oh, yes—whipped out."

They set out, to the accompaniment of thrashings and rustlings in the bushes and trees. A thin, reedy voice sang a chorus of a tune that John had never heard before, and instantly the woods erupted into song. It was a wild song and, for it, the lunatic mix of voices singing it was right. Their progress became a parade—as experienced by a blind man. For all the ruckus, the only marchers John could see were Faye and Dr. Spae.

But it didn't matter. They'd beaten Quetzal and saved the world from—from what, exactly? Maybe knowing the nature of the threat didn't matter, either. It had needed doing, and he had been part of the doing. And maybe—just maybe it wouldn't have been done without him.

At the riverbank John walked them back into the sunlit world; it was time to go home.

Robert N. Charrette was born, raised, and educated in the State of Rhode Island and Providence Plantations. Upon graduating from Brown University with a cross-departmental degree in biology and geology, he promptly moved to the Washington, D.C. area and entered a career as a graphic artist. He worked as a game designer, art director, and commercial sculptor before taking up the word processor to write novels. He has contributed three novels to the BattleTech™ universe and four to the Shadowrun™ universe, the latter of which he had a hand in creating, and is now developing other settings for fictional exploration.

He currently resides in Springfield, Virginia with his wife, Elizabeth, who must listen to his constant complaints of insufficient time while he continues to write as well as to sculpt gaming miniatures and the occasional piece of collector's pewter or fine art bronze. He also has a strong interest in medieval living history, being a longtime knight of the Society for Creative Anachronism and a principal in La Belle Compagnie, a reenactment group portraying English life in the late fourteenth century. In between, he tries to keep current on a variety of eclectic interests including dinosaurian paleontology and pre-Tokugawa Japanese history.